MW00627081

The True Sea

A NOVEL BY F. W. BELLAND

Palm Island Press

THE TRUE SEA

Copyright © 1984, 2002 by F. W. Belland

Second Edition

All rights reserved under International and Pan-American Copyright conventions. No part of this book may be reproduced in any form or by any means, electronic or mechanical, including photocopying, recording or by any information storage and retrieval system without written permission from the author, except for the inclusion of brief quotations in a review.

For information address:
Palm Island Press, Inc., 411 Truman Avenue, Key West, FL 33040 U.S.A.
pipress@earthlink.net

First edition published by Holt, Rinehart & Winston.

Library of Congress Cataloging-in-Publication Data

    Belland, F. W.
        The true sea/ by F.W. Belland -- 2nd ed.
        p.cm.
        LCCN 83-18440
        ISBN 0-9643434-9-5
        1. Railroads--United States--Fiction. 2. Florida Keys
(Fla,)--Social life and customs--Fiction.   I. Title.

      PS3552.E5332T7 1984   813'.54

ABOUT THE AUTHOR

Frederick W. Belland was born in 1944 at the Naval Hospital in Miami Beach, Florida. He spent his youth in rural Miami and the Florida Keys. After a tour with the Marines in Vietnam, Belland received a degree in Design and Literature from Florida State University.

While writing his first novel, *Fleshwound* (Dove Paperback, New York), Belland worked with his brother Chris in renovating Old Town Key West.

Belland's second novel, *The True Sea* (Holt Rinehart & Winston, New York) is based upon the construction of the overseas railroad from Miami to Key West.

Subsequent works include over a dozen short stories printed in such publications as *Tropic Magazine* (The Miami *Herald*), *The Tampa Tribune Literary Supplement*, *The Caribbean Writer* and *Key West Review*. Belland's most recent story won first prize in the South Florida Writers' Guild competition.

A compulsive traveler, Belland has settled at last under an extinct volcano in Nicaragua with his four cats.

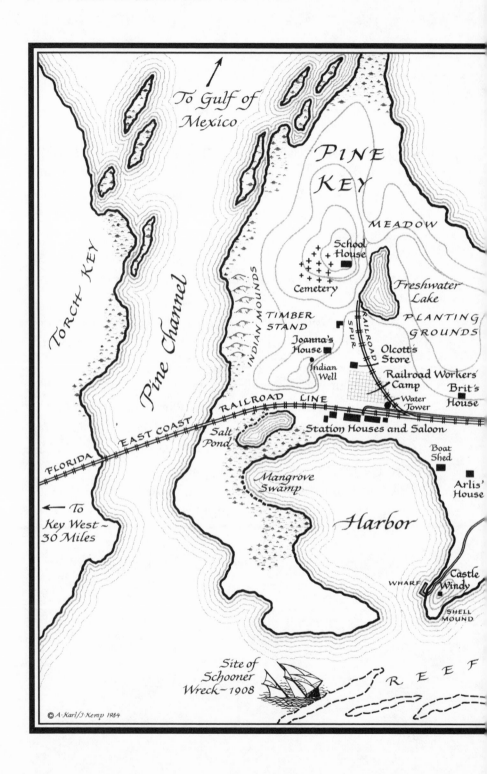

To Gulf of
Mexico

PINE
KEY

MEADOW

School
House

Cemetery

Freshwater
Lake

TORCH KEY

Pine Channel

INDIAN MOUNDS

TIMBER
STAND

Joanna's
House

Indian
Well

PLANTING
GROUNDS

RAILROAD
SPUR

Olcott's
Store

Railroad Workers'
Camp

Brit's
House

RAILROAD LINE

Water
Tower

EAST COAST

Salt
Pond

Station Houses and Saloon

Boat
Shed

FLORIDA

Mangrove
Swamp

Harbor

Arlis'
House

← To
Key West ~
30 Miles

WHARF

Castle
Windy

SHELL
MOUND

Site of
Schooner
Wreck ~ 1908

REEF

© A·Karl/J·Kemp 1984

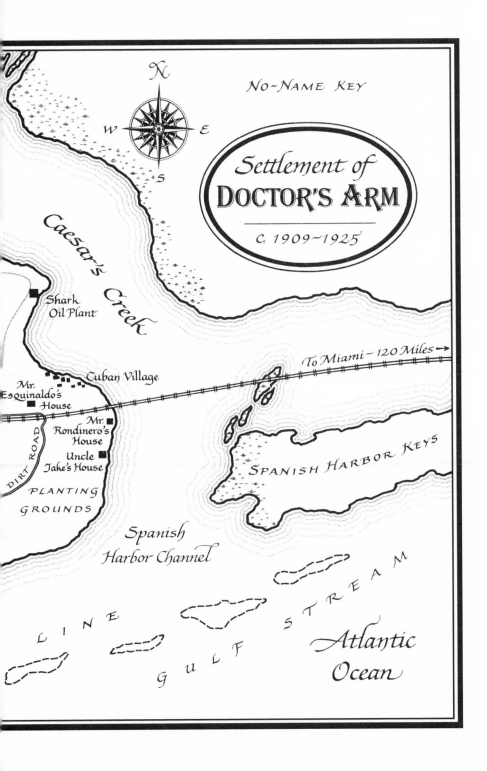

DEDICATION

This second edition is for my brother, Chris.

AUTHOR'S NOTE

Those acquainted with the geography and history of the
Florida Keys will notice that the location of some islands and
the route of the Overseas Railroad have been changed to suit
the purposes of a fictional work. Although the settlement of
Doctor's Arm and its characters are a product of the author's
imagination, the story and events surrounding it are basically
taken from truth.

Part 1
1909

1

Arlis worked the oars. On each forward stroke he saw the reflection of his own face on the little water puddled in the bilge. "Hello, Arlis," he'd say to the face, which smiled back at him, and he could see the wide-set eyes and the too-big ears and even the gaps between his teeth. Then he'd haul back, hard like a man, like Papadad. Each time Arlis pulled, the thatch rope that held the oars in their locks moaned against the wood and the sound traveled across the stillness of the morning. "Hello you, Arlis. You're ten and look how you can pull them oars." The smile from the bilge got bigger and even a little silly but he didn't mind at all. Him and Papadad were out on business together.

Without looking up, Arlis could feel when Papadad worked the long sculling oar that trailed through the notch in the boat's stern. The sculling oar worked them over the water strongly and fishlike. Papadad stood there in the stern. Arlis could feel him. Every few strokes Arlis made with the sweeps, Papadad would push down and over with all his weight against the big sculler. Arlis knew each time Papadad shifted his feet by the way the boat rocked. He would like to have watched him work the oar, but did not stare because he knew the old man would tell him to keep to his job, which was at the oars.

Since daylight Papadad had said little, and now the sun rose pretty well off the marsh. Once he'd said, "Damn fine egret over there," probably because he used to hunt them with his gun and send the plumes north, where they were made into ladies' hats. Under the seat Papadad still kept his long gun.

Arlis and his father worked the boat parallel to the new trestle the railroad men had built across the marsh that year. They hadn't built to Doctor's Arm yet, but Papadad told Arlis that Mr. Jewel Claire had sold the right-of-way to the railroad men already. Soon it would reach them and cross their island.

The railroad was a great thing to build, Arlis guessed. It would bring real civilization. That's what Jewel Claire said. It had taken them a long time to build it and it looked quite strange, so heavy and massive, like an endless table in the shallow waters. On the other side of the trestle were more shallows, then the reef, and then the blue water of the true sea, burned white now by the risen sun. Arlis stared at the huge ugliness of the trestle until his eyes burned. He had thought that to build the thing would be impossible, but the railroad men had done it. It was the greatest thing he'd ever seen. When the black locomotive crossed it, it shook the water under the boat and made Arlis feel that it was great and mighty. It impressed him more than the red brick courthouse in Key West, or the big Mallory Steamers that went to Havana. He and Papadad had taken the boat up to Matacumbe to see the train twice already. When Arlis heard the whistle, he had run to see the locomotive belching black smoke, crossing the flat savanna as if it were lighter than air; a monster on wings. In the first second when he heard the whistle, something seized up inside Arlis's breast and squeezed harder and harder until he ran close to the track and saw the train roar by. When it had gone he did not believe it really happened. The next time he saw the train he placed a penny on the steel of the track, and when the train disappeared he held the hot mashed-flat copper in his hand while he stared at the emptiness of the roadbed. From where he stood on that spot the line of the rails ran without a break all the way to New York City.

Papadad believed in the railroad almost as hard as Mr. Jewel Claire. "That there railroad's going to make us rich. Hell," he would say in the boat shed when there were three or four men hanging around. "How long it take you to make Key West under sail?" He'd slap the raw pine hull of the cutter laid up in the boat shed and answer his own question. "A day is how long. Get yourself into a blow and it's a week. That there railroad gonna get you, or the food you grow or fish you catch or sponges you rake, out and away like that!" He'd snap his finger under the faces of the others. "You cut a sweet-ripe pineapple this morning and serve it in a ice cup to a New York lady for tomorrow's supper! Hoo boy! Now what you think they'll pay for that, huh?"

"Steady on now, boy," said Papadad. "We gon' get in a little closer to the trestle." Arlis felt the boat shift as his father leaned on the sculling oar. "Mind you keep the tow sacks over them bottles, hear?"

"Yes, Papadad." He looked for a moment at his father.

"Mind to yer business now, boy," said Papadad without being unkind.

Arlis kept pulling steadily at the oars as the boat came in closer to the trestle bridge. Later, he hoped, they could get up the sail, maybe. He stroked and pushed his foot against the wicker basket closest to him. He could feel the hardness of the rum bottles packed in the straw. They were half-pint bottles, the kind the men on the section gangs liked to buy. The labels were all written in Cuban. Papadad covered the baskets over with tow sacks and sponges to hide the liquor in case a foreman came along. The railroad bosses were dead against rum-selling to the section gangs. It kept them from working.

Arlis felt sorry for the men on the gangs. They were Yankee trash from up north. With diseases. Everyone said that. Most of them didn't last long on their own, and the bosses were tough and made them work. On the first payday most of them who had worked off their passage would go back north. They had to work off their passage. A few tough ones stayed around long enough to become bosses themselves. Some of them even died.

No Conch or any man from the keys would take that kind of work. "That kind of work is too hard for a man," declared Mommer. "Even a Negro can't stand that sun all day. Poor souls. It's no wonder they take to drink like they do. Not that it excuses it in the eyes of God." Arlis's Mommer was a Temperance Lady.

"Boy," said Papadad. "Hand me up a sampler bottle."

"Mommer said. .." but he bit his words when Papadad rapped his head with the leather edge of his knuckles.

"Ne'er mind Mommer, now. Mommer's home. Mind to business and fetch me up one them bottles."

Arlis reached under the coolness of the tow sack and took out a bottle from its seat in the straw. The colored label showed a pretty sailing ship like the kind he would build someday. He loved all pictures of boats and ships and covered the walls of his room at home with them.

"Pass it up, son. I'll give you the picture later to study on," said Papadad. His voice had already forgiven him for bringing up Mommer. Arlis passed it up and looked at his father resting against the long sculling oar. He had great shoulders and a heavy neck that strained at the buttons of his collarless shirt. His black broadcloth coat had been mended neatly and shone slick with its age. In the space between the coat and the thatch-brim hat was the square of Papadad's face, pale and heavy beneath three days' beard. He wore drooping mustaches. Painted-on black brows ran in a solid line from one side of his temple to the other. Arlis handed him the bottle.

Papadad's dark fingers slipped over the small bottle. They twisted out the little cork and then covered the picture of the sailboat. He raised the rum to his lips. Arlis watched his throat move and how the sun passed through the green glass and amber liquor. His father looked handsome there.

"That's fine, son. There's times in a man's work when rum is a gift of Almighty God. But Mommer won't let on that, bless her. And don't you let on that I let on." Papadad smiled and Arlis could see the brown edges of his teeth. He shifted his quid in his mouth, spat over the side, then had a drink of water from the demijohn. He passed the water to Arlis. Without saying more they pushed on, the blinking light beneath the trestle cutting them half away from the sun.

They saw the trestle go into the bush in a wooded hammock and heard the men of the gang before they saw them. The smell of tobacco was in the air and man-sound and man-stink came differently to Arlis than everything else in the swamp. It could not even be blown away by the freshening breeze coming in from the Atlantic on the other side of the trestle.

"Ship oars, boy." Papadad's voice rumbled like chain passing out the hawsepipe of Cap'n Ben's schooner. Arlis drew in his two oars and felt the shudder as Papadad gently laid her bows up into the mangrove of the hammock.

A few mosquitoes came out, not afraid of the morning sun. They did not bother Arlis, who studied the white sails of a coasting ship as she went north in the Gulf Stream about six miles out. How beautiful she rides, thought Arlis. Like a bird, apart forever from these iron tracks.

"Poowheet. Poowheet," trilled Papadad from his place in the stern. "Poowheet." The clouds of gnats and sandflies came in now and Arlis watched Papadad scratch at his whiskers. Arlis would be glad to have whiskers too. He put his hands in the pockets of his coat and pulled his head down from the flies.

There came a rustle of brush, and from the bank the ragged faces of the first two Yankees showed directly. They stood hatless, their buttons popped. One still wore a collar on a yellow silk shirt turned black and split up the back. Their faces were raw with sunburn and eyes half closed by insect bites. They breathed through the suppressed O's of their mouths. One coughed behind a frail wrist. They tumbled down the bank, where fill had been dumped in to hold the trestle. Into the grass and water up to their knees now, they hung on to the side of the boat.

"An' I came south for my damn health," wheezed the cougher.

"Shuddup," said the other. "Hi, fellers," he said to Papadad. "You got somethin' for us?" Arlis sat in the bow by the wicker baskets. The men were so close he could smell them and see the bloodied places on their hands. Arlis felt a little afraid, but Papadad still looked big and unmoving in the stern.

"Haffa buck, silver," said Papadad and spat.

"Two for me, sonny," said the cougher in the pink shirt and handed over the coins to Arlis. Arlis passed out two bottles, seeing the battered hands close over the sailboat picture labels.

"Three for me, kid. Any discount for three, mister?"

"Half a dollar silver for one or a hundred."

"That's too damn high."

"Buy somewheres else then, Yank," said Papadad without changing anything about himself.

"Give me three, kid." Arlis watched the three silver coins drop into his hand, then put them into the box with the other money.

"Go on now, and send yer mates," said Papadad. "We can't wait for long."

The two gang men scrambled up the bank. Their brogans were full of water and made a wet sucking sound when they walked. The one with the split shirt slapped at a mosquito as they disappeared into the brush. Arlis was glad he was not going with them.

Three more men came down the bank almost before the others vanished. Two were older. One of the older men had a thatch hat like Papadad's and a beard.

"We each need two," said the one with the hat.

Arlis gave him two bottles from the basket and took the hard money. The young one crucified himself frontways against the gunwale of the boat, so that both his arms dangled inboard. He was a cougher too and looked worse for it because his head and face were shaved. "Two," he murmured." He dropped the silver into Arlis's hand and Arlis fetched him up the bottles.

"You owe me one of them bottles, Eddie," said the man with the hat.

"Aw...." But the one with the hat was already drinking at Eddie's bottle and with the other hand pulled Eddie after him. Eddie's talons seized the gunwale with a momentary determination, then let them be removed by the man with the thatch hat. As they went up the embankment Eddie coughed again.

"I want two too," said the third man, looking for a minute at Eddie and his friend. "Make it quick." He breathed hard like all the rest of them. "Hell, get something good going here and somebody has to get greedy, for chrissake, know what I mean? I ain't talking about you guys, just hurry it up, okay?"

Arlis hurried, taking the two halves and handing up the bottles. Three more men were slithering down the embankment and the impatient one pushed through them.

"Gimme one," said the new customer.

"Gimme two," said another. "How much?"

"Hey! Now what in hell's going on down there?"

"Shit," mumbled one of the customers.

"Now, I asked what's going on here." The voice came from a man who stood at the top of the embankment and wore brown tie-up leggings and a pith helmet. He had on a small black necktie under a clean collar and cradled a Parker Brothers' single-bore.

"Run aground a little, Cap'n. Your boys here's pushin' us off," said Papadad to the man with the gun. "Come astern, Arlis," said Papadad, smiling up at the gang boss. Arlis scrambled back to his seat and pushed the oars out the thatch loops.

"Hell," said the gang boss. "You trespassing on company right-of-way and selling intoxicants, is what."

"Come astern, Arlis," urged Papadad and kept grinning through his sweat at the gang boss. Arlis backed water fiercely now, watching the gang boss close the breech of the Parker Brothers with a snap that all of them could hear.

"Hold on now," the boss said. "I aim to have a look at what

you got in that boat." But Papadad had pushed them away from the bank with the sculler.

"Get away from us, mister. Company don't own the water we settin' on." But the boss had the gun to his shoulder. "Haul, boys!" yelled Papadad and dived into the bottom of the boat.

BOOM.

The boat shuddered and Arlis still sat face-to-face with the gang boss between the black cloud of smoke. Three little jets of water sprouted up from the bottom of the boat. Papadad was on his hands and knees staring at the holes for what seemed to be a long time. A terror that his father had been hit embraced Arlis only to be torn away when Papadad yelled, "Stroke, son. Stroke." As if awakening from a dream Papadad saw that they still backed water, transom first, confronted by the enemy. "Come about!" he shrieked, and Arlis held fast his right oar and wrenched his left until they pivoted neatly.

"You holed my boat, you Yankee egg sucker you," Papadad called in his fiercest voice from the stern.

"I'll hole your head you come trespassing company right of-way again, you sad-assed cracker."

"You holed my boat," cried Papadad again, as if hurling the worst curse in the world. He stood crouched, holding the wet sculling oar like a rifle. His hat was gone and a mop of black hair obscured half his face. His skin showed pale and stiff while he watched the gang boss slip away foot by foot as Arlis rowed the boat alone.

Arlis wondered if Papadad was scared as he was. Papadad saw him watching. His white lips curled back over his brown teeth.

"Keep to your business, boy, goddammit. Keep to your business and haul."

Papadad whittled some plugs from mahogany splints and sullenly knocked them into the shot holes with a maul. The leaking stopped but Arlis was still scared because the railroad boss had shot at them. Papadad stayed angry and quiet for a while, then he brightened up. He seemed almost jolly. He took a little more rum and wiped his face with a wet rag from the demijohn.

"Hell, that weren't nothing, was it? Let's put up the stick, son, and head for home. We got to clear brush for Jewel Claire this afternoon."

Arlis and Papadad stepped the pine mast, then tightened down the shrouds through the polished wood dead-eyes, so that the mast held firmly in place. Arlis rigged the fore and back stays, and together the man and the boy hauled up the patched leg-o'-mutton sail. Papadad had already set the rudder pintles into their gudgeons; now he lay the boat over to catch the wind that blew in from the sea.

They followed the trestle until it ran out, then crossed the bar and headed for the reef. The wind came almost at their backs, carrying them home.

Arlis looked in the distance where the trestle ended. Barges clustered about and a great steam hammer on a derrick mashed a piling into the mud, inching the rail line forward closer to the settlement at Doctor's Arm. Soon it would reach their home. Soon it would reach Key West. At least a hundred men scurried over the latticed scaffold and the equipment. It seemed to Arlis like a big snake that stretched over the water, eating at one end and growing from the other. He and Papadad could hear the slow steady bang of the steam hammer following them.

"We done good, son, even with gettin' shot at," said Papadad. "No need to upset Mommer with the telling of that part. God save her, she don't need no worrying. Clear?" He studied his son.

"Yessir."

Papadad took the last drink from his bottle.

"There's better times acoming, boy. We won't always have to rum-sell to them damn Yanks. It sticks in a man's craw, these things, but we got good land and when that train line comes through it, we're going to be something."

"I don't mind how things are, Papadad. I like things just fine."

"Shoo, boy, I'm going to have better for you. We're going to keep after your education. Rear you proper. How's your reading coming in Preacher's school?" Papadad's face got a little dark for a minute. Arlis knew Papadad couldn't read too good and the man felt bad for it.

"I'm trying real hard, Papadad."

"Good boy. You keep trying, you hear?"

Papadad looked out at the water, then back at the boy. He cuffed Arlis gently on the shoulder. "You love your old Papadad just a little still, don't you, son?"

"Oh yes, Papadad. I like to be with you."

Papadad cuffed him again. "Well, shucks. Let's have us some grits and syrup before our bellies dry up." It made Arlis feel all warm and happy inside when his father talked like that to him. It made him feel as if he were doing right.

Arlis put cold grits in tin plates and covered it with cane syrup from a clay bottle. Papadad sheeted in the sail and steered with his leg over the tiller bar while he ate.

They came around the point and Arlis could see the bluff at Doctor's Arm. On the end of the land spit that wrapped around the bight rose the shell mound where old Jewel Claire's daddy had built Castle Windy.

"There's Castle Windy, Papadad."

"Shoot. Ain't no castle…" Papadad squinted toward Jewel's house although it was still far to see clearly.

"I think it looks like a castle. Everyone calls it Castle Windy."

"Colored folks invented that name when Jewel Claire's daddy brang 'em over from Nassau to build it. Colored folks never seen no castle. You never seen no castle."

"I seen pictures."

Papadad laughed and still chewed on his grits.

"Maybe it does look like some kind of castle up there on that shell mound. That old Jewel Claire thinks he's a king in it leastways."

They could see Mr. Jewel's house well now, squatted low on top of the shell mound. It looked rather ordinary except for the short pointed tower Jewel had constructed so that he could look further out to sea. Being up on the shell mound did make the house look like a castle too, Arlis thought.

"Mommer says Indians built that shell mound hundreds of

years ago, Papadad. Was it that long?"

"I 'spect so, boy. Shell mound's been there long as anyone can remember and there ain't hardly no Indians left around these parts. Old Jewel Senior was right smart building it up high like that. Them Claires are right smart at just about whatever they puts a hand to. Gotta admit that." Papadad spat lightly over the side. "Clean up the dishes now, son. When you finished you can study the sailboat picture on this here bottle." He tossed Arlis the empty bottle.

In the hour it took them to reach the bight, Arlis soaked the picture off the bottle and stuck it on a piece of wood, setting it to dry in the sun. He studied it good while it dried, wondering how such ships could be made. Oh, they made good boats at the boat shed at home, but these great ships with all their fine white sail were almost too wonderful to imagine. When he'd been younger they'd built bigger boats in the boat shed. Bigger boats than this little catboat, Arlis thought. His grandfather, Cap'n Ben, had built *Eva Pearl* there before he had been born, before his Mommer had married Papadad.

"Are we going to build any more big boats at the boat shed, Papadad?'"

"Like as not, son. No big ones anyhow."

Arlis held the picture of the sailing schooner pasted on the board. He had a book at home with better ship pictures.

"Sure as hell no boats like that 'un," grinned Papadad and pointed at Arlis's picture. "Railroad's going to take the need out of it for us. The only totin' you'll have to do is to the tracks. Then the train'll take you and anything you have down to Key West or up to Miami or to New York City even. Coasting boats is dying, son."

Suddenly Arlis did not like the idea of the railroad coming, but he did not say so to Papadad because he knew Papadad prayed for it to happen.

"Will Cap'n Ben still sail *Eva Pearl?*"

"I suppose, but your grandpa is getting on, son. He's going to have to quit someday."

"Grandpa won't ever quit *Eva Pearl*. He built her." Arlis wanted to go on a trip with Cap'n Ben before the railroad made him quit.

"Well, things aren't going to change all at once, Arlis." Papadad smiled at him from the stern, where he hauled at the mainsheet. "But the change is coming."

Arlis turned forward, feeling a little bothered that change was coming when he didn't know what it was going to be. He liked things fine the way they were.

The tops of the coconut palms waved from the land spit and further beyond them Arlis could see the different-shaped leaves of the mango and pear trees that grew beside the lime grove. Inland, flowers of gray smoke rose from piles of brush that were being burned. Mr. Caine and his son Brit were working today clearing more land on Jewel's plantation, looking for potholes to plant pineapples.

"Will we work the rest of the day clearing, Papadad?"

"I reckon, son. We need to make a little money off Jewel so we can afford to work our own land. I hope the railroad gets here in time for this crop. We'll be one of the first planters to send pineapples by train." Papadad squinted at the green shoreline. "That's quite historical."

Papadad jibed the boat around past the wedge of land that protected the bay. The wind dropped off, only a little of it getting over the rise of the ground to softly belly out the old sail. Papadad steered between the mooring rock and the beach. They passed Castle Windy on the point. Below the house Jewel Claire's big pier jutted out where they loaded coasters like Cap'n Ben's for the trip to Key West. A few sponging skiffs lay upturned on the beach. Nell, Arlis's pup, came down to the water's edge and wagged her tail. She followed them along the beach as the boat glided toward their property. Arlis watched the boathouse get bigger.

"Weather's going to be good, Arlis. We'll beach her. Maybe tomorrow when the tide drops we'll plug them damn shot holes better." Papadad sounded angry for only a moment. The bow hove up a little on the sand and made a sighing sound. Arlis pulled the canvas down the mast and tied it with thatch rope around the boom.

"You clean up the boat, son. Stash them bottles away and put the money in the boathouse. Then you can give Mr. Caine and Brit and Uncle Jake a hand at Mr. Jewel's planting ground. I'm going up to the house to tell Mommer we're home, then I'll be along."

Arlis watched Papadad go up the path through the coconut trees to the house. It wasn't as fine a house as Jewel Claire's but Arlis loved it. He wished right now he could go with Papadad and sit on the big wood porch with Mommer and talk or let her read to him, but he knew he had to work. Everyone had to work, but work was good. Still, Arlis let himself think for a moment more about the cypress plank cottage with the dark porch that went all the way around.

Nell put her paws on the low side of the boat where it'd been laid up in the sand and licked Arlis's face. He scratched her ears, then bailed out the boat and stowed the oars. He took Papadad's long gun from under the seats and pulled out the charges and oiled it down before wrapping it in paper and cloth. Then he took the wicker basket of bottles packed in straw and put them in a chest in the boat shed. Mommer never came down to the boat shed anymore on account of her health. Papadad kept the rum hidden away just the same.

Arlis liked being alone in the boat shed. It was large and cool and smelled of wood and oil. Spiders built thick webs against the split shingles that turned golden and heavy with sawdust. All along one wall were hung saws and awls, mallets and chisels. On the other wall hardwoods and pine planks were stacked in tall drying bins. In the center, where she'd been laid up for as long as Arlis could remember, was the great gloomy hull of *The Reaper*. She stood there without her mast, buttressed up with rough timbers, her bow pointing to the sea beyond the closed doors. Arlis walked around her, running his hand over her clean hull. Each year Papadad and Uncle Jake wiped her down and took a bucket of linseed oil and soaked her deck planks and the inside of her hull. Mommer had told Arlis once that Cap'n Ben's wife, her mother, had been lost at sea off *The Reaper* and that Cap'n Ben had never taken her out again.

Arlis leaned against the workbench and let his eye move over the beauty of *The Reaper,* wondering at all the places she must have gone. He'd once seen Cap'n Ben looking at her as he looked at her now, alone in the dimness, with nothing around but the silent tools and high planked walls. It made the hair on the back of Arlis's neck stand up when he looked at her that way. He felt that somehow *The Reaper* called at him to take her back to the sea where she belonged.

Nell's damp muzzle pushed into Arlis's hand and he remembered that he ought to get a machete and go into the fields to help clear land.

The sun burned the top of Arlis's woven thatch hat. He snapped at the tips of weeds with the end of his machete as he walked the path across their land to the planting grounds belonging to Jewel Claire. Nell followed behind, then ran forward and turned in the path, looking back at him. Crickets shrilled; occasionally a mosquito came in and away from his ear. Everything was very green except where the land had been cleared of brush.

In the large opening of the planting grounds the first person Arlis saw was Uncle Jake, squatting on his haunches and cutting out the roots of a buttonwood tree. The rest of the buttonwood he'd stacked in a neat pile where he'd make charcoal out of it later. A piece of red rag stuck out of Uncle Jake's back pocket to scare off spirits. Mommer called that foolishness but said never to make fun of him because he was a good soul. Uncle Jake mumbled to himself as he worked.

"Hi, you, Uncle Jake," said Arlis.

Uncle Jake turned, his squinty eyes little dots in the shade of his hat. His real name was Jonah Waters but everyone called him Uncle Jake. Cap'n Ben had found him half drowned in the Savannah River when colored folks used to be slaves. Except for

Cap'n Ben, he was the oldest man Arlis knew.

"'Lo, you, child. You coming to work?" He patted Nell's head and looked at Arlis from beneath the hat.

"Yessir."

"Well, plenty clearing wantin' to be done. Pineapples need good cool holes to make their growth in. Make 'em sweet, yes Lord." His pink mouth made a smile and showed the last of his teeth.

"We going to have a good crop, Uncle Jake?"

"Sure. We get enough rain and not too much."

"And if spirits and haints don't get into them," said Arlis.

The old man stopped hacking at the root.

"What you know about the haints and spirits, child?"

"Nothing, I guess."

"Best you don't talk about what you got no idea of. You leave them to me. I know them and their ways." He waved the blade of the machete in a slow arc. "I know them and their ways, child." Uncle Jake talked slow and soft. It made Arlis feel shivery even in daylight.

"Where's Papadad and Mr. Caine, Uncle Jake?"

Uncle Jake stopped the arc of the blade and pointed with it to the other end of the field.

"I gotta go work." The old man had begun digging at the root again. Arlis said good-bye but Uncle Jake had his head down and mumbled to himself as if he were the last man in the world. Just him and the haints and spirits.

Papadad and old man Caine were standing holding machetes in an open space near a pile of smoldering brush. Mr. Caine clenched an unlit pipe upside down in his mouth. He was a bent-up sour-looking man who had land next to theirs; he had been in the Civil War with Grandpa Ben and when he got in a good humor or drunk would tell stories about goddam Yankees and running the blockade.

Arlis figured Papadad must be telling Mr. Caine about the railroad boss holing their boat because Mr. Caine had a scowl on his face. Mr. Caine scowled a great deal of the time like a dried apple, but this scowl ran even deeper. "No-'count Yankee trash," he said.

"Well," said Papadad. "S'long as they bring us down the railroad." Papadad now seemed to be a little embarrassed at telling Mr. Caine about getting shot at by the railroad man.

"Shoulda never lost the war. Hell, we coulda built it ourselfs," said Mr. Caine.

"Fact," said Papadad. "Fact." Papadad had been too young for the war but hated Yankees anyway. He told Arlis that General Sherman's soldiers had stole off all his family's horses and burned the corncrib and that's why he'd left Georgia and come south on a coaster. Arlis waited until the men finished talking and noticed him.

" 'Lo, Mr. Caine," Arlis said.

" 'Lo there, boy. Yer pappy says you was fightin' Yankees." He laughed around his pipe. Arlis shrugged and waited for Papadad to say something, but he didn't. Being close to grown men made him feel uneasy except for Papadad and Cap'n Ben and Uncle Jake.

"Where you want me to work, Papadad?" Arlis asked his father.

"You go help Brit, son. The quicker we get Mr. Jewel's land cleared the quicker we can get to our own."

"Yes, Papadad."

Arlis left the two men. He could see Mr. Caine's son, Brit, working across the clearing. He felt glad he could work with Brit so he could tell about what happened to him that morning.

"Hey, Brit."

"Where you been all morning, Big Ears? Chasing pussy?" Brit was thirteen and liked to talk tough like a man. Brit's swearing interested Arlis but did not always make clear sense to him. "Say up, now, Bo," said Brit and punched Arlis on the shoulder. "Where you been? Tell me and help me dig up this here damn root."

The two boys got down side by side and dug with their machete blades at the root pocket that impacted itself in the flinty limestone.

"Me and Papadad was selling rum to the gang men," said Arlis, then told Brit how the railroad boss had holed their boat. Brit looked impressed. He knew Arlis wouldn't lie because he would see the holes for himself.

"Hot damn, Bo. You coulda been kilt. Them Yankees is terrible. I heard Daddy say they fuck animals and get diseases." Brit sniggered. "I'd rather have me some of that Cuban stuff, though." He punched Arlis in the arm again. "Maybe we can get us both fixed up sometime, partner. What say?" Arlis felt hot across the face and something ran through his groin. He figured Brit made up a lot of stories.

"Shoot, Brit. Let's get this here root unstuck." Brit laughed and the two boys pulled and chopped at the root.

"How much further the trestle work moved toward us since last time me and you seen it, Arlis?"

"Half a mile, maybe, Papadad says. They still got that big steam hammer driving piles. Papadad says railroad's gonna be in Doctor's Arm in a year."

Both boys stopped working and looked at each other. Brit's sharp birdlike face showed real wonder, all pretense of swagger melting away. He rubbed his hands across the front of his stained cotton undershirt.

"God Almighty, Arlis. Think of that. Trains coming right here. All the way from New York City. God Almighty. It's going to make us rich. The train will just come and take our pineapples and limes and sponges and go north. And when we want something we don't have to go to Key West. We just tell them and they bring it by and drop it off to us. People are going to know where we are. We'll be on the rail line. We'll have a town here. Hell, we almost got a town already, but when the railroad comes we'll have a real town with a telegraph office." They stared at each other, having never thought of the grandness of it. They thought of a town besides Mr. Olcott's little store and Preacher's schoolhouse and the boat shed. When the railroad came they'd have a station. People could get on the train and go somewhere.

"Arlis, we could ride to Miami. And in a couple of years we can just get aboard and go clean to Key West in an hour. We can get washed up and get out of this place. Me and you'll go for a weekend in Key West just like that. They got ice cream and pretty girls. Damn!" Brit tore out the root with both hands. "Think of it. We'll be part of something, not just stuck out here on a shitty island no one knows about. We'll get mail everyday and picture books and ice if we want it. Ice!" Brit threw the root down and took Arlis by the shoulders, rocking him slowly back and forth. "Think of it," he shouted as if he'd never thought of it before. Arlis tried hard to think of it, looking into the eyes of Brit and Brit staring back at Arlis's simple features as if he were a stranger.

"Yes," said Arlis in a whisper. "Just think of that."

"Damn you boys, get to clearing." Old Mr. Caine came stumping up. "I'm going to kick you right smart I don't see that brush disappear, Brit. And young Arlis, you'd be good advised to have more industry than this lout if'n I know the mind of your pa."

"Yessir," they both said at once and began chopping. Old Mr. Caine glowered at them and went back to the other side of the field.

"Boy, your pa is mean," said Arlis.

"Yeah. It's because he's old. He's almost as old as your grandpa. He's nigh on to seventy." The boys watched the bent shape of Mr. Caine across the heat-shimmery ground of the clearing. Arlis didn't think that being old made people mean. Grandpa Ben wasn't mean and Uncle Jake wasn't mean. Mommer wasn't mean, but she looked real old.

The sun got lower. A few mosquitoes came out, and Brit blew on the smudge can and waved it around. Arlis looked at the land. Papadad said they'd have forty good acres in new pineapples besides what they had already. They'd have to get on with the planting quickly or the jungle would move in and take the land back. Papadad said the jungle didn't stand still for a day. In the distance, Arlis watched Uncle Jake and one of the Cubans who worked for Jewel pick up their bundles and walk for the edge of the clearing.

"You boys. Come on. It's quittin' time," yelled Mr. Caine from where he and Papadad stood near a smoking brush pile to be away from the mosquitoes. Nell rose and shook the gray ash from her coat and waited while the boys gathered their tools. The boys put their water bottles in woven thatch bags and loped off toward Mr. Caine and Papadad, carrying the machete blades outward so that if they stumbled they wouldn't cut themselves open.

As they ran they saw the short form of Jewel Claire emerge from the path where Uncle Jake and the Cuban had gone. He wore a rumpled linen suit and a sweat-stained sun helmet. The boys drew up so that Mr. Jewel would approach the men first. He was an impatient man. He owned half the island. They waited, scuffing their bare feet and flicking at the weeds with their machetes, not talking. They watched only with the corners of their eyes until Jewel had joined Papadad and Mr. Caine. Brit walked slowly and Arlis followed to where the three men talked.

Mr. Jewel marked on a paper with a pencil stub.

"Half a day for you and your boy. Coleman?" Jewel asked Papadad.

"I reckon, Mr. Jewel," said Papadad. He shifted his quid and spit.

"You was off this morning?" Jewel screwed up his face into the setting sun.

"Yup."

"What doing?"

"Selling half-pints to the Yanks." Papadad spit again. Jewel would like the men to work full days.

"Hope you can give me a full day tomorrow, Coleman. There's work needs doing here. Them Yanks can wait on their drinking." Papadad didn't say anything, letting the silence lay there. Jewel tried to look at Papadad for a while and finally gave it up. He knew Papadad didn't think much of him as a man even though he did respect him for being smart. Mr. Jewel scratched the round little belly that stuck out over the top of his dirty trousers.

"That rail line moving along good, Coleman?"

"She's moving right along, Mr. Jewel," said Papadad.

"That's real fine." Jewel looked back at both men. "I got the assurances of Mr. Seybold of the Florida East Coast Railroad Company that the first train's going to be to Doctor's Arm by 1910. You fellas know what that means. We'll all of us be a damn sight better off than we ever been. But we got to work together. I got assurances we're going to have a camp here and a stop." Papadad and Mr. Caine nodded. Jewel raised his face to the sky for a moment, then lowered it, shaking his head slowly back and forth. "Lord. To think of it. Civilization."

"Yessir," Mr. Caine said.

"Well," Jewel said, coming back to reality. "We still got to do things the old way until that train starts coming. Coleman, you know when your daddy-in-law's sailing down with *Eva Pearl?*"

"You can't figure old Cap'n Ben, Mr. Jewel." Papadad grinned. "He ain't regular like a train."

"That's true. But that train comes we ain't going to have to be depending on the coasters no more." Arlis felt a fear for Cap'n Ben. "I 'spect he's ready to lay up that old boat of his soon anyway, though."

"Grandpa won't ever lay up *Eva Pearl.*"

"Shut it, Arlis," said Papadad.

"Well." Jewel shrugged and looked away from Arlis. He put the paper and pencil into one of the pockets of his baggy suit. "There's always hauling for a coaster to do around the islands, I suppose. But that train line gets here I ain't wasting my time shipping pineapples on no leaky old boat." Arlis hated the snotty way Jewel talked. "I'm going on to the house, men. See you all tomorrow." Jewel hitched up his trousers and walked toward the path that led to the shoreline and Castle Windy.

"You ought not to talk out when grown folks is speaking, Arlis," said Papadad when Jewel had gone.

"I'm sorry, Papadad, but Cap'n Ben ain't going to ever lay up

Eva Pearl. And she ain't no leaky old boat either. He built her himself right here in the boat shed." Papadad smiled just a little.

"Well, son. We'll see. It's nothing we got to worry about now. What needs worrying now is getting land cleared for Mr. Jewel and taking care of our own pineapples and things. Your grandpa comes, we're sure going to have a load for him, I reckon." He patted Arlis on the head.

A single gunshot from the hammock made them all start. Papadad stared and Mr. Caine turned his wrinkly neck in its direction.

"Sounded like one of our string guns," said Papadad.

"Hope that Jewel didn't go down a deer path and kill hisself," Mr. Caine said without sounding concerned. The string guns were set on deer paths so that if a deer tripped the wire, it got shot. This helped keep the deer from eating the crops. "Why don't you boys take the dog and see if we got one? If we did, dress her down and tote it over to Uncle Jake so he can put it in the smokehouse. Me and your pappy are going to ease on home." Mr. Caine knocked his pipe on the heel of his brogan.

"Bring home a slab of that meat, Arlis. We'll soak it tonight and have it for supper tomorrow. Don't dawdle."

"Yessir." Arlis and Brit took off in the direction of the gunshot with Nell running behind. The men watched them go.

"Mind you don't trip one of them guns yourselfs," shouted old Mr. Caine and laughed.

The two boys ran like Indians or at least how Arlis thought Indians would run, steadily, not breathing hard. The dog kept ahead with her nose into the ground and the bush of her tail straight up. They saw the deer path and knew where the gun was by a wide blaze cut into a tree. Blood spattered the ground, looking red and new against the grass. Arlis felt his heart beating another rhythm, his breath becoming shallow. The hound put her nose in the blood and whined, then took off into the thicket with the boys following. A dozen yards into the brush a young doe lay across a toppled palmetto shrub, her chest smashed. It made Arlis feel weak all over to see the smooth brown fur of the hide disappear into the ragged hole.

"Let's drag her out'n here," said Brit. "You fetch the gun. It'll need a cleaning and a reload." The doe, hardly the size of a dog, thrashed with her back feet. "Mind she don't clip you, Arlis."

"I'm minding." Arlis didn't like half-killed things that would have to be killed again. Brit called him a sissy for it.

The boys dragged the deer up the path to where the gun was and then to the clearing. Arlis felt the living carcass bump over the stones and how the weight dragged on his arms.

"I guess we got to do her," said Arlis, so that Brit would not think he was afraid. He stared at the eyes of the doe; they'd gone blank with shock, as if they were made of metal.

"Let's do her different," said Brit. "Here by this pothole." Alone, Brit dragged the doe to a water-filled hole. "See how she likes drowning." Brit dropped the deer's head into the water and held the arch of his bare foot on her neck. Under the water the eyes still looked up at Arlis, shocked and alive. Arlis put his hand to his mouth.

"You damn sissy-ass. It's better'n getting strung up by your hocks and havin' your goddam throat slit. How'd you like that? This here's a more nicer way to go."

Arlis didn't reply.

"Well?"

"Well, I just don't like the doing of it." Arlis hated himself for being the way he was and that Brit could see it. The deer kicked her back legs a little, then became still. Nell sniffed at where the legs came together. A small brown turd worked itself out the anus. Brit pushed the dog away. Arlis avoided looking into the doe's eyes as they hung it onto a tree by its hocks and flayed it open. The doe was so small that the rump was the only thing worth taking. They wrapped the haunches in palmetto leaves and slabbed off some to eat for supper next day, Brit put the haunches into his thatch bag and slung the empty gun over his shoulder.

"I'll take these by Uncle Jake."

"Okay, Brit."

Brit put his hand on Arlis's shoulder. "Arlis, you got to learn not to be such a sissy about killing stuff. A man's got to kill stuff."

"I'm sorry, Brit." He was.

"Hell, Arlis. You're okay, boy." He gave him a friendly nudge. "You're going to be okay. See you tomorrow."

Arlis watched Brit until he disappeared, then walked across the clearing toward the path that led home. Some of the piles of brush were still burning: little bits of light shone from them. Through the trees, Arlis could see the orange light from the windows of the house; in the darkening blue of the sky the first stars had come out. He knew that the coons and possums and maybe even a wildcat must now be eating the innards of the slain deer. It made him tremble a bit. He wished he could be brave and tough like Brit. Brit was right. They had to kill things to eat. He shifted the damp slab of meat he carried in his hands and whistled for Nell to come along.

Arlis stood in the yard between the house and the cook shed. Papadad sat on the far end of the porch, where the light of the lamp from the window outlined him. Arlis could smell the smoke from his pipe. In the cook shed, with her back to the door, Mommer worked at the old black ship stove that covered the wall. She sang to herself. Arlis could not make out any of the words but Mommer swayed back and forth as she worked, the gray pile of hair on her head appearing shiny against the black of the iron stove. Arlis thought how small she looked there by herself. He moved to the door and leaned against the jamb watching.

"I wish my Arlis would come home," Mommer said very loudly so Arlis knew she could tell he was there. She could always tell when he came into a room whether she saw or not.

Mommer turned very quickly with a wooden spoon poised and pointing at the doorway. She smiled at her son, making fine wrinkles come to the corners of her eyes. Her face was as white as the cracked bone cameo she wore against the darkness of her old dress. The coughing sickness had made her pale and shrunken. Every night Arlis prayed to God she wouldn't die.

"Well, don't stand there like a bump, son. Come give your old Mommer a hug." She raised her arms and Arlis came to her, feeling comfort at the touch of her warm dress and the pressure of the way her hands held him. Against his cheek he could hear her breathing and feel the brittle delicateness of her body. Mommer smelled of ironed cotton and lilac powder all covered slightly in the pungent odor of the cough tonic she drank.

Mommer held Arlis by the shoulders at arm's length. looking down at him. She brushed something from the side of his face with her hand. Her fingers were cold against the blush of his cheek.

"Did you help Papadad today?"

"Yes'm. And I brought a slab of venison meat for tomorrow."

Mommer took the wrapped meat and rinsed it under a pitcher.

"We'll soak this overnight and get the gamy taste out of it, son. Tomorrow it will be as nice as a restaurant steak." She put the slab into a shallow dish and sprinkled it with soda before ladling fresh water on it.

"Did you see how far the track line has come, Arlis?" She turned back to the stove.

"Yes. Mr. Jewel said by next year it'll be here."

"Lord," she said. "Next year." Arlis couldn't see her face, so he didn't know if it pleased her or not. He didn't think it did. "You go out to the porch and wash up, now. Wash your neck and elbows and behind your ears. Then you can help me set the table." She turned back to him. "We're having cracked conch, snap beans, and leafy lettuce. And I bought a big can of peaches from Mr. Olcott and made a cobbler for you. Now go on. Take a lamp with you."

The paraffin lamp sputtered and threw long shadows across the porch. A warm wind came nicely from the east-southeast off the Gulf Stream. Arlis removed his shirt and washed his face and thin trunk in front of the spotted mirror that hung from the wall. He saw the sinews contract in his arm and shoulder as he pumped water into the basin and wondered if he would grow hair under his arms like Brit had begun to do. Arlis lowered his head into the basin. It made him think of the deer before he could force himself to think of something else.

When he lathered the back of his neck Arlis looked into the night at the Gulf Stream. Two green starboard lights flickered from packet schooners running to Key West or South America. It thrilled him to think how close the ships were and how far away they would be by morning. He buried his head in the basin once more and rubbed the cold cistern water over his skin and through his hair. The ships made him miss his grandpa. Maybe, he thought, Cap'n Ben will come soon.

He went into the house to set the table. Papadad still sat on the porch outside the front door. He did not look over when Arlis went into the room. He stared into the night, one side of his face showing in the lamplight. Arlis thought maybe he was staring at the two ships. Sometimes Papadad sat staring like that for more than an hour. Mommer always told Arlis that Papadad had deep thoughts and was an intelligent man.

Arlis set the places on the wide teakwood table. A sloop had gone on the reef in a storm three summers ago, and when she broke up the tabletop had floated into the mouth of the bight, where Papadad had fetched it out of the water. He'd made the legs for it and given it to Mommer. Papadad could make anything with the tools in the boat shed. Arlis hoped he'd build another skiff soon so he could help.

Mommer began bringing the hot covered dishes from the stove. They looked large against her but she walked straight and set each one in its place as she always did. When everything had been put on the table she went to Papadad's chair and put her hands on his big shoulders. He started slightly as if he'd been dozing, then looked at her. He smiled a little. Mommer smiled back, the skin looking tight on the framework of her face, her teeth appearing too large because the flesh lay so close to the bone. Papadad patted one of her hands and rose, standing much higher than she. Arlis drew the chair for Mommer and Papadad sat opposite her. Papadad prayed.

"Heavenly Father, we thank Thee for this Thy bounty which Thou hast set before us and please hurry along the railroad train. In Jesus Christ Our Lord, Amen."

"Amen," said Arlis.

"Amen," said Mommer, but she was looking up sharply at Papadad. "Coleman, I don't think we ought to bother the Almighty with that railroad coming."

"Now Emma, it don't hurt to ask Him to give it just a little help." Papadad grinned.

The family ate quietly. Once or twice Papadad asked Mommer about her day or she about his. The silence made Arlis comfortable and let him think about his food and about the railroad and about Cap'n Ben.

Papadad folded his napkin when he finished eating. He scraped his chair back.

"I guess I'll have my coffee on the porch, Emma," he said. He stood by Mommer and touched her arm for a moment before he let his hand drop.

"I'll bring it to you. You go sit."

"No," Papadad said. "I'll fix it. You and Arlis finish your supper."

Mommer spooned another dish of the cobbler for Arlis, then began to gather the plates.

"If that railroad comes, will Grandpa have to give up *Eva Pearl?*" asked Arlis.

Mommer had stopped working and looked at Arlis. Her eyes were like two small blue stones on the beach.

"I don't know, son."

"Say he won't, Mommer."

"I don't know, child. Only the Lord knows." She put her arm around Arlis and drew him to her for a moment. "You got to trust things to the Lord."

2

"Arlis! Come on, boy!" Brit and Poopy Esquinaldo stood in the backyard of Arlis's house. "Come on."

Mommer gave Arlis a piece of corn bread and two Cuban bananas wrapped in newspaper and kissed him on the head.

"You have a good day in school," she said. "Listen good to what Preacher says." Arlis was afraid of Preacher and hated school.

He went into the yard and fell in step with Poopy and Brit. Poopy gave him a dutch rub on the top of his head and Arlis pulled away. Poopy grinned.

"How you, Big Ears? Brit tells me the Yanks tried to kill you."

Arlis shrugged. It pleased him that the older boys were impressed. Arlis pretended that it had been nothing unusual. Poopy was Brit's best friend. His father worked at Jewel Claire's shark-oil plant on the other side of the island.

"Another morning of listening to old Preacher's horseshit. "Hell," said Poopy. "Fade back, Brit." He took an india-rubber ball from his pocket. Brit faded back and caught it when Poopy threw.

"Three-corner," called Brit. Arlis quickly stuck his two books into the front of his pants before Brit threw the ball. He missed and ran furiously after it.

"You couldn't catch it in a bucket, Big Ears," jeered Poopy. Arlis didn't mind their kidding. He didn't feel any meanness in it. Arlis caught the next one Brit threw and Poopy missed one. Arlis didn't say anything but figured that put them even.

The other children were coming along the path. Arlis and Brit and Poopy were the only three boys who lived on the shore of the bight. The others had to come across the island. Most of them were the kids of the sponge fishermen. A few of them worked at Jewel's shark-oil plant with Poopy's father.

The boys passed Mr. Olcott's store. JoAnna came out the door and down the crushed coral yard into the path. Her father leaned in the doorway. Arlis wondered why his face was so red since he stayed in the store all day. He had a big nose shot full of blue veins.

"Hi, Jo," said Arlis.

JoAnna Olcott smiled at him. She carried her books in both arms held against her chest. She was a year younger than Brit and Poopy.

"Hello, Arlis."

"Hello, Arlis!" Poopy and Brit both mimicked. Brit ran ahead and turned around. "Throw me one." Poopy threw the ball and ran further up the path past Brit. The two older boys pitched the ball back and forth and didn't look back, leaving Arlis with JoAnna. He wished he could be with them instead. They seemed to have forgotten him.

He walked along beside Jo. Next to Brit and Poopy he guessed he liked her best. The rest of the children were younger than he or much older.

"What silly boys," said JoAnna. She still carried her books into her chest and Arlis thought how nicely her shoulders moved when she walked. "Did you read up on Romeo and Juliet?"

"Some," Arlis lied.

"Good enough to read if Preacher makes you?"

Arlis said nothing.

"You could do better if you wanted, Arlis."

"I don't care about that stuff."

"You ought to try."

Arlis turned on her, "I'm just not too good on book learning, okay?" He tried to look mean. "Like you. You're his pet. He doesn't like any of the other girls."

"That's just because he works in the store for my daddy. If he ever smacked me with that cane, I know my daddy would be good and mad."

"You're his pet is all."

"Quit saying that."

Arlis looked at JoAnna. She tried not to smile at him but her deep blue eyes sparkled. Her eyes were flaked with bits of gold like a cat's eyes. Arlis guessed she was a pretty girl. She could fish good and knew how to handle a skiff better than Brit or Poopy, but Arlis would never tell them that he thought so.

The flat sound of the old dinner bell came to them. Preacher had bolted it on top of a post. Arlis and Jo could see him pulling at the rope outside the unpainted schoolhouse that sat halfway up the bluff next to the cemetery. Preacher's whole body jerked up and down like a weighted spar in the water when he pulled the bell rope.

"Come on, Arlis. We'll be late." Jo took him by the arm and pulled him after her. She's a good runner too for a girl, thought Arlis.

Jo held his arm until they got to the door of the schoolhouse.

"'Bye, Arlis," she said. She squeezed his arm and it surprised him. He watched her go to the side of the room where the girls sat.

Poopy shoved Arlis onto the wooden bench beside Brit and sat down next to him. A boy in front of them threw a paper wad over their heads to where the younger children were. The paper wad came back. Brit reached across Arlis and flicked Poopy on the ear.

A loud crack sounded and the room became immediately silent. Preacher slapped his cane once again on the top of his desk and walked to the center of the room.

"Hands folded in front of you."

The ragged tails of Preacher's coat flapped against his legs, making him look like an awkward bird. He walked in an uncertain circle then paused, raising both arms over his head. The cuffs of the ill-fitting coat drew up his wrists halfway to the elbows.

"Let us pray." Preacher kept his arms up and dropped his chin to his chest. Thin strands of waxed hair crossed the baldness of his head like inked lines. Poopy made a small farting sound. Preacher raised his head slightly and looked at the class with one eye then lowered his chin again.

"Almighty God," he sighed. "We beseech Thee to enter the minds and hearts of these children that they may gain in knowledge and follow Thy will. Guide them in the path of righteousness and let them not stray to wickedness and the sensual folly that undermines youth. Make them to obey their parents and their teacher and submit to the wisdom of experience. In the name of Our Lord and Savior Jesus Christ. Amen."

Without looking up, Preacher then said, "Lord's Prayer." The class prayed out loud.

"Amen." Preacher hitched up his trousers. "James Esquinaldo, come forward and hold the flag while we all recite the Pledge of Allegiance."

Poopy slid off the bench and shuffled to the front of the class. He took the flagstaff and held the colors diagonally, keeping a serious face.

"Rise," said Preacher. "I pledge allegiance to the flag…" he began. The class joined in. Behind Preacher's back Brit put both fingers in his mouth and pulled his lips apart. He stuck out his tongue at Poopy. Poopy struggled to look away but his gaze came back to Brit. Brit crossed his eyes. Poopy held his breath and his face got larger and dark red.

"…With liberty and justice for all." Brit touched the tip of his nose with his tongue and stuck his ears out.

Poopy's laugh exploded through his nose, causing a string of snot to fly out and hang momentarily from his chin until he quickly wiped it off with the back of his hand. The class broke into shouts and laughter. Preacher's eyes popped. He ran to Poopy, his arms and coattails flapping.

"Mr. Esquinaldo! Explain yourself. Put that flag away and then come here to me and explain yourself." Preacher waved his cane. Poopy slowly put the flag in the corner and came back to the front of the room. The laughter rose. "Silence," Preacher croaked. Preacher glared at the class, then turned to Poopy. "Hold out your hands, young sir." Poopy held out his palms. Preacher brought the cane down smartly. "Explain yourself!" He struck again. Poopy rubbed his hands together and screwed his face up. "Put your hands back out here, you young devil! Now explain yourself." The cane quivered at the ready.

"He made me do it."

"Who?"

"Him!"

"Who?" Preacher brought the cane down in a full arc.

"Ow! Him! Him! Him!"

"Who? Who? Who?" Preacher struck three times.

"Ow! Nobody." Poopy rubbed his hands on the sides of his pants. Preacher breathed hard. He rolled his bulging eyes upward.

"Take your seat, Mr. Esquinaldo. You are a disgrace. This class is a disgrace. You have mocked the flag. Mocked the flag. Take your seat, you lout!" Preacher swung but Poopy dodged the cane and scrambled for the bench.

"Take out your copy slates. All of you," Preacher panted. "Second form too. We'll spend this morning at penmanship coupled with a lesson in respect for the flag." Preacher turned to the board and wrote: Love thy country and honor thy flag.

"Each of you shall write this one hundred times."

The children groaned.

"You may thank Mr. Esquinaldo for it. Form your letters carefully or you may expect to do it again. Commence!"

The gritty sound of chalk against slate filled the room. Preacher paced uneasily for a while, then settled upon his stool behind the large desk at the front of the room. He peered over his narrow spectacles at the downturned heads, then opened a book. The room became warmer. Outside the insects began their droning as the sun struck them where they slept in the tall grass. Preacher read rapidly at first, then more slowly until his thin lips formed each word. At last he nodded fitfully.

Arlis worked over his slate, clumsily imitating Preacher's faultless script. Poopy Esquinaldo leaned across him to Brit.

"You shit-ass," he hissed. "Thanks a goddam lot."

"Love." Preacher drew the word out and stretched his bony neck. "Love is beauty. Love takes many forms. There is the manly love shared between friends as with the noble Greek heroes of mythology: the pure love of youth, elevated and unsullied by lust of the flesh." Arlis saw Preacher's gaze rest on him. His blotched lids hooded the slightly jaundiced color of his eyes.

"And there is the love of man and woman which has been decreed by the Almighty." Preacher faced the window and continued. "Without the love of man and woman there could be no procreation, no propagation of the species." Poopy winked at Arlis and Brit. He made a circle with his thumb and index finger and thrust the middle finger of his other hand back and forth through the hole. Brit smirked and elbowed Arlis in the ribs. Arlis blushed. "But there is an age of innocence that transcends the baser instincts of man's love for woman and centers on the essence of that emotion." Preacher wrote on the board: Romeo and Juliet.

"Arlis." Preacher faced the class. "Tell us who wrote that play."

Arlis froze in terror. He knew the name. It was there in his mind ready to be spoken but Arlis couldn't find it. It was William...William...

"Rise to your feet, Mr. Arlis, and be so kind to tell us please," Preacher said dryly. He dangled the cane loosely in his bony fingers.

Arlis shuffled slowly to his feet, everything around him a blur. William...William.... Oh God. He looked at the faces of the children. He looked at the little ones in the back of the class and then at the girls' side. JoAnna sat next to Wanda Rondinero and stared into Arlis's eyes. Very slowly Arlis watched her lips form the name. William. The lips formed the name again.

"William. William."

"Yes?" Preacher thumped the tip of the cane on the floor. JoAnna's lips moved again.

"William Shapespeare!" cried Arlis, feeling the relief of knowledge pouring through him.

"It's Shakespeare, you moron. Shakespeare!"

The class roared with laughter. Arlis felt the heat rising to his face. JoAnna paled as Preacher took a menacing step toward him.

"Preacher! Look! Look! Lookit down to the bight!" cried a small boy next to the window. In a rush the class craned their necks. Some rose. Slates fell on the floor.

"What! What is it now?" Forgetting Arlis, Preacher took long strides to the window, puffing out his hollow cheeks. A whistle blast covered the noise of the room, rolling heavily to them up the hill from the beach. Children left their benches and ran to the window.

"Remain seated. Remain seated," cried Preacher, pulling at the window sash. The whistle sounded again.

"It's a steam launch!" They could all see it coming into the dock in front of Jewel Claire's house. Black coal smoke billowed out of its funnel and when the whistle blew two white plumes of steam shot out at angles from either side of the stack. She shone with fresh red paint set off in black-and-yellow trim. A canvas awning covered the deck and polished brass steam fittings flashed like gold. She blew again and the first of the children spilled from the schoolhouse, running down the slope of the bluff to the beach.

"Come back here," called Preacher. But he'd lost them. The smaller children flowed around and between his legs like water and the older ones jostled him aside to get to the door. At last Preacher followed, running on pipestem legs with ragged coattails flapping behind in the breeze.

At the bottom of the slope, Arlis caught his breath. The wharf in front of Jewel's Castle Windy filled with people. He watched as more came running from the fields and from the other side of the island. The steam launch blew again, then made a low continual sighing like a small train. Arlis pushed his way to the edge of the dock to see better. Four men in blue-and-white sailor shirts were tying her off to the pilings. The boat was tidy and neat as a toy.

"Make way. Make way." Arlis heard Preacher's panting voice. "Make way for Mr. Jewel." Preacher was always sucking up to old Jewel. Preacher preceded Jewel to where the launch lay at her mooring. The crowd parted, the sponge fishermen and planters looking back and forth between Jewel and the launch. The sun reflected off the awning made Jewel squint. His suit looked rumpled and his sunhat sat crookedly on his head. He read out loud the gold-leafed lettering on the side of the boat. His puffy eyes lit up. "Florida East Coast Railroad Company."

From the waist of the launch beneath the crisp awning stepped a tall man with long sandy mustaches. His hair was parted in the middle and slicked down like two beetle wings. He looked up at the crowd, then at Jewel. His white ducks sparkled and light shone from the buttons of his coat. Smiling greatly, he crossed the gangplank to the wharf.

"Mr. Jewel Claire?" The man stood before Jewel and bowed slightly at the waist. Jewel drew back a little.

"I'm him," said Jewel and rubbed the side of his nose with his knuckle.

The man thrust out his pink spatula of a hand. "Clyde Seybold. Florida East Coast Railroad. At your service." Mr. Seybold pumped Jewel's hand and folded a degree at the waist again. He stood almost twice as tall as Jewel Claire. "I had the pleasure of corresponding with you when you sold us the right-of-way. Now it's truly an honor to meet you in person." Mr. Seybold had the whitest teeth Arlis had ever seen. He turned from Jewel Claire to the crowd. "Good day, friends," he bawled. "I bring you people of Doctor's Arm greetings from the Florida East Coast Railroad Company." Mr. Seybold looked at the launch. "Boys, go on and start unpacking." There were about fifteen men aboard and Arlis saw them start to move like a caved-in hill of ants.

"You have a lovely community here, Mr. Claire," said Mr. Seybold. "I assume you're sort of the mayor."

"Yes," piped Preacher. He stood anxiously at Jewel's elbow.

"Sort of," mumbled Jewel.

"And you, sir?" Mr. Seybold faced Preacher. Preacher fairly danced without moving.

"Preacher Scoggins, Mr. Seybold." He bowed with one hand over his sunken chest. "At your service."

"Ah. The clergy. How marvelous."

Sailors were stacking barrels and crates on the dock.

"Mr. Mayor," said Mr. Seybold, so everyone could hear. "With your permission we're here to survey the land for the right-of-way. We'd also like to provide a little modest entertainment for the folks of Doctor's Arm on behalf of the company." He paused significantly. Jewel's eyes wandered. Preacher nudged him gently.

"Oh yes," Jewel said.

"Splendid. Splendid," Mr. Seybold said. "Emmet," he said over his shoulder to a man in a khaki shirt and pith helmet. "Get your survey party going." He returned his attention to Jewel Claire. "Mr. Claire and I have business to discuss."

At this, Jewel straightened himself and looked quite directly at Mr. Seybold. He smoothed the front of his rumpled suit. Now in his own way he looked every bit as able and dignified as Mr. Seybold.

"Yes," Jewel said. "Business. That there will be just fine."

The mob had pushed its way in so that Arlis could no longer see Jewel and Mr. Seybold. He made his way off the wharf and walked a few paces up the side of the shell mound. He looked back at the narrow piece of land between himself and the beach. Two of the sailors from the launch came out of the crowd carrying a canvas package slung between them on a pole. They dropped it on the ground as two other men drove stakes into the turf with mallets.

"Some of you men there give us a hand if you want to have a proper celebration," called the nearest one. Half a dozen sponge fishermen helped them untie the bundle. The inside opened into red-and-white canvas. Others joined in, unrolling it over the grass then unfolding it lengthways. The sailors connected poles together and inserted them through grommet holes. With a shout the men pulled on long lines as the sailors directed and a great striped pavilion sprang up like a sail on a boat.

"Hooray!" cried the children. While the lines were still being tightened, the sailors busied themselves erecting a long plank table beneath the tent.

Some distance away, past the trail that went to the planting ground, Arlis saw the party of men who'd left the launch first. One was peering through a small telescope mounted on a tripod. Two others walked out in front of him with poles while the fourth wrote on a long yellow pad of paper.

The sound of music caused Arlis to look back at the striped pavilion. He'd only heard real music like this in Key West on trips with Cap'n Ben. One sailor thumped a drum while his two mates played the accordion and brass horn. The crowd gathered close, clapping their hands in time. A colored boy who'd come from the launch was setting out cakes in small tin pans on the table.

A gang of fishermen helped move boxes and casks to the pavilion. Arlis saw his father and Mr. Esquinaldo and two sailors roll a barrel up the gangway and onto the wharf. Forward, beyond the launch's awning, a man cranked the winch on the stubby mast boom. Up from the hold, wrapped in blanket-lined canvas and secured in cargo netting, rose a great block of white ice. A cry went up from the crowd. Arlis stared, then ran to see. Uncle Jake pushed a wheelbarrow up to receive it.

The ice dangled at the end of its cable. Children reached out to touch it, drawing their hands back in surprise, then touching again and licking the coldness from their fingers. Arlis heard the men laughing.

"This'll cool her down good!" said one fisherman.

"Damned if we've ever seen the likes of this here."

"There's kegs of beer and cider been cooling for you fellers all the way from Marathon," called a sailor to the men.

"Papadad," yelled Arlis. He could see his father's head over the others in the crowd.

"There you are, boy." Papadad and Mr. Esquinaldo stood beside the keg they'd helped roll up the gangway. It had been set into a cradle and Mr. Esquinaldo leaned on it as if he owned it. Arlis worked his way past the men toward his father.

"Step back, gents," said a sailor. He twisted a heavy screw into the bung and with help from Mr. Esquinaldo wrenched it out. From a sack looped in his belt he took out a spigot and tapped it into the hole.

"Knock her in there, Sammy," he called to a man who carried a wooden maul. Sammy drove the spigot home and the men turned the keg round in its cradle.

"Bring them mugs!"

The one called Sammy set out clay mugs on the table. The sailors began quickly filling them and handing them out. Another cask was opened, then another. Arlis reached his father's side.

"What's that, Papadad?"

Papadad drank long from the clay mug. When he'd finished he had a white line of foam on his mustache. He wiped his face with his hand.

"Boy, that there is beer. Cold beer that's been on ice blocks all the way from Marathon." Papadad's eyes danced. "Real ice, just like you seen." He bent at the knee so that he was face level with Arlis. He put his hands on Arlis's shoulders. His breath smelled like old too-sweet fruit. "Son, that railroad's coming sure and it's bringing all kinds of things for us. There's cold cider over there on the table for you young 'uns. You have some of that cold cider and see what you think. Have you some cakes too, son." He stood back up, keeping his hand on Arlis's shoulder but not looking at him. He looked northeast to where the rails would come. "It's coming sure. It's coming sure," he said dreamily, and his hand slid slowly from the boy's shoulder. Arlis looked to where his father had told him the train would come, and when he looked back, his father had gone.

JoAnna Olcott followed Arlis past the Indian well and a little way up the bluff. She sat down when he sat down. She ate a piece of cake from a tin plate. Arlis wished he were alone.

He watched the red-and-white top of the pavilion. Just about all the people who lived on Doctor's Arm were there. Mommer wouldn't be there because of how sick she was. Arlis saw Papadad and Mr. Esquinaldo and the other men with their clay mugs of beer. A group of them were pitching horseshoes. The ground all around the pavilion was trampled down. Patches of green were torn up, showing the rich red mold beneath it like rusty iron. Arlis wondered if anyone was working the planting grounds today. He guessed not.

"Do you want a piece of my cake?" asked JoAnna.

"No."

"Well, I guess it's going to happen for sure," she said. "The railroad coming."

Arlis didn't speak.

"Don't you think it'll be nice, Arlis?"

"Not if Cap'n Ben has to give up coasting."

"I didn't think of that part." She looked down at what was left of her cake.

"Well, I did. No one will need him to tote cargo if the railroad does it all. But I'm still going to go to work for him on *Eva Pearl*. Damn the railroad." Then Arlis felt sorry for talking tough to Jo. Sometimes if he didn't have her he wouldn't have any friends at all and he knew it. He tried to soften up his voice. "Do you really think it will be all that nice, Jo? All those changes? I mean things are okay the way they are now. We don't really need a railroad."

JoAnna waited awhile then said: "It's so hard to think of. I hope it will be all right. We have to hope so. There's not much we can do, is there? I hope it will be nice. But I'm sorry about your grandpa."

Arlis shrugged. "That's okay. We'll find cargo. Cap'n Ben's promised to take me aboard someday, you know. I'd hoped we could haul cargo from here, but a man has to go where the work is if he's aboard a coaster." Arlis felt full of pride when he talked of Cap'n Ben's promise to take him aboard. *Eva Pearl* was his dream.

"You wouldn't be gone forever, will you? I'd miss you terrible. You're just like my own little brother." When Mrs. Olcott had died bearing JoAnna, Mommer had cared for the baby. Jo called Arlis her little brother and it irritated him.

"I ain't so damn little. You're only two years older than me. That don't make you so much."

"Don't be mad, Arlis. But I would miss you terrible. No one else'll fish or go sailing with me. Not Brit or Poopy. They're so nasty anyway. You wouldn't go off forever, would you?" Her eyes were a little wet.

"Oh shucks no, Jo. This here's my home. And you're my friend." JoAnna smiled and it made him glad inside. She took the last piece of cake out of the tin plate and handed it to him.

The sun worked its way down lower to the horizon. Arlis and JoAnna watched its reflection in the water of the salt pond. The birds began settling in, large white ones, herons, who stood out on the green mangroves like awkward flowers. The fringe of the hanging branches mirrored the birds perfectly in the stillness. As the sun dropped, the herons took on a pinkish cast and the leaves of the mangroves were as if seen through the glass of an old bottle. To Arlis it had become too incredibly still until first one, then half a dozen of the herons nervously stretched their wings and as if by a signal took off at once, circling the salt pond.

"What's wrong with the birds?" asked Jo.

Arlis held up his hand without taking his eyes from the clump of mangroves where the first bird had shown its alarm. Small concentric circles radiated from the mangrove roots that disappeared into the shallow water there. The disturbance grew greater and at last there appeared the head of a man, pith-helmeted and carrying a surveying rod. He looked to the left and right, then back over his shoulder. Arlis and JoAnna watched him. He waded a few steps into the water, then stood straight as the soldiers Arlis had seen at the army barracks in Key West, while holding the rod like a rifle. Twice he waved his free hand and moved the pole slightly, then, the mud of the salt pond sucking at his boots, he waded back into the mangroves, where he paused only long enough to tie a red rag onto a branch before he disappeared.

"What was it, Arlis? Who was that man?" JoAnna sounded to Arlis as if she were frightened. Something he could not name made Arlis afraid too.

"I think they're measuring for the rails. I saw that man and some others looking with a sort of telescope." He could still see the uncertainty in JoAnna's face. He reached out and pulled her braid. "They've got to measure straight lines, dummy. You know what Preacher says."

"The shortest distance between two points is a straight line." JoAnna mimicked Preacher's voice, then laughed. She lay back in the grass and stared up at the failing sky. Her face had a peaceful look now and it gave Arlis a sense of relief that what troubled her about the surveyor had passed.

The herons came back. Only the red rag hung in the mangrove tree like a spot of blood, and a feeling of something nameless would not fully leave Arlis as he watched it. Suddenly he did not want to be there above the salt pond looking down on the herons clustered around the red cloth in the mangroves. Arlis took JoAnna's hand and pulled her to her feet. He wanted to be happy. Everyone wanted the railroad to come and it was coming. It would bring civilization and make Papadad rich. And he and Cap'n Ben could haul cargo to Nassau. Or Jamaica. Or things to South America. What difference did it make? The railroad would be good for Papadad and everyone and he could go on *Eva Pearl* someday.

"Come on," he said to JoAnna. "Let's walk up the bluff and watch the party. Then we can go eat. It must be almost time."

By now the bluff made a shadow across the pavilion. Gray smoke lay thin and flat over the beach as the wind died off with evening. From where they stood Arlis and JoAnna could see the colored boy who'd come with the sailors work over chicken pieces he'd placed on a wide iron grill above a charcoal pit. The sailors took up their playing again, the music floating up the side of the bluff to the two children, sounding strange over the distance.

"It's like the Fourth of July, Arlis."

"Yes. Better. I've never had cold cider except in Key West. Brit says the train'll bring ice here to us regular."

"No." She slapped both her knees at the same time.

"There's no reason why not."

The small valley below the bluff had darkened enough now so they could see the glowing embers in the charcoal pit. To the right, out to sea where there still remained some light, a single large packet ship went south. Her great topsails caught the last of the sun's rays and glowed pink and clean like painted birds. Again Arlis thought of the herons and the red rag and the coming of the steel tracks and wished the packet ship were *Eva Pearl* with himself aboard, carrying him away from what he did not understand. He looked over at Jo, wondering if perhaps she could understand. They stood close together watching the schooner diminish in the afterglow of day.

At the charcoal pit the colored boy rose and vigorously ran an iron pipe around the inside of a triangular dinner bell. The musicians stopped and Arlis and JoAnna watched the people begin moving to the pit.

"Let's go eat, Arlis," she said. Arlis let her walk ahead. He felt the coolness of the grass beneath his bare feet. Before descending to where the ridge of the bluff obscured the horizon, he paused for one last glimpse of the packet schooner's topsails. A weight seemed to lift up and away from somewhere inside himself.

"JoAnna! JoAnna! Over here!" called Mr. Olcott. "Come. I got some chicken and baked beans for you." JoAnna looked at Arlis and made a very small smile that turned just the edge of her lips upward. The boy watched her go to her father.

Most of the families had spread blankets on the grass around the pavilion. Paraffin flares atop poles driven into the earth gave the scene a color like a false dawn. At the end of the pavilion nearest the cookfire, men packed themselves in tight by the iced casks and drank and laughed. Arlis saw Papadad and Mr. Esquinaldo and old Mr. Caine smoking cigars. They all seemed to be talking at once. On the table, mixed with the clay mugs, were ranks of long green bottles with their corks out.

"Hey, Bo. Let's get us some of that chicken." Brit came up behind Arlis. Arlis was glad to see him, glad that Brit had sought him out. "This here is some party, don't you think?"

"Sure is." Arlis wished Brit would always be so friendly to him. He wished he were as old as Brit and Poopy so he could be best friends like they were.

Arlis followed Brit to where stacks of tin plates and wooden forks were laid out. They each took a plate and went to the cook fire. The colored boy squatted on his hams, arranging the chicken with a long steel pick. He wore a white puffed hat. The dancing fire in the pit made his face appear purple-black as if it were painted with varnish.

"What's it to be, my men? White or dark?" His broad teeth caught the light. He looked about as old as Brit.

"Dark meat for me," said Brit.

"Me too, please," said Arlis.

"Dark meat the best and I don't mean chickens." The boy winked at Arlis and Brit, then expertly speared two thighs and two legs and put them on their plates.

"How long you worked for the railroad?" Brit asked.

"Long time. Long time." The colored boy shifted so he could look up better at the two white boys. "Since I was littler than him." He pointed at Arlis with the chicken spear. Arlis hated being thought of as little.

"You from Key West?"

"Key West?" The colored boy laughed, showing his pink

tongue in the firelight. "You kidding me, white boy? I got no use for no Key West. I a city boy. City boy. I be from New York City."

"Jesus Christ," said Brit.

"You come all the way here from New York on the train?" Arlis asked.

"All the way." He threw his head back and winked again. "I like being a traveling man."

"Ain't that just the best life? The railroad," said Brit with enthusiasm. "Hell, I want to be a traveling man too." To Arlis, Brit seemed to have lost some of his dignity. He'd never seen him get so excited about anything.

"It's fine. Fine," said the colored boy. Then he paused and pushed his white puffed cap back and forth to scratch his head. "But sometimes it's lonely too. Sometimes I miss my old mammy." He looked at them and shrugged as if he were apologizing for the fact that missing his mother made traveling life something less than perfect.

"You boy," said one of the sailors as he walked up to the pit. "Fork me up two drumsticks."

"Right, boss."

Arlis and Brit moved out of the sailor's way and found a place to sit on the grass.

The wind picked up again off the Gulf Stream, clearing the air of mosquitoes. Arlis and Brit ate and picked out the stars of the constellations. Poopy came up with his plate and sat down beside them.

"That there nigger came all the way from New York City on the train." Brit nodded toward the cook.

"Shit." Poopy said.

"It's true. You ask Arlis. He heard him say it. Didn't he say it Arlis?"

"He said it."

"Maybe he lied. Niggers lie."

"Uncle Jake don't lie," said Arlis. Uncle Jake was the only colored man Arlis knew. Mommer called Uncle Jake a colored gentleman. No gentleman ever lied, she said.

"Well, Uncle Jake's different. He lives here." Poopy retreated and Arlis felt the victory.

"Besides, Poopy," said Brit. "if that boy didn't come from New York, where did he come from? There's nothing north of Miami except wilderness."

"There's Jacksonville and Atlanta and Washington, D.C," said Arlis.

"Shut up, you smart ass."

"Yeah, shut up, William Shapespeare," said Poopy.

Arlis wished he'd kept shut up, but he was mad at Poopy anyway. The boys ate in silence.

"Hell, let's go have a close look at that steam launch, boys," said Brit. "The tide's dropped. We can get up under the dock and damn near touch it." They stacked their empty plates.

Poopy had already gotten to his feet. Arlis scrambled behind the older boys.

They walked down the beach to where Jewel Claire's shell mound disappeared into the shallows. The big ironwood piles of the wharf started beyond that. Paraffin flares illuminated the launch where she bumped the rope fenders of the dock. The boys crawled out on the braces beneath the dock and sat with their legs over the water, admiring the steam launch.

"Look," Arlis said almost to himself. "All that bright work is mahogany." He knew the look of mahogany from helping in the boat shed. He wanted mahogany trim on his boat someday.

"She's sure clean," murmured Poopy. "I never seen a boat so clean. Couldn't rake no sponges with her, though. Free-board's too high."

"Sour grapes," said Brit.

"Horse apples."

Arlis was about to speak when men's voices came from the waist of the launch. There was laughter. Brit held his finger to his lips and looked at Arlis and Poopy. Half a glowing cheroot arched over the mahogany rail of the launch and winked out with a quick hiss in the water.

The thick legs of Jewel Claire waddled up the gangway and

stood on the dock over their heads. The boys could see him through the gaps in the planks. Mr. Seybold came behind him.

"Have another cheroot, Mr. Claire."

"Thank you, Mr. Seybold, I will."

A match cracked and Arlis heard Jewel suck and exhale. The strong voice of Mr. Seybold went on.

"I think we understand each other, sir. You have a fine piece of land here and my railroad crosses it. As official agent you receive a little piece of all the business that takes place."

"And for your kind considerations I give you a piece of my piece," said Jewel. His voice sounded sloppy. "That's how it should be. That's how business is done."

"Of course I expect everyone here to benefit astronomically by this progress," said Mr. Seybold. "Certainly the common people of the island will be much elevated."

"But we'll, me and you, be elevated more," put in Jewel.

"Yes, Mr. Claire. I expect you could say that."

The two men laughed and Arlis heard them walk in matched stride across the planking of the dock.

"So how about that?" hissed Poopy.

"What do you expect?" Brit said. "Old Jewel owns all the land that's worth owning. Naturally he's going to make money. A dummy can see that." He paused. "But I'm going to watch how he does it and I'm going to make me some money too. That railroad stinks of money. You just got to watch to see how to get it. You got to watch men like that fellow Seybold and old Jewel. Grubbing pineapples and salting fish is just for keeping alive." Brit jerked his thumb in the direction where Jewel and Mr. Seybold had walked. "Study on them two. They know how to get ahead."

"Well, the railroad ain't going to be here for a while yet," said Poopy. "You got plenty of time to do your thinking on it. Right now, I'm for getting me some more of that grub."

The musicians had packed up when the three boys got back to the pavilion. Most of the people who had picnicked on the grass were shaking their blankets out. Arlis saw several of the women walking toward the part of the beach where the cottages were, some of them carrying babies and others drawing children along by their hands. Beneath the canvas of the pavilion the men at the casks were laughing loudly and still crowded shoulder to shoulder, shouting over each other to be heard. Arlis saw Papadad and waved, but Papadad didn't see him. Arlis thought he would take some chicken home to Mommer. There was still plenty on the edges of the grill, though the colored boy had gone.

Arlis picked some good pieces and clamped them between two tin plates. Brit and Poopy helped themselves to more cake.

Arlis made his way to where Papadad stood and pulled at his sleeve because everyone talked so loudly.

"Ho! Arlis!" cried Papadad. His face was as red as Mr. Olcott's. His hat was gone and he looked different without it.

"I'm going to take some chicken home to Mommer."

"Good, son. You do that. You're a fine boy to think of your Mommer, God love her." Papadad laid a heavy hand on Arlis's head and mussed his hair affectionately. "You come late in life to me and your Mommer, son. Just like old Abraham and Sarah in the Bible." Papadad swayed a little and laughed. He leaned on Arlis. "But you a fine boy. Now get on home and tell Mommer I'll be along directly."

"Wait now, young Arlis." Mr. Esquinaldo was wedged in between Papadad and old Mr. Caine. One of the long-necked green bottles hung from his dirty fingers and Arlis could smell the stink of Jewel Claire's shark-oil plant on his clothes.

"Yessir?"

"Where that boy of mine?"

"Poopy?"

"James. Poopy. Whatever you call that young rascal. I'm looking for him."

Mr. Esquinaldo didn't seem to be able to hold his eyes on Arlis. He looked into Arlis's eyes, then his forehead, then at something beyond him before he pulled his gaze back down to the boy's face. He blinked. "Where he at?"

"He's over by the fire eating cake with Brit, Mr. Esquinaldo."

"You tell him to come over to me, young Arlis."

"Yessir." Mr. Esquinaldo stood crookedly, held up by the shoulders of Papadad and the man next to him. He turned up the long-necked bottle and drank. Arlis left feeling something cold and wrong like the feeling he'd had when the railroad man tied the red rag on the mangrove branch. He walked slowly back to the fire. Brit and Poopy were feeding chicken bones to Nell. The pup wagged her tail when Arlis came up.

"Your daddy says he wants to see you, Poopy." To Arlis his voice didn't sound like his own.

"What for?"

"Didn't say."

"Oh shit, God. It's for school today. Was he drunk? Oh shit, God damn."

Suddenly it was like something Brit and Arlis had known all along. They both looked away from Poopy, each feeling the other boy's dread. Poopy rose slowly and walked toward the pavilion. Brit followed some steps behind and Arlis lagged even further back, afraid yet drawn, only able to imagine what might happen. Just out of the circle of the brightest flare light, Brit and Arlis stopped and watched Poopy walk on. Mr. Esquinaldo saw him and Poopy hesitated. Mr. Esquinaldo put the bottle down on the table behind him. The other men were still all talking and laughing loudly, not noticing Poopy standing there.

"Get over here, you," said Mr. Esquinaldo. His voice was flat and Arlis could barely hear it over the sounds of the other men. Poopy scuffed his foot once, then walked the few steps between himself and his father. Papadad and Mr. Caine were talking back and forth over Mr. Esquinaldo's head and did not look at Poopy, as if he weren't even there. Poopy stared at the ground. Mr. Esquinaldo reached out and pulled the boy's chin up with the cup of his hand. Now Papadad and Mr. Caine and the men around them looked at Poopy.

"Heard from Preacher you caused trouble for the whole school today, boy." Poopy's head looked small and pale in the cup of Mr. Esquinaldo's dirty hand. The hand jerked the head up sharply. "That so? That so, what I heard from Preacher?"

"Yessir," murmured Poopy. The hand jerked Poopy's head up again hard.

"You speak up to me, you little sonofabitch. Now is that so?" The men had all become quiet now. Arlis thought Papadad and Mr. Caine looked embarrassed. Some of the other grown-ups were looking away. "Say it's so, you little sonofabitch!"

"Yessir."

"Well then, here!" Still cupping the boy's jaw, Mr. Esquinaldo swung the flat of his other hand in a full arc that crashed into the side of Poopy's head.

"Say it's so!" Mr. Esquinaldo wobbled, holding himself up by his grasp on Poopy's jaw. The side of Poopy's face puffed red and the tears made a wet sheet over his cheeks, mingling with the dirt from his father's hand.

"Say it's so, you little sonofabitch!" Again he raised his hand and swung but Poopy sprang back, slipping from his father's grip. The open hand missed the boy's head and seemed to carry with it the whole body of Mr. Esquinaldo, who tumbled forward, striking his shoulder in the dirt and rolling on his back. Poopy ran back a few steps to where Brit stood open-mouthed watching the body of Mr. Esquinaldo. The man lay there for several seconds blinking his eyes at the striped canvas of the pavilion. A couple of the sponge fishermen made uncomfortable sounds in their throats like small coughs. Mr. Esquinaldo got to his hands and knees. Mr. Caine reached down to lift him by the arm but Mr. Esquinaldo shook his hand away. He remained there on all fours, reminding Arlis of a sick dog. His head moved slowly back and forth until he saw his son standing in close to Brit and a little behind him.

"Do this to your father, will you," he said. His face bloated red and a thread of saliva dropped from the corner of his mouth. He began crawling feebly toward Poopy, who cowered behind Brit.

"For God's sake, jack, give it up." Old Mr. Caine spoke out

of the corner of his mouth, his voice muted. "Let me help you. Get to your feet, for God's sake. Give it up."

"Get away from me!" Mr. Esquinaldo shouted. There were suddenly tears in his eyes. Arlis had never seen a man cry before. Mr. Esquinaldo crawled another foot. "I'll beat you to death for this, you filthy little son of a bitch." Then his arms buckled and his forehead ground into the dirt. He pushed himself up again. A red line of blood began between his eyes and started crossing the bridge of his nose.

"Daddy. Oh Daddy," Poopy cried. He started to move toward his father and stopped. The man panted and the redness drained from his face, leaving it white as tallow crossed by the red line of blood.

"Awwhg God." Mr. Esquinaldo's spine arched upward, then slammed down flat. The hole of his twisted mouth gushed out a semisolid mass that splattered the earth beneath him. He sucked in a long gulp of air and again discharged a stream of vomit from his mouth. Arlis stood cold and trembling, watching the man on the ground and then Poopy, who now held Brit and cried into his shoulder.

"Come along, son." Arlis felt his father's arm around him and clutched at the thick cloth of his coat. He closed his eyes and felt his father leading him up the beach to their cottage, where Mommer would be waiting. Arlis began sobbing loudly into his father's coat. "Come along, son. Come along, easy now," his father said and held him close. They walked together into the darkness.

In the morning the bright pavilion was gone, along with the sailors and their shining steam launch. Long-necked green bottles and bits of broken crockery lay on the ground next to the cold embers of the charcoal pit. In a week the grass began straightening and covering the wounds in the earth. In another week all that remained was the fading red pennant tied to a mangrove branch in the salt pond where the herons slept at night.

3

Arlis watched the catboat make her last tack out past the mooring rock toward the water inside the reef. He could still see Poopy and Brit leaning against the gunwale on the high side of the boat as she heeled over. They hadn't asked him to come along. The catboat was pretty small anyway, he thought. He lied to himself. He wished he were older like them. To hell with them. He could go out by himself. They were going across the north channel to watch the railroad men work. He'd go southwest and fish. To hell with them and their railroad. That would be here soon enough.

He walked up the beach past his house. Mommer waved to him from the porch, where she sat with a blanket covering her legs.

Arlis went into the boat shed. With the door halfway open it took him a moment to get used to the dimness. There in the center, her bow pointed to the sea as always, lay *The Reaper.* "Someday I'll take you," Arlis told her. "Someday maybe Cap'n Ben and me'll fix you real proper again and take you and do you up like you ought to be done."

He and Cap'n Ben would show them all someday. He went to the corner and got his thatch palm basket with his demijohn and fishlines in it. From the wall he took down a medium length sponge hook and a water glass, which he placed in the basket. He looked once more at *The Reaper,* then walked out into the blinding sunlight.

Arlis's catboat lay beyond the high tide line. He took the

palmetto leaves off her that he used to protect the wood from the sun and put the basket inside. He pulled the cork on the demijohn and smelled the water. He figured he might as well get fresh. There was no hurry now since he was just going by himself. Maybe Nell would go. He whistled but Nell didn't appear. Darn bitch is probably laid up under the house out of the sun, he thought.

The dry grass felt prickly under his feet as he walked up the bluff toward the Indian well. Mr. Olcott sat in the shade outside his store, drinking from a teacup on a saucer. It was rum in the teacup, everyone knew that, but it was the only way Mr. Olcott ever took his rum. School was out for the summer and Arlis could see Preacher behind the counter of the store, where he helped out. Arlis hoped on hope that Preacher wouldn't come out and start in talking to him. But Preacher didn't see him and Mr. Olcott just raised his hand limply in a half wave.

The Indian well lay at the base of the limestone bluff. Even during the dry season it gushed out a little stream of clear sweet water that ran down the rock and into a pool the size of a large sponging skiff. Arlis rinsed out the wickerbound demijohn, emptied it, then filled it with the cool water. A great ironwood tree grew out of the rock ledge and cast a green shadow over the pool. Arlis sat there for a moment and looked at the joining of sea and sky beyond the whitecaps that broke over the reef. Someday he'd be sailing out past all that in the blue water of the true sea. Cap'n Ben would take him sure.

"Hi, baby brother."

Arlis turned around quickly. He hadn't even heard JoAnna come up on him. He was ashamed of himself for letting anyone sneak up on him, least of all a girl.

"I told you about that baby brother crap, Jo, now I mean it."

"Don't call me that."

"Oh, don't be so tough. What you fixing to do?"

"Jesus, fish, I guess."

"Don't take the Lord's name in vain. Can I come?"

"No. It's too rough. You might get hurt."

"Please take me, Arlis. It's not rough."

"No, I said." He still felt mad that she'd got the drop on him and he wanted to be alone anyway. He stood up and slung the demijohn over his back. "I'll see you when I get back. I'll bring you and your old man some fish maybe." The girl didn't say anything but just looked at him with the funny way she had of looking sometimes. Arlis started walking down the bluff toward the beach. Behind him he heard her footsteps following. He faced her.

"I thought I told you I was going alone, Jo."

"Well, go on. There's no law says I can't walk down to the beach if I want."

Arlis walked on, irritated at hearing the girl behind him.

He put the demijohn in the catboat and then checked to make sure all his gear was aboard. The oars, the stone with a thatch rope he used for an anchor, the mast and gaff and sackcloth sails.

"Need a hand pushing her off?" asked JoAnna. The sweetness of her voice infuriated him. It was like she'd talk to one of the babies who crawled around the floor of her father's grocery store.

"I can do it plenty easy myself." Arlis pulled out the two wedges behind the bamboo rollers beneath the keel and, heaving against the stem, shoved the boat into the water. He placed his hands on the gunwale and rolled aboard. JoAnna stood ankle deep in the water, with her arms folded and no expression on her face. Arlis decided not to notice her. Instead, he slipped the oars through their thatch loops and positioned them, then looked for any serious leaks. It always took the wood of the boat's hull a few minutes to swell up enough to seal tight. A half-dozen rivulets ran down the side. Arlis began scooping out the bilge with a split coconut shell.

The sun beat on his back as he worked. There was more water in the bilge than he'd figured on and the bailing tired him. Besides, the sea breeze was blowing the catboat broadside back toward the beach. He felt her keel touch the sand. JoAnna still stood there with her arms folded.

"Well, push her off, Jo, darn it."

"I thought you could do it yourself."

"Darn it, Jo. Come on. Please."

JoAnna reached between her legs and took the back hem of her skirt and drew it all the way up so she could tuck it into the belt she wore, exposing her legs to the knee, and waded into the water. She held the boat off the sand while Arlis kept bailing. She didn't push him out any further.

"Well, you can push me on out, I guess, Jo." The water was still coming in fast but she'd swell up and seal herself and Arlis wanted to be off. It made him nervous having Jo hanging onto the gunwale like that and staring at him while he grunted and sweated in the bilge. "Come on. Push me off. I got to get going."

"I don't think you're going anywhere."

"What you mean I ain't?"

"Look behind you, baby brother. Under the seat. Third plank up. She's sprung."

Arlis dropped the coconut shell and whirled around. Between the third plank and the rib a steady stream of water fanned delicately out.

"Jesus!"

"That's what you get for using iron nails. My daddy's got some good bronze nails up at the store for two bits. You need a hand pulling her ashore?"

"No. Yes. Damn."

Arlis knew Jo must be smirking at him as the two of them hauled the catboat ashore. He wouldn't look at her. He drove in the wedges behind the bamboo rollers with a piece of driftwood and threw it out into the water as far as it would go.

"Damn," he said again.

"You're getting to swear as bad as Brit, Arlis."

"Well I got a reason to. My pa told me to get some fish for supper tonight or he'd want to know why. Now my boat's got a sprung plank and I damn sure don't feel like walking clean across the island to fish off the rocks. Can't catch nothing but grunts there anyway and my daddy hates grunts." He kicked the sand. "Damn."

"You can use my daddy's catboat," she said coyly.

"Your daddy don't have a catboat."

"He does now. Buddy Mullins gave it to him for six months' grocery bills he had piled up. It's a nice boat."

"I guess I better ask your daddy then."

"No. Just ask me. Daddy said the boat was mine anytime I wanted it."

"So I guess you're going along then."

JoAnna only shrugged her shoulders. She looked pretty there with her dress all tucked up. digging her toes into the wet sand. "You can ask me to go along if you want."

Arlis pressed his lips together. Poopy and Brit would laugh at him good and hard if they saw him sailing around with a girl. But he had to think of Papadad and Mommer and some grouper steaks. "Will you go along with me? Please?"

"Sure, Arlis. Come on. I'll help you carry your stuff."

"Sheet her in a Iittle, Jo," said Arlis. He lounged across the tiller bar. JoAnna expertly drew in the sheet and made it fast with a reef knot on the cleat. To himself Arlis had to admit again how damn good she was around boats. It was too bad she had to be a girl.

JoAnna looked into the small live well behind the mast at the two large groupers.

"They must weigh five pounds apiece," she said. They'd caught them both within ten minutes after anchoring over Arlis's favorite rock hole. "Could we go over to the Indian mounds, Arlis? It's still early."

Arlis looked at the sun. Papadad wouldn't be back from the fields for another couple of hours. Since he had the fish, he might as well take the chance to play around some. There was a good stiff breeze blowing and that would keep the mosquitoes off them. It had been awhile since he'd been to the old mounds and suddenly the idea of poking around there sounded good.

"Okay," he said. "Get ready to come about." Arlis threw the tiller over and the little catboat pointed up into the wind, balked a second with her sail shivering, then fell off on the new tack, JoAnna sheeting her in just right without Arlis having to say a word to her.

The wind came off the beam, perfect for sailing up or down Caesar's Creek, so Arlis didn't worry about getting back as long as they started before sundown when the breeze dropped off.

"Don't you just love this, Arlis?"

"What?"

"This. All this." JoAnna made a sweeping gesture with her hand over the water and at the trees that passed them along the shore. "It's so beautiful." JoAnna's face was radiant.

"Well. Yes. It is pretty nice, I guess." Arlis faltered. He didn't want to use the word *beautiful* It was a girl's word.

"And it's all here. Everything a person could want. Look. We have fish and things that grow in the planting grounds. We can even make our own charcoal."

"Only Uncle Jake knows how to make good buttonwood charcoal," Arlis reminded her. She seemed not to hear.

"It's beautiful. Just so beautiful. It almost makes me cry sometimes. Does it ever make you feel that way?"

"Good Lord, Jo. I wouldn't cry about it." JoAnna embarrassed him. He saw the rise of the hardwood hammock, where the Indian mounds were, and shifted the tiller a few degrees.

"You know what I mean. I mean cry not because you're sad but because you're happy and everything's so beautiful."

"Get the line out. We'll tie off on a mangrove and wade in." JoAnna still looked radiantly at him.

"Well, come on. Jump to it," said Arlis. She sure knew how to embarrass a fellow with all that talk of hers. But he was happy. He wouldn't say it but he was, and things were just as pretty as they could be.

Arlis held the catboat into the wind while JoAnna tied off the bow on a mangrove root, then loosed the halyard. They both bundled the sackcloth sail against the boom as it came down the mast, and Arlis laid the gaff on top of it, looping the halyard around it several times so that the wind wouldn't catch it. JoAnna readjusted her long skirt and they both stepped into the knee-deep water.

"Doesn't the water feel divine?"

"It feels okay," Arlis said. "Watch you don't step on a sea urchin. I don't feel like carrying you back to the boat."

Beyond the mangroves the earth sloped sharply upward for a few feet. It was rich red mold. That's why the Indians camped there, because they could grow their vegetables in it. The ground was littered with ancient conch shells. The shells were so old that they'd turned chalky white and brittle. The sea breeze rattled the canopy of a great gumbo-limbo tree, causing spots of sunlight to dance on the ground. The dense shade kept out most of the underbrush and bracken fern that grew in the open.

"Arlis," whispered JoAnna. She laid her hand on his arm and pointed. On the other side of the clearing by a freshwater pool in the rock, a doe and her dappled fawn drank with their heads down. Even as JoAnna spoke both animals looked up as one. They stood frozen for a moment, their brown liquid eyes watching the humans. Then they bolted into the bush, leaping high, the white flags of their tails dancing through the deep green of the fern until only the faint sound of their hooves could be heard fading away.

"Oh Arlis!" JoAnna clapped her hands. "They were so close. Did you see how close they were?"

"They were close, all right. That fawn was a cute one. You don't hardly ever see a fawn. Even in the planting grounds."

"I wish they didn't have string guns to kill them."

"They'd eat up all the vegetables then," Arlis said. He didn't want Jo to know he felt bad about it too. "Me and Brit got us one not too long ago."

"Well, I don't want to hear about it. Come on. Let's go explore." JoAnna led off and Arlis followed her. They pushed further into the hammock, where the biggest mounds were.

"Let's dig around this one," said Arlis. They each picked up a large conch shell and began scraping at the earth. Arlis layered the dirt away, carefully moving it back to Jo, who layered it again with the edge of her shell.

"Here's an awl," she cried. She held up a tapered piece of shell that had been honed down to a rough point. They continued to dig, finding another awl and a bone sewing needle. At last Arlis sat down and threw his conch shell aside.

"Let's do something else."

"I know," said Jo. "We can get some orchid plants and take them back to your ma." Arlis knew JoAnna still thought of Mommer as part her ma too. He didn't mind this sharing. "She'd like a nice orchid in bloom, don't you think, Arlis? Do you think we can find one?" Arlis felt good about maybe bringing something to make Mommer happy. He knew how poorly she was even though she never let on.

"Sure we can."

JoAnna and Arlis followed a deer path through the thicket and out into a broad meadow. To the right, where the ground was high, tall yellow pines grew. At the edge of the stand of trees were a few stumps where people from Doctor's Arm had cut timber for ships' masts. The main and the fore on *Eva Pearl* had been cut there years ago. The other side of the meadow eased down into a swamp full of gnarled old buttonwood trees covered with air plants and orchids. Arlis and JoAnna walked carefully on the soft wet ground, stepping only where they saw the cloven prints of deer lest they stray into quicksand.

"There, Arlis." JoAnna pointed. Two emerald clusters of bulbs clung to the rotted branch of a strangler fig. A long delicate spike grew from each of the bulbs and at their tips opened three butterfly like blooms, bright yellow at the wings and darkening to purple at their centers. Arlis swung himself up on the trunk of the tree and crawled along the healthy wood toward the rotten branch.

"You be careful, Arlis."

Arlis felt the roughness of the wood through the cotton of

his trousers. Moving cautiously he tested the limb and wrenched the rotted branch away from the trunk, sending a shower of termite dust down to the damp ground.

"You got them. You got them'" cried Jo. Arlis backed down and lowered himself to the ground. He broke the crumbling log in two halves, each with its own orchid plant. He thrust them both out to JoAnna.

"Here," he said. "This one's for you and we'll give the other to Mommer." That was only fair, Arlis thought. After all, the orchids were Jo's idea.

Arlis studied the orchids that JoAnna now held. When he looked up at the girl she was suddenly crying, her blue eyes seeming wonderfully large.

"Oh Arlis. They're so beautiful." She leaned quickly to Arlis and kissed his cheek before he could pull away. "You're just the nicest boy I know."

"He's coming. The mail-boat captain said your Grandpa Ben is coming." Mommer moved around more quickly than Arlis had seen her move in months. "Oh he's coming." The color stood out in her cheeks. She ran her thin trembly fingers through the wisps of hair that had come loose across her forehead. "He said *Eva Pearl* was discharging cargo in Key West and her next stop was here." She bent down and squeezed Arlis as hard as she could. Arlis felt so happy he could fairly burst. Cap'n Ben home at last.

"Son," said Mommer. "We got to get his room ready. We got to make it good and comfortable so's he'll spend some time here. You know how we do that. I'm going to need your help."

"I'll help you, Mommer." Arlis couldn't wait to see Cap'n Ben's room again. Mommer always kept it locked when he was away, except for once a month when she'd clean it whether Cap'n Ben was coming or not. But when he was coming Mommer cleaned it extra special and Arlis always helped her. Papadad let him go from the fields or from fishing just so he could help. Every time Arlis went into Cap'n Ben's room he felt as if he were opening a Christmas package. He knew everything in the room, but each time it seemed to be different.

"Come on, Mommer."

"Lord, yes." She wrung her hands and laughed. "He might be here tomorrow for all we know. We've got to get busy."

Arlis followed her to the bedroom. From the nail on the inside of the armoire she took a brass key. Together they walked the length of the breezeway to the door of the room where Cap'n Ben stayed while in Doctor's Arm. Mommer's fingers fitted the key to the lock. Arlis heard the bolt slide back and then the door opened on its own accord as if someone were pulling it from the other side.

Mommer stood still for a minute, then became a flurry of activity.

"Arlis, open that window, son. Let the air in here." She pulled the spread from the narrow bed and then the sheets, although they were clean from last month. "We've got to put these in the pot to boil, and then we can get to dusting and mopping."

"Mommer?"

"Yes, son?"

"Before we start, can I see it? The box."

"Box? What box, Arlis?" Mommer scratched her head like she didn't know what he was talking about.

"Oh please, Mommer."

"All right, son. Just a quick look. I'm not even sure your grandfather would approve of us looking at his things, but I reckon it's okay seeing as you two bear the same name and temperament."

Arlis waited. Mommer moved to the oak dresser with the

mirror and basin and ivory brush set on top and pulled at the first drawer. It stuck, then came open. She reached in and drew out a small wooden box. She held it in both hands and carried it to where Arlis stood by the bed.

"Well, sit down, son." Arlis sat. Mommer offered him the box. Arlis took it, and after a moment, slowly opened it. Inside lay a gold disk the size of a quarter dollar. It had a ring soldered on it. Arlis picked up the medal and held it to the light from the window. "Capt. Arlis Bennington, Confederate States Navy," it read on one side. Arlis felt the prickling feeling on the back of his neck like when he looked at the hull of *The Reaper,* only now even more. He turned the medal over. "For Valor 1864."

"He was a very young man when he won that medal." Mommer had been silent for what seemed to be a long time and the sound of her voice made Arlis start. "And I was just a child." She was speaking not to Arlis anymore. "We lived in Virginia then. It was all so long ago." Mommer looked out the window some more, then she blinked her eyes. "Put it back in the box now, Arlis." She smiled and mussed his hair. She put the box back into the drawer and gathered up the bedding in her small arms. "Come help your poor old mother now, you lazy boy."

Mommer clutched Arlis's shoulder and Papadad held her under the arm. She wouldn't stay home and wait. They stood on Jewel Claire's wharf with the other people of the island, watching Cap'n Ben bring *Eva Pearl* into the bight. Everyone had harvested their fruits and vegetables on a day's notice and now waited as the great schooner moved softly with the tide. After she'd rounded the point, Cap'n Ben had struck all her canvas but the main topsails, which picked up the light air that flowed around the rise of the trees and the shell mound. Cap'n Ben handled the wheel himself. He took no notice of the crowd on the dock. The ship moved so close to the mooring rock that she seemed to touch. The man on the bowsprit stepped onto the rock and made fast while Cap'n Ben let the breeze pivot him around to the quay. Two hands threw heaving lines ashore and let the onlookers drag the heavy hawser in. The line on the mooring ring tightened as the men on the dock hauled the stern into the jetty. The bowline to the mooring rock was paid off and another bowline snugged *Eva Pearl* into the side of the pilings of the dock. The crewman on the rock swung in hand over hand, just managing to get his feet wet as his mates laughed and shouted at him.

And then there was Cap'n Ben at the head of the gangway. Arlis looked up at his mother, how pale she was in the sunlight. Cap'n Ben watched the three of them, his furious white beard fanned over the breast of his peacoat. He threw up his arms, looking like a cheerful old Christ crucified.

"Go to him, Arlis," said Mommer. Arlis ran and Cap'n Ben met him halfway down the gangway, scooping him up and crushing him against the hard brass buttons of his coat. Arlis's face became lost in the beard, which smelled like tobacco and freshly cracked pecan nuts. The old man did not miss a step but tucked Arlis beneath his arm like a sack of rice and walked to where Papadad stood at Mommer's side. Cap'n Ben put Arlis on his feet and embraced Mommer.

Mommer was crying and held Cap'n Ben with her small arms. Her arms did not go all the way around the man's body, Arlis saw. Mommer looked older than her own father.

"You look wonderful, dear," said Cap'n Ben. He held her by the shoulders and stared into her face. Mommer began crying all over again and Cap'n Ben held her, gently patting her shoulder with one of his big hands.

"Oh Father. Father," said Mommer.

"At last she stepped back from Cap'n Ben. She smiled and dabbed at her eyes with a handkerchief.

"What a selfish woman I am," she laughed and cried at the same time. Arlis couldn't tell which. "Here I haven't even let you say hello to Coleman and Arlis properly."

Papadad stepped up and shook Cap'n Ben solemnly by the hand. Cap'n Ben was bigger than Papadad. He was one of the biggest men Arlis had ever seen. When he looked up or down at anything, he hardly ever moved his head, just his eyes. He carried his body very straight.

" 'Lo, Coleman," said Cap'n Ben.

" 'Lo, Cap'n." Arlis thought Papadad always seemed to be shy around Cap'n Ben.

"See your railroad's coming right along, Coleman." Cap'n Ben turned northeast with his whole body. "She's reached Spanish Harbor. I guess they'll start mashing piles across the channel directly."

"They already have, Cap'n. You go up atop the shell mound, you can see the derrick from Jewel Claire's porch."

"I guess that makes him happy."

From where they stood on the wharf they could see a pencil line of black smoke rising from the direction of Spanish Harbor. Arlis had seen the derrick up close from sailing out to her in his catboat. She threw out lots of black coal smoke and you could hear her mashing the piles in from two miles away.

"They're going to cross that channel in six months, Cap'n," said Papadad. "In six months we can put our pineapples aboard that train and ship them north." He looked away from Cap'n Ben like he was embarrassed because *Eva Pearl* wouldn't be hauling pineapples anymore. Then he looked back. "It'll be a good chance for us. For the boy." He put his hand on Arlis's head. "With the Panama Canal opening, this whole territory is going to change. This railroad is going to bring us a life like we never had before."

"Well now." Jewel Claire came out on the wharf.

" 'Lo, Jewel," said Cap'n Ben. Arlis hadn't seen much of Mr. Jewel. He kept going back and forth to Key West on anything that would carry him. He wore a clean white linen suit that stuck to his body with sweat. A silver watch chain crossed his belly.

"Glad I caught you, Ben." Nobody ever called Cap'n Ben just plain Ben. Arlis could see by his grandfather's eyes that he didn't think much of Jewel Claire. "I been having to be away from here much of late on business. Railroad business."

"What sort of railroad business, Mr. Jewel?" asked Papadad.

"Well, Coleman, I ain't really at liberty to say. It's some thing Mr. Seybold and me've cooked up for Doctor's Arm here that just can't be divulged at the moment." He winked and tried to grin and hitched up his trousers.

"Well, Jewel," Cap'n Ben said. "If you got any bodies or cargo that wants taking to Key West you'd better have it divulged dockside tomorrow morning."

"Oh, Father. Please stay longer," Mommer said. Arlis thought she might start crying again.

"I'll come right back, child. Besides the folks'll want their produce moved out quick." He nodded to the baskets of pineapples. "And I got a load of sponges for New York to get. I'll come back and spend a little time with you."

"Well, I can sure use a ride to Key West, Cap'n Ben," said Jewel. He didn't sound so important now that he had to ask for something.

"You're welcome aboard, Jewel."

"Thank you, Cap'n." He lifted his sun hat. "I'll leave you good folks. I know you don't get to be together so much what with the way things are. Maybe when the railroad comes you'll settle down and retire here." Cap'n Ben threw his head back and laughed. He looked like a picture of a circus lion Arlis had seen once. He had the most wonderful laugh in the world.

"You be dockside tomorrow, there, Mr. Jewel, and I'll take you to Key West."

They watched Jewel walk away up the path to Castle Windy.

"I suppose that once a man's an ass he's always an ass," muttered Cap'n Ben.

Arlis took his grandfather by the hand. The man looked down without inclining his head, as if he were sighting at Arlis along the bridge of his nose.

"Can I come along to Key West tomorrow?"

"I was hoping you would, Arlis. I need a good mate to help me sail *Eva Pearl.*" Arlis burned with excitement even though he knew Cap'n Ben was teasing about helping sail. "But you best ask your pa."

"Can I go, Papadad? Please?"

"There's lot's of work to be done around here, boy."

"I'll work double hard when I come back, Papadad. I promise."

Papadad smiled. "All right, son. As a matter of fact I'll be going in myself. What do you say, Mommer?"

But Mommer was already nodding her head. Arlis hugged her waist.

"But you boys just come back to me before that railroad gets here. I think the noise of that train would scare me right to death."

5

First light brought a stirring of the land breeze. A big black sailor balanced himself on the bowsprit, holding the forestay with one hand. He blew into a conch shell he held in the other. A smaller black boy sounded the ship's bell at the base of the mainmast. Latecomers scurried aboard *Eva Pearl* and found places on deck among the well-secured boxes of pineapples. Arlis and Papadad stood at the gangway. Uncle Jake's wife, Aunt Eleuthera, held Mommer's elbow gently, as if she feared the woman would blow away. Papadad looked hard into Mommer's eyes.

"Aunt Eleuthera'll look after you, old woman. You just rest easy and wait to see what presents Arlis and I aim to bring you back." He tried to smile, then put his arms around her so as to hide his face from all of them. When he'd held her for a long time, his face looked the same as it always did, only a bit paler against the blackness of his hair. "We'll be back in a couple of days."

"You have a good time, Coleman. Take care of Arlis." She smiled a little. Her face held a cool serenity upon it. She placed her hand on Papadad's cheek and kissed him lightly. She bent down to Arlis and held his face in her hands. "I love you, son," was all she said.

"All ashore what's going ashore," bellowed Mr. Trebble, the mate. He stood in the stern by the wheel with Cap'n Ben beside him. He held a speaking trumpet.

Arlis and Papadad went up the gangplank and made their way aft to where Cap'n Ben stood. Cap'n Ben put his hand on Arlis's shoulder. He murmured to Mr. Trebble, "Secure gangway."

"Secure gangway," yelled Mr. Trebble through the trumpet. The crewmen were all Bahamians and moved like black shadows across the deck.

"The tide's on the ebb, Arlis," said Cap'n Ben. "We have to take our advantage. All right, Mr. Trebble, I'll take the trumpet, if you please. You may go forward and supervise getting under way." Arlis liked the formal way the men talked aboard ship.

"Aye, sir."

"Up the main and fore."

Hands seized the halyards and amid the squealing of tackles, yards of white sail canvas unfurled as they traveled up the mast. "Smartly, now," encouraged Cap'n Ben.

"Ho yah! Hey yah!" chanted the black sailors as they hoisted the sails.

Cap'n Ben still had his hand on Arlis's shoulder and Arlis was thrilled by his touch. "Stand by to cast off the dock lines!" In the wispy air the ship had already responded by heeling slightly.

"Gaff tops'ls, main and fore!"

The men on the pier had their lines just turned on the bollards, ready for the command to let go.

"Cast off fore and aft dock lines. Forward spring line."

Wind rattled through the rigging. Ponderously the ship swung around, her bow into the bay. In a moment the sails became fat with the light air.

"Cast off the aft spring." They were free. Cap'n Ben's hand tightened on Arlis's shoulder for a moment as if they both felt the freedom at the same time.

On the dock, Mommer's figure got smaller. Aunt Eleuthera stood on one side of her and JoAnna on the other. They waved and Arlis waved back. In the waist, Arlis saw Brit and Mr. Caine standing with Jewel Claire. Brit looked at Arlis a little jealously, but Arlis didn't care.

The ship caught the first of the real wind as she moved out of the lee of the point, the wharf and shell mound falling rapidly behind. Over a clump of mangroves Arlis could see the top of the pile-driving derrick belching its smoke. Between the rising sun and the pale morning sky Arlis tried to imagine the trestle that would cross the shallows and the new bridge over the channel that would be there in six months' time. The nagging fear of the unknown touched him and vanished as quickly.

"Well, what do you think, boy?" asked Cap'n Ben, looking fully at him for the first time.

"It's wonderful, Grandfather." He wanted to say how different it was than going in Papadad's little boat to Key West. They would hug the shore and stop endlessly to take on a few bags of charcoal here and a dozen sacks of fruit there. It seemed petty and unimportant compared to *Eva Pearl* but Arlis would never say so because it would hurt Papadad's feelings.

Cap'n Ben turned his attention to the trumpet again. "Mr. Trebble, carry all sail, if you please, then turn the off-duty watch below for breakfast. We'll keep this tack for one hour. Mark the time."

"Aye, sir," called Mr. Trebble and touched his cap.

Brit and Arlis leaned on the weather rail, letting the salt spray sting their faces.

"Christ, what a life, eh?" said Brit.

"I'll say. Too bad Poopy couldn't come along."

"Oh he'll live. You still want to get a sailing job with your grandpa?"

"More than anything."

The two boys looked out at the sea. A few dolphin rolled playfully in the schooner's wake.

"Well, if you do get aboard, Arlis, you'll be looking at the last of it, so you better see it good," Brit said. He sounded superior.

"Last of what?"

"Last of all this." He waved his hands around. "Wind-sail ships, old-timers like my dad and your grandpa."

"Don't say nothing bad about my grandpa and his ship."

"Oh take it easy, shorty. What I mean is that this is modern times. We're into real ships that got steam engines in them."

"This is a real ship."

"You're so thick, Arlis. We're into the twentieth century, boy. There's automobiles and flying machines. And then there's that God-a-mighty railroad that's going to fix our lives good. Say what you want, but this is modern times and I'm glad as hell to be a part of 'em. Don't think I plan to poke around digging potholes in coral rock pockets like Uncle Jake for the rest of my life. No, sir. I'm making me some money when Doctor's Arm gets modern. I'm going to be a businessman like Mr. Seybold and Jewel Claire and move to Key West maybe."

"Well, I kind of like Doctor's Arm the way it is," said Arlis. He wanted to defy Brit. He thought of JoAnna and the day they'd been to the Indian mounds.

"Like it? What the hell's there to like now? Bugs, snakes, and hot sun. It's got to get modern."

"I like it okay how it is. Just as long as I can sail *Eva Pearl* and build a few boats in the boat shed like they used to."

"Boats? You're crazy, boy. They build boats out of iron now. Up north is where the foundries are. You going to have an iron foundry at Doctor's Arm?"

"I don't need no iron foundry." Arlis raised his voice and Brit looked surprised. "I'm going to fix up *The Reaper* someday. She's all the boat I need."

"*The Reaper?* She's bad luck. And what'd she be good for anyway?"

Arlis thought hard and couldn't say anything for a minute.

"Sailing, I guess. Just sailing." Arlis stared at Brit until he made the other boy look away.

"You know, Arlis, you're really goofy sometimes. You really are simple. You just don't understand that modern times is here. Right now. You just got to get your thinkin' set straight."

Arlis felt tired of thinking. Modern times. Brit was probably right. He wished he could be alone in his room, with all the boat pictures he had pasted on the walls, to sort things out in his mind. But he wished this only for a second because he wanted very much to see Key West once more before modern times ruined it completely. He did not know how the ruination would take place, but he'd heard it said so many times he figured there must be some truth to it.

When they landed in Key West Harbor, Papadad and Mr. Caine gave Arlis and Brit each a half-dollar and told them to be back at the wharf by sundown. They all rode the mule trolley up Duval Street. Papadad and Mr. Caine went to see the fruit broker and Jewel Claire got off at the offices of the Florida East Coast Railroad. Cap'n Ben stayed at the ships chandlery, never leaving the wharf.

Arlis and Brit walked down the cool side of Duval Street, looking in all the windows of the stores at the newest clothing, saying wouldn't it be swell to be dressed like that or that and becoming a little self-conscious of their baggy pants and mended coats. But there were a great many people in town, from fine ladies to slack-jawed turtlers come fresh with their catches from British Honduras and the Cayman Islands. Sweating black men naked to the waist pushed trolleys of fish, calling their wares: "Grunts! Grunts! six fo' dime-you don' buy 'em dey all be mine!" Stevedores off-loaded the international ships at the Mallory docks and the passenger liners that plied from Havana to New York and Galveston.

Brit and Arlis spent a nickel each and took the horse-drawn trolley twice over its full circuit through the town, until the conductor asked if they planned to stay all day. They were going to get off but the conductor laughed and said they could ride for a while longer.

Brit kept making cracks and kidding Arlis about all the pretty girls. Arlis finally told him to quit or he would go on his own and Brit punched him in the arm and called him a sissy. Then they almost had a real fight until Brit said he was sorry and to forget it and why not go to the Armory and watch the soldiers drill.

The soldiers in their brown coats and campaign hats were grand to look at and they even had a band and marched smartly to the command of the sergeant major.

They went back down Duval Street and ate in a Cuban restaurant for ten cents, then had some ice cream that Arlis thought was the best thing he'd ever tasted. He had another dish of it and it didn't sit so well with him.

Horses and the trolleys choked the street. Once Brit yanked Arlis to the sidewalk by the sleeve as a motor car went by. It popped and gasped and caused the horses to shy and dance sideways.

"Goddam things ought to be outlawed," said the man standing on the sidewalk next to them.

"That's modern times comin', mister," said Brit real cocky.

"Who asked you? What the hell do you know about it, you damn backwoods bumpkin?"

"Somvabitch. You'll learn about modern times quick enough," said Brit as soon as they were out of earshot of the man, "Come on and let's get us a glass of beer," he said to Arlis.

"They won't serve us no beer."

"I know a place. Just pretend we're a couple of jolly jack tars."

Brit led Arlis into a smoky place off Front Street and swaggered up to the bar.

"Two beers," he said and slapped a dime on the counter. The barman slid two foamy mugs down to them and never looked at their faces, "See what I mean, kid?" asked Brit, "Now look you. When I get enough money out of the pineapple business, this is where I'm a goin'. There's chances for a fellow with brains here.

God only knows what'll happen when that railroad's done and ended here. Everything in this part of the world'll have to funnel through Key West!"

Arlis felt very grown-up talking about the world and drinking beer from an iced mug like Papadad. He thought of Mommer's atlas and how big the world was.

"Whatcha say, old Arlis? Let's make money off'n pines, then come to Key West and go in with a big mercantile house. We won't have to start at the bottom. We'll have know how and some capital. Capital. That's the word. I heard Jewel Claire talk about it. It's money. We might even have enough to get up a game of our own. Now, whatcha say?" Brit looked over at him smelling of beer. Somewhere he'd found a stinking cigar that made him look quite manly and tough standing there on the sawdust floor.

"I don't know, Brit. I just want to build boats and go sailing. I think. I like Doctor's Arm."

"Hell, you can build boats here. You could study steam engines and all and fix these tubs that come into Key West."

"Them ain't the kind, Brit. I want to build sailboats, beautiful sailboats like the ones that win the America's Cup."

"What's America's Cup? How much money do you get for building those kinds of boats? I never even heard of no such. You know, sonny," said Brit sarcastically, "you just get too many damn fool ideas out of picture books. What you need is some pussy and just you see if old Brit don't fix you up with some of the real thing one day."

Arlis and Brit came down the companionway to the salon of *Eva Pearl*. Cap'n Ben sat with a bunch of papers in front of him. Papadad and old Mr. Caine were each drinking a glass of rum, happy looks on their faces.

"Here come our boys," said old Mr. Caine. "Lookit here, son. We done real good on our pineapples. Almost two hundred dollars apiece, plus the limes and oranges." He beamed. Papadad nodded, his head lopped to one side.

"Arlis, boy. This is just the goddam beginning." His speech

was slurred. "Next year that train gonna double our money. Double it. Someday we'll have enough to get on out of farming. Come to Key West like respectable folk, get doctorin' for Mommer."

He lowered his head at this, and no one spoke. When he raised his head his eyes were wet. He took a drink. "God in heaven I wisht I could do more for her."

"Now, Coleman, steady on there," said Mr. Caine. "She's going to be fine and all right, so let's not mouth it."

Cap'n Ben looked very sad. He stood up suddenly and faced the open port. When he turned around he didn't look so sad.

"I'm loading *Eva Pearl* with sponges like I told you." He spoke as if he didn't want anything more said on the subject of Mommer. "It'll take 'em the evening to load and we sail on the morning tide. You two young'uns go to the galley now and have Cooky give you supper, then get a good night's sleep. From the barometer I fear our trip home ain't going to be as pleasant a one as coming here." Then he smiled and winked at Arlis. "But in this business, Arlis, you have to just make do."

That night Arlis couldn't sleep. The unforgiving wind shrieked through the rigging. Strange noises and the groaning of wood caused him to start out of what sleep he did have. His little berth lay behind the crew's quarters forward and twice in the night he heard the guttural patois of the colored crewmen. Beneath him Brit slept, snoring now and again. Toward daylight, when he heard three bells strike, he rolled out of his bunk and climbed the ladderway to the deck. The sky overhead loomed gray as death and a mist of rain fell. He walked toward the stern, his hands in his pockets, passing men in oilskins who were wedging down hatches on the cargo holds. In the binnacle light he saw Cap'n Ben and old Mr. Trebble, the mate, smoking and talking in soft voices. Every once in a while a gust of wind would blow the pieces of rain almost flat, so that it stung Arlis's face.

"Ah, good morning, young Arlis," said Cap'n Ben.

"Morning, sir. Morning, Mr. Trebble."

"Boson!" called Cap'n Ben.

"Suh." A large black man appeared.

"Go forward to the slop chest and see if you can find a set of foul-weather gear for the boy here. Then pass the word for Steward to bring three coffees to the wheel."

"Aye, suh." The bos'n vanished.

"Arlis," said Cap'n Ben. "We'll be running into a bit of bad weather. It might delay our return. At sea you notice the hand of the Almighty more than on the land. I hope it don't scare you none."

"Not if you're here, Grandfather."

He laughed and ruffled the boy's hair. "Well, we'll find out how being out to sea in a blow suits you."

In leaving the port Arlis stayed close to his grandfather, watching him carefully. Neither Papadad nor Mr. Caine put their heads above deck. *Eva Pearl* drifted on the tide, her sails flapping in the erratic breeze. They rounded the island and the sails filled at once, heeling the ship over and sending loose gear clattering across the wooden decks.

"Bos'n, see to that mess and turn out the watch below to trim sail," called Cap'n Ben. Arlis was afraid the big man would send him below now and so tried to be quiet and stay out of the way.

Cap'n Ben and Mr. Trebble stood in the small wheelhouse by the binnacle and studied the chart. They passed Whitehead spit and entered the main shipping channel. *Eva Pearl* hove mightily.

"East-nor'east," muttered Cap'n Ben, his teeth clenched around his inverted pipe.

"Aye," said Mr. Trebble.

"What'd you make the force?"

"I'd say thirty-five knots, Cap'n."

"Um. Very well. We'll keep this tack of 180 degrees for half an hour, then come to 110 degrees. If the wind don't change on us. Turn up the hands to take a reef in the fore and mainsails and issue a tot all round."

"Aye, sir."

The morning became more gray. Arlis could not find the sun nor could he see land. However, he felt safe being close to Cap'n Ben, who did not seem worried.

The wind moved more easterly. Arlis watched the compass. The helmsman could not keep the heading of 110 degreees..

"She's boiling up," said Cap'n Ben. "To hell with it. Helmsman, let her fall off to 140 degrees and see how she holds."

As the ship swung around a green-and-white wave broke over the bow, sending a stream of water washing across the decks.

"Nothing like a little dirty weather to make a man feel alive, eh, Arlis?" asked Cap'n Ben. It was the first time he'd seemed to notice Arlis the entire morning. Arlis pulled his oilskins closer to him, feeling dry and comfortable.

"Yessir," he said.

"You aren't having a bad stomach, are you, boy?"

"No, sir. I love being here with you."

"Good lad," cried Cap'n Ben and Arlis felt his proudest. Another wave took them across the bow and the ship pitched and yawed.

"She's a good ship and'll take the sea, Arlis, don't you worry."

"I know, Grandfather."

From the waist came a bedraggled figure in a moment of calm. It was Papadad without oilskins. His face looked pale to Arlis.

"Lord, son," he cried. "What are you doing out here?"

"He'll be all right with me, Coleman," said Cap'n Ben.

"Please. Papadad, can I stay?"

"Oh Gawd, all right." Papadad turned, looking miserable, and held tightly to each passing shroud, finally disappearing down the ladderway.

By eight-thirty they were clawing their way almost to windward. Cap'n Ben ordered another reef taken in. With a loud crack the flying jib blew to ribbons and was carried away. Cap'n Ben ordered his two best men to clear it, grumbling in his beard that it was for the better. "Never should've carried the flying jib so far to windward. Damn it all."

Two bells sounded and Cap'n Ben summoned Mr. Trebble.

"Have the watch below get as much rest as possible and that goes for yourself. Sound the well and have a man at the pumps as you think necessary. I'll send word to your cabin in case of any change. Arlis and I can see to the next four hours. You think, Arlis?"

"Oh yessir." Arlis was too excited to feel tired.

"Pass the word to Steward for two coffees, black, and some sandwiches."

"Aye, sir." Arlis realized he'd had no breakfast.

Cap'n Ben worked *Eva Pearl* into the mouth of the gale. The wind came directly at their faces, causing him to make long tacks that carried them several miles into the true sea of the Gulf Stream before they beat back landward. Cap'n Ben showed Arlis their progress on the chart and how he estimated their forward movement on each tack.

"We need for the wind to shift a little, boy," he said, tapping the chart table in the wheelhouse. "Way she's coming now is right down our throats. It's going to be a rough haul."

With the sounding of eight bells the noon watch came on. No trace of the sun showed. Another black man took the wheel from the first and listened silently as Cap'n Ben gave him instructions. Mr. Trebble and Cap'n Ben conferred over the chart table while Arlis listened, trying to understand all he could. Finally his grandfather turned to him.

"Now you, young Arlis. You'd best go below and get some rest. Have Cook give you something, then turn into your bunk. We run watch on watch in heavy weather so you'd best get your four hours' sleep."

"Are you going to your bunk too, Grandpa?"

"Never you mind that, boy. Get on like I say."

"Yes, Grandfather."

Arlis made his way to the galley, where Cook gave him some fresh white bread biscuits and cold ham. Only one small fire burned in the galley stove for coffee. Cook watched it carefully, telling Arlis that fire was more dangerous to a wooden ship than the gale blowing outside. Arlis ate in the galley while Cook fed the other black sailors as they filed in, all streaming water off their oilskin coats.

"Where the other white boy?" Cook asked Arlis.

"I don't know. Asleep, I guess."

"Maybe he *wish* he asleep about now," Cook said. "He probably need something in his belly. Seize him up. You take him some fresh biscuit. Seize his guts up for him." The other black sailors grinned, their smoky faces looking serene in the gray light from the galley porthole.

Arlis took the biscuit and stumbled down the passageway to the small cabin where he and Brit had their bunks. He opened the door and the stench of Brit's seasickness almost turned his stomach.

Brit lay on the bottom bunk with his face to the bulkhead. A reeking bucket sat next to the bunk. Arlis avoided looking into it. He didn't breathe through his nose.

"Brit."

"Awww."

"Brit. I brought you some fresh biscuit. Cook said it might make you feel better."

Brit rolled over so that he faced Arlis. His skin color looked terrible. Arlis held out the biscuit to him.

"God, Arlis," he half whispered. "Get that away from me. I got nothing left to heave and I don't want to start all over again."

"Can't I get you nothing?"

"God, no, just let me be." Brit rolled away again and lay still. Arlis took the blanket from his bunk and backed out of the tiny cabin. He closed the door softly. He was sorry for Brit but glad not to be sick. If he were sick Cap'n Ben probably wouldn't think too much of him. He wondered how Papadad and Jewel Claire were. The door to their cabin was shut. Arlis listened outside and heard nothing. He was too timid to knock.

Eva Pearl pitched and rolled. Arlis had grown accustomed to her moves. He knew they'd come about on another tack that would bring them closer to home.

With his blanket tucked beneath his oilskins, Arlis came on deck and made his way aft to the wheelhouse. He figured he could rest there where it was dry and not smelling of sickness without having Cap'n Ben be cross at him for not going below. To his surprise Cap'n Ben still stood in the same place next to the helmsman, with his eyes on the binnacle.

"I thought I told you to go and rest." The old man sounded gruff. He raised his eyes finally. They were tired and his mouth turned down.

"I'm sorry, Grandfather. Brit's not feeling so good."

"Ah." Some of the hardness came away from the old man's face. "It ain't so pleasant, is it? Well, come along then with me. You can bunk in my cabin."

"Can't I stay here with you? I'm not sleepy. Please, Grandpa. Just for a while?"

The old man looked at him overly long, his head erect and only his eyes moving, then he smiled.

"I suppose there's no harm. Foul weather and no rest builds character. So they say. If you're determined to suffer you might as well learn something while you're at it. Take the wheel." The wheel stood almost as high as Arlis. "She's geared somewhat, but a bitch all the same. Coyington," Cap'n Ben said to the big black man. "Show this boy how to hold a course."

"Aye, Cap'n." The black man placed Arlis's hands on the spokes, covering them with his own, and guided him until Arlis began to sense the relation between the helm and the compass card. Coyington stood at his back, and when the force of the sea tugged overly hard at Arlis's grasp, the heavy black hands took the pressure.

"Don't be no snake-wake," grinned the Bahamian. "Keep her steady and straight. That's right. Steady and straight and gentle like you treats a woman."

Each time the black man took his hands away leaving Arlis to handle the ship alone, a feeling of power and responsibility came over him. He felt just for a moment that he held the great schooner and the lives of all souls aboard in his small hands, which clutched the spokes of the wheel. Finally the Bahamian stood quietly behind him, helping him only with the most violent wrenchings of the wheel.

"Does it tire you, son?" asked Cap'n Ben.

"No, sir," Arlis lied.

" A normal trick at the helm in this weather is an hour, boy. Stay with it if you can. Coyington?"

"Sir?"

"Tell Mr. Trebble to turn up all hands to take in another reef. It's going to get nastier before she breaks at dawn, by my guess."

"Aye, Cap'n." The black man touched his forehead and left the wheelhouse.

Cap'n Ben sat at the small chart table, looking now and again at the compass and measuring with his dividers and parallel rule. Only twice did he gently shift the wheel under Arlis's grasp.

Pain hurt sharply then numbed Arlis's shoulders as he leaned into the great spoked wheel. Outside the glass screen of the wheelhouse, the sailors labored in the rain. Gray-green waves burst over the bow, sending knee-deep water across the deck, knocking some men from their feet.

"It can be a very hard life, Arlis," said his grandfather, breaking the silence. "But you're doing a man's work. I'm proud of you, boy."

Arlis held on to the wheel, making himself forget the aching of his arms and shoulders, feeling only the pressures of the helm and watching the dimly lit compass card before him. He looked up to see his grandfather staring at him, a look of satisfaction on his wildly bearded face.

Light came. It was the blue light of morning through the porthole of Grandpa Ben's cabin. Stunned, Arlis lay in the bunk, barely able to move in the thick cocoon of woolen blankets that covered him. Sometime in the confusion of the night the hands of Coyington had gathered him up, carried him down the ladderway, and wedged him into the warmth of his grandfather's bunk. The hands had held him gently but firmly until Arlis could fight sleep no longer. And so the storm had passed him by. Arlis knew it by the way the waves moved beneath the keel of the ship. The violence of the gale had been replaced by a smooth rising and falling as *Eva Pearl* lay over slightly to starboard. The port light was shadowed, meaning the sun was at their backs. Early morning heading west-southwest. Home!

Arlis struggled free of his blankets, feeling the ache of his muscles. He burst out of the cabin, leaving the door ajar, and mounted the ladderway to the main deck.

The sky was cloudless and the teak decks washed white by the storm. Off the starboard quarter lay Spanish Harbor Key. The naked marl embankment, topped by the steel rails sparkling in the new sun, looked out of place. In the channel the steam driver spewed black smoke, which trailed away rapidly in the blustering wind. Doctor's Arm was obscured in its dark haze.

With the wind at their backs *Eva Pearl's* sails had been loosed fully and the ship ran like a white bird across the emerald sea, the freed booms almost touching the white-capped water. Arlis looked around him once again, then ran aft to the wheelhouse. Cap'n Ben met him at the doorway.

"Arlis."

"Grandfather. We're almost home."

"The storm broke and we got our wind, boy."

"Mommer'll be surprised, us coming in from this way."

"Well, I thought I'd run far out so's we could all see how the railroad's commencing."

Arlis and Cap'n Ben looked over the starboard rail. They were now abreast of the steam hammer atop her derrick barge. Arlis thought he could hear the thump-thump-thump. Black smoke belched and mingled with the long bursts of white steam. The tide was ebbing out fast through the channel and, where the hammer worked, the water turned from green to milky gray with silt for as far as Arlis could see toward the Gulf Stream.

"The water's all chalky, Grandfather."

"I suppose that there machine tears up the seabed consider-
ably," said the old man. He did not seem too happy with that.

"You, Arlis."

Arlis looked down to the waist of the ship and saw Papadad
coming out of the hatchway. He looked puffy-eyed, but the color
had come back into his face. Mr. Jewel and Brit followed him.

"Lookit there at the water," was the first thing Brit said.
"Lookit how dirty it is with mud."

"That there'll go away soon enough, boy," said Jewel Claire.
He looked puffy-eyed too and Arlis reckoned he'd slept in his
clothes from the way they were wrinkled.

"Can't do much snapper fishing in muddy water like that. Mr.
Jewel," persisted Brit.

"Lordy, boy. I told you it'd go away soon enough. We got time
for snapper fishing later. Right now I'm just gladder than hell
them railroad boys are hard at it. We ought to have train service
in Doctor's Arm in six months. And do we got a celebration
planned." He slapped Papadad on the back. "Coleman, look at
that steam driver go, will you?" Papadad just nodded.

"Can't see Castle Windy for all the smoke, Mr. Jewel," said
Brit. To Arlis Brit seemed very chipper for someone who'd been
seasick all night.

"That smoke looks good to me," said Mr. Jewel. "That smoke
means progress. The coming of real civilization."

"Doctor's Arm pineapples to New York in a day and a night,"
said Papadad at last. "Won't be long now." Papadad put his hand
on Arlis's head. "Won't that be swell, son?"

"I guess, Papadad."

Arlis stood between Papadad and Cap'n Ben, looking at the
trail of muddy water and the smoke that threaded toward
Doctor's Arm. Suddenly he felt very sorry for Cap'n Ben. They'd
fought so hard to bring *Eva Pearl* home, and all Papadad and Mr.
Jewel and Brit could talk about was the damned railroad.
Unconsciously he moved closer to his grandfather.

"It's going to be a great thing, Cap'n Ben," Jewel said. The sun
rose behind Cap'n Ben's head and Jewel, being short, had to both

squint and look up at the other man. "Don't you think?"

"Don't much care, really, Mr. Jewel."

"Now, Cap'n Ben, we all know how you feel about *Eva Pearl* here, but don't you think it's time you came home to Doctor's Arm and settled down? You've spent your whole life at sea. You need a resting place."

"Mr. Jewel, this is my resting place." Gently he tapped the flat part of his hand twice on the side of the wheelhouse. "And almighty God willing it'll be my final resting place. Now you just excuse me, sir."

Cap'n Ben walked forward as if the others weren't there. To Arlis he sounded as cold as he'd ever heard him. The men stepped aside for him.

"Mr. Trebble," he said. "Turn up the hands. When we reach the point we'll strike all main canvas."

Arlis felt quite grown up as they walked off Jewel Claire's wharf together, the three of them, Grandpa Ben, Papadad, and himself. He could see how the gale hit Doctor's Arm. The storm tide left a line of flotsam high on the beach, though people had pulled all the catboats and sponging skiffs up to safety. Arlis figured JoAnna and Mr. Olcott must have taken care of his catboat because it sat next to JoAnna's, close, almost touching.

The settlement looked deserted. Only two old Cubans had been on the wharf to catch the heaving lines and haul in *Eva Pearl's* hausers. By the time the gangplank had been run ashore they'd vanished.

Tree limbs and leaves scattered themselves on the path leading to the cottage. One coconut tree had gone fully over but the houses stood sound and solid and yet looked as if no one had ever lived in them. All the shutters were down. The wind still made harsh sighing sounds as it rushed through the fronds of the coconut trees.

"Cap'n." Old Uncle Jake suddenly stood before them in the middle of the pathway. "Mr. Coleman." He appeared strange to Arlis.

"Hi, Uncle Jake." Arlis took a few long steps to be ahead of his grandfather and father. Uncle Jake held up the flat of his hand and did not look at the boy.

"Cap'n, Mr. Coleman." Papadad and Grandpa Ben had stopped where they were. "It's the missus," said Uncle Jake. He kept looking back and forth between Cap'n Ben and Papadad. "She gone." The words did not make sense to Arlis. He saw now that tears were coming from Uncle Jake's eyes. Neither Papadad nor Grandpa Ben would look down at Arlis but he could see the changes in their faces. He took his father's wrist but Papadad pulled away so he could move closer to Uncle Jake.

"Gone?" Papadad's voice was almost lost in the noise of the blowing fronds.

"She gone," Uncle Jake said. Suddenly Arlis understood what he meant. He clutched again at his father's wrist. The man tore his arm away and screamed.

"Emma! No! Emma!" Papadad lurched, then began running hard up the path. Arlis could hear him crying out Mommer's name as he ran. "Emma." The cries got less loud the farther he ran, like the whistle of the train once the great engine passed across the trestle where you sat fishing in your skiff. Then Arlis started to run too. Cap'n Ben's hand grabbed the back of his coat and spun him around. Arlis faced the old man, who had now dropped to his knees and held Arlis tightly by the shoulders. The old man's face looked like broken glass.

"Mommer."

Cap'n Ben pulled the boy into his heavy chest and held him as he wept. Arlis felt the old man rocking him gently while they both cried.

"Grandpa Ben?"

"Yes, son."

"Mommer?" he asked.

"Yes, son. Yes." The old man rocked Arlis like a baby.

"Mommer. Oh Mommer." Arlis cried into the wool of the old man's beard. "Yes, son. Yes. Yes."

The wind dried up all the tears Arlis had in him. They lay on his face like an extra skin, cold and dead. Arlis walked close to his grandfather but did not try to touch the old man as he had his father. Together they approached the front porch of the cottage. It seemed bigger and more hollow to Arlis at each step.

JoAnna stood beside Aunt Eleuthera in the open front door. How pale is her skin, thought Arlis. He thought how pale had been the skin of his mother. Aunt Eleuthera folded, then unfolded her arms across her breast. She sobbed only once, then covered her face with her black hands for a second, pushing the palms back toward her hairline as if to push grief away. JoAnna still did not change. She looked at Arlis as he came near. Aunt Eleuthera drew a deep breath. When Cap'n Ben stepped onto the porch she curtsied, which Arlis had never seen a woman do before.

"Cap'n."

"Morning, Aunt Eleuthera," Cap'n Ben said.

There were wet streaks down Aunt Eleuthera's face but her voice sounded as it always did to Arlis. She always spoke very plain and steady, not like other colored folks.

"Morning, young Arlis."

"Morning, Aunt Eleuthera." Someone else inside Arlis spoke; someone who lived inside him that he never knew about.

"She ready to be put down, Cap'n," said Aunt Eleuthera. The two of them stood there stiffly. "I wash her and dress her good. She ready. The box been made. We prayed you'd be back in time. She still all right for you and the boy to visit, Cap'n, but she got to go down today before the heat come." Aunt Eleuthera kept the same stone face but Arlis saw the tears reach the rims of her lower lids and begin to fall all over again. She refused to sob. "She went easy like, Cap'n." Arlis's grandfather shuddered just for a moment, as though a chill had passed through his body. "It's all right, Cap'n. She resting with Jesus now."

The wind gusted, turning up the silver undersides of the palm leaves. To Arlis everything had become unbearably cold save for the warmth of JoAnna's hand, which slipped into his own and gently held him as if she'd never let him go.

Part 2

1910

6

Jewel Claire took Preacher's place behind the pulpit. Preacher put in the schoolhouse for Sunday meetings. Preacher sat and folded his hands in his lap. Very faintly through the window Arlis could hear the sound of the steam hammer. It worked all day and night seven days a week. When the wind came from the northeast you could smell the sulfur stink of burning coal.

"Folks," Jewel said. "Before we sing our last hymn I got an announcement to make. It's something I've kept under my hat 'til now but now's the time I think you all should know it. Mr. Clyde Seybold of the Florida East Coast Railroad Company has told me personally that the first train will be in Doctor's Arm in under three months' time from today."

A patter of applause broke out led by Preacher.

"And when that first train rolls in here, we're going to have one heck of a celebration. Better than the first one even." More applause. Arlis thought of Mr. Esquinaldo crawling drunk in the dirt.

Aunt Eleuthera shifted uneasily beside Arlis. She took Arlis to church since Papadad didn't go anymore. Papadad hadn't been to church since they'd put Mommer in the ground. Poor Aunt Eleuthera couldn't get Uncle Jake to go to church with her, so each Sunday she took Arlis saying that's what Mommer would have wanted. Arlis guessed it was probably so.

"We going to have one fine celebration and to liven things up I'm setting out a purse of twenty-five gold dollars for the winner of a boat race. Now how 'bout them apples?" Jewel Claire beamed from the pulpit, waiting for the applause. It came. "Okay, folks. That's all the time I'm going to take. I'll post the boat-race rules after the service." Jewel relinquished the pulpit to Preacher.

Preacher raised his scrawny hands to embrace everybody. "My dear friends, I wish to bring up one more worldly matter before we close. It's a delicate matter, but one that needs tending to. We're about to receive what we have all been so long awaiting. The railroad and the great changes it'll bring. The Almighty's going to have a hand in our destiny. Doctor's Arm will never be the same. I think it's high time we had ourselves an official representative in the form of a mayor." Arlis watched old Mr. Jewel trying to look surprised and modest and to stop from squirming with excitement. A fool could see what was coming. Preacher was a natural born suck-ass.

"Mr. Jewel Claire has long been our leading citizen and has worked closely with the railroad people for the benefit of us all," said Preacher. "I move that we should elect him mayor by acclamation." No one said anything. Arlis did not know what acclamation was. Preacher cleared his throat. "That is to say, are there any objections?" Nobody objected. "Then we have a new mayor for a new and prosperous time. Let us all rise and sing that old favorite that's so appropriate for the occasion: 'Bringing in the Sheaves.' " Preacher nodded to the pump organist and the congregation rose and sang.

Over it all Arlis felt he could hear the steam hammer striking piles like loose earth hitting the top of poor dead Mommer's pine box.

"Sailing boats twenty feet and under," read Brit aloud. Most of the young people of the island stood reading the large hand-painted poster Mr. Jewel had tacked to the side of the school-house. "Crew of two." He punched Poopy on the arm and Poopy grinned back at him. Arlis's heart sank. "To start from the bight, sail around a designated mark, and return. First across the line to receive twenty-five gold dollars' prize. Signed: Mr. Jewel Claire."

Brit jostled Poopy again. "Can we win it?"

"Dang straight."

"You going to try for it too, Arlis?" asked Brit.

"Don't bother, kid. We got it in the bag, huh, Brit," said Poopy. "You can help us get our boat ready, though. We might cut you in for a few bucks."

"What say, Arlis?"

Arlis was glad that they'd thought of him at least. He wished that it could be him and Brit but somehow he had to be in that race and not just help with a boat.

"I don't know, you guys. I got to think on it some. I got a pretty good boat, you know."

"Not's good as mine," said Brit. It was true. For now. "Who you got to sail with?"

"I don't know. I got to think on it." Arlis had nobody to sail with him, but he wanted to be in the race. He knew he could win it because he had a plan about fixing his boat that he'd studied on for a long time. If he fixed his boat right he'd take that prize. He knew it.

"Well, you got three months to think on it, old son. Maybe one of the kids'll sail with you," said Brit, trying to be kind.

"Come on, Brit," said Poopy. "Let's go have a look at the boat." The two walked off and left Arlis. Arlis felt alone but his head began to work. He'd had it in his mind to fix his boat for a long time before this. He'd been studying pictures and reading about boats that won the America's Cup and he had a plan. He just had to keep up his thinking to put it all together.

The Italian, Mr. Rondinero, did not work very often. He did not like to. He lived with his daughter, Wanda, on the far side of the island near the Cuban sponge rakers. He raked sponges too, occasionally, if it pleased him. But he was a stone cutter by trade and his only real work came in making ironwood markers for the cemetery on the side of the bluff behind the schoolhouse.

Mr. Rondinero stood facing Arlis. Between them lay his entire stock of marble: two small pieces he'd foolishly bought years ago. Weeds grew between them where they lay in the dirt. No one had ever had a marble headstone on this island and now the boy wanted one for his mother.

"It's too expensive for a boy. It's too expensive for anybody," said Mr. Rondinero. He threw both his hands out and let them flop down.

"How much?"

"Your papa already had me make her a nice marker outta ironwood like everybody else. Why you want to be different? Ironwood last damn near as long as marble anyway. Last longer than me and you and you're just a kid."

"How much?"

"Too much, I tell you. How many letters on it?"

"As many as on the wood marker, Mr. Rondinero."

Mr. Rondinero made a disgusted sound and threw his hands around some more. Arlis listened to his heart beat and heard the thumping of the steam hammer as finally Mr. Rondinero held his hands still long enough to count on his fingers the number of letters in Mommer's name.

"Nineteen letters. Eight numbers. And one of these." He slashed a hyphen in the air with the edge of his hand.

"So how much is that?"

"On this piece of stone"- Mr. Rondinero touched a weed covered slab of marble with his bare toe-"twenty dollars."

"Okay," said Arlis very fast. He heard his heart begin settling again. He took one of the five silver dollars Cap'n Ben had given him before the old man had sailed north and put it in Mr. Rondinero's hand. Mr. Rondinero looked like he'd fall over.

"But I want a little cross cut into it too," Arlis said. just like on the wood marker."

"Wait a minute now." Mr. Rondinero thrust the dollar back in the direction of Arlis. Arlis retreated. "Wait a minute. Where you going to get the rest of the money?"

"I'm going to win me the sailboat race Jewel Claire's having." Arlis began walking away, leaving Mr. Rondinero holding the dollar like something hot to touch.

"That's three months." Mr. Rondinero took a step after Arlis. "Three months." He took another crippled step as if his feet were chained to the stones.

"That's when I want the stone, Mr. Rondinero."

"What if you don' win the race?"

"I'll win it." The distance between them became larger. Mr. Rondinero stopped following Arlis. He brandished the dollar at the boy.

"Okay. I cut the stone, kid. But you know why? Because your grandpa pay me if you don'. Then he break your neck."

"Thanks, Mr. Rondinero."

Arlis laughed to himself all the way home because he knew he was going to win the race and how he was going to do it. All he had to do was keep thinking hard.

In his room Arlis carefully turned the pages of his sailboat book. Cap'n Ben had given it to him. Before him too lay a large pad of newsprint paper with his sketches. There were many of them. Each showed the rough lines of his catboat hull fitted with different sail patterns. Arlis had cut sail shapes out of paper and overlayed them on the hull silhouettes. He read for the third time about the jib sails carried on bigger boats and ships. Catboats and sponging skiffs in Doctor's Arm didn't carry jibs, just the big, dumpy gaff-rigged mains. Arlis figured on changing that.

"Arlis."

"Yes, Papadad?"

Arlis got off the bed and went to the outer room, past the table where he and Papadad had eaten dinner. One small lamp burned on the table. He and Papadad tried to keep the house very clean but everything looked awkward and ill fitting now that

Mommer was gone.

"Son, go down to the boat shed and fetch me a small one, would you?" Papadad sat in the dark corner by the open window. Arlis could smell his pipe smoke.

"Yes, Papadad."

Arlis went down the path. He didn't need a light. The moon showed more than half and the sky was clear. Nell came with him down the path to the boat shed. The sand felt cool on his feet, and Arlis heard the wavelets on the beach and the sound of Nell snuffling at the ground when she paused. He could also hear the steam hammer. It was coming fast. He had a lot to do before that train got to Doctor's Arm.

Arlis slipped through the door of the boat shed. The opening let in enough of the moon to show the bow of *The Reaper*. Arlis fumbled in the darkness until he found the burlap bag full of half-pints. Papadad had laid in a good supply of them for when the railroad men got to Doctor's Arm. He stuck the bottle in the pocket of his trousers and leaned back against the unseen wall to look at the pale shape of *The Reaper's* bow. As long as he could see her, Arlis told himself, he'd know what a wonderful boat looked like.

One cold star hung above the beginning of the day. The sky began to lighten on the eastern side. The island still slept.

From the high-water mark where the catboat lay to the wide open doors of the boat shed, Arlis had set a pathway of bamboo rollers. He put his arms through the loops of a thatch-rope harness tied to the line running from a ring bolt in the stem of the catboat. Lowering his head like an ox Arlis began hauling the boat uphill to the shed.

She slid hard on the rollers, her keel crushing some of them as it passed over, cracking them and grinding them into the sand. Arlis felt the sweat begin to come. It was strange to sweat when there was no sun. Arlis thought how things looked flat and two-dimensional without the sunlight. He kept digging his feet into the sand, going forward, not wanting to have to start the momentum of the boat's dead weight all over again.

It's hard work. I should have put more rollers down. But if I stop now and put more rollers down it will be just as hard to get the boat started moving again. Shoot, I'm more than halfway, almost two-thirds.

The rope cut his shoulders and he wished he'd wrapped rags around them, and then he was into the darkness beyond the open doors of the shed. Arlis kept pulling the weight behind him, trudging slowly by the dim hull of *The Reaper*.

When he'd gotten the boat well into the shed he rested, before using a block and tackle to turn her over. He might have pushed her over with a long prying bar but he wanted the boat to come down easy. With her bottom up he raised her a few inches more with wedges so she wouldn't be resting in the dirt.

Roosters crowed outside. Now enough light came in the doors for him to see his boat. She looked small next to *The Reaper*. Arlis figured he could get all the planks refastened in one evening. He might even get started cutting a slice through the keel for the center board. He'd need help for that from someone who knew what he was doing. He knew he'd have to get some help lined up today.

Arlis looked at the bottom of the boat once more real good to get the image set in his mind so he could think on her during the day, then he closed the doors of the boat shed and walked through the coconut grove toward the house.

The sun rose. From the porch Arlis heard the clanking of the hand pump. He heard Papadad blow his nose and snort and spit.

"Morning, Papadad."

Papadad was drying his face with a towel.

"Morning, Arlis." Papadad looked tired and beat down even after he combed his hair.

"What field we going to work first, Papadad?"

"I reckon we'll work our own 'til lunchtime, boy. Then we'll go over and put in some hours on Mr. Jewel's place." Papadad smiled at his son. "You up and anxious this morning. You going to give me a good day's work?"

"You know I will, Papadad."

"Good, son." Papadad drew Arlis into him for a moment, squeezing him gently as if he were afraid the boy might shatter in his hands. "Let's get us some breakfast under our belts and then we'll you and me head out for the planting grounds."

Arlis and his father worked their own land until past noon. Then they went to Jewel Claire's planting ground. Uncle Jake and half a dozen Cuban sponge fishermen scattered themselves between the pineapple rows.

Arlis got in beside Uncle Jake early on and stayed with him. When he saw that the old man looked hot or thirsty Arlis went and fetched the water bottle without Uncle Jake having to ask.

Arlis kept old Uncle Jake talking too. When Uncle Jake sat back on his heels to tell a story Arlis cleared the brush around him so he wouldn't have to work as hard. Arlis knew Uncle Jake would rather tell stories than work. He could see how glad Uncle Jake was that he had someone who wanted to listen to him. He told Arlis how he'd been a slave when he was a boy and how Cap'n Ben had found him half drowned in the Savannah River. Arlis knew it all by heart but listened carefully to the telling of the story again. Arlis wanted to get Uncle Jake softened up so he'd come visit the boat shed.

"Uncle Jake," he said finally.

"What, boy?" Uncle Jake looked dreamily at the sky, smiling at the story he'd just told. His machete dangled from his fingers and Arlis scampered around raking up loose brush.

"I got me a little problem."

"What that problem be? You tell your Uncle Jake."

Arlis looked around and made his face as serious as he could.

"Spirits," Arlis said.

The old black man snatched the bait like a hungry fish. His wrinkly mouth pursed up and his eyes grew large.

"Spirit troubles?"

Arlis nodded.

"What kind of spirit troubles?" Uncle Jake murmured.

"I'm working on my boat for the race in the boat shed. Atnight. Alone."

Uncle Jake waited, never taking his eyes from the boy.

"Uncle Jake. I'm scared the spirits might come in the boat shed."

Old Uncle Jake unpursed his lips. He startled Arlis by throwing his head back and laughing, the white stubble on his face catching the sunlight as if he had a beard of silver wires.

"Don't you be scared no more, you young Arlis. I come by tonight, fix that shed up plenty quick. You gots to know how to fool 'em. Fool 'em good, yes Lord." He laughed again. It made Arlis happy to see him laugh. Everyone on the island knew how Uncle Jake could outsmart spirits. "You be to the boat shed tonight after supper, boy. I come by, fix things up right."

Arlis worked beneath the light of two paraffin lanterns in the boat shed.

He scraped the hull planks where they butted, to find the old rusted iron nails, and used a dried triggerfish skin to sand the paint away. It chafed his hands raw but he didn't care. He figured he'd be getting some help. He prayed Uncle Jake wouldn't forget him.

Where the planks butted over the mahogany ribs, Arlis drilled holes and drove in new bronze boat nails. He didn't hear Uncle Jake come up from behind. The old man materialized in the dimness more quietly than any spirit Arlis could imagine.

"You Arlis."

"Uncle Jake! You're here!"

"Course I'm here, child." The old man grinned, showing the last of his teeth. Under his arm he carried a rusty colander with broken handles.

"What's that, Uncle Jake?" Arlis pointed to the colander.

"That's the spirit fooler." Uncle Jake held it up to the light for Arlis to see. He kept grinning away.

"How does a colander fool spirits?"

"Can you count how many holes in the bottom of this?"

Uncle Jake waved the colander.

"I don't know. There's a lots."

"That's right. Lots of holes. Now bring me a ladder outside." Uncle Jake took Arlis's hammer from where it lay and picked up a few nails. "Come on, boy."

Arlis shouldered a ladder and followed Uncle Jake out the door of the boat shed. Uncle Jake carried one of the lanterns.

"Set that ladder over the door so's I can climb up there." Uncle Jake pointed to the beam over the doorway. He held the lantern while Arlis placed the ladder against the face of the building and wedged its legs into the sand so that it held tight. Uncle Jake handed him the lantern.

"Hold the light high, let me see good." Arlis raised the lantern. The old man slowly ascended the ladder, climbing higher to meet his own shadow on the weathered boards of the boat shed.

When Uncle Jake reached the top he held the colander against the wood above the lintel of the door. With Arlis's hammer he fastened it with two nails, driving one in at top and bottom. He mumbled to himself while he worked, then studied what he'd done for a few moments before he backed down the ladder.

"Well, it's finished," Uncle Jake said. He still looked up.

"How's that supposed to fool the spirits, Uncle Jake?" Arlis tried not to sound doubtful.

"Lord. Don't you see nothing, boy? The spirit come looking for a hole to let him in the boat shed. He see the colander and all them little holes, he get confused and give it up. A door hole and a little round colander hole all the same to the spirits. That spirit just scratch his head and give it up. Go somewheres else to devil people. You see, boy?" Illuminated from beneath by the flickering lantern, Uncle Jake looked a bit frightening.

"I guess I see, Uncle Jake."

"Well, it's so. Simple child like you don't need to understand. Just you believe no old spirit going to bother this boat shed." Uncle Jake rapped his knuckles on the door. "I see you tomorrow, young'un." He started to walk away.

"Wait, Uncle Jake."

"What, boy? You still ain't ascared is you?"

"No. Not me," Arlis said. "Not since you fixed everything. I wanted to thank you proper. I got a present for you. In the boat shed."

"For me? A present?" The old man pointed at himself and raised his eyebrows.

"Sure. Why, you fixed up my boat shed against spirits. I ought to give something good to you."

"Oh, you ain't got to do nothing for me, young Arlis." But Uncle Jake had already come back. He followed Arlis into the boat shed.

From the box near the catboat Arlis took a half-pint of rum and a small demijohn of water he knew Uncle Jake would want to drink with it. He handed the bottles to the colored man, then pretended to busy himself with rehanging the lantern. He knew Uncle Jake would think it was a fine present but would need an explanation before he drank it.

"Where you get this rum, boy? You been stealing from your own pa? I'll snatch you bald-headed and he do you worse you been stealing from him."

"I didn't steal it, Uncle Jake. I bought it for you. Sort of."

Uncle Jake laughed. "Your daddy don't sell you no rum."

"Not exactly. But I put money in the box for it."

"Where you get money from?"

"I held some back from Sunday school each week." It wasn't exactly the truth but Arlis knew that it would secretly please Uncle Jake because he didn't like Preacher and his church. Arlis could see too that Uncle Jake wanted to believe him and drink the rum. He kept hefting the bottle in his hands.

"Go on drink it, Uncle Jake. I put the money in Papadad's box for it. Honest."

"But you stole money from Preacher and God." A little smile came across Uncle Jake's wrinkled face.

"You don't believe in Preacher's god, do you, Uncle Jake?"

"Darkies got a different god," Uncle Jake said. "Real darkies goes to the Animal Kingdom when they dies. Preacher's god's for white folks and darkies raised by white folks. Like your Auntie Eleuthera. She damn near white folks anyway."

"Well, I want to go to the Animal Kingdom too. With you." Arlis brightened. "So it's okay if I hold back a little on Preacher. And that makes it okay for you to drink the rum as long as I put the money in Papadad's box. Don't you figure it's okay?"

Uncle Jake looked hard at Arlis. Arlis didn't flinch away from the look. Finally the old man softened as Arlis knew he would all along.

"I guess you right, child. Especially if you figures on going to the Animal Kingdom. I guess they's some white folks can go to the Animal Kingdom if they wants." Uncle Jake uncorked the bottle the way Papadad did. He sniffed at the rum, then tilted his head back and took a big swallow. He shook himself all over like a wet dog and whistled. "Damn, that's fine."

"Sit down, Uncle Jake, and rest. Tell me a story." Arlis had gotten back to work as unobtrusively as he could. He sanded slowly on the catboat hull. Uncle Jake sat on top of a nail keg Arlis dragged up. He had another swallow and his eyes were hawk-bright again.

"I been storying you all day, boy. What story you want now?"

"Tell me again how you met my grandpa and how you and him used to sail together and build boats. Cap'n Ben says you're the best boat builder on the whole island." Arlis watched Uncle Jake swell up with pride, just like someone was pumping him full of air.

"Well now. Cap'n Ben be about the finest man I knows anywhere. He save my life and tell me I don't be a slave no more. Long, long time ago. Him and me been lots of places in the world and done lots of things."

"Tell me, Uncle Jake," prompted Arlis. He kept rubbing the boat hull. Uncle Jake moved the keg nearer. He picked up a piece of triggerfish hide and began rubbing too. His face took on that detached look he had when he told stories.

"I be a child just older than you when the bottom fell out 'un the Confederacy States, the ones in the South. I belong to a blockade-runner cap'n then. Mean man. We all the time running from West Indies to Savannah..."

Arlis listened and worked and could almost say the old man's words in his mind while Uncle Jake talked away. He spoke in a singsong voice as if to someone in another room, stopping now and then to have a pull at the bottle, until it was empty.

Arlis waited for the rum to settle fully on the old man before he very deliberately picked up the brace fitted with a wood auger. He straddled the keel of his boat and began to bore a hole. Uncle Jake stopped midsentence.

"What the hell you doing, child?"

"I'm fixing to put in a dagger board on this boat," Arlis said. He tried to make his voice like JoAnna's. JoAnna always sounded innocent.

Uncle Jake sputtered. He got up and snatched the brace and bit from Arlis.

"You don't know nothing about no dagger boards, boy."

"Maybe you could show me a few things I ought to know about it."

"Somebody better show you something before you ruins your boat." Uncle Jake brandished the brace and bit.

"I guess you're the only one on the whole island knows how to really rig up a boat. That's what Cap'n Ben says. I'm sure lucky to have you show me." Then Arlis said all at once, "Cap'n Ben'll be surprised when he sees how we rig this boat. I'm just so proud to have you to show me. Will you help me, Uncle Jake? There's nobody else good as you are." Uncle Jake still held the brace and bit. He looked a little confused.

"Well, I guess I could help you some."

"Promise?"

"Course I promise," snorted Uncle Jake. "I said so, didn't I?"

Arlis seized him by the hand and shook it the way men do. Uncle Jake still looked a bit befuddled.

"Then it's a deal. Uncle Jake, we're going to win us a boat race. I just know it."

7

From the fields, Arlis could see the derrick top rise above the treeline. It looked peculiar sharing the same sky as the topmast of *Eva Pearl* where she lay at the wharf being fitted with new canvas by Cap'n Ben's seamen.

The derrick's hammering had been stopped since morning. At midafternoon someone sent word that an engine was actually on the trestle. The news went from man to man, and when they heard they stopped work to look past the derrick for the engine's smoke. They saw it and heard the long blowing of the whistle.

Jewel Claire walked up and down the rows of pineapples. Arlis saw how he tried to grin and how the sweat popped off his face. He knew he was going to lose the men for the rest of the day to the train, just like Preacher had lost the children the day the steam launch had come.

"It's just the train, men," Jewel said when the first workers got to their feet and slung their thatch bags over their shoulders. "Hell, you've all seen the train."

"But we never seen it here, Mr. Jewel. Mark me off. I got to have a look."

"Mark us off too, Mr. Jewel. We want to see her on the trestle," Papadad said. "Lord, we waited long enough for her to get here." He looked at the pineapples. They were close to being ready. That made Mr. Jewel nervous, Arlis guessed. "We'll get those pines in, Mr. Jewel. Don't you worry none," Papadad said.

Arlis wished he could help Mr. Jewel even though he wanted to see the arrival of the train. Mr. Jewel had sure been helping him and Uncle Jake. Plenty. He'd come to the boat shed one night and when he heard what Uncle Jake was going to do to the boat for the race and seen Arlis's pictures, he'd pulled at the flesh under his chin for a long time, then snapped his fingers. Since then he'd come around almost every evening to see how the work was going, and each time he came he brought something for the boat. Paint, nails, and last night a bolt of real sailcloth. Arlis never figured Mr. Jewel liked him so much. He brought Uncle Jake a half-pint on each visit and once gave him a dollar. But he got mad when he saw JoAnna in the shed, then got nice again. He made Arlis, Jo, and Uncle Jake promise not to tell anyone else about what they were doing to the boat because it was their secret. Not even Cap'n Ben.

"This works out even better, having JoAnna to help," he'd said. "You come around anytime, JoAnna. You're going to be real useful. But let's keep the secret here." He winked craftily at Arlis. "That way folks, especially Cap'n Ben, is going to see how you done things on your own. Now won't he be proud?" Old Jewel'd let go his shrill laugh and handed them each a quarter.

Arlis felt sorry for him as the workers moved off in a body toward the marl embankment, where the tracks came off the trestle onto the dry land of Doctor's Arm. Counting the day lost, Jewel left the planting grounds too, following the last of his workers. Arlis caught one more look at him and wondered at the strange interest he'd taken in the boat.

"Boy, it's hard to believe the train's come at last," said Brit. He fell into step with Arlis, behind Papadad and Uncle Jake.

"Yes," Arlis said.

"That yacht of yours going to be ready for the race?" Brit had a smirk on his face. What did he know?

"You never mind. You'll see when it's time."

"Oh sure," Brit said.

More people from the other fields met on the path. The path opened to the clearing on the other side of a slight rise. Below on the beach gaped the naked treeless space where the railroad men had built the embankment. Workers' tents were scattered along the shoreline. Beyond, the water had turned white as milk in the channel from the dredging. Anchored in the shallows were half a dozen rusty barges surrounding the derrick barge. Coming across the muddy water ran the straight line of the trestle.

"My God, look," Brit said.

Moving slowly over the trestle, a large black engine pushed a carload of marl before it. The engine looked too big to be held by the delicate structure, yet it advanced implacably. Arlis could hear the steam escaping from its great boilers.

The people who had emerged from the wooded path surged forward, some half running ahead toward the railroad camp. Brit gave Arlis a push and the two of them began to trot. The train whistle sounded as loud as Arlis could ever recall. It seemed like the engine was knocking at their door.

Arlis dropped back while Brit went on. Finally, at the edge of the camp, Arlis stopped and stood staring at the heaving black locomotive. People brushed by him, walking past the tents to the place where the trestle ended at the shore. Arlis felt both attracted and repulsed by the huge piece of machinery that moved toward him. Everything here was so different from the rest of the island. All the big trees were gone and the ground of the camp had been churned into muck that splattered itself against the sides of the gray tents. The remaining scrub at the camp's perimeter lay scarred and broken. It's just all so dirty is what it is, Arlis thought. That's why it's different.

"Arlis!" JoAnna ran up to him, holding her skirt so her bare feet wouldn't catch in its folds. She was out of breath and panted his name. "Oh Arlis. Would you look at it?" She pointed down the track. "It's so big." The whistle sounded again, causing a murmur to ripple through the crowd.

Workers moved around the ugliness of the camp. Everyone seemed to have something to do except Arlis and JoAnna and the people of the settlement who'd gathered to watch the train come in. It looked to Arlis as if at least a couple hundred men were scurrying around the clearing, carrying planks and steel rails or pushing an endless circle of barrows from the pit where a steam shovel lifted out mounds of wet marl and stone to fill in the roadbed.

"Come on, Arlis." JoAnna took his arm. "Let's go to Pa's store. I'll bet he'll give us both a limeade."

Arlis shook his attention from the train. A limeade sounded good.

"Thanks, Jo," he said.

Arlis and JoAnna walked to a big tent where Mr. Olcott had set up his second store, to be close to the railroad workers. Arlis had heard Papadad say Mr. Olcott had to pay Jewel Claire and Mr. Seybold a lot of money to set up shop on the right-of-way. But Mr. Olcott seemed to be selling plenty. Everyone who had anything to sell was selling plenty whether they were on the right-of-way or not. Each night Papadad took a tow sack full of half-pints and sold them all except what he drank himself.

"Hello, Mr. Olcott," Arlis said. "Hi, Daddy."

"Hey, darling. Hello, Arlis."

Mr. Olcott stood behind a plank table at the mouth of his store tent. A worker strode up, white muck caked on his shoes and legs. He put a nickel on the plank table.

"Gimme a can a tobacco and some papers."

Mr. Olcott gave the man what he asked for and put the nickel away.

"Got any whiskey?" asked the man in a lower voice.

"No whiskey," said Mr. Olcott. "Against the rules."

"Well, sell me some of whatever you're drinking." The worker pointed at Mr. Olcott's teacup.

"You know the rules," said Mr. Olcott.

"Shit on the rules," the worker said. He leered at Mr. Olcott, then at Arlis and Jo. "On your kids too." He waited another moment, daring Mr. Olcott to say something, then walked away, dragging the bottoms of his shoes in the mud.

"Damned impertinence," said Mr. Olcott when the man had gone. His face was all red. He stared out at the camp. "Have to put up with this rabble for a while, I suppose. The price of progress." Then he looked at Arlis and JoAnna. "How's about a cool limeade for you two?"

The children drank the limeade Mr. Olcott gave them and leaned against the plank counter.

"How's that boat of yours coming along, Arlis?" Mr. Olcott had a needling way of talking sometimes. He made Arlis sore. He winked real big like it was a fine joke.

"Me and Uncle Jake are going to win the race, Mr. Olcott."

"You and Jake?"

"Yessir."

"I don't think you know what you're talking about, boy."

"Well, we are."

Mr. Olcott stared at Arlis for a long time. "But Jake's a nigger, son." Arlis stared back at Mr. Olcott, not able to make the connection between niggers and boats. He thought that Mr. Olcott maybe didn't hear too good. Finally Mr. Olcott looked at him no longer and turned away with a shrug. Arlis felt Jo tugging at his arm and he allowed her to lead him away.

Arlis and Jo walked back to the wooded path above the camp. They sat in the grass, finishing up their limeades. Below them, workers, still surrounded by the curious onlookers, began to shovel marl out of the car that the locomotive had pushed across the trestle.

"It's sure some big camp they got themselves," Arlis said.

"I'm glad it's not close to our houses," Jo said. "I don't like those men. They scare me."

"I guess they'll be gone soon enough."

"Maybe. I hope so. But I heard they might keep a camp here because of the fresh water. There's no other freshwater wells between here and Key West."

Arlis thought on that. It was so. When the railroad had been further north he'd seen them carrying big water tanks on flatcars to feed the steam engines. He wondered if there was enough water in the Indian well for them. That was close to the right-of-way. It was also on Jewel Claire's land. He hoped the railroad men would just finish and leave. They frightened him too.

"I hope they just finish up and go on," he said. "Shoot. Look how they tore up the bottom of the channel out there." Arlis pointed to the white-streaked water that moved toward the Gulf Stream with the tide. "You can't fish in muddy water."

"Pa says we could use the business. But things will be better if those people move on. I just don't like them." JoAnna sat silently for a while, looking out over the channel. Then she asked in a small timid voice: "Do you really think you'll win the race, Arlis? I hope you do."

"Hell yes, I'm going to win it. Nobody can rig boats like Uncle Jake. Cap'n Ben says so. And do you know what else?"

"What?" Jo's eyes were wide at Arlis's outburst.

"Jewel Claire says I'm going to win too. He told me that. And last night do you know what he brought us?"

"What?"

"I'll tell you since you're part of the secret and you've been helping us. Jewel gave me a roll of real sail canvas."

"No!" JoAnna clasped her hands together.

"Yes. All I got to do is sew it."

"I'll do it, I can sew canvas, I've got Pa's sailmaker's kit."

"Oh hell, Jo. You don't have to."

"Yes I do, Arlis. That's a lot of sewing and the race is this week."

It was true. And old Uncle Jake's fingers were too bent up to sew good. He complained about it all the time.

"Would you, Jo?" asked Arlis taking her arm.

"I will. I will. I'll come tonight."

Jo smiled prettily at Arlis. Arlis thought what a great friend she was. It was too bad God had made her a girl.

The night before the race they all worked late. Jewel Claire came in and walked around nervously. He didn't say much. At last he drew Uncle Jake into the corner by the arm and Arlis could see Jewel mumbling to him. Uncle Jake nodded a few times. Once Jewel pointed to JoAnna, who sat working on the sail. Jewel took Uncle Jake's hand and Arlis saw him put some money into it. Mr. Jewel left without saying anything more.

JoAnna kept working on the sail in the light cast by the

paraffin lanterns. Uncle Jake and Arlis silently erected the mast, now almost a third of the way back from its old place in the bow. It looked odd, that mast and the big balloonlike jib sail that would be fastened to the forestay. There had never been a rig like her in Doctor's Arm but Arlis had pictures of it, and from the beginning Uncle Jake said he'd seen plenty of boats like that in the North when he sailed with Cap'n Ben. Arlis and Uncle Jake tightened the stays and hauled up the mainsail. It was made of the new canvas Mr. Jewel had given them and not of patched tow sacks.

When the sail rose Uncle Jake looked at it sullenly. He'd been quiet and sulky since Jewel left.

"Look at her, Jo," Arlis said.

Jo stopped sewing and stared at the boat. They'd painted the hull light blue like a turtle boat and trimmed the rest of her out in red with a red rudder.

"That's just the prettiest boat I've ever seen," said Jo. "It's prettier than the railroad company's steam launch."

"Well, I wouldn't exactly call her pretty, Jo. I mean boats ain't supposed to be pretty."

"Okay. She's beautiful. Who's going to man the tiller? You or Uncle Jake?"

Uncle Jake straightened slowly from where he had been tightening a stay. His eyes were smoky and sad.

"Maybe you should be on the tiller, JoAnna," said Uncle Jake.

"I'll be on the tiller," Arlis said flatly. "Uncle Jake is going to handle the sheets. He's got the experience. We got to be practical about this race, Uncle Jake. We got to get serious."

"You the one got to get serious, boy. I can't be in no race with you."

Arlis felt his heart jump into his throat.

"What you mean? Don't you be fooling with me like that. Uncle Jake. That's not funny."

"I don't be fooling no one." Uncle Jake appeared quite somber. Arlis knew he wasn't fooling.

"You promised, Uncle Jake. You got to do like you said, dammit." Arlis's voice rose to a squeak.

"Calm yourself, boy." Uncle Jake leveled his finger at Arlis. "I said I'd help you fix your boat. I can't be in no race with you."

"And how come not?"

Uncle Jake kept looking serious-faced at Arlis, then smiled a little.

"You really don't know, do you, child? Bless you. I guess I did fool you. I fooled myself." He paused. "I can't be in no white folks' race, don't you see that? And this boat bound to win. That make it all the worse."

"What difference does it make?" Arlis felt tears coming to his eyes.

"Cause I'se a darky, son. White folks don't want no darky in their race."

"But you're different, Uncle Jake. You sailed with Cap'n Ben. You're not no real darky." Arlis remembered Mr. Olcott, and the reality of what Uncle Jake said made him cold and afraid. "You just got to go with me. I won't let you not go with me."

"You fool boy," Uncle Jake said not unkindly. "Look at my skin. Touch it." He stood close to Arlis. He took the boy's hand and placed it on the flesh of his forearm. "That's nigger skin, child."

Furiously Arlis felt the meanness and stupidness and unfairness of it all. He tore his hand away from Uncle Jake.

"You ain't no nigger neither. My Mommer said you wasn't no nigger. So there!" he cried. He felt JoAnna beside him. He heard her crying too.

"I'm sorry, young Arlis. Your Mommer told you wrong. Nobody can change that. It's just the way things is. When you gets older you'll understand."

"Oh Uncle Jake." Arlis threw his arms around the old man's neck. "I can't win without you. I just got to win." Uncle Jake took him gently by the shoulders and held him a little away from his body. "Uncle Jake, I can't win without you." Arlis saw little tears in the corners of Uncle Jake's eyes and it made him all the more miserable and afraid.

"You can do anything you puts your mind to, Arlis. You just got to have the want-to. You got enough want-to inside, you can do anything."

"Want-to?"

"Want-to. You want to bad enough, you can do it."

Arlis sat down on a nail keg and leaned to rest his forehead on the gunwale of the boat. The smell of the fresh paint made him think of how hard they'd all worked and how wonderful they'd made the catboat.

"I don't know how I can do it without you, Uncle Jake." Arlis kept his eyes squeezed tight shut. "I'm scared."

Arlis felt Uncle Jake's hand caress his hair, brushing it the way Mommer used to.

"You study on it, boy. The answer come." Arlis kept his eyes shut, yet he could sense that the old man had gone. He knew Uncle Jake had to go, could never sail the boat with him. When he made himself look up, JoAnna stood alone, holding the sail maker's needle and leather palm cover.

"It's not fair, Jo. It's not right," Arlis said. With the saying of it he felt an anger rising within him. He got up and kicked the empty nail keg. "It ain't fair. Can you tell me it's fair?" He shouted. JoAnna looked a little frightened at his rage.

With his fists knotted until they hurt, Arlis walked past Jo and through the doors into the dark cool of night. He took great strides, almost breaking into a run, vaguely aware of Jo's mothlike presence as she scrambled after him.

Arlis marched up the gangway of *Eva Pearl* where she lay against the wharf. He looked neither right nor left as he crossed the deck to the lighted well of the companionway, where he took the steps down two at a time.

Cap'n Ben raised his eyes over the book he read and studied Arlis when the boy drew himself up before the old man. Arlis realized how he must look, his face red with crying and still making his hands into fists. Cap'n Ben took off his rimless spectacles and carefully placed them on the open pages of his book. At once Arlis relaxed himself and it made him begin to weep helplessly. Cap'n Ben pulled Arlis in and kept his arm around the boy's shoulders until he quit.

"Now then, sit down," said Cap'n Ben. "Drink a little of this." He pushed a saucer and cup across the table to Arlis. Arlis drank the sweetened coffee and kept his eyes cast down until he felt better. He made himself look at Cap'n Ben.

"It ain't fair," Arlis said.

"What ain't fair, son?"

"Uncle Jake says he can't be in the boat race with me because he's a nigger. And he's the one helped me fix my boat all up and now he won't race because he says he's a nigger." Arlis bit the sides of his mouth to keep from bawling.

"Uncle Jake isn't a nigger, Arlis."

"He thinks he is. Mr. Olcott says he is."

"Uncle Jake's as fine a person as I know."

"Then please tell him it's all right to be in the race with me," Arlis pleaded. "Uncle Jake doesn't figure white folks will let him race." The old man kept a long crushing silence. "You could tell him it's all right, Grandpa."

"You're a young boy, Arlis. There's things you don't know now that may make better sense later on. One of those things, I suppose, is the queer notions people have about colored folks and white folks." He became pensive and silent again. "No, Uncle Jake couldn't race with you and no, it ain't fair. Not a bit. But that don't change how some people are and how they think."

"But if it ain't fair, how come God lets it happen?" Arlis stared at the old man's wonderful face when he asked the question, like he was God Himself. Cap'n Ben's eyes reflected both sadness and a small amusement.

"God has it so people make up their own thinking. And it isn't always right thinking." He took his cup back and drank. "Look. Growing up is learning to sift through things like sifting sand to find shells. You have to take the good and let the rest fall away. It's something like that, I believe. Because life ain't always just so. A lot goes on that's not right. Old world's a hard place, Arlis. People are hard in their ideas, especially the stupid ones. Sometimes you have to live with things and ideas you know inside to be wrong. But a man deals in facts, in what is, and so you do the best you can. Sometimes you can put things right. Not most of the time, but sometimes." He smiled. "At least you have to try to do right, you see? You have to sift through things and make the best out of the good you find."

"There's nothing I can do about Uncle Jake?" Arlis asked, knowing there wasn't.

"Only love him, son, because he's a good man and he's been your friend."

While Arlis felt some sense of ease, a puzzlement still lay in his mind. Only when he'd reached the top of the ladderway did he realize once more that he had no one to sail with him in tomorrow's race. It shook him. All the labor was for nothing. He'd have to admit to Cap'n Ben and Papadad what he'd had Mr. Rondinero do and ask them to pay for the stone. Who could help him now? Who? He walked, dragging his feet slowly across the deck until he reached the head of the gangway. Without someone to help him sail the catboat, he was lost. Arlis looked down on the wharf. JoAnna sat there patiently waiting for him, her face serene and knowing in the light of a new moon.

8

Arlis figured the company had brought their best engine down for the first run from Doctor's Arm. The big shining locomotive sat there steaming in the special siding they'd built for her so she could be turned around to head back north. Behind the engine were coupled three boxcars full of pineapples and everything else that could be harvested from the island and the waters around it. They'd worked most of the night to get the cars loaded. Now almost everyone had gone down to the water's edge for the race.

Arlis saw the engine from where he sat in his boat. They were holding the train until after the race, when the celebration would begin. Arlis tried to smile at JoAnna, who sat next to the mast ready to haul up the sail. Arlis tried not to be afraid. JoAnna looked calm as ice.

Nearly twenty small boats lay in the harbor waiting for the start. Ashore, bright bunting fluttered and the crowd pressed together on the beach to get a good look. The boatmen were having a bad time keeping out of each other's way. Twice Arlis had to fend off with an oar. Most of the boats in the race were ordinary catboats with patched sails. Some of the older men who'd entered hooted when they saw how Arlis's boat was fixed up and painted and how the mast had been stepped so far back, unlike theirs. Others laughed when they saw JoAnna sailing with him. But Arlis could feel something uneasy coming from all of them when they saw his boat. They'd never seen anything like it. The betting ran heavily against him. Gambling men walked the beach calling their odds.

Arlis wished it could all be over one way or the other. The waiting made him sick and drained his strength from holding his place in the mass of boats that formed a ragged line across the harbor. Ashore, he saw Uncle Jake. The old man gave him a small wave of his hand and Arlis felt a little better.

Anchored three miles out beyond the reef Arlis could see Jewel Claire sitting in his boat beneath the shade of a black umbrella. The racers were to sail out, cross his bow, and tack back to the harbor entrance. Mr. Seybold and Preacher stood on Jewel Claire's front porch, which had been cordoned off for a starter's box. Mr. Seybold held a revolver in his hand.

Arlis calmed himself by thinking of his strategy again. He'd worked it out all morning as the direction of the wind and the placement of Mr. Jewel's boat became fixed considerations. Jewel lay to the southeast. The wind came briskly from north of east. With their shallow keels the catboats would all have to sail wide of the marker boat, tack to port for a short leg, then come about to starboard before they could pass in front of Jewel. The less handy boats might have to try this twice. Below his keel Arlis felt the stability of the daggerboard he and Uncle Jake had painfully cut from an old piece of boiler plate. It was heavy and sliced the water like a knife, keeping the boat straight on her path while the others would slip sideways with the wind on their beams. On the return, the other boats would be forced to go far north to have the right angle for the wind to push them back to the harbor.

"Arlis." JoAnna pointed. Preacher had raised a red flag at the end of a pole. "Get ready." Her hands gripped the halyard of the mainsail. Mr. Seybold looked out across the small harbor mouth. The eyes of the sailors were on him. He raised the revolver, paused for an agonizing instant, then fired.

The echo of the shot became lost at once in the raspy rattling sound of twenty mainsails being run up their masts. Line squealed through blocks. JoAnna pulled in long measured strokes while Arlis stood on his feet and supported the gaff until it left his hands. Even as Jo tied off the halyard the little boat heeled over and Arlis steadied the tiller. He looked quickly about him. At the end of the line of boats he saw Brit and Poopy moving slowly forward before they were blotted out by a leg-o-mutton sail on the boat closest to Arlis. JoAnna had the jib halfway up the forestay. Arlis thought he heard a few shouts of amazement when people saw how large the canvas was. As the boat began catching the full strength of the wind and leaping toward the mouth of the harbor, all of Arlis's fear turned to a thrill of elation. He pointed his bow up into the wind closer than anyone else dared.

Two large sponging skiffs, flat-bottomed and with center-boards, struggled to stay with him. Off to the right Brit and Poopy were still even.

Arlis turned to glimpse the slow starters. Two boats had

collided in the confusion and lay at odd angles, locked together, the boom of one piercing the sail of the other. The faint sound of cursing and laughter could be heard over the water.

Brit and Poopy made it through the break in the reef first, with Arlis and the two sponge skiffs behind. The wind and sea picked up outside the barrier. White-capped waves threw their spray against the windward sides of the boats. As Arlis expected, Brit's boat had already begun falling a little off the wind. The sponging skiffs dropped slowly behind yard by yard. The rest of the pack clustered behind Brit and Poopy.

Once they'd crossed the full length of the reef it took less than fifteen minutes to make it halfway to Jewel's boat. The more timid racers started their first tack, moving laterally so that they might once again receive the wind favorably. Brit and Poopy passed just astern of Arlis, with the other shallow draft boats in pursuit. The spongers were still waiting. With luck Arlis thought he wouldn't have to tack at all, so well did the daggerboard hold the water.

Led by Brit, the catboats now far to the left came about as one on the final leg that would bring them across Jewel's bow. Arlis could make out Jewel's ruddy face beneath the shadow of the umbrella. The two sponge skiffs had managed to keep the same course as Arlis but had fallen almost a quarter-mile behind. The catboats, the wind on their beams once more, scudded toward Jewel. But Arlis saw that he was by far the closest.

With his free hand he loosed the reef knot that held the main and sheeted it in, feeling the boat grow more rigid as she sliced the waves.

"Sheet in the jib some, Jo," he called. She untied the jib sheet and drew it in. Another wave disintegrated against the bow and flung a cold mist over them. Arlis knew he had the fastest and handiest small boat on the island. None of the others could point into the wind like this and keep their speed.

"Arlis," screamed Jo. The little boat shuddered and Arlis heard a snapping sound. "The sheet line broke, Arlis. Come into the wind quick."

Half paralyzed, Arlis threw the tiller over and pointed the bow directly into the wind. He tied a line around the tiller bar and scrambled forward on his hands and knees, not feeling himself being thrown into sharp edges as the swell lifted and dropped the boat. Sailing away from the forestay like a giant white flag flapped the jib, filling mightily with wind, then discharging it with a crack. JoAnna flailed with her hands, trying to catch it. From the loose corner of the sail a few feet of ragged thatch rope dangled, showing where it had separated under the strain.

Side by side Arlis and JoAnna clawed at the wildly flying canvas. At last Jo grasped a fistful and Arlis another. As their boat dropped away into the breeze once more, the sail was almost torn from their hands.

"Go back and hold the tiller, Jo." Arlis bunched the canvas into his body as JoAnna stumbled aft to hold the bow into the wind.

Arlis looked up in time to see Brit and Poopy sail across in front of him toward Jewel Claire. Jewel clutched the side of his boat, his head out from beneath the shade of the umbrella. Brit did not yell, but the men in the boats following did. With his teeth Arlis gnawed the wet knot in the rope. Out of the corner of his eye he saw the two sponging skiffs overtake him, one close to the other.

Everyone had now crossed Jewel's bow and made their port tacks, the sponging skiffs first, then the catboats, all jockeying for the angle that would take them most directly back to the harbor.

Arlis swore, then prayed as hard as he could. "Forgive me for fooling Uncle Jake, Lord," he whispered. "Forgive me for wanting to go to the Animal Kingdom and holding out on Preacher. Just please let me get this damn jib sail fixed and I'll never do nothing dishonest again."

From the bottom of the boat Arlis took the end of the anchor line and threaded it through the grommet hole of the sail. Holding the makeshift sheet tightly he yelled back to JoAnna.

"Head for Mr. Jewel." He felt the jib fill and the little boat heel over and gain momentum once more. He tied off the sheet and came astern to where JoAnna crouched over the tiller. Her face looked strained and white.

"Get forward, Jo. Trim that jib sail out when she needs it."

"Can we make it without tacking, Arlis? If we tack we don't have a chance," she cried over the wind noise.

"We'll try, Jo. Now go on."

They'd been pushed several hundred feet downwind of Jewel. Now Arlis held the catboat into the wind until she balked, then eased off a fraction. They moved closer and closer to Jewel. Behind them, Arlis could see the mixed sails of the others. They were gaining now. Arlis ached with each yard. The little boat worked hard to point her bow into the wind without falling off. JoAnna could not see their progress from behind the canvas of the jib. Arlis stared at Jewel Claire across a painfully short span of water. He gauged the distance carefully. It had looked as though they could make it at first, but the closer they came the more Arlis saw that the slippage of the little boat would not let them clear Jewel's bow. They'd lost.

Feeling crushed, Arlis got ready to make a tack. They might lose the race but at least they could sail well. Arlis prepared to shout his order to JoAnna. Once again he bent his head to look beneath the boom to see Jewel's boat. Through the small space between the boom and the side of the boat Arlis saw Jewel staring back at him. Quite suddenly, Jewel Claire slipped the excess coil of his anchor line over the side of his boat into the water. The wind immediately caught the freed bow of the boat, turning it slightly crosswise, and pushed it abruptly back from its anchorage. Before Arlis could speak his boat had crossed the few feet Jewel had cleared for him.

"Hurry, boy, goddammit," yelled Jewel. "You can still catch them."

"We made it, Arlis. We made it." JoAnna's face shone back at him. She waved frantically at Jewel. She'd not seen what he'd done. Jewel held a fixed grin on his face and waved back. "Come about, Arlis. Hurry," Jo cried. She'd already loosened the sheet and was hauling it in. Dumbly Arlis took in the main and kicked the tiller bar over so that the catboat came into the wind, shuddered, then fell gloriously off as the breeze filled the other side of their sails. She leaped through the water like something alive, the wind coming perfectly over their right shoulders.

The giant jib sail ballooned out, pulling them across the waves. They fairly flew. The boat made a hissing sound as it cut through the water. Ahead the sails of the other boats began to lose their flatness against the approaching shoreline.

As they overtook the first of the stragglers Arlis looked behind. Mr. Jewel had raised his sail. His face was indistinct, hardly more than a piece of dough above his dark coat. In his mind Arlis questioned what had happened. Had he really seen Mr. Jewel dropping the anchor line? There was no reason. If there was no reason, perhaps it hadn't happened as he'd imagined it.

"Arlis! Watch where you're going." They passed close by the stern of one of the sponging skiffs as if it were not moving at all. The strained face of JoAnna stared back at Arlis. "For heaven's sake pay attention." The sponge boatmen shook their fists and cursed in Spanish. Now Arlis paid attention. He guided his boat into the pack, leaning forward and keeping his head under the boom so he could see. Without giving up the wind, Arlis picked his way out of the grouped boats and advanced toward the three leaders, who'd strung themselves out in a line. The breeze seemed to become stronger. Arlis felt it. The break in the reef sped by, foaming white to either side. Ahead the harbor mouth loomed clear.

JoAnna and Arlis drew upon and passed the first catboat. Arlis did not look at the two men in it more than a second. They were Cubans. They sat with their shoulders hunched forward as if to offer less resistance that they might gain speed. The second boat lost itself to Arlis behind the gray canvas of the sail.

"Hurry, Arlis," JoAnna cried. Between them and the harbor entrance Arlis could see the transom of Brit's boat. He and Poopy looked around, then back at the harbor. Preacher and Mr. Seybold had come down to the shore and Preacher stood with his red flag poised.

Very surely Arlis's boat came abreast of Brit and Poopy. He did not want to stare at his two friends but he had to. Their faces were set and grim. Neither looked at him. Arlis thought he saw Brit's mouth moving. He heard nothing, then they sailed by, stretching the lead by several boat lengths before the flag dropped. From shore Arlis could hear the crowd cheering. He saw them standing on the beach. Some had even waded into the shallows. Arlis watched them transfixed.

"Help me, Arlis." The main came sliding down the mast. The halyard burned through Jo's hands before Arlis caught it. "Get the daggerboard up." She looked at the palms of her hands and glared at him. "What's the matter with you anyhow?"

Arlis hid his confusion by struggling over the daggerboard trunk. They sailed almost to the beach under the jib, then JoAnna loosed it and pulled it off the stay, bunching it against her thin girl's breast so it would not get away. A wave carried them in and Arlis felt the bottom touch the sand before they rose slightly and came to rest in the shallows. People crowded about them up to their knees in water.

"Did we really win, Jo?"

"Of course we did, you silly." She was beside him. She put both her arms around him and squeezed, then kissed his mouth before Mr. Olcott pulled her away and out of the boat, holding her high enough so that her dress did not drag in the water. He was laughing hilariously. People pulled the boat higher onto the beach. In a foolish moment Arlis realized that he still held on to the tiller.

"I guess you won that there race, son." Papadad stood before him a little ways into the water. He carried his tow sack of half-pints in one hand and a fistful of paper money in the other. He looked quite flushed, like he'd just sailed the race himself.

"Yessir. I guess we did."

"You did, son. You did." Papadad tottered a little. He suddenly shouted, "Hoo boy! And did we ever win a potful of betting money!" He came close to Arlis holding the money and the tow sack. His breath smelled rummy. "That Jewel Claire's one smart fellow. He come to me and tells me, 'Coleman, bet your money on Arlis. That boy's going to win.' Now I wonder how he knew that?" Papadad asked no one. He scratched his head, tipping his hat, and stepped back to the beach. He seemed lost in the question, forgetting Arlis completely.

"Come ashore, boy. Come ashore." Arlis felt the tentacle-like fingers of Preacher's hand close about his arm and begin pulling. The boats were all ashore. Sails flapped as they were hauled down. Tricolor bunting made it look like the Fourth of July. Arlis saw Mr. Seybold standing so he wouldn't get his shiny shoes wet. He smiled with his beautiful white teeth at Arlis and motioned to him. People clustered around Mr. Seybold like he was magnetized.

"Come on, Arlis," Preacher said, still tugging at him. Arlis stepped into the water. He didn't know there could be so many people in Doctor's Arm, then he saw that many were faces he'd never seen before, faces of the railroad men, who looked gray and unwashed and wild-eyed as if they didn't understand why they were there.

Behind Mr. Seybold and a little way up the embankment Arlis caught sight of Papadad again, his tow sack leaning against his leg, handing a half-pint to a stranger and pocketing the coin he received in return. Then Papadad raised one of the small bottles to his own lips and drank long and hard.

The crowd surged forward and Arlis could see his father no more. Preacher pulled him through the surf, the water cold on the flesh of his legs. He marched him up the beach to where Mr. Seybold stood. Everything buzzed in Arlis's ears. A cry rose when Mr. Seybold pinned a fluffed blue ribbon on Arlis's shirt and pumped his hand. Arlis looked frantically for JoAnna. She'd disappeared.

Again a cry rose from the crowd. Jewel Claire rode his boat up onto the beach without dropping the sail. Instead he let the sheet go so that it swung impotently in the direction of the wind like a weather vane. As he stepped onto dry land, children clambered aboard his skiff and let down the gaffed sail. Jewel surveyed the crowd, raised both arms in a salute, then strode quickly to where Mr. Seybold and Arlis stood waiting.

"Well, young man. You done real good," Mr. Jewel said. "Got you a blue ribbon and all." He winked at Mr. Seybold. "And up to the house I got you five gold pieces." He thumped Arlis on the back and let his fat hand rest on the muscle between Arlis's shoulder and neck. "Five five-dollar gold pieces for a winner." The tricolor bunting strung through the trees flapped and popped. People's voices droned. A flashing vision of a wet coil of anchor line disappearing into the sea came before Arlis's eyes.

"Mr. Jewel," he said. "I don't think-"

Arlis had to break off his sentence. Jewel Claire's thumb and forefinger pinched into his neck.

"Mr. Jewel-"

Arlis felt the pressure of Mr. Jewel's shoe grind into the top of his bare foot.

"Let's get on up to the house, young Arlis," he said through clenched teeth. "I bet you can't wait to get all that money." Jewel winked again at Mr. Seybold and dragged Arlis toward the steps up the side of the shell mound that lead to Castle Windy. He talked loudly as he pushed through the crowd, roughly elbowing a drunken railroad worker out of the way but always keeping his hold on Arlis's neck dead tight so that it hurt Arlis to move any way but the way Mr. Jewel walked.

Jewel pushed Arlis ahead of him up the steps. Still blustering to no one in particular, he paused to wave once more at the crowd.

Jewel shoved Arlis through the door of the house. The noise of the band and of the people yelling muffled itself inside the dark hallway. The thought of Mr. Jewel and what he had done nagged Arlis's mind.

"Sit, boy. There." Mr. Jewel pointed to a stuffed chair beside a rolltop desk. His voice was stern.

"Mr. Jewel."

"Shut up."

Mr. Jewel took a ring of keys from the pocket of his waistcoat and opened the desk. Then he turned to Arlis and smiled greatly.

"Hold out your hands."

Arlis held out his hands. Into their cup, so that they struck with a pleasant metallic sound, Mr. Jewel dropped five heavy gold coins. Arlis forgot everything but the thrilling weight of the gold. He'd never held so much money in his life.

"Are you pleased, boy? You ran a great race and you even had the good sense to beat misfortune."

The wet coil of anchor line disappearing into the water. The wind catching Jewel's boat, moving her back the few feet to give him clearance. It was true. It had happened. He'd seen it and not wanted to believe it.

"I can't take this money, Mr. Jewel," Arlis whispered.

"What you mean, boy?" Mr. Jewel laughed. "You done won you that there money. You done got it in your hands."

"You slid your boat back for me, Mr. Jewel. I'd of never cleared if you hadn't drifted back."

"Oh horse apples, boy. That's a silly technicality. You fixed a boat that'd whip all them others by a mile if your line hadn't broke."

Arlis got out of the chair and put the money on the desk. It felt awful to let the coins go. They'd gotten warm like living things in the hotness of his hands.

"What the hell you doing, boy?"

"It ain't right, Mr. Jewel. I can't take money I didn't win fair."

Jewel slammed his hand over the stack of gold coins and swept them up into his fist. He seized Arlis by the shirt front. He held the boy close so that their faces almost touched.

"I'll tell you what's fair, you little bastard. You won and that's that. I bet two hundred bucks on you five-to-one when no one else's bet a nickel. Nobody on this island knew that boat design was worth a damn but me. I got vision. I'm the only one got vision on this island. I know boats and I know that nigger Jake and there ain't nobody can fix boats like that nigger. Jesus! I live in a world of dumb crackers and ignorant Conchs." Mr. Jewel shook Arlis hard. "Something comes up they never seen before they won't touch it. Them people are goddam fools." Mr. Jewel pointed vaguely at the open window. "Hell, your own pa wouldn't a backed you lest I convinced him, and he took some hard convincing. I got to convince everybody to take what's good for them."

Arlis stared at Jewel Claire and started to cry.

"You shut that up." Jewel smacked him not hard on the cheek. "I live amongst ignorance," he raved. "It ain't just this. It's everything. Do you know how long I talked railroad and civilization to them people out there before the slightest idea of it sunk in? Years is how long. I deal with idiots. Finally a smart boy like you comes along and you turn out to be a goddam starchneck like your grandpa. You had the fast boat, you had the idea, now you take the money."

"I can't. I just can't." Arlis cried hard.

"Goddam you, you will too take it. You want me to look like a fool? Do you want to look like a fool? You want your Mommer's nice marble stone tore out of the ground because you can't pay for it? I can take care of that, you know. What's your grandpa going to think of a boy who'd dishonor his mother's resting place? You want that?" Jewel shook him so hard Arlis thought his teeth would come out. "Is that what you want?"

"No, sir."

"Then you take this money." Mr. Jewel shoved his hand into Arlis's pocket and Arlis could feel the weight of the gold.

"You take it. Do you hear me?" In his mind Arlis saw Mommer, then her poor grave. He watched JoAnna and Uncle Jake laboring on the catboat and heard his grandfather trying to explain things to him. Rightness and wrongness lay at each end of a hollow void. Arlis studied the gray area in between.

"All right," he said.

Jewel let go finally. He was breathing hard. Arlis hadn't known that he was such a strong man.

"Good," he said. "Now you're being sensible. Here." Jewel took a clean folded handkerchief from his rumpled suit and handed it to Arlis. "Stop that goddam sniveling and wipe your face." Arlis wiped his face, not understanding anything but Jewel's desperation and his own shame.

"May I go now?"

"Get out of here. And keep your damned mouth shut."

Arlis walked to the door and turned back to Jewel. "It still ain't right. I'm going to pay you back. I won't tell nobody but I'm going to pay you back."

Jewel looked tight-faced and mean.

"God help you, boy. When are you going to open your eyes and see what's happening around you?"

Arlis closed the door and went around Jewel's porch and down the steps at the back of the house so no one would see him. Most of all Cap'n Ben. Arlis's shame burned into the stuff of his being like a hot iron.

At the bottom of the shell mound he cut through the mangroves, away from the bay, until he reached Mr. Jewel's deserted planting grounds, where the pineapples had been cut. Even from here he could hear the music playing from way down on the shore. Arlis followed the trail along the edge of the planting ground into the woods and on to the other side, where he could see the schoolhouse and cemetery on the cleared face of the bluff. Below, from the water's edge, spreading all the way to the rail bed, where the great black engine and boxcars sat, were scattered settlers and railroad workers. Colored bunting and flags hung everywhere. Arlis walked to the cemetery to see Mr. Rondinero's stone on Mommer's grave.

With the band music coming up the hill the cemetery seemed quiet. Arlis gazed at the headstone Mr. Rondinero had carved and set in place where Mommer was buried. It was the only marble stone there. Most of the rest were wood; a few had been made of concrete. They looked shoddy next to Mommer's polished marble. Arlis studied the letters and numbers on the stone and they were all right. Mr. Rondinero had cut a cross into the stone with a nice leaf pattern around the border for nothing extra. Maybe, Arlis thought stupidly, because he liked doing it.

The stone shone like a piece of window glass. Instead of the sad happiness he dreamed he'd feel, he had only the sensation of cold loss. In the harbor *Eva Pearl* lay. He knew Cap'n Ben had watched the race from her deck and been tricked like everyone else. What was done was finished. Arlis knew with terrible certainty that if he had to, he'd do it all again.

From below on the roadbed a great cry went up mingling with a whistle blast from the locomotive. As Arlis watched, the first train from Doctor's Arm loaded with their produce began to slowly move north. The train said *chunk chunk chunk* and the boxcars banged into each other until they began to be drawn in a smooth straight line behind the engine. Black coal smoke belched out and momentarily obscured the pit, where the steam shovel dragged out wet marl to fill the roadbed.

By pushing a wheelbarrow in the evening at ten cents an hour Arlis thought that he might be able to repay Jewel Claire in two months' time. He would give the last five dollars to Uncle Jake and the blue ribbon to JoAnna. It was they who had really won the race and only because of what they hadn't had to see.

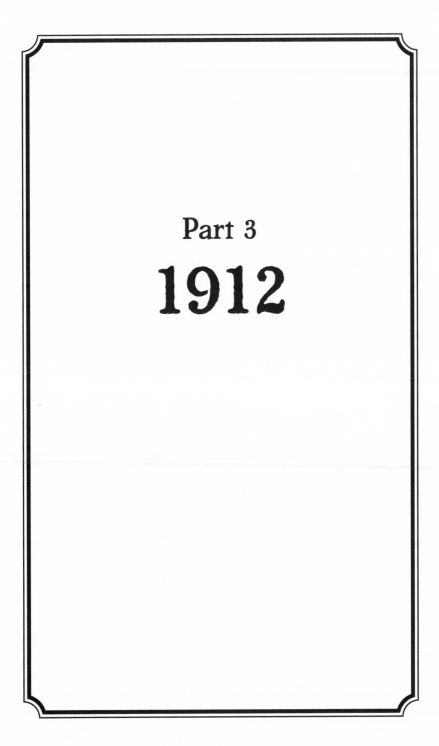

Part 3
1912

9

The railroad company had built a temporary spur in the early part of last year. It led up to the freshwater lake in the center of the island. They used big gasoline-engine pumps to suck the water and transfer it into cypress tanks on flatcars.

The locomotive drawing the empty tanks woke Brit before dawn. Now the sun was coming up. He watched the colors change on the wall. A mosquito had gotten trapped beneath the net that covered his bed and he killed it. With pineapples selling at three dollars a box everyone could afford copper screens on their windows now but Brit still liked to sleep beneath the net. It was like a tent. Brit wondered if JoAnna slept under a net. Thinking of her made him get rigid and so he stopped. It was too late in the morning to think about that. He wished it were nighttime again so he could think about her or Wanda Rondinero and feel himself get rigid.

"Brit," his pa called him.

"Yes, Pa."

"Get up, son. You got to get up and get ready for school."

"Yes. Pa." This was going to be his last year for Preacher's school. He didn't think Pa would make him go anymore after this year. He was damn near sixteen. Hell. He just wouldn't go anymore after this. But Pa wouldn't make him. Since Brit had started rum-selling to the railroad men and making some hard cash, his pa had seemed to take a new interest in him. Even with pineapples going so good his pa liked having the extra hard money around. And Brit had been saving what he didn't give to Pa.

"Come on, son. Let me breakfast you." The old man stood in the doorway with his suspenders hanging down. Brit wondered sometimes how an old man like that got around. His pa was something.

"I'm acoming, Pa." Brit got out of bed. He took off his nightshirt and got into his trousers. He could hear the old man rattling pans on top of the wood burner in the next room. The stove stunk because they didn't use wood anymore. They used coal that fell off the train.

Brit came into the kitchen. Pa stirred a pot of grits. Pork chunks sputtered in the fry pan. Brit liked the way the kitchen looked now that it had been painted. They'd paid a Cuban to paint the whole house, since they could afford it. The house was older than Brit and hadn't ever been painted before. The wood was so dry it took three coats. But they could afford it now. Two years of the railroad had brought good times. It excited hell out of Brit.

"Go wash, boy." The old man turned all the way around to look at him. "Go wash and we'll eat."

Brit washed on the porch and came back into the house. Pa was setting out the food. There were just the two of them to feed. Pa sat down without speaking and began spooning grits into his wrinkled old mouth. He cut his ham chunks into little pieces so he could gum them down.

"Arlis's Pa sold some pineapple land to Mr. Jewel," said Brit.

"He's going to regret it," Pa said, wiping grits off his chin. "Pineapples going to be the salvation of this island."

"I know," Brit said. The old man looked at him with his button eyes.

"You getting to be real smart."

Brit shrugged and ate a bite, not tasting it, feeling very excited.

"I think we ought to buy ourselves a piece of Arlis's dad's land too, Pa." Brit stared at his plate.

"You think that, do you?"

"Yessir, I do."

"And what makes you so cock sure he'd want to sell?"

"Because he can't farm it. Because he's a drunk."

The old man threw his spoon down on the table.

"Don't you talk no insults about your elders, you mutt."

Brit looked his pa in the eyes now that he'd said what was the truth.

"It's just the truth, Pa. You don't buy that land, someone else will. Mr. Jewel will. You know him."

The old man picked up his spoon and began eating again, chewing slowly. Brit could almost hear him thinking.

"What'd he sell to Mr. Jewel? How much for? You know, boy?"

"Three good acres, Pa. For six hundred dollars. And he's got another three he wants to sell for the same."

"Oh my yes. You getting real smart." The old man wiped his chin again, then looked away. When he looked away like that Brit could tell he knew his son was right. The old man would have to have the last word, but he saw how Brit was right. The old man whirled on him. "Mark you good what rum-selling leads to, boy. Watch your rum-selling don't lead to rum-drinking." Pa shook a finger at him, then thought again. "We got better'n five hundred in the bank down to Key West." He acted like Brit wasn't there. Brit laid both his hands on the tabletop.

"And I got a hundred, Pa."

Brit thought the old man would fall off the chair.

"I been saving hard, Pa. For us." Brit felt as though there were too many words to be said at once. "We'll me and you be rich. Maybe have us a two-story house down Key West someday." He waited. "Pa. I been saving for two years. Ever since that railroad come through here. When it gets to Key West they're going to have regular train service. People are going to be coming here. It'll be good to own land. Like Mr. Jewel. Look how he's doing."

"And you think he's right."

"I know he's right." It was Jewel who supplied him with half-pints to sell. Jewel taught him how to undercut Arlis's pa and the other rum-sellers. Jewel knew all about the railroad and how to make money off it.

"Well," said old Mr. Caine. He scratched vigorously at the

back of his head. "Hmmm. Hmmm." He scratched some more, then pulled on his earlobe, thinking real hard. "Well, maybe I'll go talk to Arlis's pa today, see if'n he wants to sell off that three acres." Then he stopped scratching and pulling and said: "I never figured you to be so damn smart, boy."

10

"It's different is all, Arlis. It doesn't have to be sad just because it's different," JoAnna said. Then she sighed. "Maybe it's sad too. I guess it's sad in that way."

She sounded tired of trying to make a case for the changes in the island.

They sat on the side of the bluff. The straight line of the roadbed crossed the pond where the birds used to roost. The new rails sparked off blue light and ran like parallel snakes until they disappeared into the scrub. JoAnna lay back, cradling her head in her folded arms and stared at the winter sky.

"Things change, Arlis." Arlis looked at her, then away. In the time since the train had come to the island it seemed to Arlis that almost everything had changed terribly. Frighteningly. He felt the only thing that hadn't changed lay at anchor in the harbor.

"Well," Arlis said. "Mr. Flagler's railroad's done built and we're going to see it." He looked at *Eva Pearl* in the harbor. She seemed somehow smaller than he remembered and a little dingy. The tide stood slack and the water was chalky where a dragline worked at the line of mangrove swamp, tearing it out to widen the mouth of the basin. "I'm sorry Cap'n Ben has to see it like this." Arlis heard Jo turn her head in the grass but went on staring at *Eva Pearl*. It was all so damned unfair. *Eva Pearl* had to anchor out because there was no place for her anymore at the moorings.

All along the wharf in front of Jewel Claire's house rusty barges were tied end to end. Half the wharf overflowed with a mountain of black coal that spilled off into the water. Where *Eva Pearl* used to dock there settled a partially sunken barge. The old man had to be rowed to and from his ship. Arlis hated it. The old man never complained once but Arlis knew it wasn't right for him to be treated like that. Now that they didn't need him to haul their pineapples, who cared about the old man and his boat?

"What do you think your grandpa will do now?"

"I don't know. But I want to go with him."

"No."

"Yes, dammit."

"What about school?"

"I don't need any more. If Brit can quit so can I."

"You're still too young, Arlis."

Arlis turned on her. He wanted to tell her that just because she'd grown a pair of tits it didn't make her an authority on his age. But he didn't say it. Jo's look was soft and caring. Arlis didn't think he could say anything bad to her, ever. She'd been too much his friend. No one could help growing up. That's one of the things that had changed along with everything else, he guessed.

"Sometimes I wish you were older. But then you'd just go off, wouldn't you?" She said it in a peculiar way. Arlis wasn't sure he understood her.

"Aw hell. Most of the time I don't know what I should do or would do, Jo." Arlis tore up a handful of grass and let the pieces flutter off into the wind. "But I know someday I'd like to go off with Cap'n Ben. Just to be out there in that ocean where things don't change. It just goes on and on. Not like..."

"Like here?"

"Yes, like here. Things used to be so fine the way they were. We had everything and then they changed it." He pulled up another handful of grass and threw it in the direction of the dragline. "And they just keep at it. Changing things." He paused. "It's never going to stop, you know." He paused again. "I don't feel like I really live here anymore."

"Don't say it, Arlis. It can't keep changing forever." JoAnna sounded a little frantic. "This is always going to be your home. You got your house and the boat shed and all the people who love you here. Even if you go away, you'll always come back to Doctor's Arm, won't you?"

"I guess, Jo. I don't know. There's really no place else, is there?"

"Tomorrow's the day," Papadad said. Arlis cleared the supper table between Papadad and Cap'n Ben, leaving only the rum bottle and water pitcher. To Arlis, Cap'n Ben's face and beard showed golden in the lamplight. Even his pale blue eyes looked golden. For a minute Arlis wished he could be Cap'n Ben or even one of the Negroes that worked on *Eva Pearl*.

"Have a drink with me, Cap'n," Papadad said. He spoke overly loud. "Tomorrow's the start of a new life. Henry Flagler's first train from Miami going to pass through here on her way to Key West. It's going to be very historical. Won't you have a drink to that, Cap'n?"

"I'll have one, Coleman." Papadad smiled and poured one for Cap'n Ben and the rest for himself.

"Get 'nother bottle out the cupboard, son," Papadad said. "Here's to it, Cap'n Ben." Papadad took a good drink. Arlis's grandfather had a sip and put his glass down, studying the top of it as if he had deep thoughts. Arlis went to the cabinet and brought another bottle. Papadad put his arm around the boy's waist and squeezed. He looked up at Arlis. His face was terrible; worse than Mr. Olcott or Mr. Esquinaldo. Papadad's face was sad and terrible and different and it hadn't taken even two years to get it that way. "You're my darling boy, son. Lord, you're a fine boy." He squeezed Arlis again and let go. Arlis felt like crying but didn't. "Isn't he a fine lad, Cap'n?" Papadad took another drink.

"Yes. Coleman." Grandpa looked very grave. Arlis knew Cap'n Ben felt bad because a boy ought not to be ashamed for his father. The old man never said it but Arlis knew what he felt.

"You know what I done, Cap'n? I sold the planting grounds." Papadad's grin looked lopsided and silly.

"I thought pineapples was doing quite well. Coleman," said Cap'n Ben. He still looked into the top of his glass. Papadad waved his hand at nothing.

"Hell, we made a few dollars off'n pines, didn't we, Arlis? Now we want to go into better things what with the railroad actually finished. Digging pines is no life for a man. We're going to make money by using our brains. right, son?" Papadad stared vacantly at Arlis until the boy nodded his head. "Right." He drew the cork on the new bottle. "Come tomorrow they's going to be a rail line from Key West to New York City. Running across our island just like a living thing. People in the North dying to come down here and get out of the cold. That's fact. That's how Mr. Flagler makes his money. He got him hotels in Palm Beach and Miami. What we going to have is a hotel here. And I plan to be in on it. I got money from selling that scrub land. Let some other son of a bitch dig potholes in the sun. We're going to have us a hotel. And a saloon. And a restaurant. What you think of that?" Papadad leaned forward on the tabletop. His head tottered side to side.

"Why here, Coleman?" asked the old man quietly. "Why would people come here and not Miami or Key West, where they already have big hotels?"

Papadad studied the lamp for a moment. His face grew darker in its light.

"People are coming, Cap'n Ben. You mark me. That Panama Canal's going to open. Key West'll be choked. People are coming. You watch." He poured badly and spilled rum on the table. "Hell. They're coming." Papadad covered the spill with his napkin.

"Well, I 'spect you're right, Coleman." Cap'n Ben spoke pacifically. "There's no reason why people shouldn't come here. It's a nice place."

Papadad brightened. "It is, Cap'n. And me and the boy here are going to have a fine time. Ain't we, Arlis?"

"Yessir," Arlis said, wanting *Eva Pearl* more than any hotel in the world.

"Then you see how it's going to be, Cap'n Ben?" Papadad's voice struggled for hope.

"I see, Coleman," Cap'n Ben said. He drained off his drink and rose.

"Now don't go, Cap'n." Papadad got to his feet and had to hold on to the back of his chair.

"I have to get along. It's late."

"Have another with me, Cap'n."

"No, Coleman. It's too late." He walked to the door. Arlis followed. A wind came off the Gulf Stream. "Good night, Arlis." The old man laid a hand briefly on the boy's shoulder.

"I'll walk to the boat with you."

"No, Arlis. I'll go by myself all right." He looked at Papadad. "Good night, Coleman," he said.

"Good night, Grandpa." Arlis wished he could walk to the boat with the old man. He watched him go down the steps and onto the dark path that led through the coconut trees. He watched how he walked, straight and strong, and wished he could be with him.

Papadad pushed his chair back and went to the new horse-hair couch they'd bought that year. He carried the bottle and glass and sat down outside the circle of light cast by the table lamp. The bottle clinked on the glass. Papadad drank for a while in silence. Finally he spoke.

"Do you think it's right, son?"

"What, Papadad?"

"Giving up pineapples for something else. For maybe a hotel." Papadad sounded unsure of anything. "Am I right?"

"You're right, Papadad."

Papadad had his feet up on the couch. He put the glass on the floor and lay for a long time with his head back on the cushion.

"Do you think your Mommer...what would she think?"

"It would be okay." Without seeing, Arlis knew Papadad

wept. It always frightened him.

"Papadad."

"We going to be all right, ain't we, son?" Arlis heard the terror creep into the man's voice.

"Yes, Papadad."

Papadad rolled his face into the crook of his arm.

"Oh God, son. It's so awful sometimes. It's just too awful."

Arlis waited in the dark. Papadad spoke no more. When he knew the man slept, Arlis covered him with a quilt to protect him from the cool air off the Gulf Stream.

11

The whole settlement gathered on bothsides of the tracks. They waited.

Arlis and his grandfather came out of the coconut grove. From where they were Arlis could see the new covered warehouse with its shingled roof and the loading platform where pineapples were put aboard boxcars. People milled on the platform, crowding into the shade, waiting for Mr. Flagler's inaugural train. Streamers and decorations blew from the warehouse and hung on the telegraph poles beside the track. Someone lit a string of firecrackers and their noise and pungent smoke drifted over the crowd. All the settlers and workers wanted to see this first train to make the historic run over a chain of islands 150 miles out to sea. It was an impossibility that had come true at last.

"Arlis! Cap'n! Here. I saved you a spot." Papadad waved to them from the concrete platform. He and Mr. Esquinaldo sat on empty crates, an opened bottle between them. They sat on the end of the platform just in the shade. Poopy lounged against the wall with his hands in his pockets. He wore a disinterested sneer and rounded his shoulders as if he were cold.

Cap'n Ben mounted the side of the platform and pulled Arlis up behind.

"Have one with us, Cap'n," said Mr. Esquinaldo.

"Yes," Papadad said. They'd both been hard at it since morning, starting out with their sacks of half-pints to sell. The sacks were gone now and Papadad and Mr. Esquinaldo were still hard at it.

"Too early for me," Cap'n Ben told Mr. Esquinaldo. "Not noon yet, is it? When's the train coming?"

"Eleven-thirty now, Cap'n." Papadad pulled a cheap plated watch out of his pocket. "Should be soon." He wore the new suit and watch chain he'd bought by mail. Everyone but the railroad workers had taken a holiday and dressed up. Papadad looked foreign in the new clothes. Arlis left the men and walked over to Poopy.

"Hi, Poopy."

"What say, kiddo?" Poopy spared him only a brief glance. He held a straw loosely in the corner of his mouth. Arlis leaned his back against the wall and put his hands in his pockets like Poopy. He did not try to round his shoulders. Poopy didn't talk, so Arlis watched the people.

The sun passed its zenith, compressing the air and making it hot and shimmery. The white marl of the roadbed cast its light upward, turning the people's faces unnaturally bright. A restlessness seemed to press itself on everything. Twice someone pointed at what they thought was smoke, only to be disappointed. A fistfight between two railroad men broke out and was subdued. Arlis looked down from the shade onto the sea of people beneath the stark sunlight. Most of the well-dressed men wore straw boaters that bobbed like flat yellow coins.

In front of them, crossing the rails, came Brit and JoAnna. Brit wore shoes and a pair of tight pants that rode up on his ankles. He had his arm around Jo's waist and they matched stride, he tightening his grip when they stepped over the rails.

"Cute, huh?" said Poopy. He winked at Arlis. Arlis pretended not to hear. It gave him an uncomfortable feeling to see Brit with Jo. He didn't know why. It even made him a little angry. "She's got a nice pair, huh?" Poopy winked again.

"You're a jerk." Arlis moved off the wall.

"What did you say, Big Ears?"

"I said you're a jerk."

Arlis thought sure Poopy would move off the wall too and punch him, but the older boy sunk back as if the heat were too intense for the effort. They stared at each other. Poopy looking squint-eyed and disgusted. Arlis became more annoyed with himself for making trouble. He left the older boy and worked his way to the end of the platform now. Only Cap'n Ben had stepped into the small shadow cast by the overhang on the roof. Papadad and Mr. Esquinaldo surrounded themselves with railroad men. The sun beat hotly upon them. Arlis watched a fresh bottle being passed. Papadad's face flushed dull red, almost purple, as if the new white collar were choking him. He talked. Arlis watched his lips moving, but the speech lost itself in the noise of the crowd around him.

"Hey now! Here she comes!" A ripple passed through the crowd and heads turned to the north. Arlis looked too. Above the trees, from the direction of the trestle bridge rose a black plume of smoke. The long cry of the steam whistle forced itself to be heard above every other noise.

"Listen to it," cried a man next to Arlis. Above the babble of the crowd a ragged cheer went up like a balloon. Those who had been sitting clambered to their feet. Men stood on top of packing boxes to get a better view. Arlis reached his grandfather's side.

"Well, boy. What do you think?" The old man looked quite casual, as if he were immune to excitement.

"I don't know, Cap'n Ben. I don't know what to think."

"It's the beginning of an era. Or the end of one." Cap'n Ben talked like he was talking to himself. He shrugged his shoulders. "Anyway, things are sure to be different. Come on. We'll get ourselves a better look."

Cap'n Ben led Arlis into the sunshine near Papadad and Mr. Esquinaldo. Papadad stood on top of a fruit box.

"She's acomin'!" Papadad waved his bottle, then handed it down to Mr. Esquinaldo.

Cap'n Ben set a crate on end and lifted Arlis, placing him on top of it.

"Hold on to my shoulder, boy." Arlis held fast to the old man. Grandpa was tall enough to see without standing on anything.

The big hundred-ton Schenectady locomotive came around the bend and out of the bush looking clean and large and black. Heavy smoke gushed from its stack, setting off the spurting puffs of steam that appeared at the level of the iron wheels. Behind the tender were strung five picture-pretty passenger cars draped in flags. The platform shook through the wood of the box beneath Arlis's feet. The crowd began cheering wildly. Wanda Rondinero, dressed in pink, threw a garland of flowers on the steel tracks of the roadbed. The train picked up speed. Arlis heard and saw the great brass bell clanging atop the barrel of the engine.

"Hooray for Mr. Flagler!" yelled Papadad. His jaw was unhinged. Arlis looked at him for an instant as the engine drew abreast of them. Papadad's hair fell in a tangle across his eyes. His skin looked scalded.

A cloud of steam swept across the platform to cover them and Arlis smelled the sulfurous coal smoke. Through the windows of the passing cars, half obscured in smoke and steam, came the blurred faces of well-dressed men and women. The last coach, trimmed in gold, passed them. Arlis had never seen such a pretty thing. It was Mr. Flagler's personal car. The open platform at its rear was crowded with gentlemen. In their midst, with his hand raised in a feeble salute, sat an old man. He was still and dignified as death. He waved slowly over the flag-draped railing as the train began receding, its great noise deafening, then diminishing.

"Mr. Flagler. That's Mr. Flagler!" cried Papadad. Another great cheer covered the sound of the train.

"Hooray for Mr. Flagler!"

Arlis stopped watching the train and looked to where his father tottered on the fruit box. Papadad seemed to be strangling. Arlis dug his hands into his grandfather's shoulder.

"Hooray for President Taft!" screamed Papadad. His arms, draped in the heaviness of his new coat, flailed at the air. His flesh glistened with sweat. "Hooray! Hooray!" Papadad's eyes turned up into their sockets. Arlis could see the gleam of white through the strands of wet black hair. "Hooray," he croaked hoarsely, then Papadad clutched at something invisible and pitched forward, his mouth sagging. He seemed to fall very slowly at first. Arlis wondered stupidly why someone couldn't catch him. Then he fell fast. Papadad disappeared headfirst among the bodies around him and Arlis heard a loud knock above the other noise, like a coconut being broken open on a rock.

Arlis screamed his father's name until he had no more breath in his lungs, knowing with certainty that the man had been lost to him forever. Papadad was gone and no amount of screaming or anything else could bring him back.

The two black oarsmen waited patiently for their captain. Both men wore identical expressions of solemn indifference while the old man tried to tell Arlis good-bye. The blacks held the bow of the small cutter into the beach so Cap'n Ben wouldn't wet his shoes when he stepped aboard to be taken out to *Eva Pearl*.

"There's some money," said Cap'n Ben. It was the first time Arlis could recall the man sounding lame. "And I've asked Uncle Jake and Aunt Eleuthera to move into the house with you."

Arlis nodded and tried to keep his face set, but he could feel it going fast until he finally had to seize hold of his grandfather's coat.

"Oh please don't leave me. Please."

The old man gently took the boy's small hands from the coat.

"You're still so young yet, Arlis. You need some kind of looking after that I can't give you." He gave a short laugh that sounded all sadness. "In a way we're just the same, you and I. Both going into something all different from what we've known. We're each sort of starting over. You with a new life, and me looking for a new way to make my living."

"But you'll come back to me, Cap'n Ben."

"I'll come back, Arlis. I can't say when, but I'll come back. You know I will. Meantime learn what you can from Uncle Jake. He's a good boat builder." Cap'n Ben held out his hand to Arlis just like a grown-up and Arlis took it. "Always be a man, son," said Cap'n Ben.

"Yessir," said Arlis. Then he was gone. Arlis could see his big back and white hair in the stern of the cutter, handling the tiller while the two black men hauled gently and strongly as if they were one flesh. The old man did not look back, and at last Arlis knew he did not want him to. The boy went up the path through the coconut trees to the house.

12

Arlis heard Uncle Jake hobble up the stepsand the screen door slap shut.

"You Arlis. Where you be, boy?"

Arlis came into the living room. From the big windows the gulf wind relieved the hot August day. He could see that Uncle Jake had been down to meet the train, because he carried a cardboard box and a copy of the Key West newspaper.

"Bet you glad to get these." Uncle Jake slid the box across the worn table. "You keep bustin' out your britches we going to have to build twice as many boats just to keep you dressed proper." But old Uncle Jake seemed proud every time Arlis needed a larger set of clothes. And he was growing fast. No one dared to call Arlis "Big Ears" anymore.

"Thanks, Uncle Jake." Arlis took the box. His hands were as big as a man's and blunted and callused from building skiffs in the boat shed. The railroad company seemed to have an endless need for them and the sponge market was bringing in more money than pineapples. Last year, 1913, Arlis and Uncle Jake built six skiffs. This year, seven so far, and they were back-ordered.

"Let me make you an iced tea, Uncle Jake."

"Well, we got our work, boy."

"It'll wait. Come on. Sit down." Arlis pulled out a chair for Uncle Jake. It was a small game they played, old Uncle Jake pretending he didn't have time for an iced tea. Arlis watched the black face relax as he stretched out in the chair. Then Uncle Jake pursed his mouth and ran his eyes over the lines on the newspaper. Arlis went to the icebox and made two iced teas. He brought them to the table and sat with Uncle Jake. The old man drank.

"You got a card in the mail." It was from JoAnna. She was going to the convent school in Key West so she could help teach at the school. Arlis didn't go to school anymore. Neither did Brit nor Poopy nor any other boy old enough to do a man's work. "What she say?"

"Oh, just how smart she's getting."

Arlis played the game out to the last with Uncle Jake. The man kept his head down studying the print on the newspaper, then without looking up pushed it across the table for Arlis to read to him.

"Well?" asked Uncle Jake at last.

"England declares war on Germany. Germans attack Belgian towns." Arlis read. "Damn!"

"I hope they's a long way off," said Uncle Jake. Arlis laughed. Uncle Jake looked up at him very serious-faced. "I seed the war in 'sixty-four, boy. Nothing to laugh at."

"I'm sorry, Uncle Jake. But this war's all the way across the ocean."

"Just as long as it's farther than Atlanta, boy."

"I'd 'spect it is." Then Arlis went on to read the other articles to Uncle Jake. In not too many minutes the man's chin had lowered itself to his bony chest and a soft rhythmic snore came with his breath. Dear tired old Jake, who'd loved and taught him so much. Carefully Arlis moved his chair back and went across the porch and down the steps to the path that led to the boat shed. He had a rudder post to finish mortising out and he figured he could do it before Aunt Eleuthera called him up for dinner.

The train lay gasping at the siding while the men carefully stacked the pineapple crates on board. When harvest and loading time came everyone took a hand in it because of the delicacy of the fruit itself. Even the children were let out of Preacher's school to pack boxes, which were then placed in the wood-sided cars.

Arlis worked beside Brit and Poopy. Because of his new size Arlis had suddenly become their friend and equal in swearing, smoking hand-rolled cigarettes, drinking Tropical Havana beer, and once even in sharing the legendary pleasures of Wanda Rondinero. Now they labored together, not minding since the pay was double for fast, strong boys like themselves. They put the last crate from the loading dock into the boxcar and two trainmen rolled the heavy door shut. Women were tossing garlands of sheep's-wool sponges through the opening of the end car. Wanda Rondinero winked at the three boys as they walked by. Some of the other girls laughed. Arlis was glad that he didn't blush like he used to.

"You coming to the dance tonight, Wanda?" asked Poopy. He always tried to act like a real sport.

"I might," she said carelessly.

Brit gave Poopy a dig in his ribs.

"I hope you can come, Wanda," said Brit. For Brit, Wanda smiled prettiest. It was easy to see how she liked him best.

"Come on now, girls. We got to get the rest of these sponges aboard. Train's due out soon so the tank car can get down the spur," said the agent. The girls began tossing the sponge garlands up again, ignoring the boys now. The boys watched them work for a while longer. They stood in the shade of the water tower at the foot of the temporary spur that came down from the freshwater lake. The water car would have its load transferred by a big Fairbanks-Morse-driven pump into the cypress tank, which stood on legs and fed water to the engines when they stopped at Doctor's Arm. Doctor's Arm had one of the few good supplies of fresh water in the keys and the steam engines used plenty of it.

"Let's go have a cool drink over to the guesthouse," said Brit. Poopy and Arlis followed him down the platform to the "guesthouse" Jewel Claire had appended to the station warehouse the previous year. It was a straightforward, two-storied building with a wide porch and shingled roof built like most other FEC structures. Upstairs were half a dozen rooms where railroad crews and implement salesmen stayed the night. The space below served as an eating place and saloon, the concession for which had been sold to Mr. Olcott. At night he stood watch on his bar and Wanda Rondinero waited tables, sometimes with help, if there were patrons for supper.

The boys each had a cold cider. Mr. Olcott would not serve them beer at the bar yet, but would sell it to Brit or Poopy from the back door.

Arlis drank his cider with Brit and Poopy, feeling quite manly. They sat at the window, where they could watch the girls load the last sponge garlands. On the platform Mr. Jewel and the agent were sorting out their papers along with the other growers and spongers. Everyone looked pleased. The boys counted in their minds their fees for the loading job they'd done. The agent closed the door on the last car and the train moved forward with a jerk as the man waved his hand. It moved slowly at first and the agent swung aboard. Mr. Jewel and the men on the platform watched it pullout, then came down to the guesthouse to the bar. Old Mr. Esquinaldo was first through the door, but none of the men paid attention to the three boys sitting at the window. They were ordering up drinks and getting paid off by Mr. Jewel, who had a stack of papers and his metal cashbox under his fat arm.

Through the window Arlis could see how the tents of the railroad workers had mostly been replaced with tin-roofed huts to house the gangs staying permanently on the island now to maintain that section of track. The huts had grown-up gradually, hardly noticed, until they formed a little town of their own, laid out on wide crushed coral paths, naked of vegetation and looking hot and dusty under the sun. Beyond the tall pines Arlis could see smoke from the engine bringing the tank car down the spur.

"Here comes the water car," said Poopy. "Them trains sure do take plenty water."

The spur was shored up by big raw timbers. It led down the slight incline of the bluff. turning gradually, so that it passed the old ironwood tree at the Indian well and ended almost perpendicular to the main line at the base of the water tower. A shed covered the pump and the steel pipe leading up to the tank.

The boys watched the old work locomotive slowly letting itself be dragged down the incline. Brakes squealing, the engine was preceded by a flatcar with the two water tanks sitting like giant washtubs atop it.

"She's coming kind of fast," said Poopy. They could see the wheels reverse themselves, turning madly for a second and sending out sparks. The work engine coughed hard and threw up black smoke. "He'd better slow down some."

The tanker came into the turn too fast. A brakeman on the end of the car began frantically screwing down the hand brake to lock the wheels. The engine reversed herself completely but was dragged along as if she were nothing.

The first timber cracked like a gunshot and went flying end over end high into the air, followed by a succession of pops as the timbers holding the embankment disintegrated. The horizontal logs bulged out under the weight of the packed marl and came loose, dropping several lengths of rail on one side. The flatcar slued off the track and twisted loose from the engine.

"Jesus Christ," cried Brit. The men from the bar ran to the window to see.

The two water tanks slid from the flatcar and hit the ground below the embankment. The weight of the water exploded the tanks, bursting the steel bands holding their slatted sides together, and a broad river of knee-high water rushed down past the Indian well. The water cut a trench of marl a hundred yards long, until it eventually allowed itself to be sucked up into the earth.

The work engine still stood precariously close to the broken track, breathing like a wounded animal. Nothing remained of the water tanks but broken hoops and enough cypress slats to build a large house. The engineer, fireman, and brakeman stood on the tracks with their hands on their hips as if they could somehow undo what had been done.

The boys and the men from the bar jostled out the door and ran up the sodden embankment to survey the damage.

"I could of told you," said Mr. Esquinaldo. "I been studying the building of this railroad ever since it started and I could of told you that temporary spur from the lake would bust out sooner or later. It was a waste of time, you ask me." No one paid attention to him. Instead they watched Mr. Seybold and the two engineers he'd brought down with him the day following the disaster. Jewel Claire followed anxiously behind them and a few steps back huddled a bunch of railroad workers and settlers. The sky had clouded up.

Arlis could only hear murmurs from Mr. Seybold, the engineers, and Jewel. Once Jewel's voice had risen loud enough to say, "The railroad serves us and we'll damn sure do anything to serve the railroad." When it came to the railroad old Jewel could be a bigger suck-ass than Preacher. That damned railroad means everything to him, Arlis guessed.

The knot of men followed Mr. Seybold's party from the wreck-strewn bend across the short meadow to the shade of the ironwood tree that covered the Indian well.

The engineers walked around the well together, making

notes on the pads they carried and looking very professional. The clear water reflected their images as they stood on the limestone outcropping and stared into its shallow depths. The ironwood tree dropped leaves at this time of the year and they sailed like little boats on the still surface of the Indian well. One of the engineers pointed at the water tower by the siding and the other one nodded. In a moment it became very clear to Arlis what they meant to do. He figured it was probably the best practical plan. He wondered why they hadn't done it before. It made him sick. It began to rain. Arlis stood there as the first drops hit him.

Most of the settlement came to watch the ironwood tree go. It took six charges of dynamite to get the roots out of the limestone and almost a week to clear it so they could pull a small dragline up on a sledge. When the face of the well had been shaved off fully down to the rock, the train brought in a special auger from Jacksonville. The engineers angled the drill into the stone like a needle under flesh and set it to turning. The engineers used words like *hydrostatic pressure, aquifer,* and *artesian well,* and the people of the settlement began using the same words, never knowing quite what was meant.

In the end it didn't matter. Built up next to the limestone was a tin-sided, tin-roofed shed covering a six-cylinder gas pump, much bigger than the Fairbanks-Morse. It had an iron flywheel as high as a man and an electric starter. Through a four-inch pipe it could directly fill the elevated tank at the siding in thirty minutes flat. Arlis heard Mr. Jewel say that Clyde Seybold had timed it. Mr. Jewel terraced off the whole face of the slope and planted it with pineapple suckers and watered them off the pump. He said this was the best year they'd ever had for pines and it was going to get better. He brought in half a dozen Bahamian darkies to work the new field. The train thundered through twice a day. Doctor's Arm got a post office and telegraph and on Christmas, 1915, JoAnna came home.

13

"No. I guess it didn't turn out like folks expected." Arlis looked at Jo, then past her to the workers' shacks and the pump house. She had become so beautiful and everything else on that side of the track was so ugly. Jo cried when she saw what was left of the Indian well and it almost made Arlis cry to see her that way.

"But if the people are doing well, I guess there's some justification." She looked like a woman and talked like a woman but Arlis could still see her as she'd always been. When she turned to him her face appeared in the light as if it hadn't changed since they were small children, "It's so ugly, though, I wish they hadn't done it that way. They could have left the tree."

"No," said Arlis. A tinny Gramophone played from the dining room of the guesthouse. Through the window Arlis saw Poopy dancing with Wanda Rondinero. Brit had dropped her like a hot rock the minute JoAnna stepped off the train from Key West. Now Brit courted JoAnna every day. He waited to walk her home like some great dandy after she'd finished working at the school in preparation for the new term. Arlis found that he hated him for it. "They'd never have gotten that auger through the roots." He smiled a little at remembering. "That old tree didn't want to come out of there. It gave them a real hard time in taking her out."

"What do you hear from your grandfather?"

"He's working *Eva Pearl* between New Orleans and Panama."

"You're still set on going off with him, aren't you?"

"I'd go, I guess. If he'd take me."

"But there's so much happening here now, Arlis."

"Yes. But I'd go. I want to go, I don't like it here too much."
He wondered if he sounded stupid to Jo.

"But you're a success, Arlis. Everyone tells me how you're
building so many boats. That's what you like to do."

He tried to smile at her and couldn't. "I've been here all my
life, Jo. Now I just don't like it so much. I want to do something
else. I don't like what it's becoming here." He couldn't find the
words to tell her how he hated the dirt and noise of the train and
how he would stare out to sea sometimes while he was working
in the boat shed and watch the packet ships going in the Stream.

"I know," she said. She placed her hand on his arm the way
she used to and it sent something electric all through his body.
"You're a restless boy."

Arlis took his arm away. "I'm not a boy anymore, Jo." He
wanted to tell her how he felt like a man, how he'd been with
some of the Cuban girls, and how he'd been with her own
friend, Wanda.

She kept looking at him. "No," she said. "I guess you're not."

Brit came out on the porch with a bottle of Tropical Havana.
Mr. Olcott would serve him at the bar now that he turned
twenty. Brit put his foot on the low railing and lit a cigarette
before he spoke, blowing out a long stream of blue smoke and
looking as handsome as a picture advertisement.

"How's school today, Jo?" he asked, staring off to where the
sun went down beyond the workers' shacks. He dressed nicely.
He and his daddy were doing well with their planting grounds.
Inside the Gramophone had gone down and some fishermen
were singing:

"Sponger's money never done,
Cigar-maker money on the bum…"

"Oh my." JoAnna's voice took on a different tone when she
spoke to Brit, Arlis was sure of it. "It's just the same as when we
were there." Who was the real JoAnna? Something inside Arlis
ached. He could still feel the place where her hand had rested on
his arm.

Brit tugged at his necktie. Arlis made up his mind to buy a necktie too.

"Well, we're going to break through the top in pineapples this year," Brit said. "How many acres you got in pines, Arlis?"

"Just one." Brit knew that. Why did he ask?

"Well, you'll make some money. You and old Uncle Jake too busy making boats anyway, huh?" He thumped Arlis on the back and took another drag off the cigarette. "We just got to watch we don't get into this here war. But you can't say what that would do to business. What you think, old Arlis?"

"I don't know. I don't know but what's in the papers." Arlis felt ignorant and bewildered.

"Mr. Wilson says we'll not be a part of it," said JoAnna. "And I quite agree. It's dreadful. They're slaughtering each other while industrialists capitalize on it. On human suffering."

"That's radical talk, Jo," said Brit. "I mean, for God's sake, a man's got to do what's right morally. Even Preacher says so. Them Germans done things that can't be mentioned in a woman's presence. If we go to war I think a man ought to do his duty, don't you, Arlis?"

"I haven't thought about it that way."

"Well, you're still too young." He flipped the cigarette off the porch.

But I'm damn sure big enough to kick your ass, you son of a bitch, Arlis thought.

"I think it's dreadful," said Jo. "I think we ought not even talk about it."

"Good," said Brit. "Then you can come in and have a dance with me." He put his arm around Jo's waist. "Here, Arlis." He gave him the green Tropical bottle. "You can finish my beer, kiddo." Arlis watched them go inside; even when JoAnna was out of sight, he felt a dull ache when he thought of her. The fishermen sang on:

"Let everybody know in town
Me an' my gal gonna dance 'em down.
Sponger money lot of fun–sponger money never done."

Arlis squatted over one of his Spanish reds, looking for any sign of mealy bugs. But the pineapple was fat and healthy, shining under its hat of green leaves. He ran his eye down the carefully tended row, thinking how they had only been little slips when he and Uncle Jake planted them last summer. He thought too of how when you watch growing things you see them change little by little until you almost come to love them because you know all about their lives and how they change over time. He wondered how he could love changes in the growing pineapples and hate the changes that happened on his island.

Arlis liked this piece of planting ground. Even in the hottest part of the day he liked to leave old Uncle Jake in the boat shed and come up to see the pines and the wild trees. There was a small depression, a break in the natural foliage, where if you stood up you could see the ocean like a short blue dash in the trees. The jungle around the cleared place made a curtain that shut everything else out: the rail line, the settlement, the houses of the people and train workers, the new concrete viaduct that came across the channel. Once Arlis had taken off his clothes and lain faceup between the rows of pineapples, feeling the sun all over his body. He thought about Adam naked in the Garden of Eden. He'd placed his hand on his rib and thought of God and Eve, then JoAnna. And then he'd felt a little ashamed of what happened between his legs. There had been no help for it. There had been no rib, no God, no Eve. Just JoAnna.

Arlis chopped the brush away from the base of the pineapple plant. It would not be long before harvest again. They would do all right for themselves even with this one little acre. It was about all he could work by himself along with the boats they built. It was enough, he thought. Cap'n Ben might be coming home soon too. He would go this time. He would be ready, after this harvest, to go.

"Arlis." He heard her voice come from the edge of the field where the path led in. He stood up. He could see her there looking for him among the planted rows.

"I'm here, Jo." She saw him and came toward him holding her skirt so that it didn't get snagged on the sawtooth edges of the pineapple leaves. She didn't wear a hat and she seemed a little out of breath when she came to where he worked. Arlis had gotten back down and cleared the brush. Jo stood over him for a minute, then sat down too.

"How's doing, Jo?"

"Okay, Arlis. I just thought I'd come see how you were. Uncle Jake told me where to find you."

"It's nice up here. I like it."

"Yes. This has always been my favorite planting ground. Cut off from everything. Hidden."

"Yes."

"My father used to tell me not to come up here by myself. He said if I came up here alone that the gypsies would get me and take me away. Sometimes I would come and wait for them. For the gypsies."

"And?" Arlis looked at her full in the face. She wore a peculiar little smile that turned her mouth up only a shadow at the corners.

"The gypsies never came."

Arlis chopped at the brush, thinking of it.

"Arlis. I need to tell you something." He quit chopping and looked at her again. "Brit asked me to marry him." Her face stayed the same but became very full of the colors around them. "Did you hear me?"

"Yes, I heard you,"

They looked at one another.

"Well, what do you think?" she asked.

"I think you should ask your father. I'm not your damn father," he said, hurting because he could see what he was doing to her.

"I did ask him, Arlis. He wants me to do it."

"Do it, then."

"I mean, isn't that what people are supposed to do?" Some desperation came into her voice. "Isn't that what happens when you grow up? I'm nineteen years old, Arlis. Aren't I supposed to do it? Brit's a good person, isn't he?"

"Do what you want to, Jo."

She'd begun crying a little now, and Arlis couldn't look at her.

"Can't you help me, Arlis? Please? Aren't you my friend? I don't know who else to ask."

"You do what you want to, Jo."

"Oh Arlis, I don't know what to do." She'd made her hands into little fists.

"I'll tell you what to do. Why don't you just go away?"

She got quiet, then began crying harder, and when Arlis wouldn't look at her he heard her get up and walk away. He started chopping at the brush again, mechanically, feeling how the sun burned the back of his neck. When he couldn't stand it any longer he got to his feet and threw his machete as hard as he could at the treeline where the edge of the planting ground met the jungle. The day stayed quite still until he heard the whistle of the train coming down from Miami.

In the last weeks of the season it got good and hot, and it rained almost every afternoon, making the pineapples turgid and polished as if they wanted to burst. The same as last year, Mr. Jewel opened the warehouse, and growers marked their names on the ends of the wooden boxes and carefully packed in the pineapples and stacked the full crates in the shade of the loading dock. Everyone made sure Mr. Jewel got the right count of how many boxes they had. They argued and fought if they didn't think it was right. With everyone in the settlement working, it took two days to get the first load ready to be put on the train. Mr. Jewel wired the agent in Key West that they were ready to go. But when the next day came, the train north went right on through. It trailed its coal tender, four passenger cars, and eight new green-and-white boxcars ahead of a caboose. Mr. Jewel got very red in the face, then pale, and then went into the telegraph office. The people waiting in the shade of the concrete loading dock started talking among themselves, not knowing what to make of anything.

On the following day, Mr. Jewel sent two of his darkies up the line to where the switch to the siding was and had them pull it. The train came in on time and stopped because the switch was pulled. The train hauled passenger cars with people looking out the windows and standing in the vestibules, and behind a string of the green-and-white boxcars. The green-and-white cars looked brilliant and sterile in the sunshine because of the dirt around the siding. They appeared as if they'd been brought along as someone's afterthought.

The fireman and the brakeman and the engineer got out of the cab and came up to the shaded platform where Mr. Jewel and the planters waited. They were very angry.

"Who pulled that goddam switch?" said the engineer.

"Where's our fruit agent? Where's our cars?" said Mr. Jewel.

"Who pulled that goddam switch?"

"I pulled it," Jewel piped up. "I want to know where our cars are. I want to know where's that fruit agent."

The engineer, a big man, took hold of Mr. Jewel's suit front and shook him back and forth so his hat fell off.

"Don't you never never pull a switch on my goddam train again. You hear me? Don't you never never do that again. You do that to my goddam train again and I'll knock you down."

The engineer let go of Mr. Jewel and started to walk back to the train with the fireman and the brakeman following. Everyone stayed quiet because they couldn't understand what was happening: where were their cars for the pineapples?

"Wait," cried Jewel. He ran after the trainmen. "Our pineapples. We're supposed to get our pineapples carried out of here. Where's our cars?"

The engineer turned on him. They stood out together in the dirt of the siding right between the heavy concrete of the loading ramp and the steel of the train track. The sun was hot on their heads. The steam engine made a slow grunting sound even when it didn't move.

"Where's our cars?" repeated Mr. Jewel. He'd lost control.

"There ain't no cars for you. You can't afford no cars." The engineer got back up close to him like he wanted to grab him again but instead jerked his thumb at the new green-and-white boxcars. "These here are Cuban cars with Cuban pines. Fruit agent pays Cubans six bits a box for their pines already loaded in the cars and ferried to Key West and put on the tracks. Now if'n he pays them six bits a box, how's he going to afford to pay you three and a half dollars? Huh?" The engineer spoke loudly right into Jewel's face and waited. "God, you're a stupid son of a bitch." He stared at him for another half-minute before he got back into his cab. "What you think they built this railroad for anyway? For you?"

They backed the train down the siding and the fireman and brakeman got off and moved the switch back. The train started up slow, kicking out its black smoke and making the cars buck together. The planters who had gathered around watching Mr. Jewel and the trainmen just stared at the train. They looked like dumb animals. No one said anything until Mrs. Esquinaldo started crying. She was a wiry little woman with unkempt hair. Her dress was all dirty from working at packing pineapples. She wore an apron like a man's. She didn't put her hands up to cover her face. She only blubbered openly, the tears making clean lines down her dirty face. The train got up a little more speed. The new green-and-white boxcars passed one by one, then the brick red caboose. Mrs. Esquinaldo's crying got louder but no one else could think of anything to do. All of a sudden old Mr. Caine broke out of the crowd. He had a big rock in his hand. He ran down the railbed after the caboose on his skinny legs. When he saw he'd never catch the train, he threw the rock right through the rear window of the caboose. Everyone could hear the glass break. There must not have been any trainmen inside the caboose, because no one came out on the platform. Old Mr. Caine stood in the middle of the hot roadbed watching the train going north with the Cuban pineapples.

"You son of a bitches," he screamed. "You ruined us."

The people waited around for a little while longer. Mr. Esquinaldo took his wife home and pretty soon people began going away somewhere. Jewel Claire sat alone on the platform, his suit all rumpled where the engineer had grabbed him. Mr. Caine kept standing in the middle of the tracks in the sun.

Then he walked to Jewel Claire. He looked at Mr. Jewel and pointed up the tracks. "There goes your goddam civilization. Some civilization."

The trains going down to Key West stopped for water at the tank. You could hear the big pump working at the Indian well. But the ones going north for the next few days went right on through, dropping the mailbag and never stopping. Mr. Jewel tried at the telegraph office for a while before he quit. He watched the trains pass by until the pineapples started to go, then he went up into his house and wouldn't come down.

When pineapples start going, they go fast. The gnats and flies went at them and the smell became bad. You could smell them all over the settlement. Finally, without being told, the people carried the boxes down to the wharf and dropped them into the harbor. After that the tide would carry them out to the harbor mouth only to draw them back in, washing them up on the beaches until the next tide. There were thousands of pineapples, more than the crabs or the birds could eat, lying on the beaches and up in the mangroves and even in the marl pits that the railroad dredges had cut out of the shoreline. They lay there 'til they rotted. Of course, no one bothered to pick the rest of the crop beyond what they figured they wanted to eat for themselves.

In a week the smell began to die down. One afternoon the Miami train stopped for water. The men drinking inside the guesthouse at the bar could see it. Some of the passengers came in for a drink and to stretch their legs.

Mr. Esquinaldo came in the door and walked right up to the bar. He slapped his hand down on the bar so everyone would notice him.

"Gimme a double, jack," he said to Mr. Olcott. He drank off

the double and wiped his mouth with the back of his sleeve. "Better gimme another," he said. "Better all of you have one." He turned and faced the men in the bar. "You'll need it when you hear this: Mr. Jewel's Indian well just run out of water. She's sucking mud and salt slime." He drank off his drink while the other men watched him, their faces stupid and slack. "Hell," said Mr. Esquinaldo. "I just knew that goddam thing wouldn't work for long. I could've told them that."

14

"It's a tragedy. A tragedy," said Mr. Clyde Seybold. He looked over his small audience of depressed settlers. His handsome face seemed very sad in the light of the guesthouse saloon. But Arlis thought he didn't look near as sad as Mr. Jewel who sat next to him. Mr. Jewel's skin hung in folds, like all the juice had been sucked out of him.

Mr. Seybold clasped and unclasped his hands and made his face intense. The planters gathered in the bar watched each of his gestures as if he were on one of the new Key West movie screens.

"You've been victimized by foreigners!" he shouted. A mutter of approval went through the settlers. Mr. Seybold stared around the room, giving the impression of looking each man right in the eye if just for a fraction of a second. He rose abruptly and took a couple of steps in each direction, stopping beside Jewel's chair again. His voice rose.

"But I'm here tonight to tell you that this settlement is not lost. I'm here to tell you that this settlement has been reborn." Arlis thought he sounded more powerful than Preacher when he got wound up. Mr. Seybold laid a hand on Jewel's rounded shoulder. The crowd and Mr. Jewel showed signs of coming to life.

"There's times of trouble ahead for this mighty country of ours. We're even now girding up our national loins for a global conflict with the forces of evil. Make no mistake!" Mr. Seybold shook his fist in the dumb faces of the planters. "There's plenty of evil out there!" He waved the fist at the window. "And as such, our country must have raw materials in the struggle for democracy." He paused and lowered his voice dramatically. He touched himself on the breast of his pin-striped coat.

"It hurts me. It hurts me to hear the cry of the unfed child or of the strong man willing to work." Arlis tried to think of anyone who had unfed children. "But I'm here tonight to tell you good people that those times are over. There ain't no reason for willing hands to be idle in the settlement of Doctor's Arm ever again. Your whole island is a national resource." A silence followed.

"What we got, Mr. Seybold?" asked Mr. Esquinaldo. Mr. Seybold's eyebrows went straight up.

"Timber is what you got, my dear friend. Lumber. This island's got one of the biggest stands of timber between Key West and Miami. And you got no idea how that lumber is in demand. There's a war coming. Now that you got a railroad to tote it, you're living on a gold mine!"

"But that there's government land."

Mr. Seybold showed his pretty teeth. Arlis could almost count each one in the bad light of the bar.

"You men get ready to start cutting trees. We'll take care of the government." He jerked Jewel Claire to his feet. "The saws are coming this week along with the mule teams. You can believe anyone who wants work is going to have it. Lumber's going for ten dollars a thousand. There's year's worth of work up the middle of this island." He pushed Jewel in front of him toward the door. "Mr. Jewel and me's going to just plan out the details. We're putting Doctor's Arm back on the map again. I guarantee it!" Jewel's wasted face seemed to fill out all at once. The men gave a ragged cheer and Mr. Jewel and Mr. Seybold were already talking, their heads almost touching, as they went together out the door.

"Crap," said Brit. He made himself look unimpressed and stared at the door through which Mr. Seybold had taken Jewel. "Railroad done screwed us good for our pines. What makes you think they're not going to screw us again?"

"Weren't the railroad's fault," said Poopy.

"Was." He drank his Tropical. "Them and them cheap-working Cubans. Six bits a box. Shit. We lost a fortune thanks to them." Brit was very bitter. The pineapple bust about killed his old man. Mr. Caine stayed in bed all the time now, leaving Brit to do everything. "I'm getting sick of this place," Brit said.

"Well, if we got some work it'd be maybe okay. What you figure, Arlis?"

"Crap," Brit interrupted. "Arlis and old Jake can just build skiffs and not worry about nothing. Me, I got to find a job."

Arlis stayed quiet. He didn't feel like arguing with Brit. He didn't feel too much interest in anything now. To him the days had each one become very much like the other. He didn't care about pineapples. He didn't care if they cut timber or not or if he and Uncle Jake finished the skiff in the boat shed. Uncle Jake would sleep half the day while Arlis sat and stared out past the bow of *The Reaper* at the dark ribbon of the Gulf Stream, thinking of JoAnna and of running away.

"Well. I'll try it out," Poopy continued. "Lumber cutting. Hell. I'll try anything once." He waited for what his friends would say to that. They said nothing.

"Crap," said Brit. "It's all crap."

Mr. Jewel sent the Bahamians home. He was right in figuring there would be plenty of workers in Doctor's Arm. The people had become used to money. Except for a millwright and a mechanic who moved into one of the railroad cottages, all the men working the sawmill came from the island.

Mr. Jewel and Mr. Seybold set up the first saw next to the siding. It had a forty-inch blade on it and an all-steel chain-drawn carriage. The men worked two shifts, so Arlis could hear the cutting sounds from sunrise 'til after dark. A dynamo off the saw engine lit up the whole siding with electric lights.

The trees closest were cut first. The mules, two to the team, dragged the logs off the bluff side through Jewel's old planting ground and down to the mill. If the trees were terribly large the men used a winch to get them onto the steel carriage. When the lumber had been slabbed into one-inch thicknesses it was left in covered drying piles. The semidried lumber went north to Miami or south to Key West, where the navy base was being greatly expanded.

From the door of the boat shed Arlis watched a mule team drag a log sledge over the rutted side of the meadow past the ruined Indian well. At that distance he couldn't make out who drove the mules. The ground seemed to rise up hot and dry and shimmery in the sun. From beneath the discolored iron roof of the sawmill came the whine of the ripsaw. Arlis sat on a nail keg and let his hands hang in front of him.

"What is it, boy? You sick?" asked Uncle Jake.

Arlis had not fixed him an iced tea in days and when the old man went off to sleep Arlis just left him lying in the shade and would not awaken him until suppertime. Arlis could see it made him sore and even a little afraid, but how could he help the way he felt inside?

"I ain't sick, Uncle Jake. I'm tired. I just feel tired."

"Young boy like you ought not to be tired. I think you sick."

Arlis got up. Uncle Jake watched him. Arlis walked to the hull of *The Reaper*. He'd been looking at her and feeling her and climbing up the ladder to get inside her for weeks. Arlis touched her hull and ran his hand over her planking.

"How long is she, exactly, Uncle Jake? Thirty-four?"

"Thirty-six and six inches, don't count the bowsprit."

Arlis continued walking in the sand, barefooted, letting his hand trail on the hull.

"What'd it take to get her ready for sea?"

"What you talking about, you fool lazy child? I can't even get you to finish a damn sponge skiff anymore and you want to put *The Reaper* to sea."

"What'd it take?"

The old colored man screwed up his face. He studied the palms of his hands.

"Time, boy. Something you don't know much about. She fastened good but need to have her seams packed and caulked with red lead. Needs new sails. Cabin ain't much but you rebuilds the cabin to suit what purpose you got in mind for her."

"She's a pretty boat, Uncle Jake."

"She pretty, but she Cap'n Ben's boat. Not yours."

"I know."

"She got something wrong with her, though," Uncle Jake mumbled.

"What you mean?"

"I don't know. Nothing."

"Tell me, Uncle Jake." He was tired of the old man's superstitions.

Uncle Jake squirmed. "She a bad-luck boat. Bad luck follow a boat, you know, boy." He avoided Arlis's eyes.

"You make your own luck, dammit."

"You think what you wants to," he pouted.

"I will. About that."

"That the way childrens be."

"I ain't no child."

"Yes you is. You a love-sick child is what's wrong with you."

Arlis glared across the dimness at the old man, damning him for what he could see. The new steam whistle from the sawmill shrieked, changing the shift and breaking the contact between the boy and the old man.

"I'm going down and see Brit and Poopy."

"Go on. You sure don't be no good stewing around here."

Arlis turned to go.

"Wait." Uncle Jake came to him. He put a quarter in Arlis's hand. "Buy a cool drink for your friends, boy. Your granddaddy coming back soon. Maybe take you off here. I think that's what you needs. Sit on a rock too long make a man crazy as hell. That's a fact."

Arlis left Uncle Jake. He followed the beach for a while, then cut up toward the station and the sawmill. From the rise of the roadbed he could see the harbor on his left and the sawmill and station ahead of him. He searched the empty horizon, half hoping to see *Eva Pearl*, then looked back at the harbor. The wharf had been cleared of work barges that were still fit. The old ones were abandoned and lay at different angles, rusting and rotting against the greenness of the mangroves.

The men from the offgoing shift scattered themselves, some going home, others for a drink at the guesthouse. Arlis went inside and found Brit and Poopy already slouched at a table. He sat down with them. Wanda brought three Tropicals.

They look really whipped, Arlis thought. The both of them. Poopy could hardly crack a joke with Wanda. Brit seemed worse off. He had sawdust on his hair and face, which made the wrinkles at the corners of his eyes look deep, like they'd been cut in with a knife. Arlis paid Wanda for the beers with the two bits Uncle Jake had given him.

"Thanks," said Poopy. Brit kept staring off as if he didn't see either of them. Arlis wondered when he figured to marry up with Jo. The thought of it seemed unreal, like something children play at. Brit looked plenty unhappy with everything. Maybe, Arlis thought, they won't get married now.

Poopy took a long drink of the beer and it seemed to put life back into him.

"That's about the hardest damn work I ever done, old Arlis," he said. He grinned. "Don't you think, Brit? But we did it all right, didn't we?" He nudged Brit. "It ain't so bad."

Brit swiveled his eyes back from nowhere to the two of them.

"Oh no, it ain't so bad," he mocked. "And it ain't going to be so bad tomorrow or the day after." Brit spit his words out as if something bitter had gotten into his mouth. "But how you going to feel in a month? Or a year or five years? How you going to feel doing the same thing over and over and over again? Work eight-ten hours a day six days a week, pick up your crummy pay and get drunk on Saturday night. Every week the same. How you feel about that?" His eyes squinted when he spoke, closing down the dust-coated wrinkles. "You don't even see what I'm saying, do you? I mean, where the hell we going? We ain't going nowhere. There's some blight killing the sponges. The Cubans sell better pineapples. You want to fish? Nobody wants to buy fish they can catch for themselves. You see what I'm talking about? We're stuck. We can't do nothing but just what we're doing. We ain't going nowhere. We ain't never going nowhere. And you're both too stupid to know it." He drank off his Tropical all at once. He drank it like he was angry, throwing his head back and letting it pour down him. Brit put the empty on the table and flashed at Arlis, then Poopy. The rims of his eyes looked bloody against the yellow of the sawdust powder.

"People talk war this and war that. I tell you I'm going to be damn glad to see it come. Just to change my life. Just to get me off this island." Brit got up and looked at them hard, as if he'd hated them all his life. "Just you think about that one," he said. Then he left.

"Hell," said Poopy. "What's wrong with him? He don't have no call to get snotty. I mean, life's hard sometimes. A man's got to expect that, right? Hell. I'm having another beer. Come on, have another beer, old Arlis."

Something long before dawn caused Arlis to awaken, troubled in his mind. He awakened clearly and all at once, as if his name had been called. He could not tell the time, only that it remained dark except for the starlight. Arlis dressed and walked out of the house. Between the coconut fronds he saw how the constellations had moved around the North Star.

In the coconut grove he recognized the path more by its feel beneath his bare feet than by the masses of watery tree trunks. He knew if he was blinded he could find the path just like he could smell a summer rain squall coming across the water.

Arlis sensed another thing. It felt like a need to reason inside, to ask something. He followed the path that went on down past the boat shed to the edge of the water and could see the harbor and the true sea beyond.

He sat in the sand, resting his back on a tree, and watched the dark cup of the sky over the sea. He stared long and hard into blackness and wondered if the Lord was there in the true sea and in the cup of the sky watching him on the beach, one Arlis sitting under a tree. ...Arlis believed He was. Mommer always said it was so, that the Lord watched us and would help when things weren't right. Things in Doctor's Arm weren't right to Arlis. Things weren't right to Brit. Maybe they weren't even right to Jewel Claire, but Arlis could not tell that.

I don't know why things are different, Lord, Arlis thought. Maybe because of the railroad...But that's something done and finished. It's just here, a fact. What I need to do is get out there. There on the true sea. I'm going out there, Lordy. Help me to get out there, and when I get there I can look back and see things better. I know. I maybe can't change things but I could understand them. I think it would be better to at least understand things. I might not be happier but it would be something anyway. Arlis paused. He bet old Uncle Jake understood things. He bet Cap'n Ben understood things for sure. Let me out there, Lord, and I'll understand too.

Arlis stared long and hard into the night and knew it was a fine way to make himself sleepy. He felt glad he had come down here now. Thinking about the Almighty, which he hardly ever did, had been the right thing. It made Arlis feel quite at rest.

False dawn. Mosquitoes cried into Arlis's ears. He could hear them through his sleep. They came because not a breath of air blew off the water. In the dead slack tide the sea barely moved against the shore. Coming faintly with first light a sound moved toward Arlis, gradually louder, gently pulling him to consciousness. It popped with regularity. It was a boat engine, a one-lunger, one of the slowest Arlis had ever heard. He opened his eyes and raised his head.

On the oil of the water, through the still break in the reef, stood *Eva Pearl* under full sail, her canvas hanging wet and limp and flat as the face of the harbor. She moved into the harbor mouth, showing no disturbance off her bow. From her stem, stretched wire-tight, she was dragged by a thick hemp-towing hawser tied to the stern of the laboring cutter from which the slow engine noise emanated. A black man, still as the ship, slumped over the tiller bar of the cutter.

The first of the dawn turned *Eva Pearl*'s topsails pink, and through the wonderful light Arlis saw that the topsails and all the rest of the hanging canvas were dirty and patched. Long trails of rust wept from the chain plates and discolored the once-white hull.

The cutter dropped the towing hawser and made a wide circle around the harbor's stillness. Under her own momentum *Eva Pearl* moved quietly and perfectly to lay beside the wharf before the cutter pulled under her stern and disappeared. The engine died and Arlis heard the clicking of mast hoops and squealing of halyards running through blocks as the ship's canvas was struck. The boy rose to his feet. He saw his grandfather standing alone on the deck, withered but unbent, as if his blue greatcoat were stuffed with straw and burned ash.

15

To Arlis an odor of defeat hung over the ship, and worse, over the old man himself. From the instant he saw *Eva Pearl*'s sad, limp, dirty sails Arlis could not deny it. It pervaded the ship and everything around her like a lost piece of bait-shrimp rotting out of sight.

Arlis carried the old man's things ashore. He followed next

to him, seeing how he stood as tall as Cap'n Ben now. It gave him the sensation that the old man had somehow shrunk. Cap'n Ben flatly spoke of Panama and New Orleans and all the while his point of focus seemed to be retreating to an unseen place inside his head. His great beard had become utterly wild and his expression reminded Arlis of Mommer before she died.

Unlike in older days, Cap'n Ben came to the house and stayed there. He did not sleep aboard *Eva Pearl*, as he had since Mommer died. He slept for long stretches in his little room, especially the first few days he was home.

Arlis took the chance to go down to the ship. For crew there were only four now: two old darkies and two somber boys, black-skinned and younger than Arlis. The prime seamen, along with Mr. Trebble, had been pressed into the British Merchant Fleet. To make up for her lost men *Eva Pearl* had a gasoline-driven donkey engine bolted into her deck in front of the foremast. By means of an interchangeable system of snatch blocks and pulleys the engine could both haul sail and raise an anchor. It was ugly and efficient.

Arlis looked around him. He tried to look at everything and make some sort of judgment about what he saw. It came hard to know that there was no one or nothing to guide him, only his terrible want. He watched each morning how Cap'n Ben came down to *Eva Pearl* for a few minutes and then left the crew to fend for themselves. The crew in their turn did little but fish from the cutter or buy a few greens from a settler's wife. Cap'n Ben didn't seem to care. He moodily spent the day stumping over the island carrying a stick to lean on. He walked north on the railbed to see the huge concrete viaduct and visited the disused planting grounds or observed the timber being brought to the sawmill. Each night Arlis made sure he had fresh fish, and the old man would talk a little, then sit quietly on the porch and stare at the Gulf Stream. Arlis had a vision of Cap'n Ben doing that forever. It was a frightening idea he could not allow himself to think about. In a week Arlis recognized one truth. If he ever wished to sail out of Doctor's Arm aboard *Eva Pearl* he'd have to do something.

On the next day, after Cap'n Ben's visit aboard, Arlis rowed his skiff out and tied up alongside. He secured a coarse brush to a pole and scrubbed the tailing marine weed off the hull for as far down as he could reach, working around the perimeter of the ship. The day following that, Arlis stripped off his clothes and swam with the brush beneath the keel, scrubbing until he thought his lungs would rupture before struggling to the surface. Barnacles tore off patches of his skin but the work went fast and Arlis did not mind. At night Aunt Eleuthera rubbed aloe gel into his wounds and Arlis slept as if he were dead.

Next Arlis convinced Uncle Jake what they had to do, then he counted on Uncle Jake to convince the four darkies in the crew. Arlis knew the darkies might not listen to a white boy, but by tact and bribery they would follow a smart man like Uncle Jake.

In the boat shed Arlis found half a dozen bars of pumice stone, a cask of tarred oakum, and several gallons of pitch. He and Uncle Jake brought it aboard *Eva Pearl* along with a tow sack of half-pints from Papadad's old stock.

Arlis told the crew what he wanted. From their smoky sullen faces he could not know if they understood or even spoke the same language. Then Uncle Jake took one of the bottles from the sack, uncorked it, and had a drink. Not speaking, he handed it to the oldest crewman, who drank and nodded and passed it along.

The six of them holy-stoned the deck, pushing the light blocks of pumice back and forth with the grain of the teakwood, moving on hands and knees in a line. Surely they wore down the stained and discolored patches to show the lightness beneath. Arlis swept carefully, then Uncle Jake directed the men at tapping tarred and twisted strips of oakum between the gaps in the planking. When the gaps had been filled Uncle Jake himself layed in a bead of pitch over the oakum and Arlis swabbed hot linseed oil into the parched wood.

Arlis bought several gallons of white enamel from Mr. Olcott with his savings. Uncle Jake supervised the men and they painted the hull as far down as they could reach on deck. Arlis worked from his skiff around the waterline.

With Uncle Jake, Arlis went over the rigging. Uncle Jake knew everything there was to know and just how things should be. He couldn't climb anymore but he shouted instructions to Arlis, who scrambled in the ratlines. It confused Arlis at first until he realized that in principle the rigging was just like a catboat or any other sailboat. Together he and Uncle Jake tightened the shrouds down and remade or spliced worn line. It relieved Arlis to know nothing else major needed repair. The stock of rum had almost given out. He just wished he could replace the patched and shabby canvas but figured it would have to do.

With the last of the enamel Arlis painted the chain bobstay beneath the heavy bowsprit. He wondered how long it would take for rust to bleed through. It didn't matter to him. He wanted *Eva Pearl* to look as best as she could right then.

"You done a fine job, Arlis,"

Arlis looked up at the voice. Cap'n Ben stood on the wharf. Arlis pulled the skiff in by her line and climbed up beside him so they could both look into *Eva Pearl*. He felt unsure of what to say now that he was done.

"She's a pretty little ship, Cap'n Ben."

"She's about worn out, son. She's old."

"That's okay, Cap'n Ben. There's nothing wrong with old. She's still good." This made the old man laugh. He could still laugh better than anyone. It made Arlis feel good to hear him laugh and to stand next to him just as tall. From the other side of the tracks they could hear the whine of the sawmill.

"I been walking around the settlement, boy. I walked all the way to the new concrete viaduct and back. I seen the sawmill and the gasoline pump on the old well."

"They don't work anymore. The pump and the well."

"Yes, I know, son. It's too bad. That was a good well."

"I miss the ironwood tree."

"That was some tree. I bet that tree was two hundred years old. At least."

"You think, Cap'n Ben?"

"At least."

The boy and the old man remained silent for a time and the old man spoke again.

"It's bad out there, son." His blue eyes were on the Gulf Stream and the true sea. Tanned, weathered skin folded and hooded his eyes. They peered out like lanterns, as if they could see through anything. "I wasn't going back, you know. I was going to stay here and die. Things have changed for a wind-sail man. I don't need to tell you that. You see the train with its big engine coming through every day. You know how it's changed things here. Things have changed all over. So. Well." All the defeat had gone at once. "It's still better out there."

"I've got to go and see it, Cap'n Ben," Arlis said quietly. "I got to know and have someone to show me before it's all gone."

"Yes. We got to go out again, I believe. We will. I couldn't stay here anyway. It's too damn strange." Arlis hadn't been prepared for the finality of it. Cap'n Ben did not even look at him when he spoke. He looked from *Eva Pearl* to the Gulf Stream as if each of them had known what would happen all along. The imminence had the effect of a small terror on Arlis.

"When should I be ready?"

Cap'n Ben shrugged. "You'll know when you're ready. Now send the two boys up to the house. I'm putting my things back aboard. I think I'll sleep on *Eva Pearl* tonight." The blue lanterns finally looked on Arlis.

"Yessir," he said.

Two drunks fought by the siding until one pushed the other into the water trough. No one paid attention. The payday crowd swirled around the station platform and in front of the guesthouse saloon. Electric bulbs off the dynamo formed great cones of light in the darkness. Up the slope past the cemetery, light from the second sawmill burned its yellow circle. Arlis could see the forms of men moving and the way the smoke rose from the tall coal stack. Mr. Jewel kept a shift working there until

midnight because it was farther out of town. The landscape all
the way down the slope interrupted itself with jagged slash piles
and sawdust mounds and hastily built drying sheds from which
the train took vast loads of lumber north and south each day.
Men walked out of the rows of huts the railroad had built for
them. They came for drinks or to buy from Mr. Olcott's store.
When the second mill opened people arrived from up the keys
and even from Key West to take the jobs and to move into the
huts. The sponge market had been going bad for almost a year
from the blight and spongers needed to find other work. Arlis
guessed it was good business for Doctor's Arm. There was even
talk of running a new line down from the freshwater lake. Arlis
did not know. He looked out at what he could see from the
height of the platform. There were so many lights and people.
Cap'n Ben called it strange. It was. Arlis felt glad to be leaving
even if it was his home. It didn't feel like a home anymore.

Arlis left the platform and went into the sea of faces. Some
were unknown to him; some were those he'd known all his life.
To them all Arlis seemed to go unnoticed because of the way
they hurried past. But he didn't care. He only hoped now to see
the face of JoAnna. He didn't want to go away without saying
good-bye. He wanted to see her once again.

Arlis went into the bar. Mr. Olcott stood at one end wiping
glasses and placing them upside down on a towel. Two other men
worked the bar. Preacher sat next to Mr. Olcott. He looked thin
and sickly and unwashed. He drank something from a tumbler
Mr. Olcott set in front of him.

" 'Lo, Arlis."

" 'Lo, Mr. Olcott. Preacher." Preacher nodded, his moist lips
remaining unchanged while he looked past the boy.

"You seen JoAnna, Mr. Olcott?"

"I seen her." Mr. Olcott thumped down a glass on the towel.
"I better be seein' her again soon too. She's off with that damn
Brit. Going off alone like that only leads to trouble. Marriage or
no. Where you think they are, Preacher?"

Preacher, who had been nodding in agreement, hunched his

shoulders.

"Go ask Poopy," said Mr. Olcott. "Them two roughnecks ain't never far apart." Arlis saw Poopy at a table with his father. "You find her, tell her to come here. I need help. Can't run the damn place by myself and besides, she got no business running loose at night alone with that Brit. Marriage or no." Preacher began nodding again and drank what Mr. Olcott had given him.

Arlis walked to Poopy's table. Poopy was drunk. He still had sawdust all over him. His father was drunk too and talked to the spongers at the next table. Poopy leaned forward on his arms. He looked up and smiled real big when Arlis came to him.

"Old Arlis."

"Hi, Poopy. You seen Brit and Jo?"

"Old Arlis." Poopy pulled Arlis down into the next chair. "Have a beer, pal. Wanda. Get Arlis a bottle a beer." Wanda brought a beer, looking all the time very plump and inviting. Poopy tried to touch her as she moved off. He missed.

"Thanks, Poop. You seen Brit?"

"He's gone off. For a while. With old Jo." Poopy giggled. "What you want with Brit?"

"I come to tell you guys good-bye."

"That's good of you, old Arlis. How'd you know?"

"Know what?"

"Why, that we're going. Wish you were old enough to join up with us. Me and Brit's going to miss you, boy."

"But I come to say good-bye to you."

"Well," said Poopy. "You done said it."

"It's me that's going, Poop. I'm going off on *Eva Pearl.*"

Poopy looked at Arlis and then began laughing. He laughed until moisture appeared in the corners of his eyes.

"Hell. I guess we're all going, then. Me and Brit's going soldiering." He lowered his voice. "It's supposed to be a secret. Had enough of this shit-hole island." Arlis drank his beer. Mr. Esquinaldo turned around and saw Arlis. He put his hand on Arlis's shoulder.

"My boy's going off soldiering, Arlis. What you think of

that?" Mr. Esquinaldo looked all flushed and full of pride.

"That's good, Mr. Esquinaldo. I'm going off with Cap'n Ben on *Eva Pearl*." Mr. Esquinaldo did not hear.

"He's going to be a great soldier." Mr. Esquinaldo's hand fell on the table. He looked long at Poopy, his face fat with satisfaction and sweat. Poopy grinned stupidly. "God damn, I'm proud of you."

Arlis finished his beer. "I got to go. I guess I better say so long to Brit. It's late."

"Well, Arlis. Good-bye." Poopy rose and solemnly shook Arlis by the hand. He looked sad for a moment. Mr. Esquinaldo pulled him back down and put his arm over the boy's shoulder. They looked like two clumsy bears.

" 'Bye, Poop," said Arlis. He walked through the noisy tables. Behind him he heard Mr. Esquinaldo say something again about "good soldier." Arlis hoped Poopy would be all right in the army. He passed the bar. Mr. Olcott and Preacher glared at him as if they knew something he did not. Arlis went out into the cool air of the night.

Arlis looked down the tracks in both directions as far as the electric lights would allow him to see. He saw neither Brit nor Jo.

The moon was down. A few quick clouds scudded in from the sea. Arlis walked out of the light and off the slope toward the beach. It became very dark, only the faintest star reflections striking small fire on the water's surface. A single figure loomed up before Arlis, silhouetted poorly against the white sand beach. The figure staggered.

"Brit."

"Arlis." He fell into Arlis and brought them both down. Arlis sat and Brit sprawled in the sand. He was drunker than Poopy.

"Poopy tells me you and him are going away."

"Yeah." Brit panted. "We got to get off." He lay there panting for a while, then rolled over to face Arlis. "Nobody understands it, Arlis. This place is choking me." He spoke in a sloppy voice, almost pleading. "Nobody'll understand."

"I understand. I'm going off too."

"You going off? You ain't old enough for the army. I'd a asked you along if you was, Arlis."

"I'm going off with Cap'n Ben on *Eva Pearl*."

"Then you understand. Jo don't understand."

"JoAnna?"

"She don't understand how it's choking me, Arlis. I got to get away for a while before I die." Brit's head weaved violently for a second. "Hell. You tell her the way it is. Maybe she'll listen to you. You just like her brother." The small hairs on Arlis's neck prickled up.

"Where is she?"

Brit made a drunken sweep with his arm in the direction of the water.

"Down there," he said. "I left her down there. I shouldn't of left her, Arlis. I'm a bastard. But she just won't understand." Brit mashed his fist into the sand. "You tell her, Arlis. Tell her how it is."

Arlis got up. Brit stretched out his hand and Arlis pulled him to his feet. He wavered and put his arm on Arlis's shoulder to steady himself.

"I guess I got to marry up with her, Arlis. You think I ought to marry up with her before I go off? I mean, I owe it to her, I guess. What you think?" Arlis hated the way he talked about her.

"I don't know nothing about that, Brit."

"I mean we been together. Hell. I mean I been screwing her, for chrissake. I guess I owe her."

Arlis thought how good it would feel to hit Brit's upturned face with his fist.

"You got to do what you think's right, Brit." He shrugged the arm off and turned away toward the beach. He couldn't stand the sight of Brit anymore.

"I'll do it, then," said Brit to his back. "I'll do what's right, Arlis. But you see her, you tell her how things are. Tell her this place is killing me. I mean, what else can I do?"

Arlis did not answer. He didn't give a damn about Brit. He

walked until he reached the water, then went along the shore. The sound of the gentle wavelets on the sand made him less angry. He had no right to be angry with Brit anymore than he had a right to be mean to Jo the day she came to him at the planting ground. Things had their way of turning out and that was just the way they were. And yet the image of JoAnna would not leave Arlis's mind. On the other side of the harbor one small porthole light showed where *Eva Pearl* lay. Even when looking at *Eva Pearl* Arlis still saw JoAnna in his mind. He guessed he'd always think of her and when he thought that, he saw her there in the sand. She sat leaning with her shoulder against the side of Arlis's catboat, the one they'd won the race in. The other upturned skiffs surrounded them like turtles on the beach. Both Jo's hands covered her face and her long hair was partly undone. Arlis saw how it hung in strands along her face. Jo's dress was crumpled and she'd drawn her bare legs up against herself. In the poor light Arlis saw her blouse had been opened to the waist.

"Oh Jo." Seeing her seemed to squeeze all the strength out of his body.

"Arlis. Arlis!" she cried. Arlis dropped to his knees beside her, the sand cool to his touch. Jo took her hands from her face. She looked broken. She held her hands and arms up to Arlis in a small half-circle that showed her breasts. The circle closed and she drew Arlis's head into her and Arlis's face rested on her warm flesh. He held on to her tightly and felt her crying and rocking him back and forth. "Oh Arlis. I hurt. I hurt so bad."

Arlis felt the roundness against his cheek and the swollen nipple. He placed his lips on it and Jo drew him harder against her body as his own hands pressed her sides and forced the breasts fully into his face. He breathed the mixed cotton scent of her blouse and the hot skin smell into his nostrils. JoAnna's hands held the back of his head, urging him against her flesh. Her fingers tangled themselves in his hair. One of her legs slowly moved away from the other to clamp itself against the boy's flank.

"Oh God, Arlis. It's you. It's you. Arlis. It's always been you and I couldn't make you see."

Arlis moved his lips onto her neck and across the thick hair of her temple until they reached her mouth. The tenderness of her love touched him. Jo's mouth opened to him, sucking at his lips and tongue. Beneath his hand JoAnna's thigh tensed and firmly smoothed as he felt the soft skin all the way up until it grew its small garden of curled hair above the damp slitted mound. He cupped his hand over it as though it might escape and heard the girl groan. She pushed herself into him while at the same time her trembling fingers opened the front of his trousers. She held him gently and firmly and for an instant they breathed together and looked each into the other's eyes. Still holding him, JoAnna slowly reclined, her back sliding over the smooth hull of the upturned boat until they lay together in the sand. Wordlessly, hearing only the small waves on the beach mingled with their breathing, they once more gazed at each other. JoAnna drew Arlis close, holding him and guiding him into her wet channel. A fine strength spread in Arlis's stomach and groin as he let himself in deeper and deeper until he reached the bottom. Jo and Arlis clung together and then each began to move, slowly like the train, then faster and faster. Arlis's eyes were shut tight while red and blue stars burst into his vision. He moved deeper and faster and felt JoAnna's arms squeezing him and the wet film of her tears between her face and his. She squeezed him mightily and he could feel her suddenly convulse deep inside and cause a pent-up torrent to burst through his loins and pour like hot, boiling honey into her emptiness. They locked themselves, tightly molded together, holding the moment infinitely suspended between them. At last she trembled all over and then lay still. They both lay together breathing. JoAnna kept her arms around him, loosely now, and her hand gently moved over his back, cooling the heat that came off his sweat-soaked body.

"Arlis," Jo said. "Dear, dear Arlis. Oh, dear Arlis."

Arlis began to move his head up so he could again look into her face, so that he could gently place his mouth against hers. In his weakness he raised his weight upon his arms to see her. He wanted to tell her about the love he felt.

A line of fire burned itself across Arlis's shoulders, causing him to cry out. He heard the crack of the knotted cane as it hissed through the air and struck him again.

"Fornicator! Fornicator! Here. Olcott! Come quickly and get her away." The cane slashed Arlis's face as he half rose to his knees. He lifted his hand to shield himself and JoAnna. The girl screamed, clutching her arms to her breast. Arlis saw the pallid face of Preacher high above him, his wet lips peeled back over his long teeth. The cane fell again and Preacher's eyes seemed to be fired from within. Another man had his arms around JoAnna and pulled her away as she screamed and struggled. Arlis heard Mr. Olcott grunting as he dragged JoAnna over the sand.

"Arlis!" she screamed.

The cane fell on Arlis's face, then stopped. Preacher stood trembling over him, poised to strike, and peered closely.

"Arlis? It's Arlis! Not Brit." But Mr. Olcott had already dragged and shoved his daughter down the beach beyond hearing.

"You filthy young conniver. Oh you filthy, filthy boy." Preacher quivered, then brought the cane down with renewed fury. It struck, but Arlis caught the man's bony wrist and wrenched it so hard that Preacher fell into the side of the boat onto his back. A horrible rage screamed inside Arlis. He knew he would kill the man.

Preacher scrambled sideways, like a crab trying to get to his feet. Arlis could hear his rasping breath. He leaped and grabbed him, feeling his fingers tearing flesh, twisting the man's shoulders violently and straddling his chest. Pinned flat, Preacher heaved out gasping sobs. Arlis's fist closed on the front of his coat, jamming into the throat. Wild eyes stared up at him from the dimness, as if drawn on paper. He brought his open hand down with all his strength and smashed the face, returning in the backswing to strike the other side. Arlis, trapped by the vacant eyes, smashed and smashed, watching the face snap from side to side. Preacher's lips were pulled back from his horrid teeth in a grin. Each time Arlis struck, the grin became tight and masklike. Tears poured from the man's eyes and he moaned, the moan ceasing only at the moment of impact, then resuming. Preacher made no attempt to struggle free. As Arlis beat him he could only feel Preacher's whole body arch beneath his weight. And then a single word formed at the skeletal mouth. At each stroke of Arlis's hand the tight-grinning mouth said, "Please."

Arlis stopped. Preacher's wild eyes stared upward.

"Oh please. Please. Please," he cried, and Arlis knew instinctively it was not mercy Preacher begged for. Revulsion passed through him. Arlis rolled off the man's body and jumped to his feet, stumbling backward. He stared at Preacher lying between the boats almost perfectly still, his legs a little apart. Preacher's back arched up slightly off the sand, raising his hips. Only they moved. He lay curved like a piece of spring steel, trembling with the effort. Preacher's face glistened with tears, always showing the long clenched teeth. The battered lips murmured again-"Please. Please."-toward Arlis and toward heaven.

Arlis kicked Preacher in the side as hard as he could. He heard the breath go out of the man and saw the body jackknife like a burned leech. He watched Preacher writhe and then ran blindly down the beach.

A small crying noise from Aunt Eleuthera. Forms inside the house flattened in the lamplight. Arlis presses a few pieces of clothing into the tow sack, aware of Uncle Jake and Aunt Eleuthera behind him, watching. The clean warmness of Aunt Eleuthera holding him against her and the cold when she lets go. Uncle Jake's soft murmuring. The touch of his bony hands all callused and then the sand beneath his feet on the path that leads under the rustling palms past the dark boat shed to the wharf

The old man wears a nightshirt. His beard is lost in it and the cabin around the lantern is close and airless. He looks into Arlis's eyes.

"I'm ready, Grandfather."

He is quiet and then he says:
"Yes. Yes. We should go now whilst the tide's on the run."

16

To Arlis each island that turned over the horizon shone like a jewel. Cap'n Ben knew their names and if they were inhabited with enough people to make it worth their while to stop. It was grand.

Arlis handled the spoked wheel. He opened all the tall windows on the pilothouse to feel the breeze that seemed to always blow just right for them. Everything went just right. Cap'n Ben was jolly and laughed and the crew became transformed once they were at sea again. Arlis liked them all and they liked him. Sometimes, when his work was done, Arlis would take part of someone else's wheel watch just for the joy of it. He could not remember being so happy ever.

Cap'n Ben came on the quarterdeck. The men waited in the waist.

"We'll make a port tack, Arlis," he said. "Stand by to come about," he shouted. The men stood two to a sheet. "Cut her over, Arlis." Then: "Helm's alee," he cried. The bow crossed the wind. The sails luffed, then caught, and the tackle clattered as the men sheeted in the main and fore, then the jib. Cap'n Ben gave Arlis the new heading.

He went to each sail and had the men fine-tune the sheets so they'd get the most out of the wind. Arlis could feel the water passing around the rudder. They heeled over tightly and once in a while a wave would hit the bow flat-wise and send its spray onto the deck. The old man came back to the wheelhouse.

"We'll make Grand Turk Island tomorrow, Arlis. Early, with

this wind."

"Yes," said Arlis. It would be their last port. For three months they'd worked their way down the Bahamas and on to San Juan, discharging dry goods and hardware at small islands off the steamship routes. In return they loaded rum, sugar, molasses, thatch rope, salt, starch, and dried coconuts. "I love the little islands, Grandfather. They're just like Doctor's Arm. The people are so glad to see us."

"I suppose they still need us, boy. It's not much of a living but we don't need a lot, do we? Just a good wind and a quart of rum to pour in the bilge to keep the worms from letting go their hands lest our bottom falls out." Cap'n Ben thought this was a fine joke.

"The bottom ain't going to fall out, Cap'n Ben."

"Can't say, boy. I keep telling you this is an old ship." He looked at his watch. "My spell at the wheel, son."

Arlis turned over the helm to Cap'n Ben but stayed in the wheelhouse watching the gray billowing sails and the sea. Far off on the horizon there showed two bits of islands. There were no other ships in sight.

"It's just all so darned beautiful." The saying of it made Arlis think of JoAnna and the way she saw beauty in things. It did not embarrass Arlis to say it now. He felt filled up with the beauty of everything and how happy he was so that he almost couldn't stay still. Last night he had written it very carefully in a letter to JoAnna. He wrote he was coming back to her.

"When it's this way it is a fine sight, boy. Even bad weather has its beauty, though it's frightening. But you'll see it all in time, I expect. If you go to sea long enough you have the chance to see all of it."

"This is the best life a person could have."

Cap'n Ben looked at Arlis and gave him a little smile.

"I suppose it don't tire a young boy like you to stop and go all the time-to take on cargo and discharge the consignment, then up anchor and make for another island." Cap'n Ben's smile got bigger. "It's hell on an old man like me. But having you along's brought my strength back. I ain't felt so good in years." Arlis loved him for the way he talked and for the way he made him feel so wonderful.

Arlis stayed in the wheelhouse with his grandfather for a while longer. When the old man's gaze was off on the horizon Arlis studied the hard bones of his features and wondered if he'd look that way when he got old. He wondered exactly how old his grandfather was. Mommer told him once but he'd forgotten. He'd ask him sometime. He was old, though. Arlis knew that.

Arlis went forward on the windward side. He held the shrouds and let the salt breeze push through his hair, then crawled into the netting that went over the water to either side of the long bowsprit. He lay there dreaming. He pulled his shirt off and placed it between the coarse hemp of the net and his face. Running the decks half naked had turned him almost as dark as the Negroes. Arlis loved to see his brown skin in the mirror in Cap'n Ben's cabin.

The bow rose and fell, bringing the brilliantly clear water so close Arlis could almost touch it. The chart in the wheelhouse showed nothing less than ten fathoms, yet Arlis could make out rock patches and coral heads on the white bottom. Schools of porpoises twice rolled in the waves cut under the bow, their button eyes and glistening hides throwing the sunlight back in Arlis's face.

He thought of the islands he'd visited and how they were marked on the charts and how by compass headings they had their predictable relationships to each other and how when Cap'n Ben explained it, it all seemed so reasonable and clear. He thought how his great want had been satisfied and that now new wants came into his mind. He thought of JoAnna and her touch and the smell and feel of her flesh, until he made himself stop it because it hurt. Arlis watched the water then and only thought of JoAnna's face. At last he fell asleep in the sunshine.

Bluejay, the youngest Bahamian boy, pulled Arlis's ankle. Arlis awoke. The sun almost lay on the horizon. He shivered and rubbed his face, then pulled on the shirt. In his hand Bluejay held a dolphin, so fresh its rainbow-colored flanks had not yet faded the way they do when all the life goes away from them.

"Ahlis. Help me cook this up, won't you?" asked Bluejay in his lilting voice. Bluejay was quite handy at cooking and the men liked the way Arlis could cook fish. Cap'n Ben said Arlis cooked fish better than anyone else.

"Sure, Bluejay. You slab him out and I'll get the fire going."

Bluejay walked to the leeward side, the fish hanging from his fist almost to the deck. It was a fine fish.

In the galley Arlis set the dried peas boiling over the iron stove. They would take the longest to cook.

Everyone ate on deck. They always did in good weather. Only Rubin, who stood at the helm, had to wait for Bluejay to relieve him.

At dusk Arlis and Bluejay made sure the running lights were full of kerosene and that the wicks were trimmed. They lit them in the sheltered lee of the deckhouse and placed the red lantern to port and the green to starboard in their brackets on the main shrouds. The large clear lamp with the prismed lens sat in the stern. Arlis lit the binnacle light in the wheelhouse.

Arlis waited for Cap'n Ben to finish his evening pipe. The old man smoked on the leeward side of the quarterdeck. He would pace up and down, then rest with his hands on the rail and gaze across the water. At last he knocked the pipe out. Little embers blew off into the dark. He went to the wheelhouse and looked over Bluejay's shoulder, then came out.

"Arlis," he called as he did every night.

"Here, Grandfather."

"Let's go down and study on Mr. Bowditch."

In the cabin Cap'n Ben took the heavy volume of Bowditch's Navigation and Seamanship from the bookshelf and opened it on the table before them. The place was marked where they'd stopped the night before. He read with Arlis aloud for an hour, stopping and explaining so that Arlis could understand. Some of the material came easily, some with difficulty. But Cap'n Ben repeated himself gently and clearly for the boy until Arlis could grasp each point.

They finished the lesson and Cap'n Ben carefully closed the book as if it were a Bible and replaced it on the shelf.

"You'd better get to bed, Arlis. Bluejay goes off at midnight and you have the watch."

"All right, Cap'n Ben."

His grandfather placed both hands on Arlis's shoulders.

"It pleases me how you're learning, Arlis. You're a good lad. I hope you're happy in what you're doing."

"I never been so happy, Cap'n Ben."

His grandfather held the boy a moment longer then he smiled and let Arlis go. "Get on to bed now, son."

Arlis lay in his bunk in the alcove across the narrow passageway from Cap'n Ben's cabin. Each night it was hard to go to sleep. Arlis had to catch and compress all the happenings of the day and go over them until he felt satisfied. Then he would allow himself to wander into the past and the future. He wove complex patterns in his mind that excited him, dreaming of what he would do and the places he planned to go. In half-sleep he surrounded himself with images of *The Reaper* and JoAnna. They were powerful images Arlis knew he could make real. He knew it. He reached for them and wanted them. The ship rose and fell and lulled Arlis into sleep until Bluejay woke him at midnight for his four hours at *Eva Pearl's* helm.

"I could do this forever." Arlis rowed Cap'n Ben across the harbor toward the beach.

"What? Row an old man around in a boat?"

Eva Pearl lay at anchor while Arlis and his grandfather went ashore to present the ship's papers to the resident commissioner on Grand Turk Island. Arlis laughed.

"No, Grandfather. This." He tossed his chin at the white sand beach. "What we're doing right now."

"Don't lose your oars, boy." said Cap'n Ben. He held the tiller bar of the little boat under his arm. The ship's papers were in an oiled canvas pouch on the seat beside him. Cap'n Ben smoked his pipe. To Arlis he looked magnificent in his dark blue coat with its double row of brass buttons.

"Steady now, boy. Ship oars." But Arlis had already done so. With his trouser legs rolled up he stepped into the water and pulled the bow of the boat gently onto the sand and smooth stones. Two curious children watched Arlis help the old man out. He tied a line onto a tree limb.

The morning sun gave the village a clean washed look as if it had been tinted in pastels. The shops were opening on the side streets. Children made their way to the school. On the path next to the road, lines of donkeys carried bagged salt toward the wharf next to the old prison. Arlis and Cap'n Ben walked to the government office, where a smartly dressed constable informed them that the commissioner had not yet arrived. Cap'n Ben said they would return. At that the constable saluted Cap'n Ben and Cap'n Ben returned the salute quite naturally and Arlis felt very proud of how important his grandfather was.

They stopped at the post office, where Arlis mailed his letter to JoAnna. Cap'n Ben did not ask who Arlis had written to. He just smoked his pipe and looked around the building while Arlis bought the stamps at the window as if it were quite normal for Arlis to send letters to America from Grand Turk Island.

"Well," said Cap'n Ben. "We may as well do a little shopping, Come along." He led Arlis into a clothier's.

"This gentleman needs a pair of shoes." Cap'n Ben told the clerk. "And some hose too, of course. He needs shoes, mind. No brogans. A good pair of dress shoes." Arlis hoped the surprise did not show overly on his face. He'd never had any kind of shoes in his life except brogans. The clerk measured Arlis's foot. Arlis was glad his feet were clean from wading in the harbor. He'd hate for the clerk to think he was some no-account cracker, but the clerk seemed much impressed, almost intimidated by the presence of Cap'n Ben.

Arlis selected a modest pair of tan shoes that were molded into a slim point and laced to the ankle. Next, Cap'n Ben bought him two shirts, one white and the other robin's-egg blue, with two celluloid collars and a black necktie. He paid with a ten-pound note and collected his change, leaving the clerk a half-crown for a tip.

Arlis wore the blue shirt and tie and the shoes. He carried the other shirt and collar, which the clerk had neatly wrapped for him. He walked along, keeping the long stride of Cap'n Ben, feeling the uncomfortable newness of the shoes and the sensation of the necktie on his throat. He caught glimpses of himself when they passed store windows, realizing quite suddenly that he saw a grown man staring back at him.

At the government building the constable showed them into the commissioner's office at once. It was a high-ceilinged cool room with louvered shutters and a picture of the king on the wall. Cap'n Ben knew the commissioner and introduced Arlis as his first mate. They shook hands all around, confirming Arlis's notion that he had at last become something more than a child.

The commissioner, a heavy-faced Englishman with pink skin and long white mustaches, looked casually over *Eva Pearl's* papers and the log book.

"Where did you last put in, Captain Bennington?"

"San Juan. A week ago, commissioner. We're half loaded in cask rum."

The commissioner looked up from the papers. His face showed just a shade less color.

"You've been at sea a week? Then I suppose you don't know."

"Know?"

The commissioner coughed politely behind his hand and reached in his desk drawer. He laid a newspaper in front of Cap'n Ben. Arlis caught the word WAR in boldface type.

"As of the second of April 1917 the American government has joined the Allied cause." The commissioner sounded as if this were the greatest thing that could ever happen. "Needless to say we're quite pleased."

Arlis could see his grandfather working his mouth around beneath his whiskers. His brows had drawn themselves together.

"I suppose it was bound to happen," Cap'n Ben said at last.

"With the weight of America on our side we should be able to bring the war to a quick end. They're already mounting an expeditionary force. A terrific boost for the morale of our chaps, what?" The commissioner looked at Arlis. "I suppose they'll be calling you up, young man. I'm sure you can't wait to have a crack at the Huns."

"He's not old enough," Cap'n Ben said shortly. "Besides they ain't started conscription yet."

"Oh they will. But I'm betting there will be volunteers aplenty."

"Maybe you and me should volunteer, commissioner." A faint bit of acid stuck to the old man's words that only Arlis could sense. The commissioner threw his head back and brayed like one of the donkeys that carried salt bags from the drying ponds.

"My dear captain. What a sterling wit. They'd never have old fellows like us."

"They took everyone in 'sixty-five. Everyone they could get." Cap'n Ben had turned bitter this time. It was not lost on the Englishman. He quit his braying laugh.

"So," sniffed the commissioner, becoming formal once again. "You load salt here and return to…" He ran his finger over the document before him. "Norfolk. Virginia. Lovely place."

"For the winter," said Cap'n Ben.

The commissioner scribbled something on the paper with a noisy pen and thumped it with two rubber stamps. He slid them to Cap'n Ben. They all rose at once. The commissioner kept acting formally.

"You've been officially notified of the commencement of hostilities, Captain Bennington." He took another piece of paper from his desk and handed it to Cap'n Ben. "As a member of the Allied merchant fleet you are requested and required to comply with full blackout procedures and regulations covering cooperation with proper naval authorities as outlined herein." He relaxed a bit. "There have been no reports of enemy submarine or surface vessels in the Caribbean. But Norfolk is a long way off. Use caution, please." Suddenly he seemed too happy to contain himself again. "Blast! It's splendid to have you Americans in the war. Just think, if you winter in Norfolk, it'll probably all be over by then. Won't that be jolly?"

Cap'n Ben had carefully supervised the loading of the salt bags. Arlis followed him and listened when he explained how he distributed the weight so that *Eva Pearl* would sail well under her load. The hold was packed over the keelson with great fruity-smelling kegs of Puerto Rican rum. Bins shored up with wood poles held the sacks of salt.

"Once we're loaded, son, nothing had better come adrift down here. You can imagine being heeled over and suddenly having five tons of salt shift to leeward. You'd go over on your beam ends and stay there until you filled up and went to the bottom. The heavier the cargo the lower you've got to stow it. And secure it fast." The old man hit the flat of his palm on one of the retaining bars.

Very suddenly he turned to Arlis. "We'll be at sea quite a while, son, going to Norfolk. This here business with the Germans don't trouble you, does it?" The idea had not fully settled on Arlis.

"I don't think so, Cap'n Ben." Even reading it in the news-papers had not brought the idea much closer to him. France was clear across the ocean. Cap'n Ben tugged on his beard.

"Look, boy, don't get angry now, but what would you say to my getting you a passage to Cuba? Then you could go home for a while. Take the train up and meet me in Norfolk. How would that be? Would you like that?" The old man seemed embarrassed. Suddenly it became clear to Arlis what he was driving at.

"Well, I ain't going to no Cuba. I'm staying here on *Eva Pearl*. What would the Germans want to fool with us for anyway? Dang it, Cap'n Ben, they're all the way over in France."

"They got submarines. You read about submarines in the paper. Them German submarines don't give a hoot in hell who they fool with, if you can believe the newspapers."

"You think I'm scared," cried Arlis. He felt terrible that Cap'n Ben might think he was afraid.

"I never said such a thing." The old man sat with a grunt on a salt bag. "Hell," he said. "Sit down there, Arlis. We got to talk. I might as well tell you everything I'm thinking and it don't have anything to do with you being scared because I know you're not." Arlis sat down. Cap'n Ben stared for a minute at the backs of his hands. The hold of the little ship was dark and gloomy. A small patch of light fell from the open cargo hatch and lay like a garden on the bags of salt. "I've been thinking about a couple of things and now this damn war gave me something else to consider." He drew a breath and said strongly and very quickly: "I hate to tell you, son, but *Eva Pearl's* heading for the boneyard. This is her last trip." He pushed Arlis back down when the boy tried to jump up. "I suppose I should of told you right at the beginning but I figured it could wait. Anyway I'll tell you now. Her bottom's gone bad. Worms. Happens to all old wood boats and you know it. It won't be today or next week, but it's coming, getting worse all the damn time and that's that. She's shot. Now since you're set on staying aboard there's things we got to do, so you listen to me good."

Cap'n Ben let the words hang there so Arlis understood.

"You're eighteen years old and we got to get you some third mate's papers so you'll be in the merchant marine. We can stay together for a while. That way the conscription won't catch you for the trenches. And that's what's fixing to happen. I spent most of my time at sea in the Civil War but I seen the trenches. I seen them good. They're mindless slaughter pits, boy, and they ain't changed. You're too precious to me to lose that way because it's a stupid way. Now you get your papers and in the spring we'll put *Eva Pearl* into timber hauling up in Maine. It's not pleasant to see a grand old ship like this die in timber trade, because they'll chop the bow out of her and level the deck house, but at least she'll die in harness. We'll be on the coast, so when her bottom gets to taking on more water than we can pump out, we'll just put in for good and let the salvagers break her up."

Cap'n Ben's eyes sort of stuck out of their sockets. "By then you'll have enough experience to get on as number three with a steamer. You can get on with making your career and goddam it I'll go have a rest somewhere. I need a rest!" Cap'n Ben shouted because he felt bad about *Eva Pearl* and didn't want to show it. He grinned.

"Don't you think I need a goddam rest? I'm over eighty years old." He wore a very comical look on his face. Arlis felt like crying.

"I just want to stay with you, Grandfather. I want for us to be together on *Eva Pearl*. I know it's got to end. But I wish it could be for always."

"Things change, boy. But we'll make it as easy as possible on all of us. On us and *Eva Pearl* and the crew. We'll find the answers." He drew out a long sigh. "Now we still got a lot of sailing to do but I wanted for you to know just how things are. You understand, don't you, boy? Try to understand as best as you can."

"I'll try, Cap'n Ben," Arlis said.

Fully loaded *Eva Pearl* left Grand Turk. She sailed heavily but well. The weather held and the seas were moderate. Each morning Arlis sounded the well in the hold with a long rod, and if there was more than eight inches of water over the keelson they started the donkey engine and engaged the pumps.

At night they ran without lights as the blackout directive ordered. An extra hand had to stand as lookout beside the helmsman.

In the airless cabin, its portholes covered in black cloth, Arlis cleaned and assembled the ship's sextant while Cap'n Ben watched. Arlis had made his first near-correct sunsight that noon northeast of Bermuda. It had been hard and he had done it by rote, not fully understanding it all. Cap'n Ben encouraged him to keep practicing.

"It's a good feeling to know where you are in the middle of the sea, Arlis. You and I can do that all right, can't we?" Then he mused, "I know where we are. I wish I could know where we're going, the two of us." He tousled Arlis's hair. "Things usually work out the way they're supposed to. Sometimes it's quite a surprise." Arlis polished the sextant and placed it in the mahogany box.

"What will you do with *The Reaper*, Grandfather?"

The old man looked at him, surprised, as though he had forgotten the hull in the boat shed far away in Doctor's Arm.

"My Lord," he said. Then he laughed. Arlis loved his laugh. He could always laugh better than anyone Arlis knew. "Why, nothing, I suppose. Not now. Do you know I had *The Reaper* built I guess as a toy? When I was making plenty of money running cargo, I thought, Why don't I have a nice little sloop built for fun? But you should take your boats serious." Cap'n Ben's demeanor changed. "When she was built in Honduras the keel slipped and crushed a man to death. It was a terrible thing to see. They're a superstitious lot down there. I had to hire a whole new gang to finish her. But she's as fine a boat as I've ever sailed. I sailed her all over." Cap'n Ben's voice got quiet. "Your grandmother and your mother, when she was only a child, would come along. One day I went below for a moment and when I came back your grandmother was gone. In calm clear weather. She just disappeared. God, how I looked and looked for her. For a long time it was the end of my world, I thought." The old man wasn't speaking to Arlis anymore. His face had lost itself in the memory. Slowly he returned. "I never took much interest in pleasure sailing after that. One or two men could make *The Reaper* into a good island cargo boat but I had *Eva Pearl* and just kind of let go of *The Reaper*. You know how things keep cropping up in a man's life. I suppose I forgot her and there she sits waiting for someone to take her. Maybe you'll do something with her, Arlis. She's yours, son. She's a fine little sloop. Just take her serious. Sailing's a serious business. Any man who'd go to sea for pleasure'd go to hell for a pastime." Cap'n Ben found enough humor in that to chuckle over. Arlis loved him so.

"Let me make you a toddy, Grandfather. I'll make you a

toddy, then we'll go to bed. I take the watch at midnight."

"Yes, Arlis. Would you make me a good one? The weather's fine, the wind's steady, and the barometer ain't moved in three days. I think I might sleep right on through tonight."

Arlis went to the galley and stirred the embers in the stove. He made a small fire under the black water pot. In a mug he poured a double measure of brown rum, mixing it with lime and sugar, and topped it off with boiling water.

Cap 'n Ben lay in his bunk, half sitting with the blankets up to his big chest and his head on the bolster. He held the toddy beneath his nose and breathed in the vapors before he drank it down. He sighed. He looked very old and tired there in his bed.

Arlis sat and waited for him to speak.

"There's times when you just don't think life could get no better," he said. He yawned and made his beard bristle like a circus lion's. "We'll work *Eva Pearl* up north for a while, son, then I believe I'm going to buy me a cottage on one of the islands. A nice flat island like Grand Turk where I can see the water all around. Hire me an old woman to cook fish and make a good toddy at night. That's all I can do with a woman anymore. Hell. You know, I might even go back to Doctor's Arm and get a place on the far side of the island, where you don't hear that damned train going through twice a day. That's even a better idea." The old man began fading. He reminded Arlis of his Uncle Jake the way he talked and faded into sleep. "Then you could come and visit, boy."

"I'd come and visit all the time, Grandfather."

The old man's eyes were closed. Arlis got up and turned down the lamp.

"Everything's going to work out just like it's supposed to, Arlis." His eyes were still closed. "It always does…"

Arlis lay in his bunk unable to sleep. He'd slept for a while then awakened, so he had no idea of the time. He sensed that Bluejay would not come for another hour at least. Arlis tried to build things in his imagination but restlessness overcame him. The whole night seemed to be charged with something. Even the face of JoAnna refused to stay before him and faded into the rounded corners of the small sleeping alcove. The ventilator in the overhead was turned in the wrong direction, making the air stuffy and thick. Arlis threw off the covers and got into his trousers and shirt.

He climbed the ladderway, seeing the canopy of stars over his head. The air smelled sweet and clean and almost cold. At the head of the ladder, he listened to the familiar sounds, the water beneath the hull, the creaking of timber and rope. He mounted the deck and saw the trail of ghostly phosphorescence that marked their wake.

As he drew closer to the wheelhouse he made out the small form of Bluejay's head. The faint red glow from the shaded binnacle lamp defined the boy. Arlis called his name so he wouldn't be startled. He suspected that Bluejay was frightened of the dark.

"You come up early, Arlis," Bluejay said sleepily. The whites of his eyes stood out in his black face.

Arlis opened the locker beside the wheel and lifted the lid on the chronometer's box. The radium-faced dial said 11:15.

"Rubin up forward, Bluejay?"

"Yoh, he forward." Arlis could see the white teeth of a smile. "I bet he sleepin'. Say he don't believe no submarine boat can go under the water. Say they go under the water, they sink. Say you fill a bottle with water, drop it overboard, it don't come up. No way it come up. It sink, it stay sunk. What you think, Ahlis?"

"Just what I read in the papers."

"I don't read nothin' in the papers cos' I cain't read." He laughed.

Arlis leaned on the door of the wheelhouse, then walked to the side and spit before he returned. The feeling of restlessness got worse.

"Go on, Bluejay. Turn in. I'll take the rest of the watch."

"My eyes closed already. Thanks, Ahlis."

"Go on."

Arlis took the wheel, glad to feel the spokes in his hands. Their light pressure held his feet to the deck, held his body from flying off into the air. He didn't know what in hell was wrong with him. Arlis watched the shadow of the boy walk forward. Bluejay showed well against the bleached planks of the deck. He stopped and leaned on top of the forward cabin, where the crew slept. Arlis strained but could not see Rubin. Through the open windows of the pilothouse the pressure of the silence grew more intense. He listened for noises that couldn't be there hundreds of miles out at sea. Sounds of crickets on a hot afternoon filled his ears and then the call of a night bird. The weight of the wheel began to drive him into the wood beneath his naked feet.

Arlis saw it at the same time Rubin cried out of the darkness. A white streaking line of phosphorescence bore down on them, straight as the rail line, fast as the train, sure as if it were drawn on the water by the hand of God.

"Port bow," cried Rubin. "Port bow. Jesus. Cap'n, come!" His voice wavered with terror in the blackness. Arlis threw the wheel over in a futile gesture. He ran out the wheelhouse door feeling *Eva Pearl* sluggishly drop off the wind. Bluejay stood on the cabin top right above the open hatch. His little head bobbed around like a bird's so that he might fully see the thing. It came incredibly fast, faster than anything Arlis had ever seen move in the sea, then disappeared beneath them.

Arlis braced himself. The mild shudder that went through the ship came as almost a disappointment. He could still see Bluejay's thin form above the open companionway hatch. Everything stopped except for Rubin's moaning wail. Seemingly slow, a dull red light leaked from the open hatchway. It spread silently and all at once, so that Arlis could see it seeping even between the now-separated deck planks like an iridescent paint. Planking lifted. The whole forward deckhouse rose in one piece and the explosion that had been occurring during this time burst violently over Arlis, shredding his clothes and flinging him across the deck into the railing. From where he lay stunned, Arlis watched everything on the foredeck being carried into the air. A dark bag of salt traveled up and backward, end over end, and landed near where Arlis lay just as the foremast shivered into splinters and crashed over the side. The entire front of the ship disappeared. The mainmast slowly tipped forward and eased itself down into the burning vacuum. Arlis pulled himself up and staggered. The deck listed sharply to the stern. With the bow completely blown off, *Eva Pearl* floated like a long drinking glass that spouted fire from her open end. The main topmast had broken off and lay with all its rigging across the quarterdeck. Arlis looked at the ragged mass at his feet, trying to see what it was.

"Bluejay! Bluejay!" Cap'n Ben spun Arlis around by the shoulders. "Bluejay," he yelled into his face.

"It's me, Arlis, Grandfather." The old man held Arlis's face close to his. Arlis hurt where the man's fingers dug into his naked shoulders.

"Arlis!"

"It's me, Grandfather."

Cap'n Ben reached out and touched Arlis's face.

"Arlis, It's you, son. Your damn face is singed black as a darky."

Arlis knew then what lay on the deck, what he'd mistaken for a bag of salt.

"That there's Bluejay, Grandfather." Arlis looked and quickly looked away. There wasn't anything but the boy's skinny trunk, ragged and damp, puddling on the deck in the reflected light, half covered up in the torn rigging. Arlis vomited on his own feet.

Cap'n Ben had run to the rail. He turned back to Arlis. He wore his great blue coat over his nightshirt. Cap'n Ben's hair and beard burned gold in the blaze.

"Where are they? Did you see them, boy?" The old man's voice burned like the fire, flaring up every time one of the rum barrels popped off. Arlis could hear them blow and see the renewed wave of light. The floating half of the ship belched fire like a roman candle.

"Who, Grandfather?"

"The Germans, boy. The Germans." Cap'n Ben turned his back to the flames and leaned over the rail into the night. He held on with one hand and shook his fist. "Come out so's we can see you, you bastards," he yelled. Another rum cask blew and the deck shifted beneath their feet. "Show yourselves like goddam men!" Cap'n Ben waited for a reply. Arlis could feel the heat on his face from the fire. He went to the old man's side and took him by the arm.

"What is it, son?"

"We better do something, Grandfather. We better get the boat over or something." Arlis had begun to tremble violently. He knew Cap'n Ben could feel him shaking. Cap'n Ben blinked a couple of times and then looked at the burning ship as if he'd never seen it before.

"Jesus Christ. Yes, boy. Come on quick." He pulled Arlis past the wheelhouse to the stern. There they could see how *Eva Pearl* had settled. The small boat in the stern rested on her chaulks. Arlis and Cap'n Ben hooked the fore and aft tackles from the davits to the boat and hoisted until she cleared the chaulks. It was easy to swing her out. The water had risen almost to the railing.

"Arlis, get in the boat and tie off. Let her drift back so she don't get fouled in this mess of rigging. Then get the mast up and hoist sail. Get plenty far off, though."

"What about you, Grandfather?"

"Do what I tell you, boy. I got to get a keg of water and some biscuits and some blankets and things for us. Now go on. Hurry."

Arlis tied the boat off and let her drift back. Each time a rum barrel blew up a great fistful of fire went into the sky and dropped hot cinders into the water around him. He got the short mast stepped and rigged the sail. He still trembled all over with cold and shock.

Cap'n Ben appeared, his arms full. Arlis pulled the boat into him.

"Here, boy. Get this." Cap'n Ben passed him a water cask and a large bread tin and a canvas bag. He was puffing and grinning in the weird light. "Goddam Germans," he said, but he kept grinning.

"Get in, Grandfather. Let's get away."

"Drift back, son. She ain't going down yet. There's still plenty of stuff I can get. Now, I put a compass and some charts in the bag." As he spoke, he ticked off things on his fingers with maddening slowness. He grinned all the time. Another barrel blew. Cap'n Ben ignored the rain of sparks settling over his coat and beard.

"Please, Grandfather. Please get in. Let's go." Arlis was frantic. The fire burned into the wheelhouse. His grandfather began laughing.

"I wish you could see yourself, Arlis. You're almost naked and blacker than your Uncle Jake." He took his coat off and threw it to Arlis. "Put this on, son, before you die of cold" The old man laughed harder. "Imagine that." In his white nighthirt and beard the old man looked like a Sunday-school picture of Moses. "Drop back now, boy, so your sail don't catch afire." He still laughed. "That's a good boy, Arlis. You're a good boy." The little boat drifted back away from the ship as the wind caught it. Arlis watched his grandfather. The old man looked across the water at him and waved. Arlis could still hear him laughing. When the boat drifted back as far as the line would allow, Arlis saw the old man do what Arlis knew he would. He bent down and untied the line and dropped it into the water. Still laughing he waved once more and climbed the steep list of the deck and disappeared into the door of the companionway.

The wind blew straight down on Arlis. It would catch the sail and make a flailing racket, then be still. There was no way he could ever get back to the ship. The wind just blew him further and further away while *Eva Pearl* hung burning in the water. When she went, Arlis figured it was the cargo of salt that took her down so fast. It was as if she carried a load of stone. She went down fast right in the middle of all the fire, and when the water closed over where she'd been broken in half, the long streamers of flame went out like a snuffed candle. Not even an ember stayed lit. There was just darkness. Arlis didn't move. He bundled the blue coat with the brass buttons around him and stared at where *Eva Pearl* had gone down. The wind kept catching on the damned sail, pushing the little boat around in no real direction before it slacked off. For a long time Arlis didn't think about anything. He didn't even cry. Then he thought about his grandfather laughing. His grandfather could laugh better than anyone he ever knew.

Part 4

1925

17

"I'll have a bottle of beer."

The bartender looked hard at the man. He wore a thread-bare merchant marine coat with a small foreign military decoration on one lapel. The bartender didn't take him for a kidder. He could tell by the man's face that he wasn't any kidder.

"Can't serve you no beer, mister. We're in Prohibition. Don't you know we're in Prohibition?"

"I'll have a cider, then," Arlis said. "Anything cold."

"Oh hell," said the barman. "You look all right. I'll sell you a beer. If you want a rum or some bonded stuff I can sell it to you too, but you got to drink it in the back room." He pointed with his thumb at a door on the other side of the bar.

"Just a beer. A Tropical." The barman got a green bottle of Tropical from the icebox under the bar.

"You really don't know about Prohibition?"

"Not much."

"Hell. We don't pay lots of attention to it here in Key West. But I got to be a little careful. Just for appearance." The barman sopped up a spill. "I'll serve anybody if they look all right. That your ship out there? The one that come in this morning?" He nodded to the beat-up freighter anchored on the edge of the channel.

"It was. She paid off."

"English?" The ship flew a dirty British ensign off the stern.

"Yes."

"But you ain't English. I can tell."

"No." Arlis drank his beer.

"You looking for another ship?"

"No, I'm going to Doctor's Arm. My home's there."

"Doctor's Arm? You're kidding."

Arlis looked out the window.

"Not much going on there these days," said the barman. "I mean, there's things going on all right, but things on the Q.T."

He winked. "You catch my drift."

"No more lumbering?"

"Hell, they ain't lumbered since the armistice. But the folks keep busy. In their way." He winked again.

"How much for the beer?"

"Fifteen cents."

"That's high." Arlis put the money on the bar.

"You must a been gone a long time, mister. I tell you, we're in Prohibition."

The side door next to the bar opened. Three men came out, two white men and a mulatto of some sort, Arlis thought. The mulatto was very drunk. He had an ugly purple birthmark that started below his shirt collar and spread up the side of his face.

"You want to know about Doctor's Arm, these boys can tell you," said the barman.

"Who wants to know about Doctor's Arm?" asked the first man. He walked over to Arlis and the barkeeper. "What you want to know about Doctor's Arm?"

The man stood in front of Arlis with his hands on his hips. He wasn't very big. He stood with his legs slightly apart. Arlis noticed how small his feet were, almost like a woman's.

"Nothing. I used to live there is all."

"Hey," the small man said to the others. "This fellow used to live in Doctor's Arm."

"What a shithole," said the second man. He leaned on the bar and stared at himself in the mirror. The mulatto sat on a stool with his head in his arms.

"Shut up, Riff," said the first man. He held out his hand to Arlis. "I'm Treat. That there's Riff and the drunky's Indian. We spend time up to Doctor's Arm, sort of." Arlis shook the slim hand, not wanting to. It felt resilient and cool like the hand of a man who's just been killed. "Have a beer."

"I just had one."

"Have another. Give us all a beer," Treat said to the bar man. "Make Indian drink one too." Arlis watched Treat. He looked ridiculous and dangerous at the same time. He dressed nice all except for the jacket. It was a woodsy jacket with big pockets that he wore over a shirt and tie and light creased trousers. On the small feet were mustard-colored shoes with high dancing heels. Arlis figured the heels must make him stand two inches taller.

The one called Riff pulled Indian up by the back of the collar and put the beer in front of him.

"Get him to drink it, Riff," said Treat. Little bits of saliva were beaded in the corners of his mouth. He turned back to Arlis. "Indian's a riot when he gets really bagged. What kind of work you do?"

"Merchant marine," said Arlis. He drank his beer. "What do you do?"

"Us?"

"Yeah. What do you do in Doctor's Arm?"

"We're sportsmen." He smiled. "You know. Hunt. Fish."

Arlis noticed how small and washed-out Treat's eyes were, almost wholly lacking in pigment. "We're kind of on a long vacation."

You're a lying son of a bitch too, thought Arlis.

Riff had Indian drinking the beer now. Riff held him while Indian poured the beer straight down. When he emptied the bottle he slapped it on the bar.

"Ooooow!" Indian raised his head to the ceiling and howled keeping his eyes shut tight.

"Give him another," said Treat.

"You got to keep him quiet," said the barman.

"Shut up and give him another one," said Treat. He looked at the barman until the barman gave the Indian another. "Gimme another too. You want another?" he asked Arlis. "What's your name, anyway?"

"My name's Arlis. No. I don't want another. I haven't finished this one."

"Get one for Arlis here for when he finishes the one he's got."

The barman looked disgusted. He put the beers down.

Indian sucked on his. Arlis could see his Adam's apple bobbing up and down. The purple birthmark lay like a stain of ink on his face. Riff whispered in his ear while he drank and kept his arm across his shoulders.

Indian finished and slapped the empty down. Riff took his hand away and whispered again in his ear and tilted his head toward Treat and Arlis. Indian looked at Riff, then over to where Treat and Arlis stood at the bar. Indian came over to them slowly. He waited for a second, then pushed himself in between Arlis and Treat so that he faced Arlis very close.

"You saying something about my face?" Indian stood as big as Arlis. He looked like an Indian, not like a mulatto, because his hair was fine and lay close to his head.

"I didn't say nothing about your face."

"You're a fucking liar."

"Why don't you go cool off," said Arlis. "Go sit down."

"You're a fucking liar." He pushed Arlis's shoulders.

Arlis jerked his knee up and heard Indian lose all his breath. When Indian doubled over Arlis hit him on the bare spot behind the ear. Indian went down and lay still.

"You really cold-cocked him." Treat nudged the body with the toe of his mustard-colored shoe. He laughed in a short series of high notes. "I told you he's a riot when he gets bagged." Arlis ignored the man. He stepped over the body of Indian to Riff.

"That wasn't very funny."

"What you talking about?" Riff was a stupid-looking man with red eyes. He needed a shave.

"You set him up is what I'm talking about," said Arlis.

"Hey, Treat. This guy thinks I set Indian up." Riff looked pretty nervous. Arlis moved so he could keep his eye on both of them.

"You did," said Treat. He drank his beer and looked away

from Riff.

"Hey. I was only kidding."

"I didn't think it was funny," Arlis said.

"Come on have another beer," said Treat. "Riff's a shit-head. He was only kidding. Right, Riff?"

Arlis walked over and picked up his canvas duffel bag. He looked at Treat and Riff. Riff seemed relieved he'd gone away from him. Arlis couldn't tell from Treat's face what he was thinking.

Arlis heard the door open behind him. Treat's thin lips split into a smile.

"Brit," Treat said. "What say, crip?"

"Don't call me crip. I told you that."

Arlis turned. Brit stood in the doorway.

"What's wrong with Indian?" asked Brit, looking beyond Arlis to where Indian lay.

"Brit," said Arlis.

He looked at Arlis. Brit had grown taller and thin, even a bit frail, but Arlis recognized him. His face showed that something inside him had been broken to pieces.

"Arlis?" Brit took a couple of steps forward, his eyes fixed on Arlis. He had a limp. "Arlis, boy? It's you. It's really you." He came to Arlis. His lips were slightly parted. He placed both his hands on Arlis's shoulders and kept staring. A strange emotion went through Arlis he hadn't felt for years. It was a warm comforting feeling of having a lost part of his life returned. Arlis put his arms out to Brit. The two men held one another for a long moment. Arlis tried to speak and couldn't. Brit held him away, then drew him close patting his back and speaking his name. The warm skin of their stubbled cheeks were together like two Frenchmen. Arlis realized he'd never touched Brit before in his life except to shake his hand. They parted still staring.

"Arlis. You're home." Brit said his name as if he couldn't say it enough.

"Yes. Yes." Arlis was full of joy.

"Come on," said Brit. He took up the duffel and held Arlis's arm. Treat and Riff still looked surprised. Treat paid for the beer and the two of them picked up Indian and followed Brit and Arlis across the street to the train office. Arlis noticed how badly Brit favored his right foot. Brit held tight to Arlis's arm.

Key West had grown. There were many navy men in whites and the streets were clogged with nice cars. Arlis thought there were an awful lot of saloons for being in Prohibition, but he knew Key Westers always lived somewhat apart from the rest of the country, holding to an ingrained sense of good commerce that superseded the law.

The green-visored man in the ticket cage looked curiously at the five of them when Brit said they wanted one-ways to Doctor's Arm.

"You'll have to jump it," said the ticket man. "Train don't stop today."

"I know," Brit said impatiently. "We'll jump it." He turned to Arlis. "She slows to about ten miles an hour off Pine Channel. We'll jump it there. Train don't stop much at the old station." He wore a crooked smile. "Things ain't like they used to be, Arlis."

Arlis shrugged. "I don't mind jumping off."

Indian had come to. He wobbily kept a place between Treat and Riff, his puffy face showing no remembrance of anything that had gone on. The men went into the rest room and Treat splashed water on Indian's face. Indian rubbed himself with both hands like he wanted to rub the purple stain off and then took a long piss into the trough along the wall. He said nothing.

The men walked down the street to where the train departed. They waited in the terminal building until boarding time. Treat took a pint out of his jacket pocket and everyone had a drink except Arlis and Indian. Arlis sat next to Brit.

When they looked at each other it was as if they could not believe what they saw.

"We thought you'd been killed, Arlis. We got the news about *Eva Pearl* when I got back from basic training. Said there were no survivors. You know JoAnna took it awfully hard. We married right after that." His face wouldn't change. "Me and Poopy was sent to France. While I was gone JoAnna got your letter that you were in France too with the English."

"Yes. They found me at sea." God, he thought. JoAnna. JoAnna. "Where's Poopy?"

"Killed. Right after we got there. I wasn't over there too long either. Got half my foot shot off." A peculiar look passed Brit's face and disappeared. "I wish you'd of written more."

"I wrote some," said Arlis. "Maybe the letters didn't get here." He shrugged his shoulders and told the truth. "I guess maybe I didn't write that much." He faced Brit, trying to explain the confusion inside himself. "I don't know what happened to me, Brit. After the war I kept going and going and looking for something until I figured the thing I wanted must be back here. The island. Doctor's Arm. I had to come back. I wanted to come home. Does that make any sense to you?"

"It makes sense," Brit said. "I'm glad you're back, Arlis. Things are kind of hard right now with us but I'm glad you're going to be around. Jo's here in Key West. Her pa's dying in the hospital. But she's going to be so glad to see you, you know."

Arlis felt his heart begin to pound and tried to smother it. "She really thinks the world of you. We got a kid, a little boy. She wanted to name him after you. So we call him Arlis."

Arlis waited. "Yes," he said. "She wrote me that."

The call came for the Miami train. They left the wooden benches in the waiting room and got aboard. Arlis and Brit took a seat together. Riff and Treat sat across the aisle. Indian sat by himself and went to sleep. A conductor whistled and the train pulled away from the station. Beyond Garrison Bight Arlis began recognizing the island. A great deal of fill had been put in but beyond that things had not changed too much. The low mangrove islands looked as they always did.

Arlis asked Brit about the people in Doctor's Arm.

"Old Uncle Jake and Aunt Eleuthera still take care of your house and the boat shed. They ain't neither of them changed much. My pa died while I was off in the army." They watched the telegraph poles go by.

"Wanda works the saloon. Her pa joined the Italian army. No one ever heard from him again. Preacher and Jewel's still around but there ain't any more school. Not too many kids on the island now. It's kind of deserted."

"But you're there."

"Yes."

"Well. What do you do?"

Brit raised his hands and dropped them. "There's only one thing we can do now. We're loaders. Me and them." He nodded at Treat and Riff and Indian.

"Loaders?"

Brit lowered his voice. "It's something Mr. Seybold and Jewel rigged up since Prohibition. Every so often Mr. Seybold sends down an empty boxcar on the night train. A ship comes and we go out and offload it. You know. Cases of bonded stuff. Good liquor. Then we pack it into the car and cover it with pineapples or limes. Anything to make it look good. We do okay."

Arlis looked at his friend. A tiredness covered Brit like a sheet.

"Aw hell, Arlis. Don't look like that. There's nothing else left to do."

"And the other people on the island?"

"There's a few hangers-on. Squatters mostly. Some ex-railroaders, a few mustered-out soldiers and drifters. Some of the spongers are still around. They fish. Sometimes they make a few dollars helping us load. It's a living. Mr. Jewel says better times are coming."

"Jewel's always figuring on better times."

"Even he's not the same, Arlis. Nothing's the same. But we're holding on. I guess you'll see how things are." He made an attempt at a little smile. "It's still your home."

"I want to fix *The Reaper*, Brit,"

Brit stared.

"She's still there, isn't she?"

"Yes. She's there. Old Jake takes good care of her."

"I'm going to fix her up."

"Yes." Brit stopped. "But you'll stay on, won't you?"

"I don't know."

"We want you, Arlis. It would be nice for me and JoAnna if you'd stay on."

They rode in silence. Arlis watched out the windows, feeling JoAnna and everything about her press through his mind. He tried to concentrate on how there were no houses or hotels or towns along the track. Just a few shacks and scrubby patches of neglected melons, split by the gash of the rail line. The train hadn't changed things up the keys at all. But to him it didn't make any difference now. They crossed the Saddle Bunch Islands.

In his mind Arlis thought of how at first he'd planned to come back for *The Reaper* and have a look around and leave. Then he'd heard the spoken name of JoAnna. She lived there inside him still after all the years. He'd tried to kill the remembrance but it kept living in a secret part of him. He saw the truth now. Coming back for *The Reaper* didn't make any damn difference, just like nothing else made a difference but her. Arlis looked at Brit, how tired and beat down he was. It was wrong, Arlis knew, but he could find no help for it, just a small sense of self-loathing. He felt like a thief.

"We'd better get ready," Brit said. He kicked Riff lightly. "Get the Indian up."

The train went over Nile's Channel bridge and picked up speed again on the Torch Keys. The five men walked forward and waited in the open vestibule. Arlis held the handrail and stood on the bottom step, watching the ground go by. Across Pine Channel he saw the island. The trees were gone, almost all of them. Toward the middle, where the ground rose near the settlement, some second-growth turpentine pines had sprung up. The land sloping down to the water was covered in scrub, and behind it a long line of fire burned low and fast toward the channel.

"What's that fire?" asked Arlis.

"Them son of a bitches," said Treat. "They started the deer kill without us."

Arlis looked up at his thin hatchet-shaped face. It had distorted itself with anger. Treat craned his head out the open door, watching the fire.

"What's happening?"

"They're having a deer kill is what."

The train slowed as it reached the bridge to Pine Key. Arlis could see the blue water beneath the tracks.

"Tell me what a deer kill is."

"Lookit," said Treat. He hadn't taken his eyes off the fire. "There on the beach. See them fellas with the skiffs? The other bastards waited for a good northeast wind and lit the brush. When the deer run out and make a swim for it, the fellas in the skiffs get 'em."

"They said they'd wait for us," whined Riff.

Well the fire's pretty far back. We might still have a crack at 'em. I don't see no deer in the water yet, do you, Riff?"

"No. Them boys still got the skiffs up on the beach."

Arlis looked at Brit. His face stayed grim and set, trying to ignore the brush fire. He kept looking at the sky or the water. The train crawled slowly over the trestle. Arlis held his canvas bag tightly.

"We'll get off as soon as she's across the bridge," Brit said. "She picks up speed when the ground's under her." Brit got down on the bottom step beside Arlis. A few men with clubs stood on the embankment watching the shallow line of fire close its circle and approach the water. A small buck leaped through the dense thicket by the embankment, shying away from the noise of the train. One of the men pointed and two others threw rocks into the bush. The men on the shore dragged their boats into the water.

"Goddammit, they said they'd wait for us," Riff said again.

"We'll be in time," said Treat. "Just in time." Treat and Riff leaned their heads out over Brit and Arlis. Indian stood behind them.

"Come on, Brit. Jump," urged Treat. They were off the trestle.

Brit swung down and hit the ground running. He stumbled

badly on his lame foot but kept his balance. Arlis followed. He caught up with Brit and they stood together watching the fire. Treat, Riff, and Indian dismounted a few yards up the track. The men with the boats had already gotten into the channel.

Treat came back to where Arlis and Brit were. He watched the channel, squinting with the sun in his eyes.

"They done went without us, Treat," said Riff.

"Shut up. We'll still have some fun. Come on." He walked up the track where the rails went onto the trestle, Riff following. Indian sat on the embankment and stared into space.

Two does broke from the bushes and stopped at the water's edge. The men with the clubs whooped and the does bolted into the channel and began swimming for the other side. The men in the boats were very still until the deer were well into the water. Down the beach about two hundred yards the fire reached the shore. Three men were stationed there to cut off any escape. The ring of fire began closing fast. Half a dozen raccoons wandered nervously back and forth on the beach. As the fire got closer more came out and in a panic they all made for the water.

The men in the boats closed in on the first two does. They clubbed them and dragged the bodies over the sides. They clubbed the raccoons too but left them in the water. Arlis and Brit could hear the men laughing and shouting to one another. More deer broke from the smoking thicket, almost two dozen, more than the boatmen could get at. They began swimming in divergent lines. The three men down the beach started walking quickly along the water's edge, driving the animals toward the tracks or into the channel with their clubs. They killed the raccoons and fawns who would not go into the water.

A few of the deer swam under the bridge away from the skiffs. Arlis heard cursing from the boats. Treat unbuttoned his jacket. From the waistband he took a German Mauser. Arlis had seen one like it in the war. It had a long barrel and took a clip in a magazine forward of the trigger guard. Treat sat down and pulled the slide back. Using both hands he aimed at the closest deer, who tried to make the protection of the bridge. The pistol went off with a loud crack and the deer, a young pronghorn, disappeared beneath the water. Treat aimed carefully at the next one, bracing his arms on his knees. The pistol cracked again and Arlis saw the sunlight reflect on the empty cartridge case as it was ejected from the chamber.

"Shit. Gimme a shot, Treat. Come on," said Riff.

Treat handed him the pistol. Riff fired twice and missed. He killed a doe with the third shot at close range. He fired two more times, missing, sending spouts of water up near a terrified raccoon.

"Shit."

"Gimme that goddam thing back," said Treat. "You ain't worth a piss." He shoved in a fresh clip. The deer had been frightened by the shooting and swam back toward the boats. The boatmen reached them easily and beat them with clubs before dragging the carcasses aboard. Treat sighted again at a doe close to the nearest skiff. He fired and hit her.

"Jesus Christ," cried the boatman. "Don't you shoot so fucking close."

Treat smiled. He aimed again. "Teach you to start without us next time." He fired, flinging up a geyser of water. He and Riff laughed as the men in the boat rowed hard away from the bridge and back to shore.

"Filthy bastards," Brit muttered. "Come on, Arlis. Let's go have a drink, for God's sake."

Arlis picked up his bag and followed. They walked between the rails, stepping on the wooden ties where the ground was rocky, the crushed stone white as old bones under the sun. The brush had all burned down to the water's edge. Arlis saw some deer and raccoons far out in the channel close to the other side. He was glad they'd gotten away.

"It's not very nice, I guess, is it?" said Brit.

"No."

They walked, listening to the crunch of the coral under their shoes. From the height of the embankment Arlis could see the Gulf Stream, deep blue like it had always been.

Jewel's house, Castle Windy, rose above the scrub on top of the shell mound as they approached the settlement. It looked neglected. Arlis remembered when Jewel'd had it painted. The paint was nearly gone. One shutter hung halfway off its hinge. They walked around the bend and could see the station and guesthouse. The tin enclosure around the Indian well had collapsed into a maze of rusted sheets. Near the tracks the cypress water tower lay on its side, a ruined pile of slats.

"Storm blew the water tower over last year," said Brit.

No trace remained of the two sawmills except mountains of slash. Crushed coral paths between the workers' shacks were littered with pieces of lumber and crates. A few strings of drying laundry gave color to the flat emptiness of it. Most of the shacks stood deserted, their windows and doors staring like eyes. Two old men, strangers, sat on the loading dock next to a rusty T-model truck and did not look up when Brit and Arlis passed.

The ruts on the face of the bluff where the logs had been dragged to the mill had turned into small eroded gullies and dust blew off them and onto the porch of the guesthouse. When the wind rose, the dust billowed up in a choking cloud. Arlis followed Brit through the door of the guesthouse saloon.

"Shut the goddam door," cried a woman's nagging voice. Wanda Rondinero stood behind the bar smoking a cigarette. Her face was worn. She'd become a little heavy.

"Wanda," said Brit. "Look who's here. It's Arlis."

Wanda came out from behind the bar. The cigarette stayed in her mouth. She squinted, making crow's feet at the corners of her eyes.

"Well, I'll be," she said. "Arlis."

"Hello, Wanda."

Wanda looked at him, wiping her hands on the apron she wore. Then she reached and touched the material of Arlis's coat lightly, as if she thought he might vanish.

"Lord. We thought you was dead for a while there. I'll be darned." One of her bottom teeth was missing and when she spoke she tried to hold her lower lip rigid so it didn't show. It made her face look crooked.

"We need a drink, Wanda. Bring us a pint and two Tropicals. Bring a couple of glasses too," Brit told her.

"Tropicals ain't cold. They're cool, though. No ice."

"That's all right."

Brit and Arlis started to take chairs by the window.

"I'm sure glad you're home, Arlis," Wanda said.

"Thanks, Wanda." She smiled at him as best she could while hiding the missing tooth, then went for the drinks. They drank until they felt better.

"It's funny sitting here again in the same place after all this time," Brit said. "You and me and Poopy used to sit right here. Remember? Remember the day the tank car fell off the spur?"

"Yes. It's been a while."

"So much has happened and here we are, you and me, right back in the same place. It's some world. Hell. Here's to it." Brit took a drink. He smiled a little but his eyes were sad. He's dying and he knows it, Arlis thought. This place is still killing him. I better watch out that it doesn't kill me.

Some men came in the door. They were all bloody from cleaning the deer they'd slaughtered.

"Shut the goddam door," said Wanda. The door slammed and opened again. Treat came in with Riff and Indian, followed by Mr. Esquinaldo.

"Jesus," Wanda said. She wiped the dust off the face of the bar.

Treat sat at the bar with Riff and Indian. Mr. Esquinaldo picked up an empty glass and walked across the room to Brit and Arlis. His gut hung over his belt but the rest of him was skinny, his head seeming too big for his body.

"Hello, Brit. Hello, Arlis," he said. "Spare an old man a drink?" He spoke vacantly like he'd just seen Arlis yesterday. Brit poured him one. "You boys seen James, Poopy, whatever you call him?"

"We ain't seen him, Mr. Esquinaldo."

Mr. Esquinaldo drank his drink, then stood fiddling with the empty glass. His clothes were torn and dirty.

"You boys want to buy my boat?"

"No, Mr. Esquinaldo," Brit said. "We got a boat."

"Oh." He fiddled with the glass some more. Then he started to walk back to the bar. "You see that boy of mine, tell him I got to talk with him."

Arlis looked at Brit. Brit touched his temple with a finger. Mr. Esquinaldo sat at the bar beside Treat.

"Spare a drink, Mr. Treat?"

Treat poured him one.

"I'll sell you my boat."

The men at the bar laughed as if it were an old joke.

"Your boat's got a crack in the bottom, Mr. Esquinaldo."

"So does a woman have a crack."

"Your boat's like a woman after she's shit out a couple of babies. Her crack's real big," said Treat.

"Quit that dirty talk," Wanda said without conviction.

"Shut up," Treat told her.

"Hell, that's so the water runs out of her," Mr. Esquinaldo said. "You see how that works, don't you?" He looked around at the men. They thought he was very funny.

"You always trying to sell that broken-down boat of yours," needled a young man wearing a battered army campaign hat.

"Next thing I'll sell is your broken-down ass and I'll be the one to break it," bristled old Mr. Esquinaldo.

"Relax," Treat said. "I'll buy you a drink. I'll buy you two drinks. Here." Treat took two glasses off the bar and poured rum into each glass from his bottle. "Hold out your hands." Mr. Esquinaldo held out his hands. "Like this." Treat turned the hands palms down and placed a glass on top of each. Mr. Esquinaldo sat there with the drinks on the backs of his hands, looking baffled.

"Hell. I can't get at 'em," he said. The men were laughing at him. Even Indian laughed.

"Try," Treat prompted.

Slowly, trembling, Mr. Esquinaldo moved his left hand to his mouth and caught the rim of the glass in his lips. He tilted his hand up to drink. Half the rum spilled down his chin into his lap. He sucked up what he could, then dumped the empty glass off onto the bar, where it broke. The men howled as he greedily took the second glass.

"Well, you get one and a half, anyway," Treat said.

"You made me wet myself," Mr. Esquinaldo said indignantly.

"Looks like you pissed in your britches," said the boy in the campaign hat.

"You watch out how you talk to me, sonny."

"Oh relax," said Treat. "Here, have yourself another drink."

Arlis looked at the bloody-shined men in the room, realizing they were all strangers. There was one old Cuban at the end of the bar he thought he remembered, but when he caught the man's eye the other showed no sign of recognition. Arlis watched Wanda serving them and Mr. Esquinaldo trying to cadge another drink from Treat. A deep terrible sadness settled on him. He wondered what living here had done to JoAnna. He watched Wanda's face in the last of the daylight and prayed that Jo hadn't gotten like that. It was something too awful to think about.

Wanda lit the kerosene lamps, and the next person who came in the saloon was Jewel Claire. No one paid any attention to him except Treat, who casually nodded his head in Jewel's direction. Arlis watched Jewel stand in the middle of the room and look around. When he saw Arlis he came directly to him.

"Arlis. Arlis." He sat down uninvited. "Arlis." He looked genuinely happy. "I heard you came home."

"Hello, Mr. Jewel," Arlis said. He felt a little uneasy, as if he expected a trick from the man. But Mr. Jewel just stared, marveling at him. Mr. Jewel himself looked much the same. He still wore a rumpled suit and silver watch chain. His face had become a little thinner, the orbits of his eyes more wary, seemingly on guard against hidden attackers. At last he said:

"Arlis. I'm glad to see you. I'm glad. I just thank God you're home safe at last." Jewel signaled Wanda and insisted on buying drinks. Arlis didn't want any more. He wanted to go home and see Uncle Jake and Aunt Eleuthera. He felt very tired and a little drunk.

"What are your plans, Arlis?"

"I'm going to fix up *The Reaper*, Mr. Jewel."

"Are you now? That's wonderful. She's a fine little boat. I remember her well. And you're going to stay here, aren't you?"

"I don't know. I haven't made any real plans about that."

"Arlis, we need you. The island needs you. Hell. Things are beginning to happen. Do you know there's a land boom up there in Miami? People are paying thousands of dollars for a building lot. Fifty-by-a-hundred-foot lots. Can you imagine that? And it's going to happen here."

"I seen what's happening here. I seen it this afternoon." Jewel looked hurt.

"You got to have a little faith, Arlis. Patience. There's good things coming. Still. I've never given up hope that the railroad's going to change things for the best."

"It's changed things plenty."

And it's been wonderful. Parts of it, anyway." Jewel grinned like he had shit in his mouth. "You got to keep believing in the good times to come."

"It stinks," Arlis said suddenly. He felt himself becoming angry and drunk and didn't care. "Where are the settlers? Where are the children and the planting grounds? Where's the trees? The trees are all gone, Mr. Jewel. Have you seen that? Now you got some cheap smuggling deal set up, you and these nice people." Arlis waved his glass at the men drinking at the bar. He knew it hurt Brit's feelings but he had to say it. "They're really nice folks, Mr. Jewel. They're going to make you a swell town when the land boom comes here." Arlis slumped in his chair. He was sorry he'd said it now. Brit looked empty. Jewel seemed as if the air had been let out of him. He and Brit were silent.

"We're holding on, Arlis. We got to hold on."

"I know, Mr. Jewel. Hell, I'm sorry. I'm just tired is all. I'm going up to the house. That's what I need to do. I'm tired. I'll see you all tomorrow." Arlis couldn't look at them. He stood up and took his canvas duffel to the door. He didn't walk too well. He fumbled with the latch.

"Hey, Arlis," said Mr. Esquinaldo. He looked all shiny faced in the lamplight. "You want to buy my boat?"

"No, Mr. Esquinaldo."

"All right."

Arlis got the door opened.

"You see that boy of mine, you tell him I need to talk to him, hear?"

Arlis breathed deeply, glad to be outside. A few lights came from the shacks. He walked slowly down the embankment to the beach. It was only here in this place that he felt so good to be home. The harbor looked the same except where the draglines had torn out the mangroves. From the silhouettes it seemed as if they were growing back. That gave him hope. He went along the beach, listening to the waves on the sand. The old boat shed loomed up heavy and unchanged before him. Arlis put the duffel bag down and savored the great shape of the building.

Uncle Jake's rusty collander still hung over the lintel and Arlis noticed there was a lock on the doors. With all the strangers around Uncle Jake probably had to lock it.

Footsteps came up behind. Arlis turned. By the quarter moon he saw Jewel Claire.

"Arlis. Arlis. I just couldn't let you go off thinking bad of me." He paused, his round head looking comical in the silver light, like a child's ball.

"I don't think bad of you, Mr. Jewel."

"Look. I know everything I done hasn't been right. I wanted lots for myself but I wanted for the island too. I wanted for this island to be an important place. Civilized like Key West and not just a pisshole full of backwater crackers. I got dreams too Arlis. I got vision."

"You got a lot of money out of here too."

Jewel laughed bitterly. "Oh yes, I'll tell you about that. That's a good story. When the timber went I figured we could go back to sponges. Blight killed all the sponges, you know. I had me a biologist from New York City to come here. We was going to grow sponges. I swear. You know, you can grow sponges just like plants. You chop 'em up and stick 'em on little weights and plant 'em in the bay. We planted hell out of a big patch of the bay, and let me tell you them little suckers were really growing." Jewel raised both hands in the air. "We'd of been rich in sponges." His voice died. "Damn storm washed the whole mess to hell and gone. Cost me ten thousand. But I didn't give up. No. No, I looked at all that land where the timber had been logged off and I got a homestead paper on it. Me and Brit and Mr. Olcott. But being on the leeward side of the island it's thick with mosquitoes. So I thought, How can I get rid of the mosquitoes so folks'd want to buy that land to live on? Bats, I thought. A bat eats hell out of mosquitoes. You know that. Well, I got a fellow down here from Texas who was supposed to be an expert on bats and he built a tower with scientific pockets where bats would naturally want to live. I had a whole carload of bats brought in here and we put them in that damned tower. And what do you think? In two weeks every goddam one of them had gone off. Them and the expert both. That cost me the rest of my money." He laughed again, not bitterly now, but as if it were a good joke on himself. "I think the mosquitoes ate them up. Don't kid yourself, boy. If I'd made a fortune off this island, I'd have me a two-story whorehouse down in Key West right now. Christ," he sighed. "Arlis, let me tell you something I never told anybody before. It makes me look like a fool. I don't even know why I'm telling you." Arlis thought old Jewel was drunk. "When I was a boy and my daddy had those Bahama darkies build the house on the shell mound, I wanted to live in an important place. It was me that invented Castle Windy. I read about castles in a book and I got the darkies to call it Castle Windy so everyone would call it that. I figured having a castle here would make the island important." They walked a little ways past the boat shed together before Jewel stopped. "I want for this place to be important. Like Key West. Ain't nothing wrong with that, is there?"

"No, Mr. Jewel. There's nothing really wrong with it." Arlis started again in the direction of the coconut grove. Jewel hurried up behind him.

"Don't you want something big for Doctor's Arm?"

"You can't see it, Jewel. That's the difference between me and you. I liked it the way it was. It was all here. Everything I wanted. It was all here and no one could see it. You think it's got to be different to be good. But it's good just like it was. You don't want to see that." Arlis could feel how puzzled Jewel felt, even though the man's face showed only as a pale splash. After a long while Jewel spoke:

"Well, I'm still glad you're back, Arlis, I want you to stay. I need you to stay. We all do."

"I don't know, Mr. Jewel. I love this island but I don't like the way some things are now."

Jewel again waited. "I know JoAnna wants you home, Arlis. She never forgot you." Arlis thought Jewel sounded sly. "Not after all this time. She's got a fine young son too. Pretty blue-eyed, yellow-haired boy. She named him for you, Arlis."

"What the hell are you saying?" Arlis stopped in the path. He felt the beating in his chest.

"Why, nothing. It's just that this is your home here. These are your folks. We want you to stay." Arlis gave up trying to make out Jewel's face. The moon's small light danced through the fronds. I'm too tired for this, Arlis thought. I'm too tired for anything but sleep. The wind came in cool off the Gulf Stream as it always did.

"I'm going up to the house, Mr. Jewel."

"Good night, Arlis," Mr. Jewel said. "It's real good you're back home."

18

Arlis lay beneath the hull of *The Reaper* waiting. He kept his
hands busy tapping lines of twisted oakum into the seams of
the boat, but he was only aware of the waiting. Today the train
stopped at Doctor's Arm Settlement. JoAnna, God, please,
JoAnna.

From where he lay in the sand Arlis could see the long lines
of thick red lead that Jake had painted in the seams of the hull.
It gave *The Reaper* a new look, a changed look, as though at last
something were happening to her.

The small iron grew heavy in his hand because it had to be
continually held upright without rest. Arlis thought how
boatwrights made a saying that the slight wedge of a caulking
iron is heavier than the hammer that drives it. Arlis's hand
trembled.

He cast the iron aside and pushed his body roughly from
beneath the boat, raising himself quickly and nervously, still
holding the mallet like a useless extension of his arm. Arlis
walked to the door and looked seaward.

On the beach Uncle Jake landed the catboat. Arlis had seen
him approaching for more than an hour. The old man rarely
hoisted the jib, and Arlis felt that Jake had only rigged the fast
racing sails so as not to insult them both. Given his preference,
old Uncle Jake would be equally happy with the simple, patched,
leg-o'-mutton sail customary to the island.

Shouldering a wicker basket of cleaned fish, Uncle Jake
slowly walked to the open doors of the boathouse.

"Good catch, Uncle Jake?"

"'Nuff to feed us, Arlis." His face, polished ebony in the sun,
remained steady as his walk.

"You made that catboat the best on the island." Arlis felt the jerkiness inside himself, the need to talk, the waiting tearing at his insides.

"That be the best. Yes." The old man permitted himself to smile. "That catboat outsail anything in these waters."

"And you made her that way, Uncle Jake," Arlis prattled, waiting, waiting all the while.

"You done all the thinking on it, boy."

"Thinking, doing. They're the same in their way..."

From the southwest, far beyond the channel, Arlis heard the whistle of the train. He wondered if Jake saw him flinch as if he'd been burned. Uncle Jake only yawned and placed his fish in the terra-cotta cooler.

"Guess I'll go watch the train come in. Maybe buy us a little ice, make some iced tea. JoAnna coming in today. She'll be surprised to hear you home. You coming?"

"No." Arlis felt choked.

"I'll tell her you home." Jake smiled big.

God, Arlis thought. Is it that obvious to everyone? He watched the old man pad through the dust and leave by the front door. When he'd gone Arlis put the mallet down and sat quietly. He closed his eyes and made himself breathe slowly. He counted his breathing and when he reached a hundred he got up and brushed off his clothes.

The train blew once more and the bell clanged monotonously. From the sound Arlis knew the train had stopped at the station. He walked to the door and went outside far enough to look through the leaves of the hibiscus bush up the embankment. The guesthouse and the old station blocked out the engine and most of the cars. Black smoke and steam rose over the shingled roof of the guesthouse. Maybe I should go, Arlis thought. No. I don't know. When I see her I don't know what I'm going to do. He looked out to sea. A freighter headed south in the Stream. She trailed black smoke like the locomotive. Arlis tried to remember all the grand old ships that used to ply that route. They came so close to the island, he remembered, especially the ones going south. They'd stay right on the edge of the Stream so they could buck the current and get more headway. Arlis guessed steamers were the same. Of course they were. It saved them fuel to stay out of the current, but they could still make their speed pretty much. Keeping clear of the current didn't make nearly the difference to them that it did to the old wind sailers. He shook his head. Christ, he thought. What in the hell am I thinking about? I don't have any claim to this. To her. What am I doing? He prayed to God that he was right, that she hadn't changed. That she was the same. I'm crazy, he told himself. And then he saw her.

He drew against the wall of the boat shed. It was a stupid reflex. He tried to tell himself he wasn't afraid. He watched her come. JoAnna did not see him. She walked slowly, carefully stepping over the rough ground of the embankment's slope. Her eyes were downcast. Even if she looks up, Arlis thought, she won't see me. He could see her well through the thick green of the hibiscus shrub. It was as if he waited for her in ambush. She came close enough now for Arlis to see her face. He wrapped his arms around his chest and tried to crush himself, never taking his eyes from her. Her hair was cut short, almost like a boy's. The neck seemed longer, as did her whole body without being lanky but rather softly rounded. The girl's face stayed unchanged. It was only the body that had found some magnificent gentle grace, the grace a woman acquires when she stops being a girl.

At the bottom of the embankment where the sand of the beach path began, JoAnna stopped. She shaded her eyes against the sun and looked toward the boat shed. Arlis could not force himself to move. Deliberately she stood on one foot, then the other, removing her slippers. She began walking toward him.

Arlis stayed close to the wall and moved back through the door into the gloom of the building. You're running from her, he thought. You're insane. At once he felt like laughing hysterically. A trembling began working at his center and radiated outward. He stood alone in the middle of the great room, almost beneath *The Reaper's* bow. He faced the door, not breathing, staring into the light.

"Arlis." The light surrounded her. It showed through her frail cotton dress and outlined her legs where they joined her body. Neither moved, and then Arlis realized that coming in from the brightness of the day made her unable to see him.

He walked to her, feeling numb, not able to take his eyes from her face as it became more and more clear, the backlighting of the day wrapping it in illumination the nearer he got.

"Arlis."

The eyes. The soft line of the slightly parted lips. The roundness of the chin. Mechanically his hand raised itself and rested on the side of her face.

"You cut your hair," he said lamely.

JoAnna barely smiled, keeping her eyes always on Arlis. She reached and touched him.

"A mustache. You've grown a mustache." She laughed and stopped as suddenly, not taking her fingers from his face.

Together, each with their fingertips on the other's face, they were as two blinded people. Arlis felt Jo's fingers trail from his mustache and fall gently across his lips. They rested there and softly traced the outline of his mouth. The warmth of her tears burned his hand. Very carefully he drew her close, until she rested against him. Each felt the rare gift of the breathing and heartbeat of the other.

"Arlis. Oh Arlis. What will happen to us?"

"I don't know, JoAnna. I just don't know."

A yellow scab of cloud lay across the moon. From the other side of the tracks Arlis and JoAnna heard the T-model truck start up. It backfired and then its engine idled unevenly until it warmed up. JoAnna seemed to shrink closer to Arlis when its headlights went on, stabbing impotently into the night sky. From where they were in the boat shed they could not see the truck itself but they could see the outline of the small darkened ship that lay beyond the mouth of the harbor. Earlier it had shown a masked light at two brief intervals and now it lay still and dark.

The gears of the T-model clashed and the engine noise changed as it started off. The headlights bounced erratically, marking the truck's progress on the washboard road that ran parallel to the tracks on the other side of the railbed. The road led around and crossed the tracks further to the east. Jo and Arlis lost sight of the headlamps but could still hear the motor. JoAnna let her head rest on Arlis's chest until the light again became visible, shooting up and down at the crossing. The truck crawled like a luminous insect, now plainly in sight, heading toward Jewel Claire's wharf, where the loading boats were.

On the wharf Arlis saw the mingled shadows of the men getting out of the truck. They were too distant to see clearly or to hear. JoAnna kept her eyes averted anyway. Arlis watched the two large cutters move out from the protecting shadow of the pier. They trailed a faint line of phosphorescence from their sterns and to each side where the oars were dipped and pulled. The cutters moved toward the harbor mouth and the waiting ship, carrying Brit and the other loaders away, leaving Arlis and JoAnna in their secret silence.

Arlis felt JoAnna trembling against him. Still holding each other, they went into the blackness of the boat shed. Arlis kept his arm tightly around her and let his free hand pass over *The Reaper's* hull to guide himself until they reached the back of the building.

Arlis heard the flurry of JoAnna's dress as she took it off. They threw their clothes from their bodies, seeing now in the dimmest of light from the door their own white forms. Arlis and JoAnna came together, each breathing fiercely as if they were one person. Arlis pulled her down to the bed of sailcloth. They lay together, burning where the surfaces of their flesh touched. Arlis began to speak but JoAnna covered his mouth with hers, urgently taking, as though she needed to draw some life-saving substance from within him. Arlis let his hand find each part of her body, envisioning what the fingers of his hand touched. He held her breasts into his face while Jo arched her neck back and made a small sound in her throat. The mound between her legs was wet. She held his hard penis in her hand. They each wanted to wait and savor the moment but were driven on more and more quickly. Jo allowed Arlis to force her legs back as far as they would go to fully open herself to him and then she guided him in. Arlis felt the soft resistance of her slippery dampness before it gave way and he plunged deeply inside her. JoAnna drew a sharp breath as he went in and her arms circled his back in a crushing embrace. They moved together in quiet hard desperation, unable to wait for anything now, ruthlessly grasping their pleasure. Arlis drove hard, withdrew, and then went deeper with each thrust. They lost all control. Jo's legs crossed themselves high up around his waist, pulling, contracting, demanding, each time he drove into her. Jo and Arlis moved faster and harder, grinding their limbs together, both needing more than they could take and wanting to give more than they had. They struggled almost violently in a hopeless attempt to lose themselves within one another, pushing, twisting, crushing, until the climax came to surprise them both, causing each to give a strangled cry and collapse, still locked together in an exhausted tangle of sweating limbs and flesh and hair.

"I wish you hadn't come back." They lay in the dark, not touching. Then she said: "That's not so. I'm a liar." Arlis heard her turn on the sailcloth. He could feel her breath on his face and moved so he could kiss her. "It's wrong, Arlis. It's wrong and I don't care. I won't care. I won't even think about it." Arlis let his fingers rest on her mouth after he'd kissed her.

"Let's not think about it then. Not now. We can't let ourselves think about anything more than this one minute." They became quiet, touching again, enjoying their closeness in the dark.

"And I didn't even tell you about my father," she said. "It's a bad thing. When I found out you were here I forgot him. I just forgot everything." An edge of hysteria crept into her voice and she killed it. "I buried him in Key West." Arlis knew she wept quietly and held her to himself, stroking her hair and kissing her gently until she could stop.

"Why did you come back, Arlis?"

He lay in silence, trying to form an answer.

"Before I came I didn't know. I wanted to know but I didn't. When I saw you coming down the embankment I really began to know. I came back for you. For the child. When I saw you again I knew for sure what I thought I'd known." JoAnna drew in a long breath.

"He's our child, Arlis. He's yours and mine."

"Yes."

"You never doubted that, did you?"

"No."

"I'm glad about that part, Arlis. I'm happy. The rest is terrible. The island. Those people. What I'm doing to Brit. I'm ashamed, Arlis. What can you think of me for what I'm doing?"

"That I love you. That I was dead inside myself and you made me alive."

They lay listening to the faint sounds of the waves and the breeze in the fronds.

"Do you believe in fairness?" she asked him.

"No. I don't think so."

"We only have this little time. Now. That's all we have. We can't live this way too long, Arlis. It's going to catch us sooner or later."

"Don't think that."

"But it's true, isn't it?"

Arlis didn't answer her. Instead he held her carefully, her head in the cradle of his arm. so that in a while she lightly slept. He kept his eyes open staring at the dark of the ceiling, knowing what she said was true. An answer lay somewhere beyond what he could see. Arlis lay that way, motionless, thinking, until they both heard the engine of the T-model start again.

They rose, JoAnna as if she bore a great weight. Arlis heard her dressing, her movements showing as a silver blur.

"Tomorrow," Arlis said.

"Yes."

"At the old planting ground."

"Yes," she said. There was no joy in her voice, only a necessity. "In the afternoon. I'll leave little Arlis with Aunt Eleuthera." He felt her touch and then her hand slipped away.

Arlis walked with her to the door. Their eyes had become quite used to the dark now as if they'd lived in it all their lives. They ignored the sounds of the truck being loaded across the harbor.

"I'm sorry it can't be better than this," Arlis said.

Jo didn't answer. They clung together for one more moment before JoAnna went over the sand path and up the embankment. her figure floating half seen until it vanished into the shadows of the earth.

It is something begun, Arlis thought, that has to have an end. Just like that tank car sliding down the rails. It has the feel of disaster all over it and I've got to be ready. I let her go once when I was young and stupid and afraid. I'm not that way anymore. I've got to think of her now. And the boy. Things are going to get broken and hurt and I won't be able to help it. I hope I can do it because that's the only way it can be now.

Far down the tracks, coming from Key West, Arlis heard the cry of the night train.

19

"Come on, old Arlis." Brit clapped him on the shoulder. He acted goofy and good-natured like he had it made, like he didn't have a care in the world. "You been working too hard on that boat. You got to have a good drink and a sit-down dinner and I'm going to see that you get it. Hell, you ain't even seen your namesake yet. I told that boy about his Uncle Arlis and he won't believe that someone else has the same name as him. Wait'll you see him. He's some kid. Smart as a cricket too." Brit led Arlis up the slope. Arlis followed, feeling a mixture of anger and pity. He could almost still taste JoAnna's kisses from a few hours earlier when they lay in a thicket in the old planting ground. Brit was so damned happy now because he'd hauled a few miserable cases of whiskey ashore and loaded them on the night train. What would he say if he knew about me and Jo, Arlis thought. I can't let myself get to feeling sorry for him. People who can afford to give out sympathy are never the desperate ones.

They walked through the shack town where the railroaders used to live. The newer shacks had been built as far up as Olcott's store, though they now stood mostly deserted. The squatters had moved into the best ones and scavenged parts from the others to improve their accommodations. When Brit and Arlis came abreast of Olcott's store Brit put his hand on Arlis's arm and nodded at its front. The windows were boarded up but the door opened like a black hole. Sitting squarely in the middle of it, in Mr. Olcott's old chair, was the sleeping form of Preacher. His jaw hung down, showing all his ghastly teeth, long and yellow. Everything about him had a sunken look except the eyes. They protruded like large marbles seeming ready to pop through their blackened lids. A dog-eared Bible lay open in his lap.

"He's gone crazy as hell," Brit said matter-of-factly. "Look. Up at the old school. Can you make it out?"

Arlis held out his hand to block the sun and stared hard up the slope of the bluff. Beyond Olcott's store was the cemetery and the school building. It slumped to one side in a sorry parallelogram. Someone had wedged poles against the wall as braces to keep it from collapsing entirely. The shingles were blown from the roof and the door lay against a rock some distance from the building. Written across the front of the weathered boards in black paint was: REPENT. THE END IS NEAR.

"That's his work," Brit said. Arlis shivered inside.

They stopped beside the ruin of the Indian well. Arlis kicked one of the rusted metal sheets of siding with his foot. It slid off the nail that held it to a rotten board and clattered onto the ground. Arlis looked at the bald face of the limestone, thinking of the little pool and the ironwood tree.

"We had one hell of a storm. Knocked this place down along with the water tower. Washed out Jewel's sponge farm." He smiled a little. "It's strange. The storm just busted up the new things. None of the old houses got blown down. I guess the old things were built better. You think so?"

"Hell. I guess, Brit." They walked on.

Brit took Arlis up the steps of the Olcott house, where he and JoAnna lived. Arlis wondered if she'd be there. He half hoped she wouldn't, not until he could collect himself.

"Come on in, Arlis."

The place had JoAnna everywhere. Arlis's stomach knotted up. He watched the clean muslin curtains blow away from the windows and smelled the fragrance that came from a bowl of fresh-cut frangipani flowers on the table.

"Look here what I got." Brit pointed at the sideboard. There were a dozen different bottles on it. "Have a drink. Anything you want."

"I'll have whatever you're having."

"Hell," said Brit. "Try some of this whiskey from Scotland. It's different. Maybe you've had some before since you traveled a lot. You ever tried it?"

"No." Arlis lied to make Brit feel good. Brit gave him a tumbler of the scotch.

"Here's to it, Arlis." They both drank. "It's something, you know. If it hadn't been for Prohibition I'd never of tasted any of this stuff. I don't think I ever tasted anything but old Cuban rum in my whole life until they made drinking illegal. Now each time we pull a load in the skipper gives us a couple of bottles of something different. Ain't that peculiar as hell?"

"It's strange, all right," Arlis said. "Let me have another, will you?" He felt nervous about seeing Jo here in the house. Brit poured him one and had one himself.

"Shoot, Arlis. Sit down. Make yourself at home, old boy."

Arlis looked at Brit's dumb, uncomprehending face, almost wishing he could make him know that he was taking his wife away from him. "We had a good run last night, Arlis. I made myself almost a hundred dollars. That ain't bad for a night's work." Brit took a swallow. "There's a place for you if you want. You could make you some easy money."

"No. I have about five hundred up at the house that I saved for *The Reaper.* I'm putting all my time into her, Brit. That five hundred'll take care of getting her the way she should be." And then Jo and I'll sail away with the kid and leave you flat, you poor bastard, Arlis thought. He felt sick. I'm going to have to tell him sometime. What if I tell him now? I could just say it now. I'll say it and it'll be all over. Telling him will be the worst damned part, watching it tear him to pieces. There isn't much left of him to tear.

They both heard footsteps on the porch. Brit jumped up, his face all happy and stupid.

"It's them, Arlis. Wait'll you see the kid. He's a knockout."

JoAnna came in. There was a little sunburn on her cheekbones and she looked pale beneath it. She locked eyes with Arlis.

"Is this my uncle?"

Arlis broke off looking at her and saw the boy. He saw himself. It's good that I'm sitting, he thought. The child came to him and held out his hand.

"I'm Arlis too," he said. His frank blue eyes looked deeply into Arlis's from beneath his unkempt blond hair. The tops of slightly large ears stuck out from the hair. Arlis took his hand. Then he let go and held the boy by the shoulders for a moment, feeling the warm skinny body under the shirt.

"Hello," he said. "Arlis."

The child seemed to examine him, his expression completely lacking in guile. "I never knew anyone else named Arlis."

"At least you weren't born with a mustache," laughed Brit. He came over and put his arms around the boy and lifted him so that he almost touched his head on the ceiling. Jo watched. She seemed not to be breathing. "You look a little tuckered, honey," Brit said. "I asked Arlis and Jewel to come have fish with us tonight. I'd of told you but I couldn't find you this afternoon."

"I went and got some limes, Brit."

"And I got to stay with Aunt Eleuthera," young Arlis said. "I like staying with her."

"You ought to get young Arlis to help you pick limes, Jo," Brit said. "Shoot. He's old enough. Aren't you, son?"

"I'm almost eight, Daddy."

"There're snakes around those old planting grounds," said Jo.

"Fiddle," Brit said. He put the boy down. "You ain't afraid of no snakes, are you, son?"

"No, sir."

"Your Uncle Arlis and I used to run all over this island when we were your age, didn't we?"

"Yes," said Arlis.

"We had a great time."

"I'm going to get the supper," JoAnna said. She looked at Arlis briefly from the door of the kitchen, everything in her face terribly fragile.

"Was that before the train, Daddy? The time you and Big Arlis used to run all over the island?"

"Long before the train, son." Brit put the boy on his knee. Arlis thought his heart might break.

Jewel Claire enjoyed his meal more than anyone. He had third helpings.

"We had a good run last night, Arlis, didn't we, Brit?"

"Yes. I told him, Mr. Jewel. We did real good. That was one of our best yet."

"It would be nice if that sort of thing could last forever," said Jewel. "It won't, though." He took a piece of key lime pie. Brit looked perplexed. "Nice pie, JoAnna. The whole meal was the best I've had in a long, long time. You cook just as good as Aunt Eleuthera, but don't tell her I said that. Don't you think so, Arlis?" He laughed. "Big Arlis, I'm talking to." Jewel patted the child on the head.

"Yes. The meal was very good, Jo," Arlis said.

"Well." Jewel wiped off his chin and put his napkin on the table. "Well." He leaned back in his chair. Brit got up.

"I'll help you clear the table, honey. Then maybe you can take little Arlis out on the porch to play." Jo looked at the men. She looked longest at Arlis.

"All right," she said. "But I can get the things off the table."

"No. I'll help," Brit said. Arlis watched the two of them and then caught Jewel watching him.

"Work going good on *The Reaper?*" he asked, taking a cigar from his pocket. He offered one to Arlis. Arlis shook his head.

"It's going along as best as can be expected. I might get her in the water in a week. I have a mainsail. The jib and topsail are on order from Key West."

"So you might could sail her in a week or so." Jewel puffed on the cigar.

"Under the mainsail, yes. She'd sail okay. Not too fast until I get the jib and top rigged, but she'd get along basically."

"Ummm." Jewel covered himself in another cloud of smoke. Jo came out of the kitchen, little Arlis following.

"I hope you had a good dinner," the boy said to Arlis. He came to Arlis's chair. "I'm glad you came back. I'm glad you're my uncle. Maybe we can go fishing sometime soon. I got a good boat. What do you think?"

"Yes. We'll do that. Real soon," Arlis said.

"Come on, son," Jo said, "Let's go sit in the porch swing. I'll tell you a story."

They went out the door. "Tell me about when you and Uncle Arlis won the sailboat race," Arlis heard him say. The screen door closed behind them.

"He's really some kid, isn't he?" said Brit.

"Yes," Arlis said. Jewel blew smoke rings at the ceiling.

"Ummm. Well," Jewel said. He waited.

"So what's wrong with the loading business, Mr. Jewel?" Brit asked.

"Nothing's wrong with it, Brit. I just said it wouldn't last. That's what I said."

"I don't get it. Why not?"

"Because, Brit." Jewel squinted through his own smoke. "Things like this just don't go on and on. Especially when they're illegal as hell and the federal government is looking to put a stop to it. And don't fool yourself. They can put a stop to any of it in a pair of minutes." He spoke tough to Brit as if Brit were a schoolboy. Arlis saw that Jewel had never lost the gift of playing the hardnose and Brit was still simple enough to buy it. "We're all of us playing a dangerous game. You, me, Treat and his two roughnecks. Even Mr. Seybold. Maybe especially him."

Jewel let what he'd said sink in, shifting his gaze back and forth between them. "The thing I'm getting at is that pulling in a little money each week is fine, but we got to look to the future." He didn't take his eyes away from them as he reached into his pocket. What he pulled out was a folded half of a newspaper that he smoothed on the table. It listed box after box of Miami real estate. "Look at that." Jewel ran his thick finger down the page. "Just look. Now, you know about that boom. I told you both. What this place needs is to get in on that. And we can. We got land aplenty. If we survey it and parcel it and get a clearing machine and a gang of darkies to root out the brush, we can dig mosquito trenches and make it habitable. Fine land." He looked at Arlis. "We'll leave the trees. They'll be nice parcels and we'll sell to quality folk. Quality people'll come down here and we can run the squatters out." Jewel waited again. "Capital. What's lacking is just a little capital and all this can happen." He slumped back in his chair and concentrated on his cigar for a while. Brit was enthralled. Arlis wished he'd close up his stupid cracker mouth. Old Jewel is wanting to fish us in for sure, he thought. He wants my money or my boat.

"How we going to get capital, Mr. Jewel?" Brit asked. Jewel Claire ran his hand over the pot of his belly and smiled largely at Brit.

"Liquor, boy. What the whole country is thirsty for. Bonded liquor."

"Well, we're already loading liquor."

"For somebody else, Brit," Jewel said, straining to be patient. "What if we got a load for ourselves? What if we bypass Mr. Seybold and run our own load? We can triple, hell, quadruple, every dollar we invest. All we need is a good boat."

"No," Arlis said.

"Now, wait, Arlis," Brit said. He was on fire and ready to go. "You ain't even heard what Mr. Jewel's got to say."

"I heard enough. That boat's all I got and I'm not taking a chance on some federal bastard taking it or sinking it, for that matter-" he looked Brit in the face-"and you better think good on this, getting locked up for the next ten years. No, sir."

Arlis got up from the table. "I got the money I need to fix that boat and I'm going to fix her. That boat's too valuable to risk. Hell. My ass is too valuable to risk." He went for the door, not wanting to listen to any arguments. Brit look disappointed.

"All I'm saying is to think on it, Arlis," said Jewel. "We still got time. Not a lot, but we got some time. You think on it real good. I'll wait."

"Sorry, Jewel. Don't hold your breath."

Arlis went outside. Jo sat in the porch swing. The boy had curled up and slept with his head in her lap. Arlis allowed himself to look at him for a minute.

"Good night, Jo." He wanted to touch her and tell her a thousand things. "Thanks for the supper." He wanted to take her and the boy and run away into the night.

"Good night, Arlis," she said. "Thank you for coming by."

20

Arlis and Jo dressed, then sat in the shade of the single large mahogany tree that stood in the middle of the old planting ground. The brush grew almost head-high around them except where Arlis had cleared a small place for their blanket. They met there each afternoon.

JoAnna rested on Arlis's shoulder. They listened to the insects drone in the warm thicket and thought of their lovemaking.

"Why'd you bring the gun?" Jo spoke absently. She had her eyes closed. Papadad's old ten-gauge double-bore lay in the grass.

"I thought I might go after some doves later. Would you like some? I could bring them by the house."

Jo opened her eyes.

"It's hard on me, Arlis. To see you there."

"I know. But I want to see the boy. Don't you think it's hard on me?"

"Yes." She didn't want to fight. They'd both gotten edgy in the past week. She made herself close her eyes again.

The insect noises rose and fell. The greenness of the jungle showed back in Arlis's face with the shimmery hot light that comes in the late summer.

"*The Reaper's* in the water. I paid all the squatters to help me run her into the harbor this morning."

"I know. I watched you," Jo said. "I watch you a lot when you don't know it. I saw you tie her off at Jewel's wharf and put the mast up."

"Do you like watching me?"

"I like everything about you, Arlis."

"Do you love me?"

"Yes." Her voice tried to force out the little sadness.

"She'll be ready soon, Jo. *The Reaper.*"

"I know that."

"I never really came right out and asked you to go away with me, did I? I took it for granted."

"No, you never asked me that."

"Well, I'm asking you now. You and the boy. But you've got to say it to me."

JoAnna struggled with it. She'd wanted to avoid it so badly and here it was now. She moved a little away from him, trying to see as far as she could into the wall of jungle. She didn't speak for a minute. She didn't want to go to pieces on him.

"Isn't there any other way?" She kept waiting.

"You can't believe there is. You've got to say it to me."

"Oh goddammit. Why did it have to be like this?" JoAnna suddenly took Arlis's hand in both of hers. "Don't you understand that anything I do is going to be wrong? I was wrong from the start when I married Brit. I was scared and pregnant and I thought you were dead. But that doesn't make it right. Not then, not now."

"Stop it, Jo. What's done is done. Stop doing it to yourself."

She quit. In a while she stopped crying. "All right. I'll go. I've said it."

"Yes."

"There really isn't any other way, is there, Arlis? Tell me if there is." JoAnna could see the answer in his face.

"No," Arlis said.

"Do you think he'll get over it? Do you think you and I'll get over it ever?"

"I think we have to live, Jo. If we don't have each other, we don't have anything. This is our only chance. We'd better take it. If we miss it, it won't ever happen for us again."

"Yes. It's the truth and I'm afraid to death of it. It's all the truth there is."

Arlis stood in the treeline and looked onto the meadow. There are still some nice trees here, he thought. The cutters hadn't gotten this far when the armistice happened. The deer kept the grass in the meadow short. Arlis wondered how many deer were left on the island. He didn't see any.

Arlis had charged both barrels of his gun with light loads and number-six shot before he left the house. He set the hammers at half-cock and slipped a percussion cap on each nipple. The gun had a nice feel to it. It balanced well in his hands. Arlis liked to look into the burled depths of the polished walnut stock. It was a good piece. He knew they didn't make guns like this anymore. He wondered how many egrets Papadad had brought down with it in his time. Plenty, he bet.

Arlis kept in the treeline, listening for the rustle of wings. He wished he had old Nell with him to flush out the birds. She'd disappeared all at once after the tracks came to the island. Arlis always figured some railroader had taken her. Or killed her. He'd never know now.

A soft chortling sound came to him. He looked and saw the doves. They were ground-feeding under a thornbush a few yards into the meadow. He counted eight or nine. Arlis pulled back both hammers, walking carefully all the while so as not to make any noise. From here he could get maybe three on the ground and three on the wing if he was quick. He nestled the gunstock into his cheek and shoulder and pointed the black barrel down on the doves. They chortled and moved in their stupid jerky way, the fine feathers on their necks just tinted with red and catching the sunshine. Their world is so simple, Arlis thought. They don't think about anything but going around under that thornbush scratching for seeds and bits of crap to eat. Boy, are they going to be surprised when I cut loose on them.

He kept watching them, wondering why God made such stupid birds. They just walk around all rafted up with their heads looking at the ground. How many of them would be killed if he jerked off both barrels at once? Finally he lowered the gun and eased each hammer down to the half-cock position.

"Hey!" He stamped his foot. The doves fluttered and rose in a thick body, then fanned out in different directions. They were pretty the way they flew up when something startled them. Arlis wondered why the Indians hadn't killed them all off, they were so dumb. Maybe the Indians felt sorry for them.

Arlis put the gun over his shoulder and began walking back to the settlement. He had to smile at himself even though he was still worked up inside over JoAnna. He thought maybe God would make things easier because he didn't shoot the doves. He didn't think it worked that way, though. Oh, you're getting to be some philosopher, he thought. You better just shut up thinking and stick to things you know.

The deer path led to one of Jewel's planting grounds. Arlis skirted it and got onto the main trail that let out on the far side of the bluff. From there he could see the whole settlement. The cemetery was highest up, then the broken-down schoolhouse. Further down came the Indian well and near it JoAnna's house. Arlis watched her house for a time. He didn't see anyone. He looked at the store and shacktown all laid out in squares, setting now against the station and guesthouse with the tracks running between. It would have been one hell of a town, he supposed, if things had worked out. Jewel's house stood singularly on top of the shell mound. Hell, maybe old Jewel will get his town yet.

The Reaper was snugged into the wharf. If a real town comes, Arlis thought, we won't be here to see it. He saw the boat and how solid she lay, figuring that he and Uncle Jake could build a nice cuddy cabin forward of the cargo hatch. He went down the slope, pausing to stare over the settlement again. It's still a beautiful island in spite of everything, he told himself. He crossed the tracks and walked carefully over the rocky embankment toward the boat shed.

Arlis came around the corner of the boat shed just in time to see Riff trying to pour a half-pint of whiskey down the throat of Wanda Rondinero. She lay sprawled on the gravel. Riff sat with his legs pinning her arms, holding her cheeks clamped open so he could stuff the neck of the bottle into the hole of her mouth. Her skin puffed with angry red marks. Indian worked to keep her legs apart while Treat squatted over her with his hand up her dress. They'd managed to get her underthings torn off and her stockings were shredded to her ankles.

"Get up," Arlis said.

Treat had his fly halfway unbuttoned.

"Well," Treat said. He didn't move. "Mister Arlis."

"Get up and get the hell away from her."

Indian and Riff looked surprised and scared.

"Take it easy now, cracker boy." Treat's voice was slimy soft. "We just having a little fun here. Just taking for free what she usually makes us pay for, right, boys?"

The boys didn't say anything. Riff took the bottle out of Wanda's mouth.

"Please," she cried, gasping weakly. "Oh please, Arlis. Make them stop."

"You hush now, little lady," Treat said. His voice stayed oily-calm and low. "We going to have us a little fun here and Mister Arlis going to join right in, ain't you? You just got to get in line and when your turn comes you can climb aboard. Right, boys?"

Arlis watched Treat's hand moving very smoothly from the fly of his trousers up toward his waistband beneath the jacket. Arlis swung the ten-gauge off his shoulder, pulling both hammers back. They all heard the two clicks. Treat froze like a snake.

"Get your hands up." Treat's eyes were big and that was all. "I said to get your fucking hands up." He slowly raised his hands. "You too. Both of you." Indian and Riff jerked their hands into the air. "Now get up. Get off her." The three men got to their feet. Arlis could tell Indian and Riff were plenty scared now. Treat only stared dead-faced back at him, unchanged except that the skin seemed more tightly stretched over the frame of his skull.

Wanda pulled her dress down and sat up. She looked at the men and all at once started blubbering.

"You bastards. You bastards," she said. She began crawling and picked up her underclothes. She got up and tried to smooth out her dress. She kept crying hard. "You rotten bastards," she said. Clutching the shredded underclothes and sobbing into her free hand she struggled up the side of the embankment. The men watched her until she disappeared over the top where the rails ran.

Arlis looked to the three men, not knowing fully what to do with them. He still held the shotgun pointing at Treat. Suddenly Treat's slash of a mouth cracked into a grin.

"You know what you are, cracker boy? You're a high-minded, two-faced hypocrite. That's what you are." He turned abruptly and let his hands drop to his sides. He began walking. Arlis kept the gun pointed at the small of his back.

"Come on, you shitheads," Treat said to the others. They looked at Arlis, then at Treat walking away, the gun still pointed at Treat. First Riff, then Indian edged sideways after Treat. When they decided Arlis wouldn't shoot, they broke into a run. Treat never changed stride, nor did he look back. Arlis stood alone, holding the shotgun.

Arlis dragged himself into the house. It was deserted. He hung the shotgun up and poured a drink. The rum burned itself down into his guts.

I wonder what that weaselly little son of a bitch Treat knows, he thought. He knows something. I should have killed him. Something tells me I'm going to be sorry for not killing him right then. Arlis had another drink and stood at the big window. It's getting tighter and tighter around here all the time, he thought. I've got to watch out. He put down his glass and went into the breezeway.

Arlis stayed in the breezeway for a few minutes, letting it cool him down. He felt tired suddenly. Everything seemed to be crowding in on him too quickly. Maybe a rest will straighten you out, he said to himself. He walked to the end of the long breezeway, to the door of his grandfather's old room, where he liked to sleep. The door was slightly ajar. The bolt of the lock had been ripped out and hung on a piece of splintered wood. Arlis's stomach twisted up right to the pit. He kicked the door open. The inside of the room had been gone over good. The bed lay on its side in a pile of clothes and books. Arlis didn't care about that. He made straight for the chest of drawers. He knew before he reached it that he'd been ruined. The drawers all hung out, their contents scattered over the floor. In the top drawer sat Cap'n Ben's medal box. It was empty. There had been almost five hundred dollars in gold coins in the box and now it was gone. They'd even taken Cap'n Ben's Civil War medal. Arlis held the box in his hands. Treat's smug face flashed across his mind. That's what he was doing up here, he thought. That's why his goons were scared to see me. He bluffed me good, the thieving bastard.

Arlis jumped over the mess on the floor and ran out the door, leaving it open. He got down the breezeway and back into the house. From the wall he snatched the shotgun. With trembling fingers he fitted fresh percussion caps on the nipples of the gun. His whole being burned with rage. Over and over in his mind he saw the skinny face of Treat explode like a ripe fruit when he would jam the gun muzzle into his mouth and shoot.

Arlis took the front steps two at a time and sprinted down the path. The air singed his lungs and he knew he ran too fast and breathed too hard. He told himself to slow down and relax and think, but then he'd see the face of Treat again and he just didn't care about anything except killing him as quick as he could.

He swung around the corner of the boat shed, where the path led into the settlement, and almost knocked Brit off his feet.

"What the hell are you doing?" Brit looked stunned and rubbed his shoulder where Arlis had run into him.

"I'm fixing to kill that son of a bitch Treat. Him and those two other thieving bastards." He started to jog off again. Brit caught him by the sleeve and wheeled him around.

"Turn loose of me, goddammit," he snarled. He raised his fist.

"Settle down for a second, Arlis. Tell me what you're talking about. Lord, you just can't go up there and kill three people. What the hell are you talking about?"

Arlis looked at Brit, how thin he'd gotten. He could knock him down easy. Brit's face was pale and his eyes wide. He'd gotten to look as bad as one of the consumptives that used to work on the rail gangs. All at once Arlis felt deep sorrow and a tenderness for his friend. Brit wanted to help him. He was right. Arlis knew he couldn't just find Treat and start shooting. They wouldn't carry the money they stole around with them in their pockets, for heaven's sake. The futility of it hit him hard. They'd got him. He was finished and he knew it. *The Reaper* would lay there 'til she rotted and he and Jo would never get away from the island. Here was Brit, the man he intended to betray, trying to save him from committing murder. Brit standing there trying to talk sense to him. Arlis looked into his frightened face and felt like the lowest sneak in the world.

"God," he said. Arlis leaned the shotgun against the shed and sat down in the sand, holding his face in both his hands. For nothing he could start crying like a child. At least he didn't shame himself by doing that. "Oh God," he said again. Brit sat down beside him and put his arm around his shoulders.

"Damn, Arlis. Come on and tell me what's wrong, boy. Tell me everything and maybe I can help."

"Those three thieving sons of bitches took my money. All the money I had to fix *The Reaper.*"

"Jesus. Did you see them?"

"No. But I know they did it."

"How?"

"Because I just do," Arlis shouted. He was sorry he shouted at Brit. "I got a feeling. They were up here trying to rough Wanda. Hell. I just know it's them. It's got to be them, dammit. And there's no way to prove it or do anything about it."

Brit waited a little before he spoke, and then he said timidly: "You got to be sensible, Arlis. There's over two dozen squatters around here. Anyone of them could of done it."

"Hell, Brit. I know it was them. I got a feeling in my guts that they did it. If you'd seen them the way I did you'd know." Arlis knew God was punishing him.

"Damn!" He struck his fist on the side of the shed. It was bad enough being robbed, he didn't want to start in with foolishness about God. To his inner self he sounded like Preacher. It made him sick. He boiled hot until at last there was nothing else he could feel about any of it. The great anger all flowed out of him and left only a flat sense of despair. His shoulders slumped. "I'm finished, Brit. There's not a bloody thing in the world left for me to do but start all over."

Brit didn't say anything, letting the silence build, then he said, "There's something you can do, Arlis. You don't want to do it but it's something. If we do it right maybe you can get back at Treat somehow, whether he took your money or not. We'll think on that part. Me and you. If you want to do this thing you can make twice the money you lost and maybe get Treat too. Come on. You got to. I'll help you. What do you say?"

Arlis looked up. He couldn't read Brit's face because the sun shone right in back of his head. Poor old lame Brit just helping to get himself betrayed. He didn't need to be led into it. Hell. He'd lead himself. Arlis saw how fate had ahold of them both now and pulled them right along.

"Okay," Arlis said. He'd become too desperate to hate himself anymore. "A person's got to do what he has to, doesn't he?"

21

"Well?" Jewel Claire stood with his thumbs hitched into his belt. Brit waited beside him, expectantly, looking at Arlis.

"All right," Arlis said. "Count me in."

"Good. Good." Jewel rubbed his hands together. "Let's have a look at the boat." The three of them stepped off the wharf and onto the deck of *The Reaper*. Jewel examined everything carefully. "She's not very finished, is she?"

"She's as finished as she needs to be for what you got in

mind," Arlis said. They looked into the dark cargo hold that made up the only superstructure on deck. Just the high lip of the scuttle and a hatch grating that hinged over the opening. A ladder went into the hold. Below it was all open except for the stanchions that held the deck beams.

"Plenty of room, anyhow," Jewel said. "You got only the mainsail. No jib or top?"

"You knew that."

"Mmmmm. Too bad."

"This isn't any race. If the federal men want to take us they're going to do it. What's the difference?"

"None. I guess there's no hurry. We'll make Miami in a couple of days. The current of the Gulf Stream is with us," Jewel said. "My buyer there keeps an eye on the traffic and don't worry about the federal men, Arlis. Miami's a wide-open town."

"I hope so," Arlis said.

"Trust me, son," said Mr. Jewel. "Hell, this is the easiest money any of us'll ever make. You'll see. And that's only the start. We're going to make something grand out of this island."

"Let's just worry about getting the load to Miami, Mr. Jewel."

Jewel put on a look of contempt.

"All right," he said. "Treat went into Key West to get the shipment lined up."

"You didn't give him any money, I hope," Arlis said.

"Lord, do you think I'm some kind of fool? I don't trust that little snake any more than you do. This is all strictly cash-on-delivery. It's up to him to get it here. We take care of getting it to Miami."

"He's a crook," Arlis said.

"But we got a common interest. We got three thousand and he's got three thousand. I made him show me his money."

"None of it was in twenty-dollar gold pieces, was it?" Arlis asked bitterly.

"As a matter of fact, no. Now, dammit, you put that score aside for now. Like I say, we got a common interest and we can make a good profit on it. When we get to Miami and get paid off you can do what you like with those three. But we get to Miami first. You got to understand that, Arlis." Jewel spoke purposefully.

"We'll get to Miami," Arlis said.

"Fine. Day after tomorrow we all go and anchor inside the reef after dark. Unless there's a change in plan the liquor boat will meet us then. We pay for the goods when they're aboard *The Reaper* and not before. That way everyone's protected." Jewel lightened all at once. "Hell." He stood between Brit and Arlis and put a hand on each of their shoulders. "This is going to be a piece of cake. Trust me."

It's one bad thing following another, Arlis thought. It just gets worse. He waited dumbly for JoAnna to speak.

She tried. It showed there in her face and eyes, trying to get out. Arlis didn't want to help her. Finally he had to. JoAnna looked ready to break all apart if he didn't.

"I guess I expected it," he said. "We both knew it all the time, didn't we?" He spoke dryly. Things had turned in a full circle and he stood on the outside now.

"We can't destroy him for ourselves." Jo's eyes were cast down. Arlis noticed how fine and long her lashes were.

"No."

"Arlis. He's so weak. And we're strong. Aren't we strong? He's all ruined inside. I don't think either of us could finish the job on him and then live with ourselves, could we?"

"No. I suppose not. Not together. I might be able to do it myself but I don't think we could do it to him together like this. It would always be there between us, how we finished him off. It would be a terrible thing."

JoAnna sat on a piece of driftwood. The wind from the Gulf Stream came across the harbor and lifted the ends of her close-cropped hair. She looked very beautiful. Arlis thought perhaps it surprised her that he didn't argue. She'd been ready to argue for what they each knew to be right. The need for that gone, JoAnna appeared utterly crushed by the choice they'd made.

"And us?" Her lashes caught the sunlight. They reminded Arlis of the fine neck feathers of a dove, the way they were trimmed in a faint iridescence.

"We'll live. We'll try to be close." Arlis kept his voice flat and steady.

"Because we're strong, aren't we?" JoAnna clasped her knees and held them tightly to her body. "Tell me we're strong, darling."

Arlis couldn't tell her that.

"Oh Arlis. I'll love you forever." She rested her head on her knees and wept. "Forgive me for this."

"There's nothing to forgive, Jo. You can't fault life for the way it turns out."

She looked up at him. She'd broken up in spite of everything. The trouble is, Arlis thought, is that she looks so damned beautiful even when she cries. He waited until she put her head back down, and then walked up the beach toward his house.

Rain fell sporadically. The drops came down hard and fresh but far apart in the dryness, kicking up dead grass at the side of the path like bullets. Arlis saw them all waiting for him on deck, huddled together in a gray knot. Let them wait, he thought. He walked out on the planking of the dock. It was still light enough to see the tide swirling around the piles and ebbing out the harbor mouth. The tide will have to move us out, Arlis thought. There's no wind until we get beyond the lee of the island.

"Come on, Cap," Treat said. "We ain't got all night."

Arlis could just see the split-mouth grin cut across his face. He lifted the forward spring line off its cleat and threw it aboard.

"Brit. Cast off forward. Jewel. Untie the stern line." Arlis saw JoAnna standing next to Brit in the twilight. "You better get ashore, Jo."

"Now just a second," Treat said. "We going to need every hand we can get to offload out there. We got to move fast. That liquor boat don't want to hang around forever, cracker boy."

Arlis stepped aboard. He felt the weight of the revolver in his pocket. He came up and stood very close in front of Treat.

"You call me cracker boy one more time and I'm going to kill you." Treat made no answer. His colorless eyes stared through Arlis. Arlis grabbed him by the front. of the jacket. "You hear me?"

"I hear you." Arlis let him go.

"Please, Arlis," Jo said. "I want to come. It's all right."

"We need her, Arlis," Jewel said.

Arlis looked around at what he could see of their faces. The old feeling that he'd lost control haunted him and he told himself it didn't matter.

"Suit yourselves. Come on, let's get the lines off."

The Reaper allowed herself to be gently drawn along on the tide. They moved slowly until the harbor mouth narrowed. There the water went faster through the bottleneck, spitting them into the lagoon. Arlis had the men haul up the big gaffed mainsail and they caught enough breeze to take them to the edge of the reef about a mile from shore. The night closed fully on them and Treat lit a small red lantern and tied it to the forestay.

"Okay, Cap. You can drop your hook here. The liquor boat said she'd come through the reef where it'd be calm enough to unload. We got plenty of water under us? That liquor boat don't want to hit, you know."

"We got thirty feet," Arlis said. He thought about jumping Treat right then but he figured it would be better to wait. It was Treat's contact on the liquor boat. Thinking about jumping the bastard gave Arlis a small pleasure. It was all the pleasure he had now. In the feeble light he saw Brit standing close to Jo.

"Brit," Arlis said. "Go throw the small anchor off. Let out about a hundred and fifty feet of line. That ought to hold us against the tide. It's got another hour to run." Brit went forward.

Arlis stared for a long time at Jo's outline where she leaned against the rail. He could not be sure if she looked at him or not. The anchor splashed overboard and Arlis untied the main halyard from its pin and let the sail down. He and Jewel caught it and bunched it up between the gaff and boom, tying it loosely. Arlis got Indian to lift the boom on his back and set it into the crutch astern, so they could walk the deck without stooping beneath it. The rain began falling heavily.

"Oh swell," Treat said. He went to the mouth of the cargo hold. "Might as well get out of it. Indian, you stay up here and watch for that liquor boat, you hear?"

"Shit."

"You do like I say."

Indian shuffled forward and sat where the bulwark offered a little protection from the rain. Riff had already gone down the ladder to the hold. Jewel and Brit followed. Arlis helped Jo.

"You keep your damned eyes open," Treat said to Indian and went down. Arlis watched the miserable form of Indian sitting in the rain, then he held the hatch coaming and lowered himself into the hold.

Jewel lit the gimbal-mounted lamp that hung from the deck stanchion. *The Reaper* had a twelve-foot beam completely clear of any compartments. It looked quite large. Arlis could see both bulkheads to the sides but the circle of light would not fully penetrate the shadows fore and aft.

Rain splashed through the hatch grating. Everyone found a dry seat along the bulkheads. JoAnna and Brit sat beside Jewel Claire. Treat and Riff took a place opposite them. Arlis remained standing beside the stanchion post that supported the deck above their heads. He rested his foot on the small water keg. No one spoke except Brit to JoAnna and he spoke quietly, his voice only a murmur. The rain rattled on the deck, turning into a din as the squall passed overhead.

The squall brought a slight chill. Arlis pulled his jacket closer to his body. Considering everything that's happened, he thought, I should have pulled out of this. Told Jewel to get someone else. I hate like hell risking the boat. The great need for it is gone. I should have hauled her into the shed and gone back to sea. In six months I could make the money to fit *The Reaper* out. But then I wouldn't have the chance to nail that bastard Treat. The first time I wanted to do this for JoAnna and me and the boy. Now it's for revenge. That's a bad reason to have for doing anything but it's all the reason I got. It's funny, I haven't even thought about the five hundred. Just stinking revenge. What if Treat didn't steal from me like Brit said? What if it was somebody else? If that's what happened I got no reason for doing anything.

The squall passed over but the rain still pattered gently. The air became heavy, smelling of smoke from the lamp.

"When's that liquor boat coming, Treat?" said Jewel.

"Soon." He got up and came over to where Jewel sat with Brit and Jo. "I think we might as well get our accounting done up." Arlis saw Brit shift around. Treat talked overly polite and snotty. "Captain, why don't you step over here and see this so everybody knows I ain't cheating?"

Arlis left the stanchion post and walked to where Treat stood facing the others. Riff stayed seated, hunched up in the folds of his coat. Treat looked at them all with half a sneer. He tossed a packet of greasy bills at Jewel's feet.

"Count it out, Jewel, so the captain here can see how I come up with my part."

Jewel counted the money, thumbing through it rapidly and rearranging it in a neat pile.

"Well, It's all here, Treat," Jewel said. "I didn't never doubt you." He reached into his pocket. "And here's mine." Jewel laid out fifteen one-hundred-dollar bills next to Treat's pile. "Brit. Ante up." Brit shifted nervously again and took a wad of small bills from his jacket. Jewel picked them up and counted. He looked up at Brit. "There's only a grand here, Brit. Where's the rest?"

"I got it. Ashore." His glance moved around from one to the other of them. "I want to see the liquor boat first."

"What the fuck you talking about 'ashore'?" yelled Treat. "We're out here in the goddam water."

"I can row in and get it. I want to see that liquor boat first." Sweat stood in little bumps on Brit's forehead.

"This isn't what we said, Brit." Mr. Jewel's face got all clouded.

"Yeah," said Treat. "What the hell you trying to pull on me?"

"He said he'd get it." Arlis directed himself to Treat, wanting to bully him. "He'll get it when the liquor boat shows. I don't trust you for shit."

Treat looked at all of them as if he were struggling inwardly. The atmosphere turned thick and electric. Arlis tensed.

"Oh," Treat said gently. His eyes moved around the hold. "Oh that's it. So you're figuring to pull one on me."

"No," said Jewel. "It's a misunderstanding."

"You won't misunderstand this." Treat jumped back. At the same instant the Mauser appeared. Arlis dropped his hand to his pocket just as Treat pointed the pistol at his head. "Don't do it. cracker boy." His eyes had become small and bright as pieces of cut glass. "Riff! Get over here." Riff scrambled over, trying to look tough. "See what cracker boy's got in his pocket." Riff searched Arlis and withdrew the revolver.

"Well, well, well," said Treat. "Thought you'd really suck us in." He looked at the revolver, then at Arlis. With all his strength he slashed the barrel of the Mauser across Arlis's face. The force of the blow knocked him into the bulkhead.

"Arlis!" Jo screamed. She threw herself on him, crying. Arlis tasted blood in his mouth.

"Wait. Now just wait," cried Jewel. His voice trembled. "This is all a mistake. Nobody's pulling anything, Treat. We'll get everything straightened out. Brit can go get the money right now, can't you, Brit?"

"Yes." Brit sounded choked.

"Hell." Jewel tried to make out like everything was just fine. "We're all right. Just a misunderstanding. We got time. The liquor boat's not here. We got plenty of time. Brit, get your ass in that dinghy and go ashore for your money right now. What in hell's wrong with you anyway?" Jewel tittered foolishly.

"Shut your fat mouth," Treat said. "Get over there against the bulkhead. All of you. Stand up and get over there."

"Now Treat. Wait," Jewel whined.

"We'll get the damned money. The liquor boat's coming. We got to do our business."

"We're doing our business, Fatty. Our business is done."

"But the liquor boat."

"Only liquor boat is the one in your head. Now all of you get over to the bulkhead."

Arlis pulled himself to his feet, ignoring the blood that dripped down his coat. Jewel got up, looking like a trapped rat.

"You too, girlie," Treat said. Jo stayed close to Arlis. "Riff. Pat them down. Take whatever they got." Riff patted the men down. He found some more bills in Jewel's pocket. "Pat the girl down too," Treat grinned. "Pat her down good." Riff stood in front of JoAnna. Treat stepped close to Arlis and pressed the gun to his temple. "Go on, Riff. See if she's got anything on her."

Riff ran his hands over Jo's body. Arlis watched her stiffen as the fumbling hands lingered on her breasts and squeezed. Treat grinned more widely and nodded. Riff slipped his hands under Jo's dress. Arlis felt the cold steel of the gun against his skin.

"What's the matter, cracker boy?" Treat whispered.

Jo closed her eyes. She shuddered visibly when Riff touched her. Brit looked at the space on the deck between his feet. Arlis thought he was weeping.

"They're all clean, Treat. Even the bitch. She's nice and clean."

Treat snickered. "Well, that's fine. You all figured to fool me and you the ones to get fooled. You done got fooled by the oldest trick in the book." He laughed again. "Let's go up on deck. Riff, you take cracker boy's gun and go up first. Then cracker boy and the cripple can follow." He pushed Brit forward. Brit stumbled, not able to raise his eyes. "Fatty and the girl's going to be our guests for a while. They stay."

"No," Arlis said.

Treat struck him again savagely. Little lights sparkled in front of his eyes before he could see again. Treat studied him over the muzzle of the gun.

"I don't want to kill you, cracker boy. Not nearly as bad as you want to kill me. But I will if you make me. Me and my boys are going on up to Miami. Now you might get your boat back and you might not. But if there's any trouble or if there's any law waiting for us, you're damn sure not going to get Fatty and the girl back. I'll put them over the side wearing chains. You better understand that good."

"Just do like he says, Arlis," Jewel whimpered.

"That's right, cracker boy. Do like I say. Now go on up that ladder."

Arlis looked at JoAnna one more time. The light was gone from her eyes. She stared into nothing. Brit went up ahead of Arlis. Treat pushed Arlis in front of him.

Brit stood with Arlis at the rail. Arlis saw Indian still huddled against the bulwark in the light of the lantern. A small illumination rose from the mouth of the cargo hold where Jewel and JoAnna were prisoners. Treat and Riff held the pistols. Arlis would not permit the sense of utter hopelessness to settle on him. He kept thinking. It kept him from rushing Treat and throwing his life away on nothing.

"I hope you boys can swim good," Treat said. Neither Brit nor Arlis answered. "You'll get over it. The girl and Fatty'll get back. If you behave. Now, you lost your boat and your money. You try anything at all and you'll lose Fatty and that girl. You understand that, Brit?"

"Please don't hurt her, Treat."

"I asked you if you understood that."

"Yes," Brit whispered.

"Good. Now jump."

Brit made a tortured sound deep in his throat.

"Go on," Treat purred. Brit paused, then jumped feet first. They heard him hit the water.

"Now, how 'bout you, cracker boy? You understood everything I said? I know you real interested in keeping that little gal safe."

Arlis stared at Treat's face, at the filthy little beads of saliva trapped in the corners of his mouth. Arlis let the image burn itself into his brain.

"Fuck you, Treat." Treat shoved him hard over the rail. Arlis fell and the water closed over him.

When he came up Arlis saw Brit swimming ahead of him. The cold water shocked his brain and made it work. He forced himself to study how the boat lay at anchor before he swam off. It seemed to be turned by the breeze rather than the force of the water, meaning the tide had begun to go slack. It would be hard to swim against a running tide. They were lucky. The thought touched the bitterest humor in Arlis, almost making him physically ill. The worst of everything had happened; at least they wouldn't drown. Arlis struck out in the direction of Brit and the shore.

From the boat Arlis heard the sound of the mainsail being raised. Hoops clattered and the halyard squealed through the blocks. Arlis kicked off his shoes and got out of his coat. He made himself concentrate on slow easy strokes and did not permit his mind to stray from the task of getting into shore. When he got to shore he could begin a plan to retrieve what he'd lost. There were a couple of things in his favor. For now he only needed to keep swimming. He looked back to see *The Reaper*, her one sail rising like a black fin, moving away from him. Arlis then blotted it from his mind.

He overtook Brit. Brit swam tiredly, causing Arlis to slow his rhythm to stay abreast of him. He did not like the short choppy strokes Brit made. The sound of his breathing came clearly over the water that separated them and Arlis heard him swallow and cough.

"Brit. Brit. You all right?"

"Yeah." He coughed again. Arlis tried to measure the distance to the beach.

"Come on, give me your arm. We can rest."

"No. I'm okay." He chopped the water badly, just keeping afloat.

"You got to rest, Brit. You're not moving anywhere. Let me

get ahold of you."

"Let me be, goddammit," Brit choked.

"You better let me help you now while you still can."

Brit swam doggedly on. Arlis waited until he heard him swallow another good mouthful.

"You'll drown, you fool."

"I'll drown if I want to." He went head under and came up sputtering. "Let me alone." He threw up both his arms, going down and not coming up.

Arlis hurried to where the disturbance still boiled the top of the water and groped as far down as he could reach. He felt the top of Brit's head and grasped his hair, pulling him to the surface, Brit came up thrashing and clawing.

"Let me alone," he screamed. "You fucking bastard, let me alone." Arlis socked him hard on the side of the face and Brit floated still as a rag. Arlis held him up by the collar of his jacket. They didn't have far to go, It might be all right if he took it slow and steady. Arlis could see the shore well. The tide had carried them up a few hundred yards from the point of land at the harbor entrance. Trailing Brit behind him, Arlis struggled for the white line of the beach.

Brit dragged on him terribly. Arlis locked one arm under his chin and used the other in a feeble breaststroke. At last when he rested, he felt his feet touch bottom. Only then would he admit to himself how close they'd come to not making it at all. Still towing Brit, he walked up the sloping bottom until he got to the dry sand of the beach and collapsed.

When he could, Arlis watched *The Reaper* at sea becoming obscured in the dark. For some reason Treat had not bothered to remove the red lantern on the forestay. The light of it scorched Arlis like a live coal. He'd lost everything. The enormity of it was too great and too horrible to accept. Even as he fought for his breath he knew he'd better not think of it all at once or it might kill him.

Brit began choking and gagging where he lay. Arlis rolled him onto his belly and grabbed him by the belt and seat of the pants. He flopped him up and down a couple of times, then raised his body into the air. Sea water ran out of Brit's stomach as he retched and groaned. Finally Arlis let him down, listening to be sure his friend breathed all right. Arlis rested from the effort before he forced himself to his feet. He pulled Brit from the sand and bent so he could get him across his shoulder. Brit retched once more and Arlis felt the hot bile running down his back. He listened again to make sure Brit's lungs worked, then began walking inland to the footpath that led along the railroad tracks to the coconut grove.

It's wonderful how when you start doing anything it's easier than you thought, Arlis said to himself. It's strange. Arlis felt light-headed, almost drunk. Brit rode on his back like a bundle of sticks. He was so heavy in the water and now he's like carrying nothing. Just keep one foot going in front of the other like they taught you in the army. It's easy. Arlis thought some more: I lost everything important. JoAnna, the boat, my money. Please God. Help me get them back. JoAnna, JoAnna. God, help me get just her back. You can keep everything else. How about that for a deal?

Arlis felt himself weeping. If it weren't for carrying Brit and thinking of putting one foot in front of the other he might sit at the side of the path and become hysterical. He was glad of Brit's weight and his moving feet. They allowed him to think and plan only a little ahead, being careful to include all the important details. He moved his ideas just as he advanced his feet toward the light of the cottage in the coconut grove. He still wept but he could do that as long as he moved. One foot after the other, one small idea before the next. Arlis fell onto the porch, scraping his chin hard against the wood. Brit lay across the steps like a corpse.

"What in heaven's name going on out here?" Uncle Jake held the lamp high over his head. Arlis looked at him upside down. Aunt Eleuthera stood behind him. "Arlis. I thought you was going to Miami in the boat. You drunk, boy?" Uncle Jake knelt and stared at his face. "Who been beatin' on you, son?"

Arlis pushed himself up and managed to sit. His arms and legs had turned to jelly.

"We got robbed, Uncle Jake. Let's get Brit into the house. He's half drowned."

"Great God."

Arlis pulled himself up by the porch railing. He held it until things quit spinning. He felt Aunt Eleuthera's strong arm around him, holding him into her fat warm bosom.

Arlis could walk by himself. Jake and Aunt Eleuthera dragged Brit inside and muscled him onto the horsehair couch. Arlis leaned on the sideboard and drank some rum straight from the bottle. It made the blood ring in his ears. All he could do was rest there, watching Aunt Eleuthera and Uncle Jake fussing over Brit. In the lamplight they took on the same texture and appearance as performers in the stage plays Arlis had seen in Europe. The front room of his own house seemed foreign to him. His body ached so badly it might have belonged to someone else.

Aunt Eleuthera pulled the soaking jacket off Brit and placed a cushion behind his head. He looked quite dead in the yellow glare from the lamp. Aunt Eleuthera untied Brit's right brogan and tugged at it. She gave it a hard yank and when it finally popped off a shower of gold coins sprayed out of the toe. There was poor Brit's half a foot wrapped in a dirty white sock and the floor littered with gold coins.

Arlis put the bottle down and bent at the knee. He picked up one twenty-dollar gold piece, then another and another and another. He straightened, holding the coins tightly in his fist. Then he jumped on the unconscious form of Brit, grasping his throat and squeezing with all his remaining strength. Aunt Eleuthera and Uncle Jake kept a stunned silence for less than a second.

"Quit! Quit that," yelled Jake. His eyes bugged out big as saucers.

"You crazy, boy. Stop!" Aunt Eleuthera danced around the couch with her hands in her hair before she got him in a bear hug, while Uncle Jake pried his fingers from Brit's throat. Arlis held on until at last, together, Jake and Eleuthera tore him away, causing all three of them to fall onto the floor. Aunt Eleuthera's fatness pinned Arlis between the floor and the wall. She wouldn't move. She'd knocked the breath right out of him.

"What's the matter with you, fool? What's the matter with you?" she kept saying. Uncle Jake held Arlis's wrist with both hands. "What's the matter with you, fool boy?"

Arlis opened his clenched fist. In his palm lay three twenty-dollar coins and a medal with a ring soldered on it. The face of the medal read: "Capt. Arlis Bennington, Confederate States Navy." Arlis let the coins and the medal fall from his fingers. The other side said: "For Valor 1864." Aunt Eleuthera rolled off him. Arlis pointed to the medal until he got his breath back.

"That there's what's wrong with me," he said. "That."

Arlis hung two lanterns over the workbench in the boat shed. By their light he carefully unwrapped Papadad's old ten-gauge. He let himself see it one more time as a magnificent fowling piece. The barrel grew so wonderfully long and straight-blue in the light. It had a scalloped ridge that ran up the middle of it for strength. Arlis studied the deep grain of the polished walnut stock. On the bottom side of the stock near the butt plate a sterling-silver button had been set in the wood and bore Papadad's initials. They surely didn't make shotguns like this anymore.

With jerky movements Arlis wrapped a rag around the wooden grip forward of the trigger and clamped the gun in the bench vise. Looking only at the spot where he worked, he took a hacksaw and began cutting the barrel of the gun. The steel was tough, but when he got through the barrel was shortened to about thirteen inches. With a medium-toothed bow saw Arlis followed the natural line of the stock, cutting it away to resemble the handle of a pistol. With a rasp he shaved off the rough edges. Arlis removed the weapon from the vise and examined it. It would do the job.

Arlis ladled a double measure of powder into each barrel. He thought about putting in a little extra, then decided against it. He didn't want it to blow up in his face. From a box he selected a small handful of nuts and bolts. These he dropped in on top of the charges and packed them home with wadding. Though it was heavy, he could handle the gun easily now with one hand. He secured it in waterproof canvas and tied the bundle with string, laying it in the straw basket with the other things he'd gotten together. After he'd finished Arlis felt a coolness settle upon him. It killed his emotion and let him see things quite clearly and efficiently. It was a marvelous feeling, like taking one drink of rum on an empty stomach.

Arlis worked with a set of parallel rulers and dividers on one of the navigational charts that were kept in the shed. He studied the islands and channels he knew so well. In the margin of the chart Arlis made his computations and entered the numbers in two boxes, one labeled *"Reaper"* and the other "me." He worked the figures through twice so there would be no mistake.

It took him two trips to carry all the gear to his old catboat. He sat on the gunwale and rested. While he did so he rechecked in his mind everything he'd put aboard.

Back at the house he ignored Brit where he lay on the couch. Brit's eyes were open and dark-rimmed.

"Aunt Eleuthera. I need you to help me. I want you to get some food together. Whatever you can. Get me enough for a couple of days. Uncle Jake can give me a hand filling demijohns from the cistern."

"You going after them?" asked Jake. Aunt Eleuthera was walking to the pantry.

"Yes," Arlis said.

"Then pack some food for me too, Aunt Eleuthera," Brit said. He threw the blanket off his legs and put his feet on the floor.

"You're staying. You're no good to me."

"To hell with you too. What makes you think you got the only right to go? JoAnna's my wife. Maybe you forgot about that." He had an ugly way of talking and looking. Arlis wished he'd come right out and say what he had on his mind. He waited and looked at Brit. Brit only stared back, with his sickly face appearing all the worse in the lamplight.

"All right, Brit," Arlis said to him. "Get whatever you need. Go help Aunt Eleuthera with the food."

Aunt Eleuthera and Uncle Jake went with them down to the beach where the catboat lay on her bamboo rollers. Aunt Eleuthera said nothing. She'd kept mostly quiet the whole evening, looking terribly sad. She kissed Brit and Arlis on their foreheads as if they were children and stood by while Uncle Jake helped them launch the catboat into the gentle surf. They pushed out and rolled aboard.

Arlis took the forward pair of oars. He watched Brit's back as they worked in unison, rowing the boat out of the harbor against the tide that still flowed. Brit rowed like a machine. Arlis watched his narrow body going back and forth. He didn't slow down or miss a stroke until they got to the break in the reef.

"We're going to row along the reef until we get to the channel," Arlis said. "The tide'll carry us back under the trestle bridge and into the Gulf. Then we can put up the sail."

"That's your plan?"

"That's my plan."

"It's lousy."

"Look, you son of a bitch, that's what we're going to do. You don't like it, go do something yourself. What do you think we should do?"

Brit didn't say anything. They rowed until they came off the line of the reef to the channel. The catboat drifted in the current back past the island and under the trestle bridge. Brit rubbed his shoulder muscles.

"So what happens now?" Brit spoke at last. "They're going in the Stream and we're in the Gulf. We'll be separated from them all the way by the islands and the roadbed."

"The line of islands curves to the northeast. We're on the inside of the curve. That'll make up some of the distance over the long run. I figure we can average five knots. They can't do much more than four rigged the way they are. Even with two hours' lead we'll catch sight of them by first light. It'll be good to have the roadbed between us. We'll be hard to see clearly that way. With any luck we can pass them before noon. Once we pass them we got an advantage."

"How do you figure?"

"Because we can lay for them."

"Hell. When they see us they're going to know. Treat's going to know when he sees us."

"We'll worry about that when it happens. I got something figured out."

"You think you're really smart, don't you?" said Brit.

"What do you care what I think? Help me get the sails up."

Brit and Arlis stepped the mast and tightened down the stays. The wind picked them up nicely when Arlis raised the jib. He'd forgotten how good the boat sailed. Maybe they would catch *The Reaper* sooner than he'd first thought. The important thing was to get past them and not make them suspicious.

"What if they go out into the Stream? What if they're too far out to see in the morning?"

"They'll stay in close. They have to. There isn't any compass on board *The Reaper.*"

"That's pretty smart. Did you think of that?" Brit said. Arlis wondered if he was trying to be snotty.

"Yeah. I thought of that. That and a couple of other things. Why don't you get some sleep? It's going to be a long haul."

"I ain't tired," Brit said. Still, he got out of the seat and crawled forward, settling in the 'y' of the bow and resting his back against a basket of gear.

Arlis steadied the tiller under his armpit and tried to relax too. He told himself he ought to make Brit steer and get some rest for himself but he didn't want to talk to him anymore. He was sick of Brit. He could rest at the tiller or rest in the bow. What difference did it make?

The squall lines passed, letting the stars show beautifully even though the moon had gone over the horizon. If it was for any other reason the trip would be nice to make. The wind blew moderately off their beam. Arlis wondered how they would take it if the weather turned bad. There was a limit to what a person could take. Then he guessed they'd take whatever got dished out to them. They had to.

The sound of the water made a monotonous rush on the hull. Arlis shifted and checked the compass again. He wanted to do something to make himself not sleepy. His body ached plenty now. He ran the tip of his tongue over the split in his lip where Treat had hit him with the pistol. When he began to feel his eyes grow heavy he pushed his tongue into the cut and the pain reminded him to stay awake. He heard Brit move in the bow.

"I took your money for your own good," Brit said out of the darkness. "If I hadn't done it you wouldn't have wanted to make the trip, would you?" Arlis didn't answer him. He'd thought Brit was asleep. "It was for me too. And for Jo and the kid. I needed for something to happen. A success. I didn't think it would turn out like this." He laughed a little crazily. "Of course I didn't."

"Forget it," Arlis said. Brit stayed quiet. In a while Arlis thought sure he was asleep this time.

"Jewel said we'd get rich on the boom. If I didn't do something like what Jewel wanted to do with the land, what would happen to us there on the island? Nothing. I don't always want to be just a nothing. I mean, what do I got that amounts to anything?"

You got JoAnna and the boy, Arlis said to himself. To hell with Jewel and his land boom. He didn't say that out loud to Brit. Instead he said: "Why don't you quit worrying about it, Brit? Why don't you forget that part?"

"You really think you're a saint, don't you?" Brit said thickly. "Shit."

"I don't think anything. Go back to sleep for Chrissake."

"I mean, you never did anything you're ashamed of. You got nothing you wish you could hide." The note of accusation stung Arlis. It made him mad. If Brit knew about him and JoAnna, Arlis wanted to make him say it. Just suspecting, Brit infuriated him. He wanted to get it over with now.

"You useless bastard," Arlis shouted at him. "Just say what you got to say. Say it, then you can shut up and leave me alone."

Brit would not be moved. There was only the sound of the boat traveling through the water. Arlis imagined what must be going through his mind. He wondered what he would do if he was Brit. He shouldn't have taken him along. Now it was too late. The unreasonable assurance that Brit knew everything about him and JoAnna crept over him. Arlis thought how the knowledge might twist a man, and he thought of the shotgun lying next to Brit. He strained his eyes into the darkness, waiting for something terrible to happen.

Suddenly Brit began crying. "I'm sorry, Arlis. I wish I hadn't done it. I'm so damned sorry for everything. It was my fault. All of it." Brit's voice broke. "Please help me get JoAnna back. You're the only one to help me. I don't know what's wrong with me, treating you the way I been. If you don't help me, I'll never see her again."

What Brit said was so far from what Arlis had been expecting that he sat stunned. The sound of Brit's anguish came softly from the bow of the boat, overwhelming him. He tied the halyard around the tiller bar and made his way forward to where his friend lay. Brit had bunched himself up into a knot and was convulsed miserably, with his sobs like a child. In his heart Arlis knew that a man so injured and so simple in mind could never design to know what had been done secretly against him. Arlis knelt and put his arms around Brit. He held him and let him cry, feeling how well the boat sailed herself into the night.

Dawn came slowly. Arlis reached over the side to wet his hand and wiped his face with sea water. His eyes felt gritty and raw. Brit slept fitfully in the bow.

Arlis easily made out the black line of a railroad viaduct running over the channel. It disappeared into the long green mound of Windley Key. If he'd figured right *The Reaper* was a couple miles ahead of them and to the east on the other side of the island. The islands along here were small and close together.

As the light grew more intense the wind rose. It still came west northwest. Arlis brought the catboat in closer to land. It would be best to have one sure look at *The Reaper* then sail further out. From now on each time they passed an island and crossed a channel it might be possible for Treat to glimpse them. In these breaks in cover, only distance and the line of tracks would partially obscure them. The heavy concrete viaducts made an almost solid wall, but the trestles rode up on slender supports, making the boat more visible. Arlis wondered if their sail shape would stand out enough to arouse suspicion. He had a good plan but it had to wait just a few more hours before he could work it.

The catboat came closer to the north end of the island. The sun was up now, still masked by the hump of land. The break between Windley Key and the next island appeared, growing larger as their increasing nearness opened a wider angle of vision. Arlis found himself craning his neck as if he could stretch far enough to see around the small land mass. The edge of the new sun burned through the gap. Arlis shaded his eyes. He made himself look carefully, ignoring the brightness.

"Brit. Brit, get up! Look!"

Brit snapped into consciousness. He put both hands on the gunwale of the boat and raised his head over the side. Arlis was sure now that they could both see it. Before the ball of the sun, silhouetted so that it looked black, moved the gaffed mainsail of *The Reaper*. Arlis stared until the vision passed to the other side of the island and out of his sight.

"It's them," Brit whispered.

"Yes," Arlis put the tiller over, sailing closer to the wind and further away from the island. He wanted distance between them when they drew abreast of *The Reaper* in a couple of hours. If Treat had the sense to mark anything, Arlis hoped it would be the unusual pattern of their sail. If that was all he noticed it would help his plan.

Brit came back to Arlis with a demijohn and some corn

bread Aunt Eleuthera had wrapped in newspaper.

"Why don't you eat and go forward for a while, Arlis?" Brit looked as if the sleep hadn't done him much good. Maybe he hadn't slept at all.

"All right. Here." Arlis turned the tiller over to him. "Stay a ways offshore. Maybe two miles. Make sure I'm up halfway to noon." He looked at the sun, the rim of its top now rising over the trees.

"I'll wake you."

Arlis took some corn bread and a drink of water. He had a look at the trim of the sails, then began to go forward. "Arlis," Brit said.

"Yes?"

"Thanks."

He looked at his friend's worn face. "It's going to be all right, Brit. You got to believe that."

Arlis lay down on the planks. The jib sail and the side of the boat shaded him. It felt wonderful to unbend his legs. When he closed his eyes a clear vision of JoAnna came to him. They were children, sitting on the bluff where it rose up from the beach. JoAnna wore a white dress. Below them in the harbor, at Jewel Claire's wharf, the planters were loading pineapples. Big Spanish reds. Arlis and Jo could see the herons in the mangrove trees. Their forms were reflected in the salt pond. From the north Arlis heard a train whistle. It unsettled the birds and one by one they flinched, stretched their wings, and flew off, tucking their long thin legs beneath them. Arlis thought how peculiar it was because the tracks hadn't been built to the salt pond or even to Doctor's Arm yet. The whistle continued, becoming louder, and his vision faded until Arlis saw the deck planks where his head rested. The train kept blowing.

Arlis raised his head. To the northeast a black column of smoke advanced off Long Key. As he watched, the locomotive came out of the jungle and onto the viaduct, pulling her string of coaches and boxcars. She hooted long and loud.

Arlis looked astern. Far out to their right and a little behind was *The Reaper.* Her new canvas showed clean and fresh in the light beyond the rounded arches of the viaduct. The train passed slowly between them. Arlis saw Brit staring hard back at *The Reaper.*

"Do you think they see us?" Brit asked.

"Yes. But how can they know it's us? Look there." A sponging skiff sailed ahead of *The Reaper.* Arlis pointed to another catboat that approached them from the stern. "That's going to confuse them even if they have an idea we're following."

The train got over the concrete viaduct. Arlis and Brit watched *The Reaper.* They could see the top half of her mast over the tracks. Her hull appeared, then disappeared as she passed each arched opening in the viaduct where the channel flowed through.

"Well, if they see us, they better see us good, because we're going to be a different boat just as soon as we get behind Long Key."

"How do you mean?" Brit asked.

"I brought the old sail and mast. We'll rig ourselves differently. We won't be the same boat when we come out from there. What do you think?"

"I said you were smart, Arlis."

Arlis studied Brit. He could see Brit was trying to keep from thinking the worst. "I'll take the tiller for a while," Arlis said. "I had a good rest."

"You didn't sleep for long."

"I feel better," he said. "We'll change the sail in a bit."

Arlis took the tiller. Brit got back in the bow. From where he sat Arlis knew Brit could watch the sail on *The Reaper.* They couldn't see much of her hull now, just the top of her mast over the tracks. For Brit's sake he wished they'd hurry and get behind Long Key. He didn't think it was good for Brit to stare at *The Reaper.*

"Brit. Why don't you haul out the catboat sail and make sure it's ready to go? We got to get it up fast."

Brit slowly pulled out the old dirty-brown sail from beneath the bow. He untied it and refolded it carefully, making sure the gaff and the wooden mast hoops were secured onto the canvas. By the time he'd finished, the green ridge of the island stood between them and the image of *The Reaper.*

Arlis angled into shore. Brit dropped the sail and Arlis rolled over the side, standing in water to his knees. He cut the stays with his knife, and when they were free Brit lifted the mast from where it was stepped. He lay the mast on the gunwale and looked at Arlis.

"Go on," Arlis said. "Throw it over the side. Get rid of the canvas too. We don't have time to fool with it." Brit dumped it all overboard. Arlis watched the healthy-looking sailcloth floating with all its rigging for a moment. It made him think of JoAnna and Uncle Jake. Then he got back aboard and slipped the old mast in its shoe all the way to the bow. Brit had already strung the halyard through the pulley at the top of the mast. He worked now tying down the new shrouds to hold the mast up. Together they hauled up the patched leg-o'-mutton sail. They made one quick tack to get themselves offshore, then came about on the same course as before. When they sailed past the end of Long Key they had begun to leave *The Reaper* behind.

They could see her form distinctly for the brief time it took to cross the channel, then another small island blotted *The Reaper* out and Brit and Arlis sailed in silence.

By the time the sun reached its zenith, Arlis had turned the tiller back to Brit. He waited until they passed a wide channel and shinnied up the mast, *The Reaper* had fallen further away. Looking back on her, Arlis saw the leading edge of her sail rise above the hull like a dark blade. He slid down the mast and sat in the stern by Brit.

"What do you think about water, Brit?"

"Water?"

"Yes." Arlis smiled a little. Then he thought of JoAnna on *The Reaper* and quit smiling. "There's none aboard *The Reaper*. I didn't put any extra aboard." A look of slow comprehension came over Brit's face. "I opened the spigot on the keg when you said you had to go ashore for your money. I figured if Treat let you go you could always bring back some more water."

"And so you think they're going to stop."

"I think so, I'm counting on it. By this afternoon they'll have been almost twenty-four hours without a drink. What do you figure they'll do?"

"They don't have much choice." Brit scratched his stubbled face. "There's only one well until you get further north. It would be night by then. They have to stop on Elliot Key if they want water."

"They'll be there before sundown. If they want water that's the only place to get it. And we'll be waiting."

Brit finally said what they both didn't want to think about: "What if they got water somehow? What if they don't stop?"

"Then we just have to keep after them. We'll have to do like we did today until they stop and we can get at them."

Brit stayed on the tiller. Arlis sat in the shade of the sail and thought about Elliot Key. The early Spanish called all the keys Los Martires, the Martyrs, because, people said, their twisted forms were like tortured bodies. Elliot was one of the most twisted. Its thin form ran almost east to west in crooked angles, the railroad crossing it at one end. Near the center rose a small limestone formation with a shallow well at its base. A failed citrus plantation grew nearby, mostly overtaken by jungle. A footpath led across the island's width to the well. If they sailed around to the north side they could leave the boat and walk across. From there *The Reaper* would be in plain sight as she approached. Jewel would know where the well was. He would point it out. After that, Arlis figured he would have to wait and see what happened.

As the afternoon lengthened Arlis felt the tension growing in himself. He could see it in Brit. Twice more he climbed the mast and caught the hazy outline of *The Reaper's* mainsail.

Brit drew up a bucket of sea water from over the side and buried his face in it. Both of them were burned by the sun. In the distance they could see where the tracks crossed the west end of Elliot Key.

"We'll take the mast down to get under the trestle, Brit. We can put it up again and sail to where the path is."

Brit rinsed his face again, rubbing his skin vigorously, then drying himself with the sleeve of his shirt. Arlis continued: "When we cross the island we can look out and see *The Reaper* coming. It ought to take them a couple of hours to reach us, right around sunset. One or two of them will row in for the water. Better if it's two. If all three come it would be perfect, but I think it will be just one. We'll take him. At dusk we'll go out in the dinghy. I sawed off the ten-gauge. With surprise and a little luck I think we can get the drop on the other two."

"Are you afraid, Arlis?" Brit's eyes were red and puffy. When he looked at Arlis the eyes seemed a little out of focus.

"Sure I'm afraid some. I hadn't thought of it yet. We won't need to think of that until the time comes."

"In the army. . . ," Brit began. "In the war, were you afraid then?"

"Yes. I was afraid sometimes. Sometimes more than others."

"That's funny. You don't look like the type now," Brit said conversationally. "I mean, you can never tell about anyone really, but you don't look the type. Old Poopy wasn't afraid at all but he got killed so fast. I saw it. I decided then I wanted to live. You want to live, don't you?"

"I think we all do."

"You know, I wasn't there in France very long. On our second day at the front the regiment was ordered to attack on line. I don't think we got a hundred yards out of the trench. They tore us all to bits. That's when Poopy got it. I set there in a ditch just watching him. It took him all night to die, laying in a damned hole half filled with water." He paused. "In the morning I took my rifle and shot my foot off." He waited again. "What I'm trying to say is, I'm a coward. I wanted you to know that." Brit closed his eyes. "Did you bring any rum? I need to have me a drink."

Arlis and Brit lay in the mangroves. They'd rubbed themselves with oil of citronella to repel the black swarms of mosquitoes that whined around their faces. *The Reaper* moved ponderously toward them. It was still too soon to tell whether she would come in for water or continue on. Arlis prayed Treat hadn't brought water with him somehow or found any that had collected from the rain. If they were forced to chase *The Reaper* another night and day in the open boat he didn't know how well either of them would hold up. He looked at Brit's face in the light reflected off the water from the afternoon sun. His skin raised itself in raw blisters and the dark circles around his eyes had grown deeper. Arlis handed him the pint flask and they each took a drink.

"It's going to take them an hour to get here, Brit. Let's go back to the well. We got to figure out some kind of plan." Arlis and Brit crawled out of the mangroves. A path led from the high-water mark up in the direction of the well. From the pile of driftwood left by the tide Arlis picked up two short lengths of lignum vitae root. He hefted them and gave one to Brit. They were hard as iron. "We'll use these for clubs if we have to." Brit just held his. He looked as if his flesh had been dusted with gray powder. "Come on." Arlis led the way up the path to the well.

The path was fairly defined. Sponge fishermen used the well from time to time. The path ran about fifty yards in from shore, gradually rising several feet above sea level. The jungle grew thick around them, strangling the remnants of the old lime grove. The path widened at the base of the rise into a small clearing. In the center some forgotten person had stacked a low wall of coral rock around the mouth of the Indian well. On a tree branch hung a rusty bucket and coil of line.

Arlis unwrapped the shotgun from the waterproof canvas. He put the hammers on half-cock and inserted the percussion caps.

"When we know they're coming for sure, you'll hide on that side of the clearing and I'll be on this side," Arlis said. "If it's all three of them, I'll drop Treat and Riff with the gun, and we'll get Indian between us. But I'm betting there's only going to be one or two coming ashore, so we can't use the gun no matter what. If it's one or two, whichever of us they face away from when they draw the water has to rush with the club. We can't let there be any noise. You think you can do it?" Arlis thought Brit looked worse by the minute. His lips were white and he'd developed a slight tic. "Brit. You got to."

"Okay," Brit said. "If they face away from me, I'll rush them."

"Good. No noise. Hit them hard." Arlis looked at Brit. "We got to hit them hard the first time, all right?"

"Yes," Brit said. His eyelid danced spasmodically and stopped.

"Let's go back to the mangroves and wait. We'll know soon enough if we got to worry about anything or not."

The Reaper sailed slowly in the lighter breeze of late afternoon. Arlis and Brit watched her through the green mangrove leaves as she came. Up until almost the last moment they couldn't be sure if *The Reaper* would stop, then she angled in and turned sluggishly to port, gliding as close as she could to the island before the wind came over her bow. A figure in the bow dropped the anchor and at the same time the sail went down. Arlis felt the pressure of Brit's hand gripping his arm. Arlis stared hard at the boat, looking for JoAnna or Mr. Jewel. He only saw Riff and Indian. All the old terrible apprehensions began flooding over him, so that at last he had to forbid himself again to think beyond each simple problem as it came. Now he only had to wait to see who would row the dinghy ashore.

The dinghy trailed *The Reaper* on a line. Indian bent over and pulled it along the freshly painted side. Indian and Riff stood at the break in the railing. They seemed to argue; then Riff climbed into the dinghy and Indian handed him four gallon demijohns. Riff began rowing sloppily for the shore.

"Come on, Brit. Let's go back." Arlis pulled him away by the sleeve. At the path he nodded for him to go on in front. They ran up the path and stood for a moment at the well. Arlis handed Brit his club. "Remember. If he puts his back to you when he dips up the water, you got to rush him." Brit nodded, breathing heavily through his mouth. "Now go on. Hide yourself good." Arlis wished he'd say something. It would be a good sign. Brit didn't answer. He only shambled into the undergrowth. Arlis prayed Riff wouldn't face away from Brit. He was plenty worried about him. Brit was going fast. He'd seen men fall apart and that's the way they went, very quickly toward the end. Arlis wondered if Brit could hold on just for a while longer. He needed Brit. Arlis went to the other side of the clearing and crouched behind the trunk of a big sea-grape tree. The island became still save for the humming of insects and the faraway sighing sound that the ocean makes.

Riff wasn't long in coming. He walked up the path briskly, slapping at himself with one hand and carrying the tied-together demijohns in the other. Arlis knew the mosquitoes were eating him alive. Riff's stupid face was screwed up against the insects and he wore a large straw hat pulled over his ears. He looked around the clearing, not seeing the well at first. When he saw it he came and set the jugs down, peering a little cautiously over the stone rim as if he expected something dangerous to be down there. Riff took the bucket from the tree limb and dropped it into the well. Keeping his foot on the rope he pulled his hat off and swung it viciously through the air to drive away the mosquitoes. Arlis could see the black swarm around his body. Riff pulled up the bucket and squatted on his hams to fill the first demijohn.

Arlis gripped his club. Riff was turned not quite facing away from either him or Brit, but Arlis figured he'd better make the move rather than wait. Maybe Brit was in a little better position but Arlis knew he would have to be the one to do it. If you want someone dead, Arlis thought, you'd better be ready to kill him yourself. He made himself think of JoAnna and what the man squatting at the well had done to her. Arlis moved out quickly, close to the ground, each muscle of his body hardened to steel. For no reason Riff turned and looked up at the last instant of his life. His eyes became momentarily larger as Arlis brought the club down on his skull with both hands. Riff fell onto his face. Arlis watched the blood run in little rills from each of his ears. The gnats and mosquitoes swarmed in to feed. A small horror tried to grow inside himself but Arlis drove it away. Alive this man wanted to harm what he loved. Dead he would harm nothing. It was very simple like that.

Brit stood beside him, his club hanging out of his hand. A brown patch stained the seat of Riff's trousers where he'd messed himself. Arlis rolled the body over. Some blood came out of the nostrils too. The whites of Riff's eyes appeared beneath the lids. Arlis pressed his fingers under the collarbone. He didn't feel a pulse. He pulled Riff's jacket off. "See if he's got anything in his pockets, Brit. Maybe he's got one of the pistols."

"You better do it," Brit said. Arlis made himself stare very hard at Brit. "All right," Brit finally said. "I'll do it." He felt Riff's pockets and found nothing. Arlis hadn't thought he would.

"Get him by one of the arms," Arlis said. "We'll drag him back into the bush." Brit and Arlis dragged the body into the jungle. Near one of the old citrus trees they found a shallow depression in the ground. They placed Riff in it and covered him with coral rock. "The son of a bitch," Arlis said.

Back at the well Arlis picked up Riff's jacket and hat. He put them on.

"So what do you think?" he asked Brit. He had to get him talking. Brit shrugged. "Come on, goddammit. How do I look?" Arlis hated acting hard.

"Maybe you look a little like him," Brit said tiredly.

"Well, you better hope I look a lot like him." Arlis pulled the hat down closer to his ears and turned the collar of the jacket up. "Better?"

"I don't know, Arlis. Maybe that's better."

Arlis felt like shaking him. He went into the bushes where he'd been hiding and got the shotgun. "Grab the demijohns." He walked down the path to the water. He was getting worried sick about Brit. He heard Brit gather the demijohns and stumble after him.

The dusk came on rapidly. From behind the mangroves Arlis and Brit watched *The Reaper* swinging at her anchorage. One figure wandered on deck. It looked like Indian but it had gotten too dark to tell now.

"Brit," Arlis said. "Here. Have a drink." He gave him the flask. Brit drank. Arlis handed him the demijohn to wash it down. "Have another. Take a good one." Arlis watched Brit take a good swallow. Arlis drank what was left. He waited a few minutes for the rum to get working inside of Brit before he spoke. "Now listen, old Brit. I want you to take the gun and lie down in the bow of the dinghy. The sail's all piled up there. Get under the sail so you can just peek out. Have the gun ready."

Arlis thought. "Maybe you better not cock it all the way. It might go off by accident. But have it ready. When I get up alongside somebody'll be there. If it's Treat, kill him. You got that?" Brit nodded as if someone else were moving his head. "I think I can fool Indian. But Treat's the one to watch. You see him, shoot." Arlis waited. He wondered if he should slap Brit across the face. "If it's Treat I'll say his name. It might be too dark for you to tell. If you hear me say his name, give it to him." Arlis shoved the gun into Brit's hands. Brit's fingers were cold.

"Arlis. I don't know if I can do it."

"You got to. Think about JoAnna."

"I'm thinking about her. I want to do it. I don't want to screw up and get you killed. I don't want to get us all killed."

Arlis held him tightly by the shoulders. I wonder if he knows how scared I am, Arlis thought. He shook him gently just once. "Brit. You're going to do it. There's no doubt in my mind. You're going to do everything just fine." Arlis held him for a minute more, trying to calm his own fear. "Now let's go."

Brit got into the dinghy. Arlis covered him in the sail, then pushed out of the mangroves. The little boat moved into the open water. Arlis rowed, wondering if Treat saw him yet. What if Treat knew and just shot him while he sat in the boat with his back turned? Then I'd never know what hit me, Arlis thought. Even Riff saw what got him. Arlis glanced over his shoulder and lined up on *The Reaper.* He rowed hard. I got to not look sneaky, he thought. I got to act glad to get away from the mosquitoes and back aboard. Arlis tried to remember what Riff's voice sounded like. He wondered if he could fool them. He might fool Indian, but not Treat. Treat was smart and very dangerous. You better not forget that, cracker boy, he said to himself.

Arlis let the bow of the dinghy thump carelessly into *The Reaper's* side. In his right hand he held the lignum vitae club tucked up along his forearm out of sight. He stood up in the bow waiting. Indian appeared at the rail.

"Where you been?"

Arlis tossed the bowline so that it landed across Indian's face.

"Shit," he heard Indian say. Indian held the line, then knelt to tie it to a railing stanchion. Arlis had one hand on deck. He saw no one in the dimness but Indian. Indian knelt so close Arlis could hear him breathing.

"Where you been?" Indian asked again.

Arlis struck him across the temple and reached up just in time to break his fall.

"Get up quick, Brit," he whispered. Brit struggled out of the sail. "Help me."

Arlis and Brit eased Indian down into the dinghy. Arlis looked again over the deck. It was empty. Arlis pulled himself up and gave Brit his arm. They lay there, feeling the planking beneath them still warm from the sun. A light showed up from the cargo hold forward of the mast. Brit got into a crouch and, staying doubled over, made for it. Arlis followed. Carefully they looked down into the hold. The lamp burned feebly. Jewel Claire lay facing the bulkhead, his hands tied behind his back. JoAnna was faceup, her eyes closed. She had one leg bent and her arms were free. She looked like a doll someone had dropped. In the poor light Arlis saw her cheek was swollen. Her dress had been ripped open and there was blood on it.

"They killed her," Brit said out loud. He wouldn't take his eyes from the hold.

"No we didn't, crip," Treat said. He rose out of the darkness on the other side of the hatch coaming. He held the Mauser. Arlis felt ice form in his gut. "She's fine." Arlis and Brit were on their feet. Brit took a step back. "Don't go nowhere, boy." The light from the hold illuminated Treat's wedge of a face and flashed off the blue steel of the pistol. Treat's sliced mouth grinned. "Me and Riff just used her a little. The Indian's scared of women. He don't know what he missed." He stepped around the hatch coaming.

"You filthy pig," Brit said.

"Hell, Brit, what you saying? Your own pal cracker boy here's been piling her ever since he got on the island."

"I know that," Brit said stonily. The tone of his voice made Treat stop smiling. Arlis saw the muscles ripple across Brit's face. His eyes were flat and dull.

"What you got in your hand, boy?" Treat pointed, a small hesitancy in his voice.

"You got one chance to live, son of a bitch," Brit said slowly. "Give me your gun." The set of Brit's features stayed rigid. Treat failed in a laugh. He looked hard at Brit and the ten-gauge.

"You got to throw that thing down, boy. This here German gun'll put two holes in your wishbone before you can even pull the hammers back on that." He pointed again with the barrel of the Mauser. In the light from the hold Arlis could see Treat sweating. He swallowed, his sharp Adam's apple rising and falling in his throat. "Don't do nothing foolish, boy. You put that damned thing down. You make me kill you, I'm really going to fix your wife."

"I won't allow it," Brit said in the same voice. The pistol pointed at him, Treat took a step closer.

"What you say, cripple?"

"I won't allow it."

They all heard the two metallic clicks of the hammers going back. Arlis threw himself down. He saw Treat fire twice. The long tongues of flame connected to Brit's chest, knocking him into the mast. Brit slid to his knees, raising the shotgun. Treat fired once more, wildly, before both barrels of the ten-gauge went off together at the level of his abdomen. The force of the blast threw him across the deck and he crumpled into the railing. Treat squirmed and raised himself up a little. He put both hands where his guts used to be and started screaming with all the breath he had. Arlis crawled on his hands and knees and picked up the Mauser. Treat lay on his back, digging his fingers into the mess. Arlis could see close up how Treat had been hit. He'd been gutted like a spooned-out melon. An open cavity gaped from his navel to his hips. Treat got some more air and started screaming all over again. Arlis swung the edge of his hand down on Treat's throat. He felt something crunch and Treat quit screaming. He still made a rattling sound. Treat's little eyes glistened and he worked his mouth. The eyes stared at Arlis and the mouth kept up its hideous moving. Arlis prayed for him to die. It took a minute before the mouth made words.

"Cracker boy," it rasped. "Kill me."

Arlis forced the muzzle of the gun into Treat's mouth. He felt the sight blade hitting his teeth. The eyes kept staring. Arlis pulled the trigger, taking the top of Treat's head off.

Arlis had to stay on his hands and knees. He didn't think he was able to walk. He looked where Treat lay half over the side. Quite close to him, frozen like a child caught stealing, Indian crouched in the dinghy. He'd been trying to untie the line and get free. Arlis pointed the pistol between his eyes.

"Hail Mary full of grace, blessed art Thou among women and blessed is the fruit of Thy womb, Jesus. Holy Mary, Mother of God-"

"Shut up," said Arlis. "Shut up, you fool."

Indian knelt in the bow of the dinghy, his hands clasped around the railing stanchion where the line had been tied. His eyes were closed. He started whispering the prayer again:

"...pray for us sinners now and at the hour of our death.

Amen. Our Father Who art in heaven. .."

"Indian."

Indian opened one eye. Even by the light of the stars Arlis could see the stain of the birthmark across his face.

"Don't kill me, please. I didn't do nothing to the lady. I promise." Tears shined on his cheeks. "I swear to God." He shook violently.

"Get out of here," Arlis said. "Row around that island and you'll see the railroad tracks. Go north. If I ever see you again, that's when I'll kill you." Indian let go of the stanchion and slumped to the seat of the dinghy. Arlis finished untying it. He dropped the line and watched the stupid face of Indian drift into the dark.

Arlis walked to Brit. He still sat against the mast with the ten-gauge across his lap. Arlis took him by the shoulders and gently laid him down. For no reason he placed Brit's hands across his chest. They covered the wounds. He didn't fool with the eyes. They had closed themselves. Arlis looked at him lying there. He looked pretty good, like he was satisfied. Arlis placed Riff's jacket over the body so he wouldn't have to see it anymore. He hoped that wherever Brit was now he could maybe understand.

22

JoAnna and Arlis stood in the shade near the station house and watched the Pinkertons set fire to the shanty town on the other side of the tracks. A special train at the siding would take all the squatters north to Miami. Someone had even sent a federal marshal to see that it got done. The liquor business was being dried up on the east coast.

The few people who still legally lived in Doctor's Arm came to watch the Pinkertons turn the squatters out. Mr. Jewel Claire put his newspaper on an old fruit box and sat. He pushed his hat back and wiped his forehead with a handkerchief. The railroad official in charge of the burning kept glaring at him. He wore leather puttees and a righteous sunburned face.

"You ought to be put in jail, you know," said the railroad official. "The law caught up with your friend Clyde Seybold and I'll bet you're twice as guilty as him. You are. I just wish I had the proof. I'd like to see you all in jail." Jewel only shrugged. Since the night off Elliot Key an odd sereneness had come over him. It was difficult to say whether he'd lost or gained something in the experience. "It's a damned disgrace. A thieves' den on railroad property." The official looked at the burning shacks, then at the marshal for support and got none. "Christ. You people are pathetic." He surveyed the ragged group of settlers: Wanda, Jake and Eleuthera, Mr. Esquinaldo, and a couple of Cuban spongers. Preacher was absent. "The railroad brings you civilization and you behave like a pack of savages. This place got turned into a rum-smugglers' haven and you all knew it. Hell. You were part of it." Arlis got out of the shade and walked over to the official.

"Why don't you just get on with your business and leave us alone?"

The railroad official glanced at the marshal, who still remained silent, ignoring him. Arlis stood with his hands on his hips. Finally the official walked away a few steps in the direction of the burning shanties.

"The railroad's going to leave you alone for sure," he said. When no one answered, his face became redder under his sunburn. He shook a dimpled fist. "You were a bunch of no-account crackers before the railroad came and that's what you'll always be." He glared fiercely, then stomped away, his leather puttees flashing in the sunshine.

The marshal stood close to the settlers and looked after the retreating railroad official. The marshal wore an old-fashioned mustache and a battered hat. He reminded Arlis a little of Cap'n Ben.

"You all the folks that's left here?" the marshal asked no one.

"Just about," Arlis said.

"Well, that's not so bad. This ain't a bad place."

"It used to be better," said Arlis. "A lot better.

The marshal looked at Arlis, then at JoAnna. Little Arlis stood close to his mother, timid and curious at the same time, peering out at the marshal from beneath his unkempt blond hair. Sensing there was no danger, the child scampered down the embankment to play among the upturned boats on the shore.

"Fine-looking boy," the marshal said to Arlis. "He your son?"

"He's ours," JoAnna said so everyone could hear.

The marshal smiled a little absently as if remembering his own youth. He looked down at the harbor where *The Reaper* lay beside Jewel Claire's wharf.

The shantytown burned fully now, sending a tall column of gray smoke over the island. The Pinkertons stood at the train as the last squatters got aboard, some carrying little bundles, others with nothing at all. The train gave one whistle blast.

"So," the marshal said. He'd been staring away from the fire and down at *The Reaper*. "I guess they're ready to pull out." He faced Arlis. "There's nothing you need to tell me, is there?"

"No," Arlis said. "Nothing that would make any difference now."

"I suppose it's just as well," the marshal said. He held his hand out to Arlis. Arlis shook it. "Good luck, son. I 'spect things'll work out all right for you folks."

"I think they will, marshal."

The marshal gave a little wave and walked away to the train.

The engine blew again as the marshal and the last of the Pinkerton deputies swung themselves up. Steam gushed out of the boiler valves and the great wheels began to move. The black locomotive jerked against the cars and slowly pulled away from the siding. The settlers watched it pick up speed, moving past them. It went up the tracks to the bend, the engine disappearing first, pulling the cars behind. In the distance they heard the train hoot once more, then all they could see was the coal smoke. In a while that was gone too.

Jewel Claire shifted himself so he could pull out the newspaper he'd been sitting on. He shook it, letting it hang full-length in front of him.

"Land boom's finished in Miami," he said matter-of-factly. "The bank's are all failing. Dropping like flies. Hell of a thing. Hmmm."

"Looky there," interrupted Mr. Esquinaldo. "Here come Preacher."

They all gazed at the bluff. Shantytown blazed against the sky. Half running, half walking past all of it hobbled the awkward figure of Preacher, his coattails whipped up by the hot winds of the fire. It took him a full minute to reach them. He stood with his unwashed arms dangling out of his sleeves, trying to catch his breath.

"Mr. Jewel," he puffed. "Mr. Jewel. Where are those railroad men that were here?"

"They're gone, Preacher," Jewel said.

"When are they coming back? There's been a miracle."

"I don't think they're coming back."

"But there's been a miracle."

"What miracle you talking about, Preacher?"

"The Indian well. I went to the Indian well and there's water coming out of the limestone. It's a miracle from Almighty God." Preacher raised his hands and his cinder-blackened face to heaven.

"Hell," said Mr. Esquinaldo. "You leave a well set awhile. it'll come back. I could a told you that." He spat in the dust.

"Damn you filthy drunkard, it's a miracle!" shouted Preacher. He trembled, slowly lowering his hands. "We should tell the railroad people, Mr. Jewel."

Jewel Claire squinted into the dirty face of Preacher. "Tell the railroad people what?"

"That we got water again. Isn't that important?"

Jewel kept squinting. It was hard to say what thoughts he had.

"No," Jewel said. "I guess it's not important now. We don't need to tell anybody."

Preacher seemed stunned. He looked at Jewel and the others. One of the shacks on the bluff collapsed, and everyone stared toward the noise and swirl of hot sparks, forgetting Preacher. Preacher stood with his head cocked to one side, and when nothing else was said to him he finally walked sadly to the station and sat on the platform to watch the fire alone.

The fire took the rest of the afternoon to burn down. By the time shack town lay in a heap of embers, all the people had drifted away except for JoAnna, Arlis, and Jewel Claire.

Jewel rolled the newspaper into a cylinder and put it in his pocket. He stood up, not looking unhappy.

"I guess that's it," he said. "We tried, and wound up with nothing."

"No." JoAnna spoke up, doubt troubling her voice. "There is something." Her statement was more like a question.

"I'm trying real hard to see it, JoAnna." He laughed easily. "Well, I been wrong about lots of things before. Maybe if I keep working at it I can see something out of this mess." Jewel waved his hand at the blasted landscape.

"Try, Mr. Jewel," JoAnna said. One line furrowed the smoothness of her forehead.

"I'll try. I got plenty of time now." Jewel Claire walked down the embankment to the beach path that led to Castle Windy. Arlis and Jo watched his dumpy figure go along the sand. He didn't wear any shoes.

"Do you think we have something here, Arlis? Anything?" JoAnna faced Arlis squarely. "Or is that too much?" She put her hand into his. He felt all her sadness and happiness and uncertainty in the touch.

"I don't know, JoAnna." A queer sense of being unable to express himself in words, even to this woman he loved, seized Arlis violently and let him go like the fist of God. He looked from her expectant face to the blackened desolation around them. JoAnna's eyes pleaded with him in silence. She's looking to me for an answer, Arlis thought. She's got no one else to look to and I owe it to her. I owe it to myself. And to the boy too. I need to work on finding some kind of sense out of all this, out of what's happened to our lives.

Arlis took her by the shoulders. He tried to hold her gently but he could feel the strength pulsing, being generated in his heart and moving to the tips of his fingers as the seeds of thoughts foreign to him began finding life within his being.

"Get the child and go to the house," he told her. He saw that she meant to speak and placed his fingertips lightly upon her lips. "Wait for me. Will you do that?" JoAnna nodded, her eyes wide with the energy she felt coming from his flesh and the fear of what neither of them yet understood.

Arlis turned abruptly from her, lest contemplating her might deter him from the task he'd set for himself. The task had no name, only a vague shape that began to define itself as Arlis trudged away from JoAnna.

He crossed the gashed line of the railbed, noting its parallel lines of steel running north and south, not breaking his stride. Walking more quickly now, he made his way up the rutted face of the bluff. At the Indian well he paused. On the gouged side of the limestone, a sad trickle of water seeped sluggishly downward, darkening the bleached marl at the base.

On each side of the pathway, piles of smoldering shanties allowed wisps of smoke to curl upward into the heated air. Twisted sheets of corrugated roofing metal crackled as they cooled, turning from red to a flat, lifeless black. Arlis kept his head low, thrust forward like a sensor. He looked furtively left and right over the ruins.

He quickened his march, trotting several feet, then slowed before he once again doubled his pace to get beyond the shanties.

In their enthusiasm the railroad detectives had fired the old schoolhouse. They'd torched the downwind side, burning out the supports, so that the sagging building collapsed on itself, smothering the flames. The weathered boards smoldered at their edges. As if by one more miracle of that day, a portion of Preacher's handwritten admonition survived on the flattened wall. It said: "…THE END…" The rest of the message was charred to ash. Arlis gazed at the letters for a long while before he continued the small walk higher up the hill to the cemetery.

In the several weeks they'd been back on the island, Arlis had put a crude ironwood post in the ground for Brit. They'd buried him on Elliot Key, but Arlis wanted a marker for him here. It had been his home. He'd cut one for Poopy too.

He looked at the other stakes, lopsided with neglect, whitened by the sun. Mommer's stone still looked good. Some of the ash from the burning had settled on it and Arlis wiped it off with his hands so he could read the name and date Mr. Rondinero had cut so nicely in the piece of marble. He wondered if Poopy had a nice marker in France. No, he recalled. Common soldiers only got wooden ones. Poorer than ironwood even. The thought made him all cold inside.

He stared down the bluff. For the briefest of moments the devastation vanished and he saw things as they'd been. He saw Brit and Poopy throwing the rubber ball. The ironwood tree dropped leaves onto the clear face of the Indian well. JoAnna walked with him, clasping her schoolbooks against her girl's breast. When he blinked his eyes, he knew things never stayed the same no matter how hard you wished it.

He'd come here looking for something changeless, hoping to find the cemetery so, because the dead were eternally dead. He was wrong. They were merely forgotten. The wooden stakes would rot and fall, Mommer's stone would erode. The jungle would creep over it all, covering everything in tangles of impenetrable bush.

Discouraged, Arlis let his eyes wander over the sloped, ruined earth, cross the tracks, and rest on the white sand of the beach. At the wharf *The Reaper* lay snug against the pilings, bow out, the new canvas bundled against her forestay and the main-sail tied neatly to the boom. He stared hard at her, feeling the pressure building behind his eyes.

The utter simplicity sucked the breath from Arlis's lungs. *The Reaper* pointed at his answer like a dagger; no, like a great key. Beyond her bowsprit lay the true sea. Waiting. Beckoning for him to come.

Arlis felt his lips parting, moving, unable to form sounds, then he began to run down the slope. He ran fast and recklessly, hardly seeing the dying embers of the shantytown. He slipped and fell once, regaining his footing without effort, continuing his headlong race to the railroad embankment. He vaulted the rails, scrabbling down the loose stones of the other side to the soft sand of the beach. Past the boat shed and up the path of the coconut grove he ran, taking the stairs of the cottage in twos and halting only when he could grasp the doorjambs to steady himself and look at the four people who waited for him in his house.

"Arlis!" cried Jo. She stepped to him, her hands in front of her, palms apart, reaching. She touched him. "Arlis, Arlis."

In the mirror Arlis saw his cinder-scorched face, his heaving chest, the torn material of his shirt, darkened with a patch of rust-colored blood. He began laughing, thinking of the sea and of the woman who loved him. He thought of Cap'n Ben and how he'd laughed. And JoAnna laughed too, tears of happiness covering her cheeks as she allowed his arms to encircle her while Jake and Aunt Eleuthera showed a mingling of surprise and amusement. Little Arlis, momentarily frightened at Big Arlis's wild appearance, watched how his mother laughed joyously and embraced the man. Half hiding behind Aunt Eleuthera's skirt, he covered his mouth and began giggling too.

JoAnna had a hard time catching her breath. She was forced to hold Arlis away from her body at arm's length until she could speak.

"What?" she gasped. "What?" Then she began laughing again because Arlis had started up once more.

"Will you go with me?" he was finally able to shout.

"Will you be my wife?"

"Yes! Where? Oh yes, yes. Where?"

Arlis pulled her by the arm across the room. He wrenched the latch on the window that faced the Gulf Stream and threw the great shutters back on their hinges. A furious gust of Atlantic air blasted through the cottage, billowing curtains and sending loose papers across the floor like leaves. Light and wind filled the room.

"There," Arlis said. He pointed past the break in the reef. "Out there."

Arlis and JoAnna stood almost as one body, staring at the sea, held by its greatness. The child, artless in his nonrecognition of the moment, approached Arlis and tugged at his hand. "Why, Uncle Arlis?"

Arlis picked the boy up and held him so that the three of them stood in the wind and the light. "Because." He paused a while before choosing his words. "If we go out there, in time, we'll know everything that needs knowing." The child wore a slightly puzzled look that changed to seriousness. Locking his glance into the man's, he inclined his head in two slow nods of clear affirmation.

"You and Aunt Eleuthera can still come, Uncle Jake." Arlis and Uncle Jake stood a little apart from the small knot of people who'd come to see them off. He and Jake had taken a week in building a good cuddy cabin and a solid hatch for the cargo hold of *The Reaper*.

"Too old," Jake muttered. "We both knows it." The old man tried to arrange his gnarled fingers into some sort of order and pretended to study them. "I'm on the beach now. Can't be helped. Shoo. Somebody got to take care of things up to the boat shed, right?" Arlis knew he was crying. Carefully, in much the same way he'd taken JoAnna by the shoulders, he held Uncle Jake until the old man looked into his face. Arlis held on to him, the two looking into each other's eyes. At last Uncle Jake gently pushed Arlis's elbows back and away.

"Go on, boy. They waiting for you and the tide's right. You got to take the tide when you can."

"Good-bye, Uncle Jake."

"Good-bye, son."

Arlis crossed the narrow gangplank and pulled it aboard after him. Wordlessly, he and JoAnna loosed the main halyard from the belaying pin and, pulling together, hoisted the large gaffed sail.

JoAnna, the child following, walked astern and stood steadying the wheel. Arlis hauled up the white jib. The sails stretched drum-tight, the jib cracking the air as it filled, laying *The Reaper* over on her side. The small ship quivered with energy. Jewel Claire and Mr. Esquinaldo threw the fore and aft mooring lines aboard. Uncle Jake kept a turn around the iron bollard with the spring line for just the instant it took for the bow to swing out into the channel. He released them, casting the hemp rope aboard. The child had already scurried across the deck to coil the lines. A small cheer went up from those on the wharf, hung in the brisk air, and dispersed itself forever.

Freed, *The Reaper* crossed the lagoon and cut a line through the foaming break in the reef.

"They oughtn't to've gone," Aunt Eleuthera said. She stared morosely after the vessel.

"They didn't have to."

"Yes, they did," Uncle Jake said, watching how beautifully the ship sailed.

"Well, I can't understand why. Not for the life of me."

"Because it's out there." Uncle Jake raised a bent finger and pointed at the deep blue ribbon of the Gulf Stream. "It's all out there if you study on it long enough." Jake stood pointing and finally let his withered arm fall to his side. His wife looked at him with an amazing intensity for a woman of her age. Permitting a half-smile to play at her lips, Aunt Eleuthera released a sigh of resignation and turned to walk back to the cottage.

"You come along soon, old man," she said over her shoulder.

To Jake's eyes *The Reaper* had grown quite small now in the distance. Inside himself he trembled with joy in the knowledge that the three people aboard her would find out all the wonderful things they needed to know in this life and maybe the next. After all, who could really tell?